TEETH

TEETH

+ VAMPIRE TALES +

EDITED BY

ELLEN DATLOW & TERRI WINDLING

HARPER

An Imprint of HarperCollinsPublishers

Introduction © 2011 by Terri Windling

"Things to Know About Being Dead" copyright © 2011 by Genevieve Valentine

"All Smiles" copyright © 2011 by Steve Berman

"Gap Year" copyright © 2011 by Christopher Barzak

"Bloody Sunrise" copyright © 2008, 2010 by Neil Gaiman, written as a song lyric for
Claudia Gonson and recorded on the CD accompanying *The Lifted Brow* Volume 4,
published in November 2008. This is the piece's first print publication.

"Flying" copyright © 2011 by Delia Sherman

"Vampire Weather" copyright © 2011 by Garth Nix

"Late Bloomer" copyright © 2011 by Suzy McKee Charnas

"The List of Definite Endings" copyright © 2011 by Kaaron Warren

"Best Friends Forever" copyright © 2011 by Cecil Castellucci

"Sit the Dead" copyright © 2011 by Jeffrey Ford

"Sunbleached" copyright © 2011 by Nathan Ballingrud

"Baby" copyright © 2011 by Kathe Koja

"In the Future When All's Well" copyright © 2011 by Catherynne M. Valente

"Transition" copyright © 2011 by Melissa Marr

"History" copyright © 2011 by Ellen Kushner

"The Perfect Dinner Party" copyright © 2011 by Cassandra Clare and Holly Black

"Slice of Life" copyright © 2011 by Lucius Shepard

"My Generation" copyright © 2011 by Emma Bull

"Why Light?" copyright © 2011 by Tanith Lee

Teeth

Copyright © 2011 by Ellen Datlow and Terri Windling

All rights reserved. Printed in the United States of America.

No part of this book may be used or reproduced in any manner whatsoever without
written permission except in the case of brief quotations embodied in critical articles
and reviews. For information address HarperCollins Children's Books, a division of
HarperCollins Publishers, 10 East 53rd Street, New York, NY 10022.

www.harperteen.com

Library of Congress Cataloging-in-Publication Data

Teeth: vampire tales / edited by Ellen Datlow and Terri Windling. — 1st ed.

v.   cm.

Summary: A collection of nineteen original stories of teenagers and vampires.

Contents: Things to know about being dead / by Genevieve Valentine — All smiles /
by Steve Berman — Gap year / by Christopher Barzak — Bloody sunrise / by Neil
Gaiman — Flying / by Delia Sherman — Vampire weather / by Garth Nix — Late
bloomer / by Suzy McKee Charnas — The list of definite endings / by Kaaron
Warren — Best friends forever / by Cecil Castellucci — Sit the dead / by Jeffrey
Ford — Sunbleached / by Nathan Ballingrud — Baby / by Kathe Koja — In the
future when all's well / by Catherynne M. Valente — Transition / by Melissa Marr —
History / by Ellen Kushner — The perfect dinner party / by Cassandra Clare and
Holly Black — Slice of life / by Lucius Shepard — My generation / by Emma Bull —
Why light? / by Tanith Lee.

ISBN 978-0-06-193515-2 (trade bdg.)

ISBN 978-0-06-193514-5 (pbk.)

1. Vampires—Juvenile fiction. 2. Horror tales, American. [1. Short stories.
2. Vampires—Fiction. 3. Horror stories.] I. Datlow, Ellen. II. Windling, Terri.

PZ5.T294985 2011   2010018436

[Fic]—dc22   CIP

                                                                                          AC

Typography by Andrea Vandergrift

11 12 13 14 15   CG/BV   10 9 8 7 6 5 4 3 2 1

❖

First Edition

The editors would like to thank
Anne Hoppe, Merrilee Heifetz, Jennifer Escott, Heinz Insu Fenkl,
Howard Gayton, Ellen Kushner, and Delia Sherman for their
assistance with this book.

For the fantastic Merrilee Heifetz

TABLE OF CONTENTS

INTRODUCTION

by Terri Windling & Ellen Datlow

Okay, let's admit it: Vampires are hot. Not only hot as in "irresistibly attractive," if your amorous taste runs to dark and dangerous (or, in the case of *Twilight*'s Edward Cullen, rock hard and glittery), but also hot as in "spectacularly popular" in all forms of media today. There are vampire films, vampire TV shows, and so many vampire novels on the shelves that some bookstores now give them their own special section. There are vampire bands, vampire styles, vampire internet forums and journals, and even a fringe subculture of people who claim to drink human blood. Magazines tout the "new vampire craze" that has "suddenly" taken teen culture by storm. Fact is, this craze is nothing new—it's been raging for at least two centuries, ever since Lord Byron and his friends (who were in their teens and twenties themselves) created the first "vampire bestseller" . . . and in the process gave birth to the genre of English Gothic literature.

But first, let's look at the vampire's origins in the ancient tales of myth, for in this form, Edward Cullen's ancestors are very, very old indeed. Although the word "vampire" derives from the legends and folk beliefs of the Slavic peoples, vampirelike creatures can be found in the oldest stories of cultures all around the globe. Bloodsucking spirits of various kinds populated the early legends of Assyria and Babylonia, for example. Some of these foul creatures were human in origin: They were the souls of the restless dead, condemned by a violent death or improper burial to haunt the lands where once they dwelled. Others were supernatural, such as Lilitu, whose tales were once known throughout Mesopotamia. Lilitu had been a sacred figure in Sumerian goddess mythology, but over time she devolved into a fearsome demon, famous for seducing and devouring men. Hungering insatiably for the blood of infants (especially those of noble lineage), she prowled the night in the form of a screech owl, hunting down her next victim.

Likewise, the vampires of Central and South America were usually female figures. Sometimes dangerously seductive, and sometimes birdlike and hideous, they were generally the ghosts of women who had died childless, or in childbirth, and who now haunted the landscape thirsting for the blood of living children. Many of the tribes of Africa also had stories about vampirelike beings with a penchant for blood that was young and fresh. The adze, in the tales of the Ewe tribe, could appear in the form of a firefly or as a misshapen human with jet-black skin. It lived on palm oil and human blood; the younger its victim, the better. The obayifo, in Ashanti tales, was a malevolent spirit who inhabited the bodies of seemingly ordinary men and women, causing them to hunger obsessively for the blood of children. They hunted at night, when they could be detected by the phosphorescent glow from their anuses and armpits.

The ghul, a particularly nasty vampiric demon in old Arabian tales, was a shape-shifter who dwelled in the desert and preyed upon travelers. The ghul robbed and slayed its victim, drank his blood, feasted on his rotting corpse, and then took on the dead man's appearance as it lay in wait for its next meal. In India, cemeteries were the haunts of all manner of vampiric spirits who preyed upon the living; they were the malevolent souls of those buried without the proper funeral rites. China, too, had an extensive tradition of revenants caused by improper burial procedures; the ghosts created in this manner ranged from deadly bloodsucking, flesh-eating creatures to those who were merely melancholic and annoying. Rice, not garlic, was the most effective means of keeping Chinese vampires at bay, for they had a strange compulsion to *count*. Throwing rice at the ghost compelled it to stop; it would not move again until each grain was counted.

Russia and the Slavic-language countries of eastern Europe had the highest concentration of vampire tales of any region of the world, but other kinds of bloodsucking beings were not unknown in the rest of Europe. The bruxsa of Portugal, for example, was a seductive bird-woman (similar to Lilitu) who seduced unwary men, drank the blood of babes, and practiced all manner of witchery. The mullo of Romany Gypsy tales was the animated corpse of a man or woman who had died violently and unavenged (or, again, without a proper burial). There were stories in which the mullo lived undetected for a span of years and even married, but always some strange aspect of his or her behavior would eventually give the game away. The strighe and stregoni of Italy were sorcerers who ingested human blood to enhance their powers in the working of black magic. They also sucked the life essence out of crops and animals and were greatly feared. Italy was unusual in having tales about *good* vampires as well: the stregoni benefici, who worked white magic, assisted in funerary rites and protected the populace from the harm caused by their more malevolent kin.

The folklore of the British Isles contained a variety of flesh-eating revenants and ghouls, and even a bloodsucking fairy or two, but vampires themselves did not arrive on English shores (or in the English language) until the eighteenth century. In 1721, English newspapers reported that a series of savage vampire attacks was terrifying the good citizens of East Prussia. "Vampires," newspaper readers now learned, were dead people who would return to life to prey on the blood and flesh of the living—either because the dead person had sinned terribly against the church (by practicing occult magic, for example) or because an improper burial had allowed an evil spirit entrance into the body. Soon more vampire attacks were reported all across the Hapsburg Monarchy, kicking off a mass vampire hysteria that raged through eastern Europe for the next two decades. Suspected vampires were hunted down, graves were dug up, and suspicious corpses were staked, until the Hapsburg empress Maria Theresa finally put a stop to the whole crazy business by passing strict laws prohibiting the exhumation of graves and the desecration of dead bodies.

The Eighteenth-Century Vampire Controversy (as this strange slice of history became known) went on to inspire a number of famous German poems—including "The Vampire" by Heinrich August Ossenfelder and "The Bride of Corinth" by Johann Wolfgang von Goethe—which were huge hits in their English translations. Poetry in the eighteenth and nineteenth centuries was a much bigger deal than it is today—*everyone* read poetry (everyone in the literate classes, that is), and the most popular poets had fans just as avid as Stephenie Meyer's or Neil Gaiman's are now. The most popular of them all, the English poet Lord Byron, left a trail of swooning readers in his wake, as mesmerized by his dark good looks and his scandalous life as by his poetry. Although he was not the first English poet to put vampires into verse (that credit belongs to Robert Southey), it was Byron's rock-star fame and glamour that gave vampires a new glamour of their own: first when he used vampire lore in his epic poem "The Giaour" in 1813, and then, a few years later, when he conceived a horror story about an English aristocrat turned vampire. That vampire is the great-great-granddaddy of the vampires we know and love today.

Like everything in Lord Byron's life, the story had a curious twist. In 1816, at the age of twenty-eight, Byron gathered a group of friends together at a villa in Geneva, Switzerland. The company consisted of Percy Bysshe Shelley (the not-yet-famous poet, age twenty-four), Mary Shelley (his wife, the not-yet-famous novelist, age eighteen), Claire Clairmont (Mary's stepsister), and John Polidori (Byron's friend, physician, and possibly lover, age twenty-one). Bored and kept indoors by rain, they'd been reading a collection of German horror tales together, which inspired Byron to challenge each of the others to write their own horror story. For his contribution, Byron began a tale about two Englishmen traveling in Greece. One of them dies mysteriously, the other man returns home to London . . . where he runs into the friend he's just buried and discovers he's a vampire. Byron never actually finished the tale—it exists only in fragmentary form—but he talked about it extensively with the others, while John Polidori quietly made notes in his private journal. Later, Polidori took up those notes and, without Byron's knowledge or permission, turned them into a story of his own, *The Vampyre*, which he then proceeded to publish under Lord Byron's name. Byron was furious, of course—particularly as the tale's vampire antihero, Lord Ruthven, was based on Byron himself, and it was not a particularly flattering portrait. But despite (or maybe because of) this scandal, *The Vampyre* was a runaway success—first in its initial magazine publication and then in a book edition. Mary Shelley, meanwhile, went on to complete the story she'd begun that same night in Geneva, called *Frankenstein*. It, too, is now a beloved classic of Gothic literature.

Following the Byron/Polidori tale, vampire stories by other writers began to appear in print and on the theater stage in London, Paris, and Berlin—some of them (in those days of lax copyright laws) also featuring the Byronic vampire Lord Ruthven in the starring role. In 1828, Elizabeth Caroline Grey published the first known vampire tale by a woman: a Gothic confection called *The Skeleton Count, or The Vampire Mistress*. Although largely forgotten now, Grey was a prolific, bestselling novelist beloved by women readers, and this brought the vampire legend to an even larger audience. In 1847, a serialized melodrama called *Varney the Vampire* by James Malcolm Rymer caused the next big vampire sensation. It's pure soap opera, and about as well written, but Rymer's story remains an important part of the vampire canon none-theless—not only because it was hugely popular, but also because we now begin to see vampires portrayed in a more sympathetic light (as creatures tortured by the life they lead), a theme that has since been carried on by writers like Joss Whedon and Stephenie Meyer. Other major additions to the vampire canon at the end of the nineteenth century included Sheridan Le Fanu's *Carmilla* (1872), which scandalized readers with its overtones of lesbian eroticism, and a trio of books by the French author Paul Féval: *Le Chevalier Ténèbre*, *La Vampire*, and *La Ville Vampire* (1860–1874).

All these nineteenth-century tales were based on the vampire myths of eastern Europe, made familiar to readers by the vampire hysteria of the previous century. There was no attempt to stay faithful to this lore, however; each writer reshaped and embroidered the legends to suit his or her own purpose. The vampires of myth, for example, are described as hideously bloated in appearance, red of skin and unnatu-rally fat from feasting nightly on blood and flesh. The literary vampire, by contrast, is generally pale, thin, and aristocratic, with a dark erotic appeal that is largely absent from the old folktales. Many tropes now standard in vampire lore were actually invented in nineteenth-century fiction—such as the vampire's protruding fangs, his fear of sunlight, his invisibil-ity in mirrors, his association with vampire bats (which are native to South America, not Europe), and his ability to travel as long as he brings his coffin and some native soil with him.

In 1897, a novel was published that would shape our concept of vampires more than any other work before or since. The book, of course, was *Dracula*, by the Irish author Bram Stoker. Stoker spent years researching the history, myths, and folk beliefs of eastern Europe before writing the novel that would make its title character truly immortal. Stoker was also influenced by Lord Ruthven, Varney, and the other vampires of English Gothic literature—and so his own vampire, Count Dracula (like every popular vampire since), is a hybrid creature: part mythic figure and part literary invention. Dracula's name was borrowed from a real historical figure, Vlad Draculae ("Vlad the Impaler"), a fifteenth-century Wallachian prince renowned for the sadistic pleasure he took in torturing his enemies. Unlike Vlad Draculae, however, Stoker placed his Count Dracula in the Carpathian Mountains of Transylvania. Vampire legends were known in the region, just as they were known throughout most of eastern Europe and the Balkans, but prior to Stoker's novel Transylvania had no special association with the creatures of the night. (Serbia, rather than Romania, was the true hotbed of vampire legends.) Stoker's novel received reasonably favorable reviews, but *Dracula* was not an immediate success, and it was not until the tale was filmed that its power was fully recognized. Stoker himself didn't live to see the iconic status his story would attain; he never knew that he'd created a vampire myth so potent and so archetypal that every single vampire tale published since bears the marks of his influence.

In the twentieth century, the vampire craze leapt from the printed page to the cinema screen, as film began to play a major role in the shaping of the vampire legend. Feature films such as *Nosferatu* (1922), *Dracula* (1931), and *Dracula's Daughter* (1936) rekindled interest in the Gothic tales created in the previous century—and inspired new generations of writers to add to the vampire tradition. Television, too, then played its part. *Dark Shadows*, a "Gothic soap opera" series, aired on American television in the 1960s and popularized a new kind of vampire who was even more sympathetic than Varney had been: the vampire as romantic hero. Women across America swooned over *Dark Shadows*'s Barnabas Collins: a vampire who was dark and dangerous, yes, but also tortured by his fate and capable of love, perhaps even of redemption. *Dark Shadows* then inspired the enormously popular Barnabas Collins series of books by Marilyn Ross (1966–1971), a precursor of the multi-volume "paranormal romance" series of today.

Stephen King's *Salem's Lot* (1975) brought vampire fiction back to the bestseller lists, closely followed by *Interview with the Vampire* (1976), the first of the Vampire Chronicles by Anne Rice. These books, set in Maine and New Orleans respectively, did much to establish a uniquely American form of vampire literature, as did *The Vampire Tapestry* (1980) by Suzy McKee Charnas—although another great American vampire saga, the Saint-Germain series by Chelsea Quinn Yarbro (first published in 1978), remained more firmly rooted in the English Gothic tradition. All these books were influential texts in the early days of the modern goth movement—a subculture that is, remarkably, still going strong, more than thirty years later, and that may prove to be just as enduring as vampires themselves.

From the 1960s forward, the sexuality that had sizzled underneath the text of the vampire fiction published in the nineteenth century was now becoming more and more explicit—in Anne Rice's steamy novels, for example, and in books like *The Hunger* (1981) by Whitley Strieber and Laurell K. Hamilton's Anita Blake: Vampire Hunter series (1993–present). Scholars of Gothic literature point to the rise of the AIDS epidemic as a factor in the popularity of stories linking sex, blood, and death throughout this period. Another big change was afoot, however, for with the dawn of the twenty-first century came an absolute explosion of new vampire fiction—but this time it was not intended for horror fiction shelves. These stories were set in the high school hallways and small towns of modern America and aimed at teenage readers, especially *female* readers. Why and how this happened can be answered with one word: Buffy.

Yes, there were other contributing factors: the rise of the urban fantasy genre in the 1980s, pioneered by authors like Charles de Lint, Emma Bull, Neil Gaiman, and Mercedes

Lackey; the expansion of the young adult publishing field after the phenomenal success of the Harry Potter books in the 1990s; and, of course, the publication of *Twilight* by Stephenie Meyer in 2005. But it was Joss Whedon's *Buffy the Vampire Slayer* (the television series, 1997–2003, not the lackluster movie that preceded it) that blazed the trail for *Twilight* and the slew of other paranormal romance novels that followed, while also shaping the broader urban fantasy field from the late 1990s onward.

Many of you reading this book will be too young to remember when *Buffy* debuted, so you'll have to trust us when we say that nothing quite like it had existed before. It was thrillingly new to see a young, gutsy, kick-ass female hero, for starters, and one who was no Amazonian Wonder Woman but recognizably *ordinary*, fussing about her nails, her shoes, and whether she'd make it to her high school prom. Buffy's story contained a heady mix of many genres (fantasy, horror, science fiction, romance, detective fiction, high school drama), all of it leavened with tongue-in-cheek humor yet underpinned by the serious care with which the Buffy universe had been crafted. Back then, Whedon's dizzying genre hopping was a radical departure from the norm—whereas today, post-*Buffy*, no one blinks an eye as writers of urban fantasy leap across genre boundaries with abandon, penning tender romances featuring werewolves and demons, hard-boiled detective novels with fairies, and vampires-in-modern-life sagas that can crop up darn near anywhere: on the horror shelves, the SF shelves, the mystery shelves, the romance shelves. And on the bestseller lists, thanks to Stephenie Meyer's Twilight series.

Stephenie Meyer zeroed in on one of the most popular aspects of the *Buffy* saga—Buffy's torturous (and mostly chaste) romance with a "good" vampire, Angel—and spun it into a Gothic love story for a new generation of teens. Less genre bending than Whedon's tale, focused more on romance than on fantasy world building, *Twilight* works on a level of pure emotion. The series' brooding young hero, Edward Cullen, stands firmly in the literary vampire tradition: a clear line runs from Edward back through Angel and Barnabas Collins all the way to Varney, the first of the sympathetic vampires. Like Varney, Edward has struck a chord with readers of all ages and backgrounds, not just traditional fans of vampire tales; and like Varney (and every other beloved literary vampire from Lord Ruthven onward), he will help to shape the vampire legend in the years to come.

Regardless of how you feel about the Twilight books and films, whether you passionately love them or passionately hate them (and there are vast numbers of vampire aficionados in both camps), we all have reason to be grateful to Meyer. The extraordinary success of the Twilight series has placed a huge spotlight not only on modern vampire tales but on the urban fantasy genre as a whole—and that, in turn, is bringing new readers, and some terrific new writers, into the field. Some of those talented new writers can be found in the pages of this book—alongside writers who have long been working in the vein of urban fantasy fiction. (If any of these authors are new to you, we highly recommend seeking out their prior novels and stories.)

Here's the brief we gave to each of the writers we invited to contribute to this book:

Give us a YA vampire tale, we said, but make it smart and unusual. It can be funny, or frightening, or folkloric, or romantic; it can be quiet, or explosive, or brutal, or tender; it can even be all of these things at once. Give us a story we can (ahem) get our *teeth* into.

And don't be afraid to draw blood.

THINGS TO KNOW ABOUT BEING DEAD

by Genevieve Valentine

As it turns out, if a person dies badly, sometimes the soul can't escape the body and will have to feed off the living forever.

Of course, I only find this out *after* Madison Gardner offers me a ride home in her dad's Beemer after six shots of coconut rum and ends up shoving the car through a tree.

Madison pours herself out of the driver's side and teeters around on her tacky platforms, mumbling and choking and being as useless as usual. I break my neck and die before the ambulance gets there.

I'm so pissed that she's okay that it takes me a few minutes to realize I'm not dead anymore.

(Sometimes your priorities aren't what they should be.)

Things to know about being dead:

1. You have a heartbeat when a paramedic checks for a pulse. Easy to fake. It's like sit-ups with ventricles.
2. Your grandmother, who has been getting senile, takes one look at you and says, "So, Suyin, you're dead," so either something about you looks different or everyone was wrong about the senile thing.
3. Grandmother tells you you're jiang-shi, and that it's safe to go to school. "The winter sun shouldn't worry you," she says. She doesn't mention the summer sun.
4. Your parents have no idea what's going on. They're just happy you're bonding with Grandmother.

I couldn't sleep that first night. Grandmother and I had tea and played cards (she killed at poker; I'd never known), and once I was upstairs, I checked my homework twice and clicked through every online video I could find, trying to keep my mind off it.

I started wondering if jiang-shi ever slept. If not, I'd have to develop some new hobbies. And I'd have to find something I could eat. (Grandmother said I'd be drinking blood now. That was about the point I flipped out on her and ran to my room.)

Finally I counted the shadows of leaves on my wall. It helped more than anything else had, but whenever I spaced out, I remembered Madison laughing at her own joke and reaching for the radio to find a better song, just before the tree rose up in front of us.

(I hadn't wanted to say yes, but it was two miles home and it was dark, and you knew things happened to girls who walked home alone. Madison was one of Amber's crowd, but she wasn't as vicious as they were.

She could, however, drink as much as they could, which I sort of wish I had known when I got in the car.)

I didn't want to think about that. It was bad enough that I had died; I didn't want to relive the moments I had been dead in the car. What if I talked myself right back into being dead?

I must have gone somewhere when I died, because I remember coming back, blooming inside my body just before I opened my eyes. And I couldn't shake the feeling I wasn't alone; that I had brought some darkness with me.

It must have been the first night of my life I'd ever *wanted* to be alone.

On Monday, I saw that Amber and Company were meeting up outside the school at the picnic tables, even though it was still coat weather.

"Oh my *God*, Madison," Amber was saying, "I still can't even believe it. I mean, you could have *died*. Like, you could not even *be here* right now."

(Madison stumbled out of the car, and when she saw me, she laughed and said, "That was awesome, right, Sue?" before she saw I wasn't moving. Then she vomited.)

"Yeah," I said, "that would be a shame."

Madison snorted. "See if I ever offer you a ride again, ungrateful bitch."

As I went inside, Madison was saying, "Seriously, you guys, it's changed my *life*."

5. People smell like their skin. Once I get a real whiff of the beef-and-cologne on the boys and the varnish-and-perfume on the girls, I throw out all my Body Shop.
6. Refuse blood all you want. The hunger drives you insane after the third day.

That morning I couldn't go to school because I was shaking and sweating and my mouth was so dry I couldn't even speak to tell my mom I'd be fine.

"Grandmother will take care of you until I get home," Mom said, unconvinced. But I nodded. Grandmother knew the score.

My parents went, and I listened to the quiet house for a while, sucking in air I didn't even need, trying not to let my brain boil. I heard, *Hang on, hang on*, but I didn't know who could be talking; I was alone. I thrashed out—I wasn't going to let Death get me twice.

Grandmother brought with her a little bowl in each hand. She was wearing a yellow housedress, and her skin smelled like tea and lotion and fish scales and the vitamin pills Mom made her take.

I turned away, gripping my knees with my fingernails until the blood ran, so I wouldn't grab for her arm and bite down. My head was going to burst.

Then I felt something cool on my shoulder, something thick and earthy. Mud.

I tried to speak, but my throat was too dry; I lay quietly as she smoothed her fingers over my shoulders, my neck, the backs of my arms.

At last, somehow, I was calm enough to look at her without being afraid of myself.

She smiled. "Come here. I have something for you."

I didn't want to get closer, but somehow I was sitting up anyway, moving to rest my back against the headboard. The mud was soothing—it smelled nice, like sleep—and Grandmother's yellow dress filled the room.

"Here," Grandmother said, upturning the second bowl.

It was dry rice—the little white grains stood out sharply against my purple bedspread—and my mind went blank, suddenly. I started to count.

Dimly I was aware that she left and came back, but I wasn't finished, and the counting was all that mattered.

"How many?" my grandmother asked at some point, and handed me a warm mug. I counted through to the end.

"Four hundred thirty-six," I said. My throat wasn't dry anymore; I was surprised, until I looked down in the mug and realized I'd already drunk from it. There was some blood left, forming a pudding skin on top. When I looked up, I saw myself in the desk mirror, my mouth ringed with red.

"I'm disgusting," I said, on the verge of tears.

She held my hand. "Don't worry. You're mine."

After a moment, she sat back, folded her hands over her stomach.

"If you're ready for the rest, I can tell you," she said, and I scratched at the mud on my arm and listened.

7. Jiang-shi must drink blood to keep their bodies from turning into tombs; otherwise they go from strong to granite, and you're trapped inside. ("You should learn to hunt deer," she says. I ignore that.)

8. The yellow dress keeps me at bay. ("Tell your friends to wear yellow," she says, like I have any friends I'd want to save.)

9. She can get blood from the butcher, "for sausage," she says, winking broadly, so long as I give her a ride. She's not allowed to have the car anymore.

10. Blood tastes disgusting.

11. At first.

At school, I went in the back way and made it through the morning trying not to fall asleep. (Good news about the new compulsions: I took *monster* notes.)

The cafeteria was an orgy of social anxiety, and my useless heart still pounded in my chest as I walked in. Old habits die hard, I guess.

Amber, Madison, Jason, and the rest were sitting at the lunch table with their McDonald's bags, evidence that they were cool enough to leave campus. Jason was feeding Amber fries, one at a time.

I heard, *Ignore them.*

It was a boy's voice. I looked around; I was alone.

You can't see me, it said. *You can stop looking.*

"You can shut up," I muttered, but I headed through the cafeteria, trying to shake it.

We should talk, now that you can hear me, it said.

"Now, as in you were around before?"

Outside, I found an empty bench and sank onto it, checking that I hadn't been followed.

Still here.

I got nervous before I remembered I was dead, too. I probably had more in common with this thing than with any of the people in the cafeteria.

"How long have you been around when I couldn't hear you?" I asked, folding my arms like I was too cool to care if some ghost had been watching me brush my teeth.

You brought me back, it said.

I thought about my sense that there was someone in the

room with me that first long night.

"Wow, I hope you're not a pervert," I said.

12. If you're frightened enough, or desperate enough, when you come back to your body, you can drag a soul with you by accident.
13. His name is Jake. He committed suicide. (He doesn't say more than that, and I don't press him. People get to strange places.)
14. He thinks he still has it better than me.

"We should send you home," I say that night.

The idea of an imaginary friend was fun in class (I wrote snarky notes and he laughed), and it was great in study hall, when Amber and Company murmured and cast dark glances at all the nerds sitting around trying not to be seen. An imaginary friend who could secretly complain about how much they sucked was pretty ideal.

But now I was getting ready to shower, and, well.

I don't know how to go back, Jake said. *I don't think I have a home anymore.*

"Well, my room is not the place for invisible boys."

I don't look.

"Like I can tell," I said.

He said, *It's not really my thing.*

I wondered if it meant what I thought it meant; it would explain a lot about why he had committed suicide, but I didn't push it.

"All right," I said. "Hope you know chemistry."

C plus last year, he said.

I opened my textbook. "Start reading up, then."

I didn't mention sending him back again. Even if I'd known how to, he didn't seem eager to go. I guess any friend is a good friend if you're lonely enough.

I knew the feeling.

Early on, the worst part of being jiang-shi is watching my body dying, a little at a time.

It's not as bad as it could be; apparently if you don't come back right away, you have to deal with the half-decomposed body you left behind. Disgusting.

But you can tell yourself a hundred times that what you look like doesn't really matter; there's still horror in waking up every morning to see your hair going white, that you're getting paler and harder, that your eyes are bloodshot no matter what you do.

I deal. I dye my hair black even though it chokes me with the stink, and I wear those tinted sunglasses that make you look like a John Lennon impersonator.

Once, in the hallway, Madison calls me a poser, but no

one else even notices I'm any different. Death hasn't changed a thing about that.

It should make me happier than it does.

How long before someone figures you out, you think?

I shrugged and jogged across the crosswalk. "I don't go to lunch. If anyone even notices, it'll be Madison. She'll just think I'm starving down to bikini weight."

You could always eat her.

"Don't tempt me," I said, a reflex.

Then I thought about it—Madison screaming as I sliced into her neck with a plastic fork and started drinking. It would be like drinking Victoria's Secret perfume, but I'd never had blood fresh. It might be worth it, just to find out what it tasted like when it was still hot and pulsing and—

I made a note to stay out of school when I was hungry.

"It's just until college," I said.

Jake said, *So you'll go to college?*

Sometimes a normal question can stop you right in the street.

15. It will knock you sideways that everyone around you will grow older and go to college and major in art history, and they'll get jobs and date and complain and marry and have normal lives and die, and you'll be stuck at seventeen,

sucking blood out of mugs and counting the stripes on your wallpaper forever.

16. You make a note to ask Grandmother if jiang-shi can die; what happens then?

Grandmother was home making tea, shuffling quietly back and forth in her house slippers. (Over the past couple of months she had become the most comforting thing in the world; anything she did was home to me.)

"What happens when I'm supposed to be older?"

She thought about that, shrugged helplessly. "I don't know," she said, in that tone she used when she had been thinking about something with no good outcome. (She used it a lot.)

Grandmother set a mug of warm blood next to me. "You'll think of something. I know it."

That was more faith than I had in myself.

I rested my head on her shoulder, just for a second, like a little kid would. Then I cleared my throat, said, "I have homework, gotta go," and scooped my backpack over my shoulder on my way up the stairs.

Grandmother watched me go, looking lonelier than I'd ever seen her. My stomach twisted just to see it.

I dreamed that the school was empty and covered over with vines, the walkways broken with tree roots, the shelves of the library stuffed with birds' nests. There was a little river sloshing through the main hallway, and as I walked, I made no sound.

The sunlight streamed through the broken windows and through the holes in the ceiling where the beams had given in at last.

They are all dead, I thought, and I knew it was true. I was the only one there; I was the only one left.

I didn't think it was a nightmare until I woke up and heard myself panting.

Sorry, Jake said. *I was trying to wake you, but—*

My hand shot out across the bed, looking for him. He took in a breath, held it.

Then I remembered he was only a spirit, some remnant I had brought back with me because I was too angry to come back alone. I felt the lingering horror of the dream, seeping quietly through me like rising water.

"Why do you think it was you I brought back?" I asked, just to say something.

He let out the breath slowly. I wondered if I still breathed, too; how deep my habits went.

I was looking for a way out, he said finally, like the words were being forced out of him. *I couldn't—I couldn't be there anymore.*

Jesus. I asked quietly, "Why not?"

But there was no answer. He was gone.

The room was so quiet that I heard the first raindrops falling before it started to storm.

The next day in chem, Madison was sitting so close to Jason that their legs were touching, so close that when she turned to look at him they were practically kissing.

I wondered how long it would take for that to get around to the injured party. I scribbled in the margin of my notebook, "T-minus Amber?"

There was no answer from Jake. Not like I had expected one, anyway. Whatever.

I erased the note.

(Third period, Madison's car got towed. High school is more efficient than the Mob.)

Jake was silent all day. I hadn't realized how much I liked having him around. I mean, I managed—you take the notes and ask questions and draw stick-figure monarchs in your history notebook just like usual—but it was . . . strange. You get used to some people.

(You miss someone.)

17. You stop sleeping at night.
18. You get in more and more trouble for nodding off in class.

I had been drinking blood for months, but I still ended up in bed later that week, broiling and thrashing.

It was Grandmother's day at the doctor, so she couldn't help me for hours, and I could hardly move; I was going to burn, I was going to burn.

There was a cool breath on my neck. *Suyin? Suyin.*

It was Jake. Jake was back. I could hardly hear him through the grinding ache of my blood as it slowed.

Suyin, open your eyes.

I struggled to find the will, but at last I hauled my eyelids open, gasping with the effort.

There was a boy in my room. He had dark hair and slightly crooked glasses. He wasn't quite real—I could see my desk through him, and he had eye sockets instead of true eyes—but I could see the silhouette of his hands, which he was holding up, palms out.

Count my fingers, he said.

I couldn't even focus my eyes for more than a moment, but I counted, one through ten. After that I counted the threads in my comforter, and just as I was running out (and panic was coming), Grandmother knocked on my door.

Jake stepped behind my drapes.

"What's wrong?" Grandmother asked, kneeling and looking me over. My skin was clammy; my hands were shaking.

"I'm so hungry," I said. "I drank yesterday, but . . ." I couldn't finish, my throat too dry; I shook my head.

Grandmother frowned at me. Then she said, "Let me see what I can do." She handed me a book, said, "Count the words," and closed the door behind her.

By the time I was on chapter three, I had a mug in my hands. The blood was hot and rich, and when I was finished, I licked down into the mug as far as I could.

Grandmother looked tired, but she smiled at me. "We'll find a way," she said. "We'll find something."

I nodded and kissed her cheek. (She smelled like salt and lotion and talc.)

After she had gone, Jake stepped out from behind my curtains.

"Thanks," I said. "For before."

He shrugged. *No problem,* he said, not quite looking at me. *I'll let you get some sleep.* He started to fizzle around the edges, like film burning out.

"Don't go," I said.

He stopped. Now I could see him when he held his breath; I could see him nodding, his dark hair falling into his face.

Even if he'd never told me, I could tell he had died unhappy. His eye sockets were two black pits, as if sadness had swallowed him up while he was still alive. I wondered if he would ever have real eyes, or if this was how his sorrow had marked him.

(I wondered if he was sorry for anyone else; if he had seen anyone else's last moments, when he happened to be looking. Madison and the rest of them were worthless, but it hurt, it *hurt*, to think of them all being gone, and just me left behind. There were kinds of loneliness that I still couldn't name.)

He spent all night beside me. I could feel him breathing, and if I reached out my hand, there was a chill when my fingers passed through his fingers.

One morning as I was walking to school, the sun came out. It was the summer sun, hot and bright.

My blood started to boil.

I screamed, pulled my hoodie up over my head, and ran. The sun was beating down, I was aching and trembling, I didn't know where I could go that would be safe. Finally I ran past the wooded acre—FOR SALE for the last five years. It was studded with trees and brambles; it was dark and wild.

It was a beacon.

I ran until I couldn't see the street, and then I fell to my knees and pressed my face to the ground. It had rained overnight, and the smell of the damp earth was as comforting as an embrace.

I dug. My arms were like marble, like iron; mud and roots flew up under my hands.

I slid into the shallow trench, pulling mud over me until the last of the knife-sharp pain was gone; still my body trembled, and I gasped into the sopping mud, openmouthed, until I choked.

The grave got mercifully cool, as if snow had suddenly fallen on it. Jake whispered, *Suyin?*

I cried.

When it was dark, I clawed my way out and walked home, sluicing mud off my clothes with my hands. Jake was quiet, but I could feel him to my right, a patch of blessed cold in a world that was getting warmer.

(My body was room temperature these days.)

I got home just in time to catch Mom, Dad, and Grandmother cooking dinner. They stopped and stared.

"I slipped," I said into the silence.

My mom sighed. "Suyin, what's wrong with you?"

"I'll wash them," I said. "I need to shower. Sorry."

I dropped the boots in the hall and squelched up the stairs as carefully as I could.

If I turned on just cold water, it was almost nice.

When I came down, Grandmother was making tea.

"How are you feeling?" she asked.

"Better. You?"

She was looking a little drawn, a little pale, but she waved one hand and said, "Better," and we smiled.

She was wearing a yellow shirt.

My stomach dropped.

"Grandmother, are you scared of me?"

She looked up and blinked. "Oh, no. You always wear yellow when you're near jiang-shi. The priests used to ring bells to let us know they were carrying souls with them." She smiled. "You remind me of home, now. Of those days."

I thought about her home in some little town in Anhui province I had never seen; how Dad had brought her here. And her dead granddaughter was the best thing that had happened to her, somehow.

"Tell me," I said.

She beamed. Then she told me about going to the opera there; she told me how to steam stone frog.

Then she kicked my ass at rummy. Twice.

After she had gone to bed, I went upstairs, worrying with every step.

You all right? Jake was sitting on the edge of my bed, not quite looking at me.

"No," I said.

After a long time, I covered his translucent fingers with mine. He looked down, smiled.

You really suck at rummy, he said.

I pulled a face. "Quit spying!"

I was in the kitchen, he said. *You could have seen me. You just didn't look.*

"I was concentrating on not sucking at rummy," I said.

Yeah, he said, *that worked out great.*

19. Jiang-shi must seek the earth when the sun is bright. ("It's just the pain," said Grandmother. "You won't burn." Like that was comforting.)

I went back to school; it was cloudy enough that I could bear the pain, if I tried. No one mentioned that I had the shakes.

My acceptance letter came from Seattle. I sat on the empty benches at lunch and read it twice. Then I stuffed it into my backpack, grinding it into the bottom.

You should go, Jake said from beside me. He sounded more excited than I'd ever heard him. *I've always wanted to see the West Coast.*

"Sure," I said. "Crawl out of the mud in time for night class and learn things that don't matter for a life I'm never going to lead. Brilliant plan."

You just need a couple of fake IDs and some shade, he said. He was the freaking pep squad, suddenly. He grinned at me. *You'll be fine. It'll be fine. It'll be an adventure. You can totally handle it.*

I turned to face him. "You think I can get through college hoping they don't notice I only take night classes and wildlife goes missing? What sort of life is that? How can I do that?" I shook my head. "I can't even live at home for long. But where else can I go? I'm trapped."

His glasses gleamed in front of the blank sockets. He snorted, his mouth twisting. *Wow. I didn't realize you were such a coward, Suyin. You're just going to run?*

Blood filled my vision.

"Coward?" I turned to face him. "And you knew so much more about how to handle life than I do, before you killed yourself?"

Shut up, he said, so raspy I could hardly hear him.

I couldn't shut up, though, couldn't stop. "You couldn't even take being *dead*! You caught a ride with the first person who could come back on her own because you couldn't hack it in the afterlife, and you're telling *me* when I'm being a coward?"

There was a horrible silence. The words settled in between us, and still nothing happened. I was frozen. Behind his almost-there glasses, his eye sockets filled with tears, like a crack in a rock weeps.

Then he was gone, plumes of smoke that disappeared into the afternoon sky.

And that's how you take care of a lingering spirit, I thought. Annoy it until it goes back to the afterlife just to avoid you. Then you get to be alone, just like you wanted.

Go, me.

20. The school has no outside broadcast system. If you're not in the building, you don't know that you're being paged to the main office, and you're an hour late getting the news that your grandmother has died.

* * *

My parents had left a note with the address of the funeral home.

I went into Grandmother's room like I didn't believe it; like she would be there if I just opened the door fast enough.

The room was thick with smells: the bamboo in a vase on the windowsill, the detergent smell of her dresser. The bed smelled like her skin, as much as if she were still in it, sleeping, and I could reach out and wake her up.

The little nightstand next to her bed was a pile of vitamin bottles and eye drops and insulin. It seemed wrong in the room, like weapons, and I opened the top drawer to sweep them in, to leave the room the way she'd meant it.

Inside the top drawer was a needle and a plastic tube and a small glass jar with a narrow neck, like an ink bottle. Everything was clean, but the smell of blood was so powerful, I sank onto the bed.

After the animal blood stopped working, she had found something that would save me. She hadn't told me I needed human blood; I would have found some other way if I had known. Why hadn't she told me?

("Don't worry," she'd said. "You're mine.")

I wondered, if I tried, if I could bring her back. I could reach into the afterlife, I was sure—if I just brought her out, she could keep me company, she wouldn't mind, we could get out of here and go anywhere she wanted—

I bent over, sobbed into my hands.

21. You cry blood.

When I had cried myself out, I licked my hands clean and then drank what was left of the blood in the fridge. Now that I knew it was hers, it tasted strange, but it was a gift of love, and I would need strength for what I planned to do.

The glass bottle and stopper went into my backpack, along with necessities and cash from my dad's desk drawer.

I put on a yellow shirt, left a note for my parents, and hit the road.

22. You can carry a person's soul in an object of great meaning to them. No matter how far away they died, you can bring them home again, so they aren't angry or lonely; so they can sleep quietly in the ground.

I shake all the way down the highway, my hands trembling on the wheel, but I don't turn around. I owe my grandmother a favor. I know how she missed home.

Jake appears just as I'm walking into the airport.

You gonna do that to me, too?

He's solid now; if people weren't walking right through

him, I'd think he was real.

His eyes are green.

I tilt my head. "You want me to?"

He shrugs. *I'd go back if you sent me, but I thought maybe you want a friend.*

"I can do it alone," I say. It's important, now, to be able to be lonely and still survive.

He slides his hand through mine.

I know, he says. *But I'm with you, if you want.*

I wait him out for three seconds before I smile.

23. It's just as weird as being alive. You figure it out as you go.

ALL SMILES

by Steve Berman

Drowning felt like a real possibility. The cold rain came down hard, soaking Saul through each layer of clothing: the faded peacoat he'd stolen from Cotre Ranch, the Red Caps T-shirt he'd bought at their Philly concert, the waffle-weave long sleeve, and the boxers and jeans he'd been wearing for too many days and nights. His socks and sneakers were saturated sponges; every step down the shoulder of the highway made him shiver.

Every time Saul heard a car approach, he would turn back into the force of the wind, letting the rain sting his face. He would squint and, if he didn't recognize the car from the ranch, he'd raise an arm, thumb out for a ride. And the cars swooshed past, and he'd walk on.

By nightfall, the air might freeze him. But he'd been on so many forced marches the last few weeks, he imagined his corpse would keep walking.

A car stopped yards ahead of him. The passenger door opened wide. Saul blinked away the water running into his eyes. A dark sedan, sleek, with tinted windows. A New York State license plate. How he missed the East Coast! The Statue of Liberty beckoned, reminding him of that speech of hers, welcoming the poor and downtrodden.

He ran up to the car. Warm air seeped from the interior. From behind the steering wheel, a dark-haired girl in her early twenties leaned over and patted the passenger seat, now speckled with rainwater. "Need an ark, Noah?"

A giggle came from the backseat as Saul climbed inside. The vent near his face gushed hot air, a forgotten piece of summer trapped within the car. Saul slammed shut the door just as the girl stepped hard on the gas pedal.

He noticed the glove compartment hung open and stuffed with maps, folded wrong so they accordioned, and papers.

"Introductions," she said. Saul noticed she had the most dazzling smile he'd ever seen. Perfect, expressive, expensive. He caught himself staring at her smile a bit too long, which only made her grin wider.

Saul brushed back the wet hair along his head and offered his name.

"I'm Dutch, and back there," she said, stabbing behind her shoulder, "is Marley."

Marley leaned forward and offered Saul a smile that matched Dutch's in brilliance and intensity. He also had dark hair, though his was just shy of stubble compared to her longer tresses. Both wore matching white button-down shirts and black slacks. Both had the topmost buttons undone to reveal plenty of smooth skin.

Siblings, Saul was sure. Both good-looking and with the confidence that meant if they weren't rich, they had once been so.

"What's a night like this doing to a boy like you?" Marley asked, followed by another giggle that belonged to a toddler.

"Running away," Dutch said. "Well, aren't you? Only someone on the run would be hitchhiking in this weather."

Saul nodded. Cotre Ranch might tell parents it was an "outdoor behavioral health care facility," but it was really a gulag to help kids kick their drug habits through hard labor and obstacle courses. Punishment for doing a little herbal and a couple bumps of crystal meth—how else could he entertain himself? His parents hadn't asked *him* if he'd like to move from Jersey to Iowa.

The motion of the car and the intense heat made him sleepy. As an inmate of the ranch, he'd been rising at dawn only to collapse on a stiff bunk every night. And even then, sleep wasn't a guarantee: Every so often there were random night checks when a "counselor" would try to sneak up on a sleeping kid. If they could do so without waking him, it meant an hour's worth of scrubbing floors. Saul learned fast to wake at the slightest creak.

"You're not ax murderers, are you?" he asked.

Both siblings laughed. Dutch, at least, had a normal laugh. "No, no. Nothing like that."

Saul's right arm itched. He rubbed it through the peacoat. He was covered in so many bruises and scabs from all the tough love. His hands were either all blister or callus.

"No hobo bag?" Marley tugged at Saul's wilted collar. "I always loved those cartoon hobos."

"You're traveling light," Dutch said.

Saul felt too tired to shrug. "Nothing to hold me down." Truth was, the goon staff had locked away most of his things after his parents had dropped him off at the ranch. He wasn't sure if he *should* be missing things. What did empty pockets say about a guy?

He looked out the window, scratched at the cheap, tinted film with a dirty thumbnail. The thought of freedom was intoxicating. "I could go anywhere," he muttered. His original plan had been to make his way back to Jersey, but that now seemed as empty of promise as knocking at his parents' door. There was nowhere he *had* to go, which left him troubled. He couldn't imagine himself anywhere in the world, as if the cold rain had washed away his ability to daydream. When the siblings let him out, all he would do was wait for the next ride. And then the next.

"We've been anywhere." This time Marley's fingers, which

felt like icicles, moved to Saul's matted hair. "And everywhere in between."

Saul stiffened. When you're gay, you always wonder about every guy you see. What if Marley was too? But when you're right, it's still a surprise. It had been too long since another guy had even touched him. While being trapped in a bunkhouse filled with teen rough trade might seem like a wet dream come true, actually no one had the energy after the first few days to do more than brag about past lays. And by the third week—a week of digging holes six feet deep—everyone looked and smelled so scroungy and raw that the thought of even approaching a horny straight boy was too damn hazardous.

"Relax. We want to like you," Dutch said. She ran one finger along the front of her teeth, as if checking to make sure they were clean. Saul noticed she didn't wear any fingernail polish or rings, something he'd expect for a rich girl. She needed only her smile.

As Saul scratched at his arm, Marley's cold touch slipped under his collar. "Are you one of those shy boys?"

Saul didn't think "shy" was the right word for how he felt. Maybe curious or anxious. When a total stranger started stroking the side of your neck, how were you *supposed* to act?

His right arm more than itched. It felt as if ants had crawled under the skin. Angry ants that tore at the nerves with their mandibles. He tried pushing up the sleeve of the coat, but it wasn't enough. The arm burned as if soaked in acid. He began stripping off the coat and ripping at his sleeve.

The siblings laughed. "So eager," one of them said, but Saul didn't pay attention to which one.

When he finally bared his forearm, the pain ceased immediately. The skin looked so pale compared to the black, curvy Hebrew lettering of his tattoo. He had thought it so clever to get that line referring to tefillin inked on his arm. *And you shall bind them as a sign upon your hand.* As a boy, he'd often watch his zaydie, his grandfather, on Saturday mornings, wrap his arm with the phylactery's straps, which filled the room with the smell of leather. Zaydie had told him that the small animal-hide box held magic words.

Of course, as he'd planned, his parents were appalled. He remembered his mother crying, "You can't be buried in a Jewish cemetery. You can't go to shul." He thought her reaction was so hypocritical; after Zaydie died, they only went to synagogue for the High Holy Days. The only bagels in Iowa must be frozen in the supermarket.

Saul had expected the staff at the ranch would mock him for the Hebrew, but Phelps, the head counselor, had admired his tattoo and actually suggested Saul get more ink, so that it would resemble leather bands coiling all the way down to his palm.

Saul looked at the siblings. Dutch had her eyes on the road, but her face had become drawn, the lines of her jaw clenched tight. "His arm," Marley groaned from the backseat.

"I know," Dutch muttered. She glanced at Saul, and the look was one of disgust. Instinct made his hand edge toward the door latch, but he realized that she was driving too fast to make rolling out of the car a safe option. It didn't matter. She pressed a button and the locks came down. He heard them echo awhile.

"Remind me that you're not ax murderers," he said weakly. He never wanted trouble.

The last few days had been weird at the ranch; the counselors seemed distracted and kept talking in hushed voices. Some of the older boys were on edge, as if too much testosterone malice had built up in their veins. Saul was sure they planned on a game of Smear the Queer any moment and decided he had to get out of there as soon as possible.

That night, he feigned sleep in his bunk. His ears strained to pick out the whispers among the many snores. He hid his face under the crook of an arm and watched as some of the boys rose from their bunks. Saul tensed. He told himself there'd be no shame in kicking another guy in the balls if he meant to brain you. But the boys didn't even look in his direction as they opened the door (which should have been locked!) and slipped out of the bunkhouse.

He counted to a thousand. Well, he aimed that high, but somewhere after two hundred, he crept to the door. He held a breath and was rewarded when the handle was unlocked.

The grounds were dark, except for the amber glow seeping from the slotted windows of the large storage shed, off-limits to all but the staff.

Saul knew he didn't have time or the luck to afford being curious.

As he passed through the parking lot, he considered letting air out of the tires, but there were too many cars. He crept down to the end of the driveway and looked over the metal gate. Tugging at the chain that fed the motor reminded him of all the bike chains he'd broken as a little kid. He hunted around until he found a palm-sized rock, and then smashed the chain off. He tossed the rock over his shoulder, muttered a thanks to the counselors for teaching him to climb anything, and scurried over the rain-slick bars. He didn't stop running until he reached the highway.

"What do you want to do?" she asked. Saul knew she wasn't talking to him.

"I don't know. I'm hungry, though. And we were promised food." The last words came out of Marley as a whine.

Dutch nodded.

Saul leaned against the car door. Now alert, though sweating from the furnacelike heat, he didn't know where to look. Staring at the road left him feeling helpless, but eyeballing Dutch might antagonize her, like an angry dog. He risked a glance and realized she wasn't sweating. Not a drop. His own forehead felt slick, feverish. He remembered Phelps mentioning he would never trust anyone who didn't sweat.

They drove too fast past a road sign for him to read it. "There's a gas station up ahead," she said.

"We need to stop. I can't think when I'm hungry. I need to think about his arm."

Saul wondered if they were some crazy anti-Semitic pair. Just his luck to find the only New Yorkers on vacation who hated Jews. He tried to cover the tattoo with his fingers, but the skin beneath began to ache again until he removed his hand. He didn't understand what the hell was happening.

Dutch barely slowed down to pull into the gas station. She came to a screeching halt in front of a pump. A pregnant woman filling her gas tank nearby gave them a sour look as she covered her stomach with one arm, as if that might keep her safe from injury. "Looks like we need some gas."

"I need a refill." Marley's usual giggle was brief and pained.

Dutch turned to Saul. "You fill the tank. We'll be inside. If you run, we'll kill her."

Saul nodded. The flatness in Dutch's voice was more chilling than the threat. No, not a threat, but a promise of murder.

"C'mon, bro," she said, and unlocked the doors.

Saul's legs felt hollow as he stepped out of the car. He moved slowly. Marley flipped him the finger under one eye before following after his sister. Saul noticed that neither of them wore shoes, and their bare feet were dark with grime.

Saul hissed at the pregnant woman to catch her attention. She ignored him. He stomped his foot, splashing a puddle. Nothing. Then he noticed the white cord around her neck. Damn iPods. Would serve her right if he ran.

But he wouldn't be so easy to kill. He'd discovered something about himself at Cotre Ranch. Through all the hiking with heavy backpacks, the hand-over-hand rope bridge over mud puddles, the old brick wall they had to climb, he might have stumbled, but Phelps's goons had made sure he kept going. They would yell at him, insult him, and shove him forward. And he was tougher for it.

The liquid crystal display on the pump came to life. He lifted the nozzle. He needed a distraction. On the island beside the pump, a metal drum served as a trash can. The crumpled fast-food bags, empty soda cans, and discarded oil bottles would ignite fast with a little gasoline. He pulled the nozzle's trigger and splashed the top of the trash.

The pregnant woman finished and drove off. Saul turned to see if the siblings could see him through the gas station's windows and found himself face-to-face with Dutch. He jumped back. She was sucking on her index finger. The look of excitement on her flushed face dropped when she smelled the gasoline.

She popped the finger from her lips and then kicked at

the drum. The trash spilled out all around the island. Saul silently cursed.

"Inside," she told him, and pushed him toward the gas station door.

Marley stood at the back by the refrigerated shelves, juggling cartons of milk. His lips looked ruddy, as if he'd been kissing someone hard. He'd be gorgeous if not for the smirk. It was the sort of smirk that made you want to punch him before kissing him.

The register drawer was open and empty. Maybe they're just thieves, Saul thought. And they're getting off on scaring me. Then he thought he glimpsed a foot sticking out from behind the counter, and he felt the scream building within him. A scream at their madness, a scream of shock and fear. But he knew if he let the scream loose, he'd be rooted to the spot and never escape. So he swallowed the scream, as he had the aches and pains he'd earned at the ranch.

Marley tossed the smallest carton to Saul. Heavy cream.

"The Masai drink blood first and then milk." Marley let one carton drop. It smacked the floor, and milk spilled all over the stained linoleum. "Oops, don't cry." He smiled and Saul shivered, frightened and, embarrassed to realize, aroused. There was something powerful about their Cheshire cat grins.

Saul glanced around him. He stood in the midst of an aisle with chips and snack foods along one side, soda on the other. Six-packs of root beer caught his attention.

Their smiles had some sort of hold over him. He needed to break that hold, break their smiles, and glass bottles were promising. He'd always thought those scenes in the movies when a guy broke a bottle over someone's head looked hilarious. In real life, though, it had to be effective.

Marley opened the carton with his bared teeth and drank. Not a drop ran down his shirt despite the greedy gulps. Behind Saul, Dutch laughed.

Saul opened the heavy cream and lifted it as if to drink. With one swift motion he turned around and splashed Dutch full in the face. She stumbled back. When she opened her mouth to call out, Saul had already grabbed the nearest root beer by the neck and slammed the bottle into her upper jaw. A couple teeth went flying.

He didn't wait for Marley to react. That was the biggest mistake fresh meat made at the ranch. During a run, they'd look back to see how much of a lead they had and would lose ground. Or they started to trash talk. So Saul was already climbing up and over the metal shelving like he'd done so many times at the obstacle course. Bags of chips popped and crumpled beneath him as he scrambled and landed on the other side of the aisle.

But his shoes were still wet. Saul skidded on the floor. He pulled down a spinning rack of travel maps to block the way behind him.

All he had to do was make it outside. He was sure he

could lose them in the woods behind the gas station.

His mistake was noticing the surveillance camera by the ceiling. The barrel turned toward Saul, who, surprised, hesitated.

From behind, a strong hand grasped his shoulder and pulled him backward. Ice-cold nails stabbed through the fabrics to bite his flesh.

"We've been too kind to you." Marley's fingernails dug deeper into Saul, making him cry out. Marley slipped his other hand beneath Saul's shirts to stroke and scratch his stomach. "We're no better than magpies. Pretty things distract us."

Saul heard Dutch scream, "Kihl im!" though the words were blurred by her ruined mouth.

He felt Marley push his cold fingers down the front of his jeans. Marley nuzzled his ear, and the stink of curdled milk made Saul gag.

"That mark poisoned your blood, but I'll enjoy—"

Saul suddenly sprang backward, slamming Marley into the ATM. They struggled near the coffee station, but Saul couldn't reach one of the hot pots. His fingers closed around the handle of one yellowed ceramic mug stacked in a pyramid on the counter. Its fellows tumbled noisily to the floor. He slammed the mug into Marley's side and gut. The guy went down, clutching his abdomen.

Saul glanced at the mug, dusty and cracked, a relic older

than him. Black lettering on the side said IOWA, YOU MAKE ME SMILE. He threw the mug at Marley's crotch and ran.

Before he reached the door, his peripheral vision spotted the mop, its wormy head tangled and dripping, before it struck his chest. He stumbled into a shelf, the metal raking his back, cans and shrink-wrapped goods spilling around him. Dutch shrieked as she slammed the mop against his knees and sent him to the floor.

She stood over him with a slack jaw filled with broken teeth. But no blood; delicate strands of saliva webbed her lips and hung from her chin. She reversed the mop in her hands, so the blunt end hovered over his neck. Saul could see her struggle with her lips to make a smile.

Fresh light played over Dutch. When she raised her head to look out the glass panels, Saul grabbed at her leg, pulling hard. She lost her balance and fell, her head making a sickening smack as it struck the linoleum.

That should take her out, he thought, but she was lashing out, trying to stab at him with the mop. He grabbed the nearest can rolling on the floor—an aerosol, some sort of air freshener—and sprayed her full in the face. She cried out, tried to wipe her eyes as the smell of sweet faux lemons filled the air.

Saul stood. A car had pulled askew of the pumps and its headlights were aimed directly at the convenience store.

He stopped at the counter—without any urge to peer over and see the body—to grab a lighter. The other stunt from the movies he'd always wanted to try was igniting an aerosol spray.

Outside, the rain had slowed to a steady drizzle. He could still smell the gas vapors from the spilled trash drum.

The driver's side door of the idling car—no, a pickup truck, he saw—opened, flashing Saul the Cotre Ranch "endless trail" logo. Phelps stepped out.

He must have been searching the highway for me, Saul thought. He felt relief at being found. He was more battered and bloody from fending off homicidal siblings than from anything the ranch had thrown at him. And yet beneath that relief was a dismal emptiness at knowing he'd be taken back to the ranch. So much for finding a new life.

"Saul, get in the truck," Phelps said, then reached across the truck's seat for something.

Saul stepped into the headlights' beam. "Two psychopaths are in there." He held aloft the aerosol. Despite the drizzle, flicking the lighter would probably ignite the very air around him, but he couldn't let Phelps get hurt because of him.

"I know," Phelps said.

"Wait. You . . . you know?"

"Course." Phelps hefted what could only be a crossbow. "Boys watching the closed circuit told me you did good."

He began walking toward the store.

"But—"

Phelps carefully pushed open the door. "Shit, looks like I'm cleanup crew tonight." He spit on the ground and chuckled. "Get into the pickup. And don't be messing up my radio stations. They're a bitch to program."

Saul noticed that Phelps left the keys in the ignition. He told himself to count to a hundred while the man made the fatalities. If he wasn't back by then . . .

But he was, with a grin, before Saul reached sixty-eight.

As Phelps smoked a cigarette and drove, Saul had to listen to Patsy Cline walk after midnight and Merle Haggard avoiding mirrors.

"You weren't supposed to even know about *their kind* till Christmas." Phelps flicked hot ash out the open window.

"Hanukkah."

"Right. Hanukkah." Phelps managed not to mangle the word.

"So the other boys at the ranch . . ."

"Some know. We'd been luring that pair through the internet for months. The boys were supposed to go out hunting tonight. 'Cept someone messed with the gate."

"Guess I'm in trouble."

Phelps didn't say anything but kept driving. The truck's cab was bitter cold from the wind.

Phelps braked the truck to a stop in the middle of the

road. "Minnesota is a couple miles north. Just follow the road. Truck stop not far over the border." He pulled out a scuffed leather wallet. "Bounty on two of 'em—let's say two hundred." He held out four wrinkled fifty-dollar bills to Saul.

"I don't understand," Saul said.

"You're the one who ran. Thought you wanted out."

"But—"

"The boys who know . . ." Phelps crushed his cigarette into a crowded ashtray. "Well, they work extra hard 'fore they can go out hunting. What you went through before, that'll seem like a Hawaiian vacation."

Saul still had the aerosol can in his lap. He could never look at it the same way anymore. Tonight had transformed it from a cheap, lemon-scented air freshener into an aluminum trophy. And he could feel transformed, too. He didn't want to step out of the truck and keep walking down a highway. Not after what he'd seen, what he'd done. He looked Phelps in the eyes. He knew the man was ready to pass judgment, depending on what Saul did next.

He fingered the top of the aerosol. "Ever light the spray? I mean, when you're fighting one of *them*. Like a mini flamethrower?"

Phelps slipped the money back into his wallet, back into his slacks. "Never wanted to burn my face off," he said.

Saul knew he had passed the test. They'd turn around, head back to the ranch. And whatever grueling crap he'd face when he woke would be fine, because this time he'd been the one who chose the ranch, and this time as reward, not some punishment.

Still, he couldn't resist leaning out the window as Phelps put the truck in gear. His hand was steady as he held the lighter to the can and squeezed. Saul found himself grinning as a tongue of blue-and-yellow flames licked the cold night air.

GAP YEAR

by Christopher Barzak

When the vampires came to town, there was an assembly in the high school gymnasium. Retta and Lottie sat next to each other on the bleachers, like they did every day in study hall, their hands folded between their pressed-together knees. The three vampires who stood on the stage had something to tell them. "We're people, too," said the head vampire, if that's what you call a vampire who speaks for other vampires. He couldn't have been more than eighteen. A splash of freckles on his face. Mousy brown fauxhawk. A tight, too-short Pixies concert T-shirt showing off a strip of skin above the waistband of his boxers. He wore jeans with a snakeskin belt hanging loose in the loops. If you saw him in the hallway, you wouldn't suspect him of being a vampire. Retta and Lottie weren't sure if they suspected him of being a vampire now, even though he said he was.

"We just want you to know that we're not all about silk

cravats and rural villages that sit at the bottoms of eastern
European mountain ranges," he told the assembled population of freshmen through seniors. "We don't necessarily kill,
although some do, but they aren't representative of us as a
whole."

"Oh my God," said Lottie. "I cannot believe they're doing
public outreach. It's pathetic. I *want* the cravats, whatever
those are. I *want* the rural villages that sit at the bottoms of
eastern European mountain ranges. Not these losers."

"They're ties," Retta whispered. "Victorian ties. Shh."

Lottie rolled her eyes. She said, "You're too nice, Retta."

Retta isn't Retta's full name—it's Loretta; but since they
were little, people have called her Retta because she and Lottie
have always been best friends and two L-named girls who are
consistently spotted as a pair are annoying. Lottie and Retta
had once agreed: They didn't want to be like those siblings
whose parents name them all under the tyranny of one letter, like steps going up and down a staircase, the same, one
right after the other. It was Lottie who came up with Retta
For a while Retta had wondered why it was her who had to
change her name, not Lottie, whose full name was actually
Charlotte, but it was Retta that stuck.

"We would also like to disabuse you of the notion that we
are all bloodsucking fiends with fangs," the head vampire told
them. His companions nodded behind him. One was a short,
chubby boy who looked like he should be playing a tuba in

the marching band, glasses that he'd taped together on one side, a potentially obsessive thumb sucker. The other was a hyperthin girl, skin white as paper, wearing black boots, black jeans, black tank top, black earrings made of some kind of dark crystal. She had long black hair and wore black lipstick. She was probably not the head vampire's best choice in representing the unexpected in vampires. Find comfort in familiarity when familiarity is disappointing, Retta reminded herself. That's what the guidance counselor had told her at her senior session when Retta had said she didn't know what she wanted to do after high school but was hoping to somehow get out into the world. "Thanks," Retta had said upon receiving that wafer of wisdom, then told the next kid it was his turn when she left the counselor's office.

"Did that dude just say he was abused as a child?" Lottie whispered. "No doubt that's the reason for his vampirism."

"Shh," Retta said again. "They deserve to be heard, too."

"*Too* what?" said Lottie.

"*Too* like anyone," said Retta. "Lottie, will you please just pay attention? Mr. Masters is looking up at us. We're going to get detention."

That shut Lottie up. Nothing was worse than sitting in a stale classroom with Mrs. Markowitz after school. Mrs. Markowitz, who has taught freshman algebra since the dawn of time, expects you to look straight at her as she reads romance novels at her desk during detention. Retta always focused on the cover, the muscular chest of a man as he wrapped the heroine up in his arms. She'd imagine the book, the ink on the paper, make it up as Mrs. Markowitz turned each page. Lottie would spend the entire period burning holes into Mrs. Markowitz with laser eyes. She lacked imagination.

The head vampire said, "We feed, yes, but we do not always feed on blood."

A boy in the row behind the girls shouted, "Yeah, they feed on your mom!"

Lots of laughter followed. Yuk, yuk, yuk. But the head vampire did not look amused. "That's right," he said, staring up at the kid who had insulted him. "We feed on your mom. Your mom, she's really great. A little misunderstood. I don't know why people talk so bad about her."

"Who the hell do you think you are, man!" the kid behind Lottie and Retta said. He was suddenly up and rearing. Everyone in the bleachers turned to look. The bleachers creaked like a ship at sea. Because the kid stood directly behind Lottie and Retta, it felt like everyone was staring at them, all those faces a spotlight. "You better watch your mouth, dude!" the kid behind them said. His face was red and puffy, his long hair shining with the sort of grease that can only accumulate after long periods of not washing. He looked like *he* could be a vampire. Retta wondered if perhaps he was just afraid to admit it. A self-loathing vampire. Such people existed.

"No, you better watch *your* mouth, *dude*," said the head

vampire with his microphone pressed against his mouth, amplifying the challenge. Everyone turned again, a tennis audience, to look his way. Something in his voice was different. And when Retta saw him, something in his eyes had changed. They didn't glisten or sparkle, they didn't look like anything but brown eyes in a slightly freckled fauxhawked boy's face. But they held her.

"Whoa," said Lottie. "Things are getting kind of rash."

The head vampire continued to stare up at the greasy-haired kid behind them, and the longer he stared, the quieter the gymnasium got. Whispers faded until no one said anything, and then suddenly the greasy-haired kid burst into tears and sat down, covering his face with his hands. He sobbed. He wiped his face on his shoulder. It was awkward for a minute. Then the principal finally broke out of the spell the head vampire had seemingly put on everyone and said, "That's enough, all right, that's enough. We've given you people a forum—what else do you want?"

"Respect," said the head vampire. Then he walked down the stage steps toward the gym doors, his vampire cohorts following, casting glares over their shoulders.

As the doors swung shut, the principal said, "All right, everyone, sorry that got out of hand, but it's over. You can go back to your classes now and discuss in small groups."

"Discuss *what*?" said Lottie. Retta elbowed her, but Lottie had spoken loud enough for the principal to hear.

"Discuss what these young people had to say," he said, looking up at Lottie. Everyone turned to stare at the girls again. "Times are changing, Ms. Kennedy. If you don't change with them, you'll be left behind."

"Change or die," Lottie said, smirking. "I get it. Isn't there a third option, though, Mr. Masters? Why not be a vampire? Like them? That way, you never have to change. That way, you never have to die."

"That's a stereotype," a girl in the front row said. Looking back at Lottie, the girl touched the frame of her glasses, pushed them up the bridge of her nose. Lottie stuck out her tongue. Then the principal said enough is enough again, and sent everyone packing.

On the way out of the assembly, Lottie turned to Retta and said, "Only last period left. Screw it. Want to leave?"

"And go where?"

"Home," said Lottie. "We can hang at my place for a while."

"Sure," said Retta, and they ducked down a hallway that opened onto the student parking lot, where a hundred cars gleamed hotly under the mid-May afternoon sun. Someday soon, in a few weeks, I will never have to see any of this, thought Retta. She ran her hands through her hair, unsure if she should be happy or sad.

They were only halfway across the lot, though, when she saw the head vampire standing against a car, a large maroon Cadillac, staring in their direction. In her direction, actually.

His vampire friends were gone. Lottie was saying something about a video game she played online, about a character she'd made last night, someone who carried a sword and wore lots of armor. Retta kept saying, "Yeah? Oh, yeah?" but she couldn't break from the head vampire's stare. And finally, once they reached Lottie's car, Retta said, "I think maybe this wasn't such a good idea."

"What wasn't?"

"Ditching."

"Come on, Retta, are you serious?"

"Yeah," said Retta. "I'm going back in. You go. Sorry."

"You are acting so weird lately, Retta," said Lottie. "But whatever. Fine. Take notes for me or something."

Lottie got into her car, started it while pointedly not looking at Retta, then pulled away.

Retta, on the other hand, turned around and saw the head vampire was still there, leaning against that car. Still staring at her.

But instead of going to her last class, she crossed the lot toward him.

The thing to know about Lottie is that she's a difficult person to be friends with. Retta used to take pride in her patience with her. Lottie was almost always mad about something. "The world is so full of stupid people," she liked to say. Retta didn't know if Lottie really meant that or if she just said it, because Lottie did sincerely get angry with people who said and did stupid things. Like cheerleaders. Lottie hated cheerleaders, mostly because of the cheers, how strident they were, how unquestioning. Lottie once said cheerleaders would be more effective if their cheers called their own team's ability into doubt when behind in a game, rather than trying to boost morale. But sometimes Retta wanted more than sitting around with Lottie discussing the uselessness of certain teachers, the annoyance brought on by certain students who actually cared about things like prom and the commencement ceremony that they would totally regret missing if they missed it, according to their parents, teachers, classmates, Hallmark greeting cards, and certain television shows modeled on the moralizing tendencies of 1980s and '90s afterschool specials. Sometimes Retta just wanted more *more*. This is what she was probably wanting when she walked up to the head vampire in the parking lot and said, "Hi. I heard your speech. Very interesting."

"Interesting?" said the head vampire. He bobbed his head from side to side, pursing his lips, weighing her statement. "I guess so," he said. "Interesting if you've never met a vampire."

"You're the first one."

"That you know of," said the head vampire. His eyes

widened after he said this, and Retta started to think maybe she'd made a mistake, that vampires didn't deserve a chance at friendship after all. But then he laughed, and then he smiled. "Just a joke," he said. "What's your name?"

"Loretta," she said, feeling like she was giving a fake name, as if he might be a stalker, even though she'd been the one to cross the parking lot under a hot sun.

"Loretta? That's kind of old-fashioned," he said, and Retta said only if you think about it for a while. He said, "Why are we talking, Loretta?"

"Just thought I'd introduce myself. I liked what you had to say."

"Are you a vampire, Loretta?" he said, narrowing his eyes, nostrils flaring.

"Me?" said Retta. "Ha ha. I don't think so."

"Sometimes people are and don't realize," he said. "Like me. I didn't realize for a long time."

"How can you not realize something like that?"

"Because," he said. "I don't drink blood."

Retta asked what he drank instead.

"Emotions," he said. "Feelings."

Hearing him say those two words made her stomach flutter.

"What's your name?" she asked.

"Trevor," said the head vampire.

"Well, Trevor," said Retta. "It was nice meeting you. Good luck with your campaign for vampire equality."

"Wait a second," he said as she turned to walk away. "Are you going home now?"

"Why?" she asked.

He said, "I can give you a ride."

Retta stared at the cinnamon splash of freckles on his cheeks and tried to calculate the potential danger in accepting a ride from a vampire. In the end, she started nodding. And finally she said, "Okay."

The ride to Retta's house was just two miles. She could have walked it, she usually walked it, and it seemed to disappoint Trevor when he realized he only had her in his car for a total of eight minutes, almost all of which Retta didn't look at him. Instead she rolled down the window and leaned her arms across it, her head on her arms, watching the passing houses with beds of bright flowers decorating their front yards. And when Trevor asked questions, like whether or not she was disturbed by the scene that had occurred in the gym, Retta didn't bother to look at him when she answered. She just said, "I don't know," and let the wind take the words from her mouth, watched them tumble behind her, tin cans dancing across the pavement. It was only once they turned onto her street that she sat back against the hot leather.

"Do you think we'll ever be accepted?" said Trevor.

"Who? Vampires?"

He nodded.

"Sure," said Retta. "There are precedents. People of color. Women. Gay people. Wiccans. I mean, I *already* accept you. So there you go."

"So there you go?" said Trevor, smiling as he pulled his car against the curb.

"How did you know this was my house?" asked Retta. "How did you know this was my street?" She hadn't given any directions.

"Inside," said Trevor, lifting his finger to his temple and tapping. "Didn't you notice me inside, searching?"

Retta stared at him for a long second before opening the door to climb out.

"Hey. I'm sorry," said Trevor. "I didn't mean to scare you."

Retta closed the door and bent down to look at him through the window. From above, his fauxhawk made him look a little birdlike, a brown baby chick who knew how to drive. "You don't scare me," she said, and started up the walk to the front porch.

"Hey, Loretta," Trevor called after her. "Hey, can I come in?"

"No," said Retta, turning to look back at him. "That would not be a good idea. If you let a vampire into your house, they can come in anytime they want afterward."

"I'm not that kind of vampire," said Trevor, grinning, stretching farther across his seat to call out from the rolled-down passenger window.

"That's right," said Retta. "And I'm not that kind of girl."

When she turned to continue on her way, she let herself smile, just a little.

Vampires had been appearing on all the news channels and in all the papers for several months by then. They were usually sad or angry, mostly because they had all lived isolated lives, misunderstood by normal people. Some were excited, though, to finally have a chance to speak about their lives in public without threat of being hunted, staked in the heart, or burned to cinders so that they could never regenerate. "As if!" one old woman vampire had said on CNN from her living-room recliner. "I wish I could regenerate!" she told the interviewer. "I would never have had my hip replaced!"

There were so many of them, and so many kinds, more than Retta had ever imagined. There were vampires who fed on the blood of others, and there were vampires who fed on feelings, like Trevor. There were vampires who fed on sunlight (they mostly lived in Florida, California, Hawaii, and at certain times of the year Alaska), and there were vampires who fed on the dark, eating their way from midnight to morning. There were vampires who fed on tree bark and vampires that fed on crustaceans, there were vampires who fed on nothing but the sound of human voices, and there were vampires who fed on any attention they could receive (they often took up karaoke, made YouTube videos, or auditioned for reality television shows). They were everywhere, once you started looking, although it wasn't until Trevor and his friends came to speak that Retta had ever seen one in person. That she knew of, as Trevor had weakly jested. To be honest, she'd expected something different. An old-fashioned vampire with long, sharp teeth, or at least one of the less expected vampires, the sort she could watch with fascination as they ate through a meal of darkness, or one who looked as if she were carved out of ivory, with bright green eyes, or some other sexy, slightly otherworldly physical composition.

But despite the fact that they seemed harmless, over the weekend phone calls were strung from house to house, and by Sunday parents were either frowning or wide-eyed with terror. Retta's mother came into her room after receiving a call from her best friend, whose daughter was a junior and had been at the assembly, and said, "Why didn't you tell me about these vampires, Retta?"

She stood in the doorway, hands on her hips.

Retta said, "Oh, them. I forgot about them."

"How can you forget about vampires, Retta? They got into an argument with a boy who was sitting behind you! Seriously, I am livid. What did Mr. Masters think he was doing by having them in for an assembly?"

"Helping to educate us about vampires?"

"Retta," said her mother, "you are so unwitting. Listen, because I'm only going to tell you once: no vampires, young lady. Not in this house, not outside it. Understand?"

"I have no idea what you're talking about," said Retta, closing her book and sighing.

"I know you, Retta," said her mother. "You're the sort of girl we call 'susceptible.'"

When she left, Retta said, "Who's *we*?"

But her mother didn't answer. She was already down the hall in her own bedroom yelling at Retta's father about vampires, as if their existence were all his fault.

Retta wanted to disown them. She wanted to disown everything: her room, her house, her street, her town. She even wanted, after twelve years of best friendship, to disown Lottie, who sat down across from her at a picnic table during lunch on Monday and said, "You total slut," without any prelude.

Retta looked up from her cup of strawberry yogurt and said, "What are you talking about?"

"I saw you," said Lottie in a harsh, whispery voice. She leaned across the table and said, "I saw you ride home with that vampire kid last Friday. You didn't go back to class. You totally went off with him."

"What are you, some kind of stalker?" asked Retta,

twirling her spork in the plastic yogurt container, trying not to look at Lottie.

"Stalker? Oh, really? Is that how it is? *I'm* a stalker, not some kid who says he's a vampire?" Lottie tucked her hair behind her ears and shook her head in resignation.

"You are so dramatic, Lottie."

"What's his name?"

"Trevor," said Retta, who could not help but smile a little after she said it, as if she were only telling one half of a secret, keeping the rest to herself.

"Uck," said Lottie. "Even his name is a loser name. What are you going to do? Marry him and have loser vampire babies?"

"Grow up, Lottie," said Retta. "You don't know anything about him."

"Neither do you, I bet," said Lottie. She folded her arms across her chest and leaned back, sitting up straight. "I bet you don't even know where he lives."

"No," said Retta. "You're right. I don't."

"But he knows where *you* live," said Lottie, tilting her head to the side, smirking like she'd just won a game of chess.

"I'm okay with that," said Retta, and stood up to throw away her yogurt.

"Hey," said Lottie. "Where are you going? What's the matter with you? Retta?"

"I'm late for chorus," said Retta, and kept on going.

Behind her, Lottie said, "Retta! I'm serious! You should be more careful!"

"I am," said Retta over her shoulder. "I'm always careful. I'm nothing but careful."

But there was nothing for Retta to be careful about, really, because when she stepped out of her last class and into the parking lot that afternoon, he wasn't there. And he wasn't there the next day either. Or the next. It was Wednesday, then it was Thursday, and although everyone was still talking about the vampires, it seemed like they might never see one again. There were a few people who now claimed they were vampires, of course: Jason Snelling, who had been a nose picker for as long as anyone could remember, so no one was really impressed; and Tammie Galore, an ex-cheerleader who had quit cheering because she'd fallen from the top of a pyramid a year ago, and six months of wearing a cast up to her crotch and having multiple surgeries to fix her leg afterward had left her afraid to return to the happy squad. Apparently she was a vampire, too, although she never revealed what kind, exactly. Most people assumed she was lying for the attention.

And there were others who came forward: a quiet librarian who wore cat-eye glasses and white blouses with pearl buttons, tight little navy blue skirts; a plumber who lived just three streets over from Retta, who had actually been in her house to fix a toilet, but since it was for pay it probably didn't invoke the vampire right to enter a house once he's been invited, said Retta's father; an old man who played the saxophone downtown on Friday and Saturday nights, wearing sunglasses as if it were still bright out. Retta had always assumed he was blind. Go figure.

It was a week of lively discussion that followed the appearance of Trevor and his vampire friends. Even the PTA had met by that Thursday evening to discuss whether Mr. Masters should be penalized for having allowed the vampires to speak at all. "Of course he should be," said Retta's mother after she came home from the meeting. "He should be fired. We should sue him for endangering the lives of our children."

"We only have one child," said Retta's father, hanging up his Windbreaker in the foyer closet.

"It's a figure of speech, Clyde," said Retta's mother. "It's a figure of speech."

Retta left them arguing over the issue in the kitchen and went upstairs to sit on her bed and look at her room as if it would offer her something special at that very moment. But all she saw was her hairbrush, curling iron, an uncapped lipstick on the dresser, a rumpled bedspread, clothes she hadn't worn in a long time strung out on the floor in twisted shapes like the chalked outlines of murder victims. Then her cell phone rang and she reached for it with extreme zeal, glad that, finally, the world had responded in a timely manner to her request for a reprieve from her own inertia. She looked at the call screen. It was Lottie. "Hello?" said Retta.

"Hey, did you hear about the PTA meeting?"

"Yeah, my mom and dad just got home," said Retta. "Penalty or no penalty? Poor Mr. Masters."

"Sounds like they'll let it go this time," said Lottie, "but not if he screws up again."

"Lottie," said Retta, "why are we even interested? We're graduating. We're out of here. If I want to talk to a vampire, I can. We're adults, aren't we?"

There was silence on the other end of the phone for a moment. Then Lottie said, "You are so hot for that kid! I can't believe it!"

"Shut up!" said Retta. "You're not even listening to me."

"You're not even listening to yourself!" said Lottie.

"Whatever," said Retta. "Anyway, what are you going to do this summer? Or next fall, for that matter?"

"I'm thinking about finding work as one of those people who do sleep experiments," said Lottie. "They're always advertising for those. Seems like a steady job."

"Hmm," said Retta, "sounds as good as anything I've got."

"College?" said Lottie.

"Oh, yeah, that. My mom brought home an application for the community college the other day, said I could stay here if I didn't feel like trying school somewhere else. I don't know. Don't British kids go on something called gap year after high school? Where they go to some poor eastern European country or some island in the Mediterranean for a year and help people out and stuff? That's what I'd like to do. Maybe."

"Retta, you're not British."

"I know," said Retta. "It's a figure of speech."

"No, it's not," said Lottie.

Retta was about to ask if Lottie was going to pick her up on the way to school tomorrow, then maybe they could go to the mall afterward and stare at things and people, but as she opened her mouth to speak, a spray of pebbles rattled against her bedroom window. "Hold on a sec," she told Lottie, the mall forgotten, and got up from her bed to look out.

It was night out, but beneath the big oak in front of the backyard's mercury light, she could see him, his face covered in leafy shadows, the hands that had tossed those pebbles up to her window like he was out of some 1950s movie now stuffed in the front pockets of his jeans. He pulled one out when Retta showed up at the window, lifted it into the air to flick her a wave.

She told Lottie it was her mom calling her, and clicked the phone off before Lottie could argue. Then she pulled up the window, stuck her head out, and whispered, "I can't come out there. My parents would see you."

"Then can I come up?" he whispered back.

"How?" said Retta. "Do you have a ladder?"

The next instant he was climbing her mother's rose trellis, hand over hand, the tips of his shoes seeking purchase. In a minute he was three feet beneath her window. "Can you give me a lift?" he said, reaching with one hand, holding on to the trellis with the other.

"Are you serious?" said Retta. "I can't lift you."

"I'm lighter than I look."

She sighed, leaned out, stretched.

He was telling the truth. He was light, so light, in fact, that she pulled him over her windowsill not quite like a rag doll, but not far from it. It made Retta want to diet. "What are you?" she said. "On a hunger strike or something?"

"No," he said. "I'm empty."

They sat down on her floor, and Trevor folded his legs beneath him like an Indian guru. "So what are you doing here?" asked Retta, trying to keep things business formal.

"I missed you," he said.

She said, "You don't even know me."

"Sure I do," he said. "I know you better than you think, remember?" He tapped his temple like he did the day he'd given her a ride.

"So you read minds?"

"A little," he said. "Enough to know you've been wondering where I've been for the past week."

"*Everyone's* been wondering where you and your friends disappeared to for the past week," said Retta. "Don't flatter yourself."

"But you've been wondering more than everyone else,"

he said. Retta made a face that said, You are so stupid.

"You have," he said. "Admit it."

"Okay," she admitted. "Maybe."

"Loretta," he said. "Loretta, Loretta, Loretta," he said, like her name was something musical.

"What?"

"I was just thinking about your name. Do you have a nickname?"

"No," she said.

"Doesn't anyone call you Lo?"

She shook her head.

"Then that's what I'll call you. Lo."

"Loretta is fine."

"But Lo is much better," he said. "Can't you feel it?"

"Feel what?"

"The sadness in Lo. The anguish."

"I don't feel it," said Retta. "No."

"Because you don't like feeling," he said. He stood and went to her mirror, primping his fauxhawk, which wasn't really out of place. "You don't like feeling because it hurts too much," he said. "You numb yourself to feelings. But you feel more than you ever let yourself know."

"Okay, *Trevor*," said Retta. "What am I feeling right now?"

"You feel like you're going to tear this town down. You feel like you're waiting for something to happen, for someone to tell you what you want. You feel all that and more. You feel a lot, Lo," he said. "You feel so much."

Retta looked down at the carpet and didn't say anything. He left the mirror and came over to her, his red Chuck Taylors inching into her vision. She looked up, blinked, unsure whether to be angry or relieved that he'd said all that. That he'd known.

"I can help," he said. "We can help each other."

"How?"

"I can take some from you, if you let me."

"Take what?"

"Some feelings."

"You know," said Retta, "I've been very tolerant and accommodating about your condition, but at this point I think I should probably say that I never quite believed you and your friends. Nor the old woman on CNN this past week, nor the librarian, nor the blind musician downtown."

He sat down across from her again and said, "Let me show you."

"Really, Trevor," said Retta, ready to protest, but her next words surprised even her: "Okay, sure. Show me."

He reached over and grabbed her hands from her lap, his fingertips brushing against her palms, tickling. Then he closed his eyes, and Retta felt something move inside her, displacing her organs, shifting around. She shivered. Then it was in her chest. She tried to say, "Maybe this isn't something I want to do after all," but she couldn't. By then it was in her throat. She gulped, trying to swallow down whatever it was. Then she opened her mouth and began huffing and puffing. Tears formed, trembled, rolled down her cheeks. She couldn't stop them. She couldn't take her hands away from him either, even though Trevor barely had hold of them. She was stuck, breathing in short, sharp bursts, whimpering. Then he opened his eyes, licked his lips, and said, "Thank you."

She took her hands away and wiped the tears from her face, stood up, and almost fell over. Her center of balance was nonexistent. The room spun, then slowed to a stop. She felt like she could lift off the floor, drift over to the window and out into the sky if she wanted. "I think you should go," she told him.

"I won't be able to go down that trellis now," said Trevor. He stood, put his hands in his pockets again, sheepish. "I'm full now," he said. "The trellis probably won't hold me."

Retta said that he would have to go as soon as her parents were asleep. He assured her he'd leave as quietly as he'd come. "Where were you the past week, anyway?" asked Retta.

"At school," he said. "I don't go to your school. I don't live in your town. I live in the next town over."

"Do people there know you're a vampire?"

"Yeah," said Trevor. "But it's pretty liberal there. No problem."

"Am I going to become a vampire now that you fed on me?" she wanted to know.

"No," said Trevor. "Vampires aren't made, they're born."

"So I couldn't be a vampire even if I wanted?"

He said, "I don't think so. No."

"What a waste," said Retta. "What a waste of a perfectly good cultural icon."

The next day, Lottie said, "I'm afraid for our friendship."

Retta said, "Lottie, why does everything with you have to be a chick flick?"

"It so does not have to be a chick flick!" said Lottie. "Seriously, Retta, you have been a total space-a-zoid for the past few weeks. It's not cool. Everyone has noticed."

"Who's *everyone*?" said Retta. "You're my only friend. I'm your only friend."

"I've made some other friends, I guess," said Lottie. She stopped walking down the mall concourse and took hold of Retta's arm, squeezing gently. She'd brought Retta here, to the place where they'd spent most of their free time the past few years, in a last-ditch attempt to remind Retta about the bonds of their friendship, to surround her with shared memories of shopping and telling each other they looked good in certain outfits. But as Retta looked around at all the neon commerce and mass-produced entertainment surrounding her, she couldn't help but sigh and wonder why none of any of it made sense to her any longer.

An enormous man eating a Frisbee-sized chocolate chip

cookie passed behind Lottie as she waited for Retta to react to her declaration of having made other friends. The fat man was the sort of thing Lottie usually would have seen coming a mile away and would have commented on; and, at one time, the two of them would have bonded over making fun of him. Retta felt her face flush, embarrassed. She didn't want to be the sort of person who boosted her sense of well-being by laughing at other people's addictions, just because she herself didn't know what she wanted so badly. And though she would have disapproved of Lottie's blithe nastiness, now she just wanted her to say something terrible. It would have made ignoring her plaintive grasping easier.

"You've made other friends," said Retta. "That's nice. Who are they?"

Lottie winced. She was wearing a T-shirt Retta had bought in a store for boys a year ago, lent Lottie six months ago, and never gotten back. It had a yellow smiley face smack dab in the middle, stretched across Lottie's ample chest. Lottie folded her arms over the face, as if to emphasize her unhappiness. Even the smiley face wasn't allowed to be happy.

"It doesn't matter who they are, Retta," said Lottie.

"Loretta," said Retta.

"What matters," said Lottie, "is me and you. Us! What happened? We've spent our whole lives together and now we're graduating next weekend and you're all like, Whatever whatever, I'm in love with a vampire!"

"I am so *not* 'Whatever whatever, I'm in love with a vampire!'" said Retta. "I'm . . . enlarging my environment. That's all."

"I can't believe you will stand here and lie to me like that, Retta."

"Seriously, Lottie?" said Retta. "We're standing in front of Victoria's Secret, not some hallowed monument to truth telling. And I'm not lying! Vampires are retarded. I could live for the rest of my life without seeing another vampire and be totally happy. Why won't you let me be happy?"

Lottie's jaw dropped. "I don't even know you anymore, Retta."

"*Loretta.*"

"Whatever," said Lottie. "I can totally do without Loretta. Call me when Retta comes back." She turned, arms still folded over the smiley face, hands clamped on her forearms like the mall air conditioning had just gotten way too chilly, and walked away in a hurry, leaning forward as if she were trudging uphill through driven snow.

Retta couldn't feel the chill, though. She couldn't feel anything, or wouldn't allow herself, like Trevor had told her. And it wasn't until Lottie had disappeared from sight that Retta remembered Lottie had driven them to the mall, that she was stranded.

She called her mom on her cell phone to ask if she would pick her up, but all she got was voice mail, her mother's happy voice singing out the obvious fact that she couldn't answer the phone. Retta looked at the time—six o'clock—and realized her parents had probably just arrived at their Friday Night Out, drinking wine in a restaurant with a bunch of people going *ha ha ha*, fanning their faces with their hands because something someone had just said was way too funny.

So she started walking.

Walking was what Retta did for the next few days, for the final week she would spend in that building that had housed her throughout her weekdays for the last few years of her teenaged life. She walked through her neighborhood, looking up through the new leaves at the sun, daring it, trying not to blink. She walked down the newly edged sidewalks on Monday and Tuesday, heading to school with her head hanging, watching her feet go back and forth. Lottie drove past both days, on the way to school, on the way home, but never looked at Retta, even though Retta looked at her, ready to wave. Lottie only sat in her car face forward, windows down, the wind blowing hair around her face.

Maybe it was better that way, spending the last week of classes getting used to not being around Lottie, who used those same last-minute days of their secondary education making an attempt at fast friendship with Tammie Galore, of all people, the ex-cheerleader turned vampire, which, it turned out, had been completely fabricated, as everyone had suspected. Retta supposed that Tammie's backpedaling on her declaration of vampirism, along with her previous defection from the cheer squad, was what probably made her seem like a potential candidate for Lottie's new best friend. In fact, by Thursday of that week, Tammie Galore was no longer Tammie but Tam-Tam, which everyone thought was cute and why hadn't they all been calling her that for ages? Retta could have told them. Because Tam-Tam is not a cute name. Because Tam-Tam reeks of the desire to be someone you're not.

She was walking home on Friday, taking long steps—trudging, really—when Trevor pulled alongside her in his car. She kept walking, though, so he began to follow, driving slowly, revving his Cadillac's engine every now and then. "Hey, Lo," he called out his window.

Retta looked over and said, "What?"

He grinned before saying, "Well, *someone* isn't very happy."

"That's right," said Retta. "I'm not happy. I'm not sad either, though, Trevor, I think you should know that."

"What are you then?" said Trevor, and Retta stepped over the devil strip to the road, opened the passenger-side door even as his car idled forward, hopped in.

"I'm nothing," she said, slamming the door shut. "I don't feel anything. I'm affectless, a sufferer of ennui, apathetic, a-emotional."

"That's not true," said Trevor. He pushed down on the

gas to go faster. "I tasted your feelings. You filled me up. I was full for days."

"There could be a banquet inside me and I wouldn't be able to taste any of it," said Retta. She wanted to cry, because now was the sort of moment a person would cry, at a crisis point, confessing to their own flaws and weaknesses. But she couldn't. If she had any tears, they weren't raising their hands, volunteering their services.

When they pulled up to her house, Retta said, "I wonder if I could feel someone else's? What if you were right? What if I'm like you and just don't know it? What if I'm a vampire, only I can't feel my own feelings?"

"I guess anything is possible," said Trevor.

"If I was like that," said Retta, "would you let me have some of yours?"

"Who? Me?" said Trevor, pointing at his chest, eyebrows rising higher on the slope of his shiny forehead.

"Yeah," said Retta. "Is there anyone else in the car?"

"Sure," said Trevor, shrugging. "Yeah, you bet."

"Can we try then?" said Retta.

"You mean now?"

"Yeah," said Retta. "Now. Why do you keep answering my questions with questions?"

"Sorry," he said. "I guess . . . I just wasn't prepared for this."

"Because you came to feed on me, didn't you?" said Retta. "Not the other way around."

"Um . . . ," said Trevor. "I guess?"

"Don't worry," said Retta. "If you're right and I have more feelings than even I'm aware of, there should be plenty. There should be more than enough for both of us."

Back at her house, they sat down on the floor of her room, guru-style again, where Trevor showed Retta how to hold his hands properly, how to push forward, he explained, into someone else. "If you're a vampire," he said, "you'll be able to do it. It's not a trick. You'll just be inside me with the slightest effort. Then, well, you'll know what to do. Trust me."

Retta touched her fingertips against the palms of his hands and pushed forward, as he'd instructed. Immediately the room went dark and she couldn't even see the outlines of sunlight around the blind covering her window. She was inside him. And when she pushed a little further, she found them, his feelings, all tied up in the most intricate of knots. She took hold of one, unraveled it, slipped it inside her mouth, and started chewing. It was glorious between her teeth, bitter-sweet, like her mother's expensive chocolate, soft and sticky as marzipan. It was the way she'd always imagined feeling should be. Visceral. Something she could sink her teeth into.

She untied another, and another, and another, until finally she felt herself lifting up, up, up.

Then—out of him.

She opened her eyes. Light hit her in the face, so much light she felt she might go blind like that street musician downtown. Is that what this did to him? A moment of blinding brilliance after his first taste of something wonderful? Then things began to readjust and her room was her room again, its peach walls surrounding her, and Trevor sat in front of her, sniffing, wiping the backs of his hands against his eyes like the greasy-haired kid had done at the assembly.

"That was hard," he said.

"Then take some from me," said Retta. "Take all of them. Just let me take some back when you're finished."

He stared at her for a long moment. The ridge of his fauxhawk looked like it was wilting. Finally he said, "Lo, this could be the start of something beautiful."

She grinned, all teeth, and nodded.

In the morning, she rose with the first coos of the doves and thought about how symbolic all her actions were, how quickly everything she did now took on sudden significance. It was almost as if she could see everything, even herself, as if she were a benign witness to the actions of others and to the ones she herself was taking, as if she were someone else altogether different from the girl she had been. It was as if she floated above the town where she'd spent the first eighteen years of her life wondering how she'd gotten there, where she was, where she was going. Now she could see everything, as if it were no more than a map she'd hung on her wall, sticking bright red tacks into the places she wanted to visit.

Trevor was passed out on her bed. She'd drained him a few hours earlier, taken what he had and what she'd given, untied all but one of those bright little knots in his stomach, and left him empty. As she stepped carefully down the stairs with his keys in one hand and a bag of clothes in the other, she wondered what he would do when he woke, wondered what her parents would do when they, too, woke to find a vampire in their daughter's bed instead of their daughter.

On the way out, she stopped in the kitchen to scrawl a message on the dry-erase board magnetized to the refrigerator. *It's been fun,* she wrote in purple, her favorite color, and realized even as she wrote the message that purple was her favorite color. *You are all lovely people. But I'm off to start my gap year. XO, Loretta!*

When she was twenty hours away, drinking coffee as she drove down the interstate, eating up mile after beloved mile, her cell phone rang. It had been ringing for the past seventeen hours, but each time it had been one of her parents, and each time she didn't answer, knowing that as soon as she pressed the talk button, nothing but hysterical screams and shouts would come out. This time, though, it was Lottie's name on the screen that kept blinking. Retta answered, but before she could say anything, Lottie spoke in a sharp whisper.

"Retta," she said. "I am sitting in a commencement assembly next to an empty seat with *your* name on it. Where *are* you? Your parents are freaking out and that vampire kid has filed a stolen vehicle report, so you'd better watch out. I guess I was wrong about you. You weren't hot for him. You totally ditched him. But I still don't understand. Tell me one thing, Retta," said Lottie, and Retta imagined Lottie, arms folded over her chest, cell phone pressed to her ear, her plastic black gown and that square little hat, the golden tassel she would flip to the other side in half an hour, her legs crossed, the one on top bouncing furiously. "What happened? Why are you being such a bitch?"

"It's *Loretta!*" screamed Loretta into the phone, like some rock star in the middle of a concert. "And it's because I'm a vampire, Lottie! Because I'm a vampire! Because I'm a vampire!"

She flipped the phone shut and threw it out the window.

It was late morning. The sun was high and red all over. She snarled at herself in the rearview mirror, then laughed, pushed down on the gas, made the car go faster.

BLOODY SUNRISE

by Neil Gaiman

Every night when I crawl out of my grave
looking for someone to meet
some way that we'll misbehave

Every night when I go out on the prowl
And then I fly through the night
With the bats and the owls

Every time I meet somebody
I think you might be the one
I've been on my own for too long
When I pull them closer to me

Bloody Sunrise comes again
leaves me hungry and alone
Every time

Bloody Sunrise comes again
And I'm nowhere to be found
every time
And you're a memory and gone
something else that I can blame on
bloody sunrise

Every night I put on my smartest threads
and I go into the town
and I don't even look dead

Every night I smile and I say hi
and no one ever smiles back
and if I could I'd just die

But when I'm lucky I do get lucky and
I think you might be the one
Even though the time is flying
When we get to the time of dying

Bloody Sunrise comes again
leaves me hungry and alone
Every time
Bloody Sunrise comes again
And I'm nowhere to be found

Every time
And you're a memory and gone
something else that I can blame on
bloody sunrise

FLYING

by Delia Sherman

Lights dazzling her eyes. The platform underfoot, an island in a sea of emptiness. The bar of the trapeze, rigid and slightly tacky against her rosined palms. Far below, a wide sawdust ring surrounded by tiers of white balloons daubed with black dots, round eyes above gaping mouths.

She stretches her arms above her head, rises lightly to her toes, bends her knees, and leaps off as she has a thousand times before, the air a warm, popcorn-flavored breeze against her face. Belly, shoulder, and chest muscles tense as she cranks her legs up and over the bar. She swings by her knees, her ponytail tickling her neck and cheeks. The white balloons below bob and sway, and a tinkling music rises around her, punctuated with the uneven patter of applause.

Her father calls, "Hep," and she flies to him, grasping his wrists, pendulums, releases, twists, returns to her trapeze, riding it to the platform. She lands, flourishes, bows. Applause swells, then the music falls away, all but the deep drum that gradually picks up its pace like a frightened heartbeat. She spreads her arms, lights flashing from silver spangles, bends her knees, and leaps into a shallow dive, skimming through the air like a swallow, swooping, somersaulting, free of the trapeze, of gravity, of fear. Until, at the very top of the tent, her arms and body turn to lead. The bobbing balloons and the sandy ring swell and mourn as, flailing helplessly, she falls.

And wakes.

Panting, Lenka sat up and fumbled at the bedside lamp. Damn, she hated that dream. At least this time she hadn't fallen out of bed and woken her parents. That's all she needed—Mama patting her down, asking briskly if she'd hurt herself, Papa watching over her mother's shoulder with sleep-blurred, helpless eyes. They wouldn't yell at her—they never yelled at her these days, even when she deserved it. They'd just tell her to rest and maybe suggest talking to the doctor. Well, she wouldn't. She was finished with doctors and rest. She'd been in remission for nearly three months now. When her parents were out at work, she did calisthenics in her room, took runs through the neighborhood. Short runs—she was still pretty feeble. But she was getting stronger, she told herself, every day.

She'd be flying again, soon.

* * *

Lenka sat in the kitchen, glumly eating cereal, waiting for the slap of the morning paper on the doormat.

Mama and Papa were always talking about how getting the morning paper delivered was one of the perks of living in the same place for more than a few months. So was Lenka having her own room and a view with trees in it and a separate kitchen and living room, with a TV.

Lenka didn't care about any of it. She preferred backstage—any backstage. It was where she'd grown up, practically where she'd been born, a space variously sized and furnished, the only constants the smells—makeup, sweat, and do-it-yourself dry-cleaning sheets—and her family: the Fabulous Flying Kubatovs.

At their height, right before Lenka got sick, there had been seven of them: Mama and Papa, her two older brothers and their wives, and Lenka herself—in sweats and leotards, in tights and sequins, hands bound with tape and ankles wrapped with Ace bandages, practicing, stretching, dressing, mending costumes, arguing cheerfully with the other acts, seeing that Lenka got her legally mandated hours of English, math, and social studies. Making her strong. Teaching her to fly.

The Cleveland Plain Dealer thumped on the mat. Lenka opened the door and picked it up as Mama came in.

"You're awake early," she accused.

Lenka slid into her chair. "I'm fine, Mama, really. I had a bad dream."

Her mother rolled her eyes and turned to the refrigerator. "I'm making an egg for your father. You want one?"

"Ick," Lenka said, and opened the paper to the entertainment section.

She skimmed the movie listings. Nothing she wanted to see—which was good, since movies cost money. Her brothers and sisters-in-law sent what they could, but mostly it had to go for rent and doctors. Having leukemia was crazy expensive, even with insurance, and jobs hard to come by. Mama was temping for an accounting firm. Papa was working the register at Giant Eagle. These jobs yielded enough for food and a family membership to the YMCA so Papa and Mama could keep in shape. But Lenka noticed, every time they talked to her brothers, touring with Ringling Bros. in Florida, how Mama got crabby and Papa's jokes got even lamer than they usually were. They were as miserable in Cleveland as she was.

A headline caught her eye. CIRQUE DES CHAUVE-SOURIS CONVEYS CLASSIC CIRCUS MAGIC.

Lenka didn't want to read it, but she couldn't help herself.

> Fresh from the eastern European circuit, the Cirque des Chauve-souris is like a glance back into a vanished time. Ringmistress Battina brings the Old Country to the new

with a show that is as Gilded Age as the
antique wooden tent and the steam organ.
The kids probably won't get it. There are no
clowns or flashy high-wire acts; no midway,
no concessions, no trendy patter. There is,
however, a bar with draft pilsner and some
seriously fine acrobatics.

"There's a circus in town," Lenka said.

Her mother didn't even turn from the stove. "No."

"The tumblers are Czech—you ever hear of the Vaulting
Sokols?" Mama shook her head. "And a cat act. You *love* cat
acts. Please, Mama?"

Papa came in, hair wet from the shower, shirt half but-
toned over his undershirt.

"Please what, *berusko*?"

"She wants to go to the circus, Joska," her mother said. "I
have already said no. You want fried egg or scrambled?"

Lenka pushed the paper toward her father. He shook his
head without looking. "Your mother is right. Your immune
system is compromised. Circus means children; children mean
germs. Not a good atmosphere for you, princess mine."

"It's not a big-top show, Papa, just salon acts. Straight
from the Old Country—you'll love it. Besides, Dr. Weiner
didn't say I couldn't go out, he just said I had to take it easy."

Mama beat the eggs with unnecessary vigor. "It will not

make you happy, to watch someone else fly."

"I miss the circus, you know?" Lenka got up and put an arm around her mother's stiff shoulders. "Please, Mama? I'm going nuts, stuck here wondering if I'm ever going to be well enough to fly again."

It wasn't playing fair, but if Lenka had learned anything over the past year, it was that sometimes getting better involved pain.

Lenka and her parents drove in early from University Heights. As they waited for the house to open, they had time to examine the outside of the Cirque des Chauve-souris's famous wooden tent.

"Doesn't look like much, does it?" Mama said.

"It's antique," Papa said, not quite apologetically.

"So they can't paint it? It doesn't make a good impression, all dinged up like that."

Papa smiled one of his sad clown smiles and took her hand. He reached for Lenka's, too. Lenka squeezed his fingers gently and disengaged. Yes, it was painful to be waiting in line instead of making up and stretching backstage. But she'd rather he didn't make such a thing out of it.

Inside, as her mother claimed three empty chairs on a side aisle, Lenka cast a professional eye over the setup.

The tent was roomier than it had looked from outside, but it felt cramped to Lenka, the peaked ceiling too low to fly in, the ring a raised platform hardly big enough for a decent cartwheel. A ramp connected it to a semicircular stage curtained with worn scarlet velvet. The audience was stacked back from the ring in folding chairs. A row of raised booths against the walls was furnished with tables and velvet banquettes. Above them were faded old-timey murals of circuses past. The light wasn't great, but Lenka made out clowns in whiteface, a ringmaster in scarlet, a girl standing on a fat-haunched pony, a boy on a flying trapeze.

Lenka felt a tug on her sleeve. "They're starting."

The houselights snapped off; a portable steam organ struck up a wheezy *oompah-pah, oompah-pah*. A spot came up on a woman dressed in brown velvet with a cape to her feet. Her head was covered with a half mask sporting leaflike bat ears. The ringmistress. Battina.

She lifted her arms, and the cape hung down from her wrists like wings. "Welcome, mesdames," she fluted, Russian accent thick as borscht. "Welcome, messieurs. Welcome . . . Les Chauve-souris!"

Lenka heard a chittering overhead, and suddenly the air was full of movement, half seen and half heard, a restless, leathery flutter. A woman gave a nervous shriek, and Mama covered her head protectively as small, dark shapes flickered through the lights and down to the stage. A crashing chord, and the shapes transformed into a troupe of performers, caped and masked in brown.

Mama folded her hands in her lap. "Handkerchiefs and trapdoors. They're fast, though."

As the organ struck up "Thunder and Blazes," Battina rose into the air and skimmed over the ramp, her cape flaring out behind her. Everyone gasped, even Lenka. Between the cape and the tricky lighting, the telltale bulk of the harness and the glint of the wire were functionally invisible. Battina looked like she was really flying.

She circled over the audience and disappeared behind the curtains.

"Nice effect," Mama said.

"Shh," Papa said. "The acro-bats."

Lenka giggled.

There were three Vaulting Sokols, slender young men with white teeth and incredibly fast reflexes.

Papa watched their flipping and posturing for a moment, then whispered in Lenka's ear. "They tumble like in your grandfather's time—much skill, but little imagination."

Behind Lenka, someone got up and headed for the bar. "They're losing the audience," Mama muttered.

The next act was better—a big man in a moth-eaten bear suit and a contortionist in a scale-patterned leotard who slithered around his body with multivertebraed suppleness until he plucked her off and spun her in the air like a living ball.

When the bear man and the snake girl removed their masks, Lenka saw that the girl was about her age, with very fair skin and very dark hair cut in a square bob. She made her compliment to the audience without a glimmer of a smile, one arm raised, her knee cocked, pivoting to acknowledge the applause.

"Very professional." Mama approved.

The next act was Battina, capeless, and with black velvet cat ears sticking out of her thickly coiled hair. She swept in, proud as a queen, heading a procession of seven cats, their tails and heads held high.

Lenka had seen cat acts before—mostly on YouTube. Cats are cats. Even when they're trained, they tend to wander off or roll belly-up or wash themselves. Not Battina's cats. They walked a slack rope, jumped through hoops, balanced on a pole, and most remarkably of all, performed a kind of kitty synchronous dance routine in perfect unison, guided by Battina's chirps and meows.

"The woman's a witch," Mama muttered.

"Shh," Lenka said.

When the lights came up for intermission, Papa turned to her anxiously. "You like?"

"She'd better," Mama said.

"The cats were way cool. And the contortionist is the bomb. Can I get a Coke at the bar? I'm really thirsty."

After the break came a female sword swallower, a Japanese girl on a unicycle, and a slack-rope walker in a striped unitard that covered him to the knees. Lenka judged them all better than competent, but uninspired.

The contortionist reappeared, cartwheeling out between the curtains and down the runway, a simple effect made spectacular by the shimmering bat's wings that stretched from her ankles to her wrists. Reaching the center of the ring, she reached up, grasped a previously invisible bar, and rode it slowly upward. Lenka's throat closed in pure envy.

About six feet up, the trapeze stopped and the girl beat up to standing, bent her knees, and set the trapeze in motion, her wings rippling as she swung.

"She's going to get those tangled in the ropes," Mama muttered darkly.

She didn't. Lenka watched the girl flow through her routine, twisting, coiling, somersaulting, hanging by her hands, her neck, one foot, an arm, as if the laws of gravity and physics had been suspended just for her. She must be incredibly strong. She must be incredibly disciplined. She must not have any friends, or go to movies or play video games or be on Facebook, just train and perform and sleep and do her chores and her lessons and train some more. It wasn't a normal life. Mama and Papa said Lenka would learn to like normal life, if it turned out that she couldn't perform.

Mama and Papa were so totally wrong.

Dear Mama and Papa:

When you read this, I will be far away from here.

I'm not leaving because I don't love you, or because I think you're mean or unfair or anything. You're the best and most loving parents in the world and you've saved my life, even more than Dr. Weiner and the clinic. You've given up a lot to make me well, and you haven't tried to make me feel guilty about it, which is totally awesome.

The thing is, I feel guilty anyway. And fenced in and tied down and fed up and generally sick and tired. And it's not just all about me, although it probably sounds like it. I can see what my being sick has done to you. Temp work? Retail? Get real. Even Papa can't make it funny. You've got to go back to flying again.

Which you can't as long as you're looking after me.

So I'm going away. Please don't look for me. I'm eighteen. I'm in remission, I feel fine, I've got a little money to live on until I can find work. The only thing I'm tired of is resting. In a month or so, I'll let you know how I'm doing. I'm going to call Radek's cell phone, so you better be on the road.

Lenka

P.S. I know it's stupid to say don't worry, but really, you shouldn't. You taught me how to take care of myself.

P.P.S. I love you.

Lenka knew her parents. No matter what her letter said, they'd look for her, and the first place they'd look was the Cirque des Chauve-souris. She spent a couple of days hiding out, mostly in the Cleveland Art Museum, on the theory that it was the last place on Earth they'd expect her to be.

After the Cirque des Chauve-souris's last show, she gave herself a quick sponge bath in the museum john and headed downtown.

Lenka had been hoping to slip in under cover of the mob scene that was a circus breaking down. When she found the backyard deserted, she was a little freaked out, but she didn't let it stop her from slipping through the stage door.

A voice spoke out of the darkness. "We wondered when you'd show up."

Lenka froze.

"Don't worry," the voice said. "We won't call the police."

"The police?"

The contortionist stepped into the light. Close up, she looked smaller and paler. "They've been here twice, looking for Lenka Kubatov, age eighteen, five foot six, brown-brown, hundred fifteen, kind of fragile looking. That's you, right?"

Fragile looking? Lenka shrugged. "That's me."

"You ran away from home? Why? Do your parents beat you?"

"No," Lenka said. "My parents are great."

"Then why . . . ?"

Lenka squared her shoulders. "I want to join the circus. *This* circus. I want to be a roustabout."

The contortionist laughed. "That's a new one," she said. "Well, you'd better come talk to Battina."

The ringmistress of the Chauve-souris was helping the strong man unbolt the booth partitions and banquettes from the walls. There wasn't a roustabout in sight.

"The runaway," she said when she saw Lenka. "Hector, I need a drink."

The strong man laughed and slotted the partition into a padded wooden crate. "Later," he said.

Battina settled herself on a banquette, for all the world as if she hadn't been lifting part of it a moment before. "You must call your parents," she said severely.

Lenka shook her head. "I'm eighteen."

"The police said you are sick."

"I *was* sick. I'm better now. I need to live my own life, let them live theirs. They're flyers. They need to fly."

"What was wrong with you?" Hector asked.

"Cancer," Lenka said shortly. "Leukemia."

Battina and Hector exchanged unreadable looks.

"What do you want?" Battina asked, as if she didn't much care.

Lenka's heart beat harder.

"I want to come with you," she said. "I know I'm not up to performing, but you look like you could use some crew. I can put up rigs, I can clean cages, I can handle props. And I'm good at front-of-house stuff. You don't even have to pay me—not right away." She felt her eyes prickle with rising tears. "Without the circus, I'm not really alive. Please. Let me come with you."

Her voice broke. Disgusted, she fished in her shoulder bag for a Kleenex and blew her nose. "Sorry," she said hoarsely. "That was unprofessional."

"That was truth." Battina tapped her teeth with her thumbnail. "I can't deny we could use help—someone who understands American *chinovniks*, who can talk on the telephone, who can make plans." She cocked a dark eye at Lenka. "Are you such a one?"

"I've never done it," Lenka said truthfully. "But I can try."

"Our manager we lost in New York," Battina said. "He left us with big mess—papers, engagements in cities I have never heard of. I am artist, not telephone operator. You think you can fix?"

Lenka wanted to say she was an artist, too. But she wasn't—not while she was sidelined. "Yes."

Battina's gaze shifted over Lenka's shoulder. "What do you say?"

Lenka spun around to face the performers of the Cirque

des Chauve-souris, who had gathered behind her so silently that she hadn't even known they were there. Skin pasty under the work lights, they measured her with narrowed eyes.

The contortionist spoke. "I say we take her. It isn't right for an artist to be stuck in one place."

The equilibrist nodded gravely.

"Why not?" the ropewalker said. "Might be time for new blood."

The sword swallower giggled. "Boris is right."

The acrobats exchanged looks. "Can we trust her?" one of them asked.

Battina glanced at the strong man. "Hector?"

The strong man examined Lenka, his deep-set eyes glinting under the shadow of his heavy brow, then leaned toward her. Not sure what he was up to, Lenka stiffened but held her ground. He sniffed delicately at her hair, then straightened and nodded.

Just like that, she was in.

"In" is a relative term.

The snake girl's name was Rima—"like the bird girl," she explained, and then had to explain that it was the name of a character in an old book. Battina's real name was Madam Oksana Valentinovna. The Vaulting Sokolovs were Evzen, Kazimir, and Dusan, the equilibrist was Cio-Cio, and the sword swallower was Carmen. The ropewalker said his name was Boris from Leningrad, but Lenka thought he sounded more like Bert from Idaho.

None of them was remotely interested in making friends.

In Lenka's experience, all circus people were family. Even when they hardly had a language in common, they shared everything: war stories, opinions, meals, personal histories, shampoo, detergent.

The performers of the Cirque des Chauve-souris, not so much. They didn't chat among themselves. They didn't hang out, they didn't even eat together. On the road from Cleveland to Columbus, Madam Oksana filled Lenka in on the terms of her engagement. Lenka must keep to the office truck, not only to work, but to sleep and eat. Lenka must watch the show from the front of the house, keeping an eye on the local bartender and ushers hired for each venue. Lenka must never, ever bother the performers. Practices were closed; the back-yard was off-limits. If she objected to any of these conditions, she could go back to Cleveland.

Lenka gritted her teeth and agreed. Papa had told her about the hoops First of May circus virgins had to jump through, back in the old days. Jumping through hoops was better than going back to Cleveland.

Things Lenka learned in Columbus, Ohio:
Circuses need a lot of permits.

You can do almost anything if the support staff likes you. Madam Oksana's cats fed themselves.

In Lenka's experience, animal acts were incredibly work intensive. Animals have to be groomed, fed, and watered, their cages cleaned, repaired, and hauled into place. A cat act should mean, at the very least, tiers of cat carriers stacked in the backyard and bags and bags of kitty litter and cat chow.

Not at the Cirque des Chauve-souris.

When they weren't onstage, Madam Oksana's cats were free to wander where they pleased. Lenka saw them lounging on coiled ropes, sleeping on banquettes, prowling the backyard, perched on the artists' trailers. One night, she saw the big gray tom with a rat in his jaws, trotting toward the tent. A couple of nights later, she was about to climb into bed when she saw a young calico stretched luxuriously across her pillow. She scratched Lenka when Lenka tried to cuddle her, then licked the scratches penitently and settled down to spend the night in a furry coil by Lenka's feet, purring like a boiling kettle.

Lenka had never had a cat of her own. And she was lonely. She shared her bed with one or another of Madam's cats almost every night, ignoring their scratches and love nips even when she woke with a throbbing ear or nose, blood on her pillow, and a rough pink tongue busily licking her clean. It was a small price to pay for the company.

* * *

The second week in Columbus, the audience started to trickle away like coffee through a filter. People who liked highly produced glitz were bored. Even people who liked boutique circuses came once and didn't return.

Madam Oksana didn't seem to care.

"They do not appreciate true art," she said. "The fashion now is crude humor, terrible music, costumes that show everything. It is the same in Europe. Still, we will contrive."

Lenka cared very much.

"It wouldn't kill you to buy new costumes. Hector's bear suit is going to totally fall apart one of these days."

Madam Oksana shrugged liquidly. "New costumes are expensive."

"If you could attract better houses, you could afford them. Your open is flashy, and Rima and Hector's act totally rocks. But the Vaulting Sokolovs are, like, stuck in the last century, and Cio-Cio's routine is totally lame. Here." She turned to her laptop, searched, and opened a YouTube video of a Cirque de Soleil equilibrist. "Look," she said, turning the screen to Madam Oksana. "Cio-Cio could do that with her hands tied behind her."

Madam Oksana watched the tiny blue-clad figure moving from backbend to handstand while balancing on a giant red ball. "The music is like dogs barking. And the ball is not dignified."

Neither is walking on your hands, Lenka did not say. "The music's negotiable. And it doesn't have to be a ball. She could use a teeter-totter. Or a flexible pole. The point is, she needs more props. There's only so far you can take a unicycle if you don't juggle."

Some time later, after watching dozens of videos of tumblers and ropewalkers and sword swallowers and static trapeze artists, Madam Oksana looked thoughtful and Lenka was exhausted. Watching the trapeze acts was torture, especially one in which two women and a man twisted, swung, and maneuvered their way around a rigid rig like a giant skeletal cube.

There wasn't a trick she saw that she couldn't have done before she got sick.

If she could just get in shape again. If she could just practice.

Everyone slept late at the Cirque des Chauve-souris. With no matinees, there wasn't any reason for the performers to be awake before two or even three in the afternoon, and as far as Lenka knew, they never were.

At eleven one morning, Lenka crept across the parking lot to the tent, telling herself there was no reason to be nervous. Madam Oksana had never said the tent was off-limits, or even the rigs, if nobody was using them.

The tent was dark and smelled of dust and rosin. Heart

beating and palms sweating, Lenka turned on a work light, checked the guy ropes on the static trapeze, then chalked her hands and leapt up to grab the bar. Her shoulders screamed as they took her weight, and her belly muscles protested as she beat her legs up and over. She hung there a moment, then hauled herself up to sit on the bar, where she sat, swinging gently, getting her breath back. Her muscles were unhappy, and she should definitely put on a safety harness before she tried anything fancy. It wouldn't do any harm, though, to throw one simple trick.

Lenka slid her butt forward, arched her neck and back, and spread her arms stiffly along the bar in a crucifix. As she swung, staring up into the peaked roof, she thought she saw a shadowy stirring among the lights. Her vision sparkled and faded. Her ears buzzed.

I'm going to fall, she thought calmly.

When Lenka woke, her mouth tasted of metal and she hurt all over, but in a strained-muscle way, not a broken-bone way. She opened her eyes to a ring of faces.

Madam Oksana was annoyed. "You are not obeying the rules."

Lenka rolled herself to her side, pushed herself weakly upright. "I wasn't in the backyard," she said. "And nobody was practicing. I checked."

Madam Oksana's snarl made her look very like one of

her cats. "You are a lawyer now, you argue with me? You kill yourself, maybe that is the end of your troubles, but not for us. You are here to make things easy, not bring police to ask questions. You practice, you must wear a belt, *ponimaesh*?"

Lenka grinned. "I got it, boss."

Madam Oksana threw her hands to the heavens and disappeared into the shadows.

Lenka clambered to her feet and staggered dizzily.

Rima steadied her, her grip cool and strong on Lenka's arm. "Maybe you should build up those muscles more before you go up again."

Lenka laughed, embarrassed. "You know it."

The thing about working out is, you feel weaker before you start to feel stronger, especially if you're coming back from a long time away and you're impatient.

What made it harder was that suddenly, Lenka was very much in demand.

Rima and Evzen wanted to learn to navigate YouTube. Then Cio-Cio and Hector and Boris got interested, and after that someone or another was constantly dropping by the office to use her laptop and study new moves and new routines. Hector built a cube like the one in the video, and Rima and Cio-Cio started working on it. The Sokolovs obsessively practiced new tricks. Every time Lenka turned around, someone was pestering her with questions about American circuses, American slang, American taste, until she started to feel like a human search engine.

"Watch this sequence, Lenka. Is it now smoking?"

"There is a man who swallows a bar stool, Lenka. Is this cool for me to do, or lame?"

She was welcome at practices now, which was what she'd wanted, but somehow, their attention made her feel lonelier than being ignored. Lenka tried not to mind that they never asked her questions about herself. It wasn't that she wanted to talk about her family or her illness. But it might have been nice if they'd wanted to know.

After Columbus, they went to Chicago. A week into the run, Lenka took herself out to dinner. She'd been feeling kind of punk lately—too much fast food, too much pushing herself to get stronger faster so she could work herself into Rima and Cio-Cio's act on the cube rig. Possibly too much Madam Oksana and Company, although she was hardly ready to admit that, even to herself.

In any case, she needed to get out, and Madam Oksana had decided the circus was doing well enough to pay her. So Lenka borrowed a dress from Rima and took a taxi to a restaurant she'd found on the internet. It was Italian, her favorite kind of restaurant, not fancy, but nice enough for tablecloths and candles. She ordered *insalata mista*, garlic shrimp, and a glass of white wine, which the waiter brought without comment. The garlic shrimp reminded her of Papa, who always ordered it. As she ate, she thought about calling her parents. Not that she wanted to give up, of course, not when she was just starting to feel at home. But they must be worried, and she wanted to hear the voice of somebody who loved her, even if it was yelling at her.

It was nearly one in the morning when Lenka got back to the circus. She was exhausted, achy, and a lot more lightheaded than she should be on a single glass of wine. Heading for the office truck and her bed, she hoped a cat was waiting for her.

When she heard the groan, her first impulse was to ignore it. She knew the performers sometimes hooked up with townies and brought them back to their trailers, especially Boris and Evzen. It didn't bother her—it was what circus people did. But it wasn't anything she needed to know more about.

Another groan—unmistakably not *that* kind of groan. Someone was hurt. Someone was in trouble.

Lenka groaned herself, softly, and padded around the costume truck toward the back door.

Per municipal regulations, a security light illuminated the area immediately around the door, which was currently occupied by Hector, Carmen, Kazimir, Madam Oksana, and Boris, who was holding the body of a young woman in his arms.

Lenka shrank back into the shadow of the costume truck,

cheeks tingling with shock. The woman groaned again, and her head rolled back in a horribly final way, revealing a wound in the angle of her jaw. It was bleeding sluggishly.

Hector said a word Lenka would have sworn he didn't even know.

"Shut up, Hector," Madam Oksana said dispassionately. "She is not yet dead—although she may be if Boris insists on stupid clowning."

Boris bared his teeth and hissed at her, reminding Lenka strongly of a cat defending his kill.

Madam Oksana hissed back.

Boris laid the girl on the ground and watched unblinking as Madam Oksana knelt, turned the girl's head to one side, then bent and delicately licked at the seeping wound.

After a long moment, Hector laid his hand on her shoulder. "You must stop now," he said.

Madam Oksana straightened and licked her lips. Her face was as blank as a doll's.

Lenka looked at the girl. She lay as she'd been arranged, arms sprawled, neck pathetically arched to display an unbloodied expanse of white, unbroken skin.

While Lenka was digesting this, Kazimir swung the girl up and over his shoulders like a dead deer. "I'll get some water down her and sprinkle some gin around. She's already drunk, right, Boris?" Boris yawned. "Right. With any luck, she won't even remember where she's been when she wakes up."

Boris stretched sleepily. "Why risk it? Why not make sure she won't wake up?"

Hector gave him a look that would strip paint. "You are a savage, Boris, and very young. It is good for you that you have fallen among civilized monsters, who know better than to make messes where we eat. Kazimir will take your little inamorata where she will be found soon and cared for. And you . . . you will be more careful in the future."

Kazimir disappeared into the tent, the girl's dark head bobbing at his shoulder. Everybody relaxed. Carmen said, "I'm *starved*," and folded abruptly like a piece of fabric. A moment later, Lenka saw a bat drop from the edge of the tent, catch an updraft, and glide out of the light. And then, shamefully, she fainted.

Lenka opened her eyes to darkness and silence. She felt like death on a cracker—exactly the way she'd felt when her parents had insisted on taking her to the emergency room in Cleveland a year ago. There was something heavy lying on her chest.

She moaned and tried to sit up. She couldn't move.

A cat meowed right below her chin.

"Yes," said Madam Oksana. "I know. Get off, Rima. We want her restrained, not smothered."

Rima. The aerialist. Her friend. The cat. The vampire.

Rima walked down Lenka's body and flopped heavily onto her ankles.

"Lenka Kubatovna," Madam Oksana said. "What will we do with you? We have no wish to kill you. You are useful to us."

Lenka wriggled uncomfortably. "Can you turn on a light? Talking about this in the dark is creepy. I feel like I'm in a bad horror movie, you know? *Circus of the Vampires*. It's just too unreal."

"This is not a time for joking," Madam Oksana said stiffly. But she turned on a lamp. Lenka saw she was in her bed in the office truck, with Madam Oksana's seven cats huddled around her, pinning down her blanket. She should have been able to throw them off easily, but no matter how she strained, she couldn't budge them. They stared up at her as only cats can stare, their round, unblinking eyes glowing red.

Lenka suppressed a hysterical giggle. "No? It would make a great movie. Girl with leukemia runs away to join a circus of vampires who turn into cats and bats."

The biggest cat, a brown furball like a miniature bear, shook itself and became Hector, sitting sad-eyed by her hip. "Spiders," he said. "We can also be spiders and mosquitoes, but it is unpleasant to be so small."

This was too much for Lenka, who started to laugh helplessly and couldn't stop until Madam Oksana slapped her, bruising Lenka's jaw and knocking the laughter right out of her.

"I do not like hysterics," Madam Oksana said. "It is very simple. You will stay with us. We will buy a big computer and you will conduct the business of the circus and book tours and make everything smooth with the *chinovnik*. You will share your blood with us." Her scarlet mouth stretched in a feral smile. "It will be what you call totally smoking."

"No, I wouldn't," Lenka said. "I'd call it incredibly gross."

The cats turned back into circus performers and perched on the furniture. Free at last, Lenka sat up and glared at them. "I've got leukemia, remember? That's a disease of the blood, in case you didn't know."

Dusan took her hand. He'd never touched her before. His skin was cool and waxy against her fingers. "For us, it is not poison," he said. "For us, it is new strength."

"All those multiplying white cells," Boris said, "can put a real bounce in a vampire's step. We wouldn't love you half so much if your blood was normal."

Lenka tried to tug her hand out of Dusan's grip. It was like pulling against handcuffs. "Well, it is. I mean, remission, remember? I told you when I came."

Rima bent and stroked her cheek, a touch like falling snow. "Nice try. But you are not in remission."

As Lenka stared at her, stunned, Dusan lifted her wrist to his mouth, delicately nicked the flesh with a sharp canines, and licked the resulting drops of blood from her skin. "Delicious," he said.

"If you don't like hysterics," she said shakily, "then you should all get out now, because I am about to seriously lose it, and I think you'd have to kill me to make me shut up."

The office truck remained closed and silent all the next day, the door locked and the shades drawn. Carmen sold tickets from a table by the bar and flirted coolly with the bartender. The house was good, the applause enthusiastic, the chatter overheard during the blow-off promising. When Madam Oksana counted the take, she said she thought they'd be able to order new costumes soon, maybe even a desktop computer.

"It will do you no good," Rima pointed out, "if Lenka goes mad with shock."

Madam Oksana shrugged. "Then we will not buy computer."

The next day, Boris eyed the silent office and wondered aloud whether he should break down the door to check if the mortal was still alive.

"She does not want to die, that one," Madam Oksana said. "Leave her alone."

The next night, another sold-out show. Townies gathered at the back door in hopes of a smile, a word, maybe even a date with one of the performers. Carmen and Evzen fed on something tastier than rat blood. The office trailer stayed locked and silent.

* * *

The next evening, after the last show, Lenka washed, put Rima's dress on over her jeans, braided her dark hair, and went to the tent, where she found Horace and Carmen and Madam Oksana.

"I want to talk to you."

Three pairs of eyes examined her gravely. The whites looked red, as if they were all suffering from a bad case of pinkeye. Lenka wondered why she hadn't noticed it before.

Madam Oksana beckoned her closer.

"No, I want to talk to all of you. I'm only going through this once."

Madam Oksana shrugged and closed her eyes briefly. Lenka heard a flutter, and three bats swooped down from among the lights, transforming as they landed. A calico cat snaked between the stage curtains and became Rima. The big gray tom that was Boris leapt smoothly onto the ring, his muzzle dark with blood, and settled down to a leisurely bath.

"We are all here," Madam Oksana said. "Speak."

Lenka licked her lips. "I've done a lot of thinking since the other night, and I've made some decisions. First, I'm totally okay with the whole vampire thing. I mean, you're awesome performers and it's not like you go around killing people all the time—"

"Not on purpose," Evzen murmured.

"Or very often, or somebody would have noticed. Anyway.

I wouldn't turn you in, even if I left, which, before you start telling me how I don't have a choice, I actually do."

She glared around at the assembled vampires, challenging one of them to argue. They gazed back, patient and incurious.

"I said in Cleveland I wanted to join you. I still do. Make me a full member of the troupe—make me a vampire—and I'll stay."

"Or else?" Kazimir prompted.

"Or else I'll erase all my files, the bookkeeping program I set up, all the contacts in all the towns where you've got gigs, all the permit numbers—everything."

Evzen shrugged. "We will keep you away from the computer."

"You don't even know how to turn it on," Lenka said. "All you know how to do is search YouTube, and that's not going to get you very far when some policeman in Utah wants to see your paperwork. You can't figure out anything new by yourselves. You know how to do what you did when you . . . became vampires—and that's it."

Madam Oksana nodded. "True. So why should we deprive ourselves of your knowledge, your imagination, your fire?"

"Your blood," Boris added, licking his (now human) lips.

"Crude," Carmen said. "But he's got a point."

Lenka's careful poise shattered. "Because I'm *sick*, you self-centered jerks. Because if I don't get treatment, I'm going to *die* and take my special high-energy tasty *blood* with me."

She'd startled them, which was a minor triumph in itself. Madam Oksana's glance darted to Hector, who shook his head ruefully.

Rima, astonishingly, laughed.

"Oh, let her join us. She won't forget anything she already knows, after all, and we can get new ideas for our acts off YouTube."

"It would be a shame to waste her blood," Kazimir said. "Perhaps she can come up with some way to preserve it?"

Lenka was shaking, possibly with relief, possibly with horror: She felt both. Also sick and weak and in need of something more to eat than the Fritos and jelly babies she'd been living off for three days.

"Sure—why not? There's a bunch of things I want to do before I . . . turn. I need to work on a triple act for the cube rig, for one. And find someone to make us new costumes."

Madam Oksana stood up and stretched. "Well, that is decided. Good. I will come to the office now and look at the YouTube."

Lenka shook her head. "Unless you want me to die ahead of schedule, you'll get me something to eat and let me go to bed. You can watch YouTube tomorrow."

Joska and Mariana Kubatov joined the line of eager customers waiting for the house to open for the eight-o'clock show of the Cirque des Chauve-souris in San Francisco.

An Asian girl approached them. "Mr. and Mrs. Kubatov? Please follow me."

Lenka's mother saw that the tent had been painted and regilded, the faded murals artfully touched up, the brass lamps polished. The girl—the unicyclist—showed them to a booth. Two glasses of red wine sat on the table.

"Lenka said to tell you she can't come out now, but she'll see you after the show. Please, enjoy." And she glided away.

Papa laid his hand on Mama's. "You must not be disappointed. You know how frightened she is before a show."

"Frightened I will scold her, you mean." Mama turned her hand and squeezed. "I'm fine, Joska."

They sipped their wine and looked around them.

The organ had been repaired, and the player's repertoire now included old-timey arrangements of popular songs. The opening charivari was the same, but the acts themselves had been—not modernized, exactly. Polished, sharpened, refurbished.

Like the tent. Like the costumes, which were modest but sexy, well made, theatrical.

The Kubatovs smiled and applauded and waited for Lenka to appear.

Battina had acquired a new cat—a seal brown shorthair that rode a miniature flying trapeze from one upholstered platform to another, her tail sticking straight out behind her like a rudder.

"That is cruelty," Papa murmured.

Mama patted his hand.

At the end of the first half, the steam organ began to play "She's Only a Bird in a Gilded Cage." A cube fashioned of shining golden bars was winched smoothly into the spotlight. Three girls appeared, dressed in silk kimonos painted with bats: the Asian girl, the dark-haired contortionist, and finally, finally, Lenka, almost unrecognizable in a Dutch-boy bob, heavy eye shadow, and circles of rouge on her cheekbones.

The girls backflipped down the ramp, shedding their kimonos, posed a moment under the cube to show off their coy ribboned bloomers and white silk corsets. Lenka stepped lightly onto her partners' linked hands and vaulted into the cube as if she were flying, then caught the Asian girl, creating a human chain up which the contortionist swarmed.

It was a breathtaking act. The three girls wound through all the cube's dimensions, hanging from its bars and one another, folding and unfolding their bodies through a complex geometry. Their last trick was a subtle slip-off, Lenka seeming to slide through the contortionist's hands headfirst in an uncontrolled fall. The audience gasped. Even Lenka's mother, who knew how the trick was done, covered her mouth with her hands, then laughed with relief when the contortionist caught Lenka and swung her, impossibly, up and out and back into the cube again, where she seemed to float for a heartbeat in midair, hovering, trapped, like a white bird in a glittering cage.

The show was over. The audience had departed, drunk on alcohol and circus magic. Lenka's parents sat in their booth behind their empty glasses and waited for their daughter to come to them.

"I'm not going to cry," Mama announced.

"There is no reason for crying," Papa agreed.

Lenka appeared on the other side of the table. She'd changed into jeans and a sweatshirt, but her face was still masked with the garish doll paint.

"Mama," she said. "Papa. I'm glad you came."

She sounded less glad than polite. Her father hesitated a moment, then slid out of the booth and hugged her hugely. "Princess mine," he said. "*Berusko.* You have become a great artist." He held her out at arm's length. "You are well? Your hands are very cold. There is so much to say. You will come eat with us?"

Lenka looked at him gravely. "I can't, Papa. I'm sorry. I'm on a special diet—it wouldn't be any fun for any of us."

Mama joined them. She opened her mouth to scold, to question, her arms half raised to gather her daughter to her. But when Lenka turned to her, smoke eyed, solemn, self-contained, she dropped her arms and said crossly, "We were *worried,* Lenka."

"I know, Mama. I'm sorry."

"And your health?"

A smile flitted over the painted lips. "I'm stronger than I've ever been."

"And happy?" Papa asked.

"Yes," she said evenly. "Very happy."

A calico cat leapt up onto the table and meowed.

"I'm sorry," Lenka repeated.

Her mother nodded once, shortly. "You have duties. Go. We will come again tomorrow."

"It's the same show," Lenka said.

"Even so," her father said.

The calico meowed again, flowed through the air to her shoulder, and settled around her neck like a furry scarf. Girl and cat looked at the Kubatovs, amber eyes and dark equally calm and disinterested. Then Lenka smiled, a bright performer's smile, turned, walked through the stage curtain, and was gone.

VAMPIRE WEATHER

by Garth Nix

"You be home by five, Amos," said his mother. "I saw Theodore on my way back, and he says it's going to be vampire weather."

Amos nodded and fingered the chain of crosses he wore around his neck. Eleven small silver-washed iron crosses, spread two finger widths apart on a leather thong, so they went all the way around. His great-uncle told him once that they'd used to only wear crosses at the front, till a vampire took to biting the backs of people's necks, like a dog worrying at a rat.

He took his hat from the stand near the door. It was made of heavy black felt, and the rim was wound with silver thread. He looked at his coat and thought about not wearing it, because the day was still warm, even if Theodore said there was going to be a fog later, and Theodore always knew.

"And wear your bracers and coat!" shouted his mother

from the kitchen, even though she couldn't see him.

Amos sighed and slipped on the heavy leather wrist bracers, pulling the straps tight with his teeth. Then he put on his coat. It was even heavier than it looked, because there were silver dollars sewn into the cuffs and shoulders. It was all right in winter, but any other time all that weight of wool and silver was just too hot.

Amos had never even seen a vampire. But he knew they were out there. His own father had narrowly escaped one, before Amos was born. His great-uncle Old Franz had a terrible tangle of white scars across his hand, the mark of the burning pitch that he had desperately flung at a vampire in a vain attempt to save his first wife and oldest daughter.

The minister often spoke of the dangers of vampires, as well as the more insidious spiritual threat of things like the internet, television, and any books that weren't on the approved list. Apart from the vampires, Amos was quite interested in seeing the dangers the minister talked about, but he didn't suppose he ever would. Even when he finished school next year, his life wouldn't change much. He'd just spend more time helping out at the sawmill, though there would also be the prospect of building his own house and taking a wife. He hoped his wife would come from some other community of the faith. He didn't like the idea of marrying one of the half dozen girls he'd grown up with. But, as with everything, his parents would choose for him, in consultation with the minister and the elders of the chapel.

Amos felt the heat as he stepped off the porch and into the sun. But as he looked up the mountainside, a great white, wet cloud was already beginning to descend. Theodore was right, as usual. Within an hour the village would be blanketed in fog.

But an hour left Amos plenty of time to complete his task. He set off down the road, tipping his hat to Young Franz, who was fixing the shingles on his father's roof.

"Off to the mailbox?" called out Young Franz, pausing in his hammer strokes, speaking with the ease of long practice past the three nails he held in the corner of his mouth.

"Yes, brother," answered Amos. Of course he was—it was one of his duties, and he did it every day at almost the same time.

"Get back before the fog closes in," warned Young Franz. "Theodore says it's—"

"Vampire weather," interrupted Amos. He regretted doing so immediately, even before Young Franz paused and deliberately took the nails out of his mouth and set down his hammer.

"I'm sorry, brother," blurted out Amos. "Please forgive my incivility."

Young Franz, who was not only twice as old as Amos but close to twice as heavy, and all of it muscle, looked down at the young man and nodded slowly.

"You be careful, Amos. You sass me again and I'll birch your backside from here to the hall, with everyone looking on."

"Yes, brother, I apologize," said Amos. He kept his head down and eyes downcast. What had he been thinking, to interrupt the toughest and most short-tempered brother in the village?

"Get on with you then," instructed Young Franz. He kept his eye on Amos but picked up the nails and put them back in his mouth. Every second nail had a silver washer, to stop a vampire breaking in through the roof, just as every chimney was meshed with silver-washed steel.

Amos nodded with relief and started back down the road, faster now. The fog was closer, one arm of it already extending down the ridge, stretching out to curl back around toward the village like it usually did, to eventually join up with the slower body of mist that was coming straight down the slope.

He liked going to the mailbox. It was the closest thing the community had to an interface with the wider world, even if it was only an old diesel drum on a post set back twenty feet from a minor mountain road. Sometimes Amos saw a car go past, impossibly swift compared to the horse buggy he rode in once a month, when they visited with the cousins over in New Hareseth. Once a bus had stopped, and a whole bunch of people had gotten out and tried to take his photograph, and he had almost dropped the mail as he tried to run back and keep his face covered at the same time.

The flag was up on the box, Amos saw as he got closer. That was good, since otherwise he would have to wait for the mail truck to get back out on the main road. Sometimes the postal workers were women, and he wasn't allowed to see or talk to strange women.

He hurried to the box and carefully unlocked the padlock with the key that he proudly wore on his watch chain, as a visible symbol that while not quite yet a man, he was no longer considered just a boy.

There were only three items inside: a crop catalog from an old firm that guaranteed no devil work with their seeds; and two thick, buff-colored envelopes that Amos knew would be from one of the other communities, somewhere around the world. They all used and reused the same envelopes. The two here might have been a dozen places and come home again.

Amos put the mail in his voluminous outer pocket, shut the lid, and clicked the padlock shut. But with the click, he heard another sound. Right behind him, the crunch of gravel underfoot.

He spun around, looking not ahead but up at the sky. When he saw that the sun was still shining, unobscured by the lowering cloud, he lowered his gaze and saw . . . a girl.

"Hi," said the girl. She was about his age, and really pretty, but Amos backed up to the mailbox.

She wore no crosses, and her light sundress showed a

bare neck and arms, and even a glimpse of her breasts. Amos gulped as she moved and caught the sun, making the dress transparent, so he could see right through it.

"Hi," the girl said again, and stepped closer.

Amos raised his bracer-bound wrists to make a cross.

"Get back!" he cried. "I don't know how you walk in the sun, vampire, but you can't take me! My faith is strong!"

The girl wrinkled her nose, but she stopped.

"I'm not a vampire," she said. "I've been vaccinated like everyone else. Look."

She rotated her arm to show the inside of her elbow. There was a tattoo there, some kind of bird thing inside a rectangle, with numbers and letters spelling out a code.

"Vacks . . . vexination . . . ," stumbled Amos. "That's devil's work. If you're human, you wear crosses, else the vampires get you."

"Not since maybe the last twenty years," said the girl. "But like you said, if I am a vampire, how come I'm out in the sun?"

Amos shook his head. He didn't know what to do. The girl stood in his path. She was right about the sun, but even though she wasn't a vampire, she was a girl, an outsider. He shouldn't be looking at her, or talking to her. But he couldn't stop looking.

"I don't have a problem with crosses, either," said the girl. She took the three steps to Amos and reached over to touch the crosses around his neck, picking them up one by one, almost fondling them with her long, elegant fingers. Amos stopped breathing and tried to think of prayers he couldn't remember, prayers to quench lust and . . . sinful stirrings and . . .

He broke away and ran a few yards toward the village. He would have kept going, but the girl laughed. He stopped and looked back.

"Why're you laughing?"

She stopped and smiled again.

"Just . . . men don't usually run away from me."

Amos stood a little straighter. She thought he was a man, which was more than the village girls did.

"What's your name?" asked the girl. "I'm Tangerine."

"Amos," said Amos slowly. "My name is Amos."

Behind the girl, the fog kept coming down, thick and white and damp.

"It's good to meet you, Amos. Are you from the village up the mountain?"

Amos nodded his head.

"We just moved in along the road," said Tangerine. "My dad is working at the observatory."

Amos nodded again. He knew about the observatory. You could see one of its domes from the northern end of the village, though it was actually on the crest of the other mountain, across the valley.

"You'd better get home before the fog blanks the sun," he said. "It's vampire weather."

Tangerine smiled again. She smiled more than anyone Amos had ever known.

"I told you, I'm vaccinated," she said. "No vampire will bite me. Hey, could I come visit with you?"

Amos shook his head urgently. He couldn't imagine the punishment he would earn if he came back with an almost naked outsider woman, one who didn't even wear a cross.

"It's lonely back home," said Tangerine. "I mean, no one lives here, and Dad works. There's just me and my grand-mother most of the time."

The fog was shrouding the tops of the tallest trees across the road. Amos watched it, and even as he spoke, he wondered why he wasn't already running back up the road to home.

"What about your mother?"

"She's dead," said Tangerine. "She died a long while back."

Amos could smell the fog now, could almost taste the wetness on his tongue. There could be vampires right there, hidden in that vanguard of cloud, close enough to spring out and be on him in seconds. But he still found it difficult to tear himself away.

"I'll be back tomorrow," he said, and bolted, calling over his shoulder. "Same time."

"See you then!" said Tangerine. She waved, and that image stayed in Amos's head, her standing like that, her raised arm lifting her breasts, that smile on her face, and her bright hair shining, with the cold white fog behind, like a painted background, to make sure she stood out even more.

Amos wasn't home by five, or even half past, and he just barely beat the main body of the fog that came straight down the mountainside. The home door was shut and barred by the time he got there, so he had to knock on the lesser door, and he got a cracking slap from his mother when she let him in, and when his father finished his bath, he ordered an hour-long penance that left Amos with his knees sore from kneeling and made the words he'd been repeating over and over so meaningless that he felt like they were some other language that he'd once known but had somehow forgotten.

Through it all, he kept thinking of Tangerine, seeing Tangerine, imagining what might happen when he next saw her . . . and then he'd try to pray harder, to concentrate on those meaningless words, but whatever he did, he couldn't direct his mind away from those bare arms and legs, the way her unbound hair fell . . .

Amos slept very badly and earned more punishments before breakfast than he'd had in the past month. Even his father, who favored prayer and penance over any other form of correction, was moved to take off his leather belt, though he only held it as an unspoken threat, while he delivered a homily on attention and obedience.

Finally it was time to get the mail. Amos took no chances

that this plum job might be taken from him. If anyone else saw Tangerine, he'd never be allowed to go to the mailbox again. So he put on his bracers, coat, and hat without being asked and went to tell his mother he was going.

She looked at him over her loom but didn't stop her work, the shuttle clacking backward and forward as she trod the board.

"You be back by five," she warned. "Theodore says the fog today will be even thicker. It is a shocking month for vampire weather."

"Yes, Mother," said Amos. He planned to run to the mailbox as soon as he was out of sight of the village. That would give him a little extra time with Tangerine. If she came. He was already starting to wonder if he might have imagined her.

He also made sure to wave and nod to Young Franz, who was working on the roof of his father's house again. But as soon as he was around the bend, Amos broke into a run, pounding along the road as if there was a vampire after him. He didn't notice Young Franz standing on the chimney, watching him run.

Tangerine was at the mailbox, but so was the post truck and a postal worker, a man. He was chatting to Tangerine while he put the letters in the slot, and they were both smiling. Amos scowled and slowed down, but he kept going. Since he'd already talked to a girl, talking to a postman wasn't going to be any bigger transgression.

They both turned around as he approached. Amos had seen this same postman before, in the distance, but up close he saw details he'd never noticed before. Like the fact that the postman didn't wear crosses either, and there were no wrist bracers under his uniform coat. It also looked too light to be sewn with silver wire or set with coins.

"Hi," said Tangerine. She had a different dress on, but it was just as revealing as the one the day before. Amos couldn't take his eyes off her, and he didn't notice the postman winking at him.

"Howdy, son," called the postman. "Good to see you."

"Brother," replied Amos stiffly. "We don't call each other 'son.'"

"Fair enough, brother," said the postman. "I guess I'm old enough to be your dad, is why I said son. But I'd better be on my way. Plenty of mail to deliver."

"And the fog is coming down," said Amos. He was trying to be friendly, because he didn't want to look bad in front of Tangerine. But it was difficult.

"Oh, the fog's no problem," said the postman. "I'll drive down out of it soon enough, and the road is good."

"I meant it is vampire weather," said Amos.

"Vampire weather?" asked the postman. "I haven't heard that said since . . . well, since I was no older than you are now. I doubt there's a wild vampire left in these parts. With nothing to drink, they just wither away."

"My great-uncle's wife and daughter were killed by vampires, not eight years ago," said Amos hotly.

"But that's . . ." The postman's voice trailed off, and he looked at Amos more intently, tilting his head as he took in the necklace of crosses and the bracers. "I knew you folk were old-fashioned, but you can't tell me you're not vaccinated? That's against the law!"

"There is no law but the word of the Lord," said Amos automatically.

"I gotta get going," said the postman. He wasn't smiling now. "Miss . . . uh . . . Tangerine, you want a lift down to your dad's?"

"No, thanks, Fred," said Tangerine. "My grandma's coming past a bit later, I'll go back with her."

"Well, say hello to your dad from me," said the postman. "Good-bye . . . brother."

Amos nodded, just a slight incline that if he'd done it to an older man back home would have gotten him into serious trouble.

"I've been waiting for a while," said Tangerine. She leaned back against the mailbox and tilted her head, so that her hair fell across one of her eyes. "I thought maybe you'd come early."

"Everything's got its time," said Amos gruffly. He took out his key and held it nervously, his mouth weirdly dry.

"Uh, I have to . . . to get the mail. . . ."

"Oh, sure," laughed Tangerine. She moved aside, just enough that Amos could lean forward and open the lid. She was so close he almost touched her arm with the back of his hand. He reached past and quickly took out the mail. Just two buff-colored envelopes today.

Tangerine moved behind him as he locked the mailbox, so that just like the day before, she was blocking his way.

"I have to get back," said Amos. He jerked his thumb at the fog that was once again eddying down the hillside.

"Can't we just . . . talk awhile?" asked Tangerine. "I mean, I'm curious about you. I've never met anyone like you before."

"What do you mean, like me?" asked Amos.

"Nothing bad!" exclaimed Tangerine. She came closer to him and gave a little tug at the lapel of his coat. Amos took half a step back and almost didn't hear what she said next, the blood was rushing so in his ears. "I mean, you're a really good-looking guy, but it was kind of hard to tell at first, with the big hat and the coat and everything. And I never saw so many crosses—"

"I told you, it's for . . . to protect us . . . against the vampires," said Amos.

"But you don't need them," said Tangerine. "Like Fred said, there's no wild vampires left. When most everyone got vaccinated, they just died out."

"I don't know about that," said Amos. "People see them,

in the fog, through the windows."

"Have you seen them?" asked Tangerine.

Amos shook his head. He'd looked, but all he ever saw were drifts of fog, occasionally spurred into some strange eddy.

"There you go then," she said. "Besides, if you did think they were still around, you could get vaccinated, too."

Amos shook his head.

"But it's just like getting a shot for polio, or measles," said Tangerine.

Amos shook his head again. His little sister had died of measles, but everyone said that it was the Lord's will. Amos had taken the measles, too, at the same time, and he hadn't died.

"If the Lord wants to take you, then that's it," he said. "No amount of vaccinating can stand against that."

Tangerine sighed.

"I guess you hold to some pretty strong beliefs," she said. "Do you even get to watch television?"

"Nope," said Amos. "That's just a door for the devil, straight into your head."

"My dad would kind of agree with you on that," said Tangerine. "Not enough to stop me watching, thank heavens."

"*You* watch television?" asked Amos.

"Sure. You could come down and watch it too, sometime. My place is only half a mile along the road."

She pointed, and Amos suddenly realized that the fog was upon them. Tendrils of cold, wet whiteness were undulating past, weaving together to make a thicker, darker mass.

He looked up the mountain and could no longer see the sun. The two arms of the fog had already joined, and he would be in darkness all the way back to the village.

He must have made a noise, a frightened noise, because Tangerine took his hand.

"It's only fog," she said.

"Vampire weather," whispered Amos. He tried to look everywhere at once, peering past Tangerine, turning his head, then spinning around so that somehow he ended up with Tangerine's arms around him.

"I can't get back," Amos said, but even in the midst of his panic, he was thinking how wonderful it was to have Tangerine's arms around him, and then out of nowhere her mouth arrived on his and he supposed it was a kiss but it felt more like he'd had the air sucked out of his lungs, but in a good way, it wasn't something horrible, and he wanted it to happen again but Tangerine tilted her head and then settled her face into his neck, all warm and comfortable.

He patted her back for a little while, something he'd seen his father do once to his mother, before they'd seen that the children had noticed their embrace. Tangerine said something muffled he couldn't hear. Then she stepped away and disentangled herself, but she was still holding his hands.

"Don't go back, Amos. Come down to my house. You can stay with me."

"Stay with you?" mumbled Amos. A great part of him wanted more than anything to always be with this wonderful, amazing girl, but a possibly greater part was simply terrified and wanted him to sprint back up the road and get home as quickly as possible. "I . . . I can't . . . I have to get somewhere safe. . . ."

A noise interrupted him. Amos flinched, looking wildly around, arms already coming up to make a cross. But Tangerine dragged his arms down and hugged him again.

"It's just Grandma's car, silly," she said.

Amos nodded, not trusting himself to speak. He could see the car now, turning in off the main road. A small white car that sent the fog scurrying away as it pulled up next to the mailbox.

The car's headlights turned off, and the light inside came on. Amos saw a white-haired old woman in the driver's seat. She waved and smiled, a tight smile that bore no relation to Tangerine's open happiness.

Tangerine held Amos's hands as they watched the little old lady get out of the car. There was something strange about the way the woman moved that Amos couldn't quite process, how she kind of unbent herself as she rested her hands on the roof, and got taller and taller, maybe seven foot tall, with her arms and legs out of normal human proportion, and then she didn't look like a little old lady at all.

"Oh, God, Grandma, I can't do this," said Tangerine, and all of a sudden Amos's hands were free and the girl was pushing at his chest, pushing him away. "Run!"

Amos glanced back over his shoulder, only half running, till he saw that the old woman's mouth was open, and Amos wished it wasn't, wished he'd never seen that mouth, never met Tangerine, never gotten caught in vampire weather, and he was running like he'd never run before, and screaming at the same time.

The vampire stalked past her granddaughter, who held a necklace of crosses in her hand and wept, a girl crying for her grandmother the vampire, and for a boy she hardly knew.

Amos felt the cold, wet air against his bare neck, missed the jangle of the crosses, and knew that Tangerine had taken his protection when she'd kissed him. He wept, too, tears full as much of the hurt of betrayal as fear, and then something fastened on his coat, and he was borne down to the ground, sliding and screaming, trying to turn onto his back so he could cross his arms, but the vampire was so much stronger, her hands like clamps, gripping him to the bone, keeping him still, and he wet himself as he felt the first touch of those teeth he'd seen on his neck and then—

Then there was a heavy, horrible thumping, cracking sound, like a big tree come down on a house, smashing it to bits. Amos felt suddenly lighter, and with a last surge of desperate energy he rolled over and brought up his bracers to form a cross—and there above him was Young Franz, in full silver-embroidered coat and hat, a bloodstained six-foot silver-tipped stake in his hand. Behind him was Old Franz, and Amos's father, and all the older brothers, and his mother and the aunts in their silver-thread shawls, argent knives in hand.

Amos sat up, and a bucketful of tainted dust fell down his chest and across his legs. It smelled like sulfur and rotten meat, and the reek of it made Amos turn his head and vomit.

As he did so, his mother came close and raised a lantern near his head. When Amos turned to her, she pushed his head back, so that the light fell clear upon his neck.

"He's bit," she said heavily. She looked at Amos's father, who stared blankly, then held out his hand. Young Franz gave him the bloodied stake.

"Father . . . ," whispered Amos. He reached up to touch his neck. He could, quite horribly, feel the raised lips of two puncture wounds, but when he looked at his fingers, he could see only a tiny speck of blood.

"It is the will of the Lord," said his father, words echoed by the somber crowd.

He raised the stake above his head.

Amos let himself fall back to the ground and shut his eyes.

But the stake did not enter his heart. He heard someone screaming, "Stop! Grandma! Stop!" and he opened his eyes again and tilted his head forward.

It was Tangerine shouting. She came running through the crowd of villagers, who parted quickly ahead of her but closed up behind as she faltered and stopped by the mound of ash and smoking flesh that had been her grandmother. She had his necklace of crosses in her left hand and a small golden object in her right.

"Another one," said Amos's mother. She raised her knife. "A young one. Ready your stake, Jan."

"No!" shouted Amos. He twisted himself up and grabbed his father's leg. "She's human. Look, she's holding crosses! She's a person!"

Tangerine looked up from the remains of her grand-mother. Her face was wet with more than fog, and her mouth quivered before she was able to get out a word.

"I—I've already called the police! And my dad! You can't kill Amos!"

Amos's father looked her up and down, the stake held ready in his hand. Then, without taking his eyes off her, he spoke to his wife.

"She's holding crosses, sure enough."

The older woman sniffed.

"This isn't any of your business, outsider. A vampire's bit my son, and we must do what must be done."

"But he can be vaccinated!" sobbed Tangerine. "Within twenty-four hours of a bite, it still works."

"We don't hold with vaccination," answered Amos's mother. She looked at her husband. "Do it."

"No!" shrieked Tangerine. She threw herself over Amos as Jan raised the stake. Amos put an arm around her and shut his eyes again.

"I said do it, Jan!"

Amos opened his eyes. His father was looking down at him with an expression that he had only ever seen once before, when Jan had broken his favorite chisel, broken it beyond repair.

"My phone is still connected to the 911 operator," said Tangerine desperately. "Listen!"

She held up the tiny gold object. There was a distant voice speaking from it.

Jan looked at it for a long, long second. For a moment Amos thought he would throw it away, or crush it beneath his heel, but instead he reached out and took it gingerly between two of his thick fingers, as if it was a bug to crush. But he didn't. Instead he lifted it to within six inches of his face and spoke slowly and heavily.

"This is Jan Korgrim, from New Rufbah. We need an ambulance for a vampire-bit boy. He'll be by the mailbox. . . ."

The voice spoke from the phone, urgently.

"No, the vampire's dealt with," said Jan. He looked at Tangerine, and a dark, angry tone crept into his voice. "I reckon it was an old family one, let loose."

The 911 operator spoke again, but Jan dropped the phone on the ground and left it there, squawking. His wife looked at him with eyes sharper than her silver knife and turned away. The other villagers followed watchfully, lanterns held high to illuminate the fog, stakes and knives still kept ready.

Only Jan remained, looking down at Amos and Tangerine, all tangled together in the dirt.

"Father, I—"

Jan raised his hand.

"There's nothing to be said between us, Amos. You're an outsider now."

"But Father, I don't want—"

Jan turned away and strode quickly up the hill, toward the fuzzy, fog-shrouded lantern light that marked the way home.

Tangerine rolled off Amos and got to her feet. He looked dully up at her and saw that she was weeping uncontrollably, tears streaking her face.

"My name's not   not really Tangerine," she sobbed. "It's Jane."

Amos shrugged. He didn't want to know this—he didn't want to know anything.

"And I've got a steady boyfriend."

Amos just wanted to lie on the ground and die.

"Grandmother wanted me to find someone she could drink. Someone unvaccinated. She was tired of reheated treated plasma. She promised she wouldn't kill you, but then when I saw her . . . I saw her go full vampire . . . I'm sorry, Amos. I'm sorry!"

"Doesn't matter," said Amos. "You'd better go, though."

"Go? I'll help you down to the road, to meet the ambulance."

"No," said Amos. He got up on his knees and then slowly stood, pushing Tangerine . . . Jane . . . aside when she tried to help. "I'm not going down to the road."

"What?"

"There's a cold lake in a kind of hollow near the peak," said Amos. He staggered forward a few steps and almost collided with a tree. "The fog sits there, day and night. I'm going to take a rest there. Just for a few days, and then—"

"But you'll turn," exclaimed Jane. She tugged at his arm, trying to drag him downhill. "You'll be a vampire!"

"I'll be a vampire," agreed Amos. He smiled at the thought. "And then I reckon I'll go home and . . . despite crosses and silver and everything, I'll—"

"No," said Jane. "No! You don't want to be a vampire. Grandma . . . Grandma hated it, she could never see the sun, she could only see daylight through fog . . . and she was always cold, so cold—"

"Cold," agreed Amos. He was cold, too, chilled to his heart. Who needed the sun anyway?

"I'll help you," said Jane. "You'll get better. You can watch television!"

Amos looked at her with dead, unfeeling eyes. He couldn't even cry for everything he'd lost.

"Help me to the lake," he muttered as he stumbled into another tree. He couldn't see properly or work his legs. "That's not too much to ask, is it, after what you've done?"

"No," whispered Jane. "No. Here, take my arm."

Amos held on to her arm, though it was hot, so hot he thought it might sizzle his skin. But she held him up as he staggered on, mumbling about drinking the blood of girls with names Jane had never heard of, like Hepzibah and Penninah, and killing someone called Young Franz.

He was so intent on this litany that he barely noticed when they reached the mailbox and Jane sat him down against it.

"What?" he groaned as she lowered him to the ground. "What?"

"Rest a little," said Jane. "Just for a while."

She tried to stroke his head, but he flinched away, and she bit back a sob as she saw that her fingers had branded red streaks on the pallid flesh of his forehead.

The ambulance came a few minutes later, accompanied by two police cars. The police spoke to her briefly before driving on up the road to the village. The paramedics gave Amos a sedative and the antivampire shot, then began the transfusion of blood plasma. After a brief conversation with Jane, they gave her a sedative as well and put her on a stretcher next to Amos. She lay there, looking at the unconscious boy, wreathed in the fog that had extended its twining fingers into the back of the ambulance.

One of the paramedics, the older one, looked out the back and took a deep breath before he pulled the door shut.

"Ah, I like a lungful of mountain fog," he said. "Sometimes you just can't beat a touch of vampire weather."

LATE BLOOMER

by Suzy McKee Charnas

The vampires showed up the summer that Josh worked at Ivan's Antiques Mall.

The job wasn't Josh's idea. He hadn't *asked* to be there.

Ivan's side of the family were all fixated on material stuff, and what is an antiques mall about if not *stuff*? Josh's side were the talented ones. His mother, Maya Cherny Burnham, was a well-known landscape painter. His father taught higher math at the technical college. Upward strivers both, they had never been shy about letting him know that they expected great things from him.

That was okay; everybody pushed their kids. Josh wasn't the only one taking extra science, math, and creative writing electives. In fact, he was doing pretty well. He even liked the writing work. The teacher was giving him A minuses and B pluses, and he was really getting into it.

Then he broke his leg. And then Steve Bowlin's crazy dog

bit him, two surgeries' worth. Then he got mono (better than getting rabies, ha ha). A whole parade of pain. No wonder he messed up on his SATs.

His father said, "Josh, you should hear this from me first: If you had major sciences talent, we'd have seen it by now."

His mom said, "Okay, you're not the next Richard Feynman or Tom Wolfe—so what? You've got more creativity in your little finger than that whole high school put together!"

So, on to after-school classes at the Community Arts Center: oils, clay, watercolor, printmaking, even a "fiber arts" class that (despite strong encouragement from the instructor) he bailed on early. The retards at school were already spreading a rumor that he was gay. He eased out of team sports around that time, too. You do *not* want to be the weediest guy on the field with a bunch of Transformers who think (or pretend to think, just for the fun of it) that a guy who does any kind of art must be queer.

The worst, though, was when the portfolio of his best drawings didn't get him into the Art Institute Advanced Placement program. Probably he shouldn't have included those comic book pages he'd been so proud of. So he wasn't good enough; but that was what art school was for, wasn't it? To help you do it *better*.

His parents said, "Some creative people are late bloomers." They smiled encouragingly, but disappointment hung over them like those little black rain clouds that float above sad cartoon characters. Josh got depressed, too. He quit draw-ing, writing, even hanging out in the local museum (a small collection, but they had two awesome Basquiats and a set of spectacular watercolors by a local guy—he could see these things in his mind anyway, they were that good).

He shut himself off as much as he could, using his iPod to enclose himself in a shield of sound: Coldplay, a couple of rap-pers, some older groups like the Clash. And the Decemberists, at the top of his list since he had heard them in a live concert and had been blown away.

Then at the farmer's market one Saturday he heard a band performing and stopped to listen.

They were heading for a music festival in Colorado, according to the cardboard sign propped up in an open guitar case: a sturdy guy on a camp stool with one drum and a light, easy beat; a skinny, capering guitarist who wore a T-shirt on his head like a jester's cap and bells; a low-slung blonde who padded around with her eyes half closed, fiddling the sweet-est riffs Josh had ever heard; and a square-shouldered girl with a voice like a trumpet, belting out offbeat love songs and political ballads without ever needing to pause for breath.

They were too cool to talk to—in their twenties, playing barefoot on the grass for gas money—but he stayed until they started to repeat themselves. Their songs were good—quirky, catchy, wry, sad, the works. Okay, they were not Danger Mouse or the Decemberists. But they were surely what those groups had been when they started out: talented friends who went out to play whatever they could to whoever would listen, learning how to make great songs.

That was what he needed to do. That was the life he wanted.

So when the class play, an original musical, needed more songs, he volunteered to help. His reward was to be assigned to write two songs with Annie Frye. Writing verses (what was he *thinking*? Now he was *really* going to be killed in the boys' bathroom)—with Freaky Frye!

But Annie was fun to work with, and lyrics for her tunes came surprisingly easily. Didn't that mean something?

Annie introduced him to some seniors she knew who played gigs around town for beer money. They called themselves the Mister Wrongs, and they needed a writer (obviously). He began spending time with them, rehearsing in Brandon White's garage. Annie had a fight with the drummer and walked out. Josh stayed, not just writing songs but singing them. His voice was getting better. They said if he could grow some decent stubble, he might make himself into an acceptable front man.

He had two big problems. One, his mother thought pop music was stupid and destroyed your hearing, so for the first time she was carping about what he was doing instead of cheering him on.

Two, he was so far behind! He couldn't seem to get the

hang of reading music. The only instrument he could play was a Casio keyboard (secondhand from Ivan's). He existed, musically speaking, in a whole other *galaxy* from the Decemberists and their peers.

But Brandon's group liked his lyrics, and sometimes his words and their music did awesome things together. Brandon's girl Betts knew some people in Portland. They talked about heading up there to do a demo tape. Things were looking good.

Then Betts's parents moved across the river, and Brandon's house was repossessed after his whole family snuck away overnight. The others drifted away, and it was all over.

Josh holed up in his room, working on songs about wishing he was dead. He told his parents that he wasn't going back for senior year.

After the inevitable meltdown, his mom got him the summer job at Ivan's mall, no ifs, ands, or buts. Obviously his parents hoped that a microscopic paycheck for grunt work in "the real world" plus some "time to think things over" would change his decision.

As if! All he wanted was to get the hell out of Dodge and go someplace he could find new musicians to work with, someplace with a real music scene that went beyond country whining, salsa, and bad rock. He needed a fresh start, in Portland or Seattle—*someplace*. Once he got there, his nowhere origins wouldn't be a problem. Colin Meloy was from *Montana*.

Basically, though, what he really wanted was for the world to stop for a while so he could make a really good musician of himself. He needed to make up all the time he'd wasted on science and arts.

The vampires' arrival, of course, changed everything.

The first-look sale of old Mrs. Ledley's estate ran till eleven p.m. on a Friday night. Josh was posted in a back booth, with orders to keep his eyes open. The crowd was mostly dealers, but you couldn't be too careful in a huge warehouse space broken up into forty-five different dealers' booths and four aisles.

Tired from schlepping furniture and boxes all day for Ivan's renters (who all had bad backs from years of schlepping furniture and boxes), he sat at an old oak desk in booth forty-one (Victoriana, especially toys and kids' furniture), doodling on a sketch pad. He'd have worked on song lyrics ("The day flies past my dreaming eyes . . ."), but not with Sinatra blatting "My Way" from a booth up front that sold scratchy old long plays.

Hearing a little *tick, tick* sound close by, he glanced up.

A woman in a green linen suit stood across the aisle, tapping a pencil against her front teeth and studying the display in a glass-fronted cabinet. Josh sketched fast. She might work as a goth-flavored Madonna, being pointy faced and olive skinned with thick, dark hair.

Next time he looked, he met a laserlike stare. Her eyes,

crow footed at the outer corners, were shadowed in the same shade of parakeet blue as the polish on her nails (good-bye, Madonna).

He closed his pad and asked if she wanted to see anything from the locked cases.

"Have you got any furs?" she said. Her English had a foreign tinge. "Whole fox skins, to wear around the neck in winter?"

He shook his head. "Some came in with the estate, but they've already gone to a vintage clothing store."

She sniffed. "Then show me what you're drawing."

He meant to refuse but found himself handing over his pad anyway.

She flipped pages. "Jesus and sheep? Are you Catholic?"

"You can always sell a religious picture in here sooner or later," he said, folding his arms defensively. "Minimum wage sucks."

"This isn't bad," she said, tapping the top sketch, "but I would stay in school if I were you." What was she expecting, Michaelangelo?

"I'm dropping out." Not that it was any of her business.

"Then this is a good place for you," she said, handing back the pad. "One can always make a living in antiques."

"It's just a summer job," he mumbled. "I'm a musician, actually."

"Oh? What's your instrument?"

"Keyboards. But I'm more of a songwriter." She had moved closer. Her perfume was making his eyes water.

"Can you sing something you've written? My name is Odette Delauney; I know a lot of people. Maybe I can put you in touch, ah . . . ?"

"Josh," he muttered, "and I'm a song*writer*." He was not about to sing anything at a building-sized party of old farts zoned out on—Stevie Wonder, now. He avoided mentioning two blurry video clips, made with Brandon and Betts, on YouTube. He *had* to remember to take the stupid things down.

Odette Delauney's beady stare was making him feel strange. His feet kept inching his chair backward, but his head wanted to lean closer to her.

She swiveled suddenly on her high heels and pointed at a toy display: "If the donkey works, I'll take him." Then she was walking away, carrying a wind-up tin donkey that sat back on its haunches with a pair of little cymbals between its front hooves.

The ambient sound of the wide dealer space roared in as if Josh had suddenly yanked out a pair of earbuds: conversation, Julie Andrews climbing every mountain, shuffling footsteps.

Odette Delauney? Was she somebody? Had he just blown a big chance?

Too late; she was gone.

* * *

Josh stayed late to sweep up and turn out the lights. It was after midnight. His gray Civic was the only car left in the lot.

By the glow of the floodlight outside, he saw that a plump, dark-skinned girl was sitting on the sagging slat bench by the front door. She had a mass of dreadlocks, shiny piercings in an ear plugged with a white bud, and a cigarette in her hand. Wearing jeans, a tank top, and pink plastic sandals with little daisies on the toe straps, she looked about fourteen.

"Hey," she said as he locked the front door behind him, "think I could get a job here? I've got expenses, and my aunt is so *stingy.*"

"But she lets you stay out late and smoke weed," he said.

She snorted derisively and took a puff. Ivan would disapprove of her on *so* many levels. The dealers and buyers at the mall—mostly old, white, and from the boondocks—didn't run, as Ivan said, in progressive circles (har har, progressive *circles*, get it?).

"Is working here as boring as it looks?" she asked.

"Worse." He gestured at her iPod. "So, who are you listening to?"

"Amy Winehouse." She narrowed her eyes. "What'd you expect? The Jonas Brothers?"

Josh thought fast. "M.I.A."

"'Jai Ho,'" she drawled, but her expression relaxed. "You're Josh? My auntie Odette met you inside."

"She bought a musical toy, right? Funny, she sure didn't

strike me as the type for that kind of thing."

"She'll have a buyer for it somewhere. Those old animal-band sets are hot right now."

Then auntie was just another antiques dealer, not a record producer's best pal, surprise surprise.

"So—are you adopted?" he said.

Studying him with narrowed eyes, the girl blew another slow plume of smoke. "My Main Line mom ran off with a bass player from Chicago. The wheels came off and they both split and left me with a neighbor. I call her auntie to keep things simple. I guess 'adopted' works. You a musician?"

"Uh-huh," he said, and that was enough about that. He didn't want to come off as some dumb-ass poser. "You collect stuff, too, like your aunt?"

"Sure," she said, shifting aside on the bench. "Sit down—I'll show you what I found tonight."

He had barely touched butt to bench when she grabbed him with steely arms, jammed her face down the neckline of his T-shirt, and bit him. His yell pinched down to nothing in seconds. Muffled panic surged through him as he slumped, unable to move or shout for help, staring over her head at the neon bar sign across the avenue.

Am I dying?

"That's enough, Crystal."

The sucking sounds from under his chin stopped. Someone else took the girl's place. He knew that perfume. The woman's lips felt tight and cool, like the skin of a ripe nectar-ine pressed to his throat. . . .

He came to sitting behind the wheel of the Civic with a stinging sensation in his chest and a headache. "Ow, shit, what happened?"

Crystal said, right beside his ear, "Odette wants to talk to you."

It all came rushing back, paralyzing him again with sweaty horror.

"Josh," said Odette Delauney from the backseat. "I'm only in your town for a little while, buying antiques. I need an insider here to help me find the kinds of items I want and then to make sure I get them. Tonight I'll just take a quick look at the storage area. If I pick something out, you show it to your employer tomorrow—"

"Cousin," Josh croaked. "My cousin Ivan owns the place."

"Show it to your cousin Ivan and tell him you have a buyer for it. I'll come in the evening and make the purchase."

Something weird as hell had just gone down between him and these two, but *what*, exactly? Odette's calm tone made it impossible to ask directly without sounding like a lunatic.

Please go away, he prayed.

"You could just take stuff," he muttered. "I wouldn't say anything."

"Of course not," Odette sniffed. "But I don't steal. And I'm not asking you to steal *for* me, either."

Gee, thanks. His trembling fingers found a swelling, hot and pulpy wet, low on his throat. "Oh, God," he moaned. "What'll I tell my parents about this?"

"Nothing," Odette said. "One of us will lick the wounds closed. Our saliva heals where we bite."

Agh, vampire spit! His teeth began to chatter. "Are you gonna turn me into a—like you?"

"With one little bite?" Crystal hooted scornfully. "You *wish*."

"Certainly not," Odette said, ignoring her. "Do as I say and you have nothing to worry about. Our arrangement will be brief and very much to your advantage. I'll pay you a commission on every purchase that I make."

A giggle burst out of him, ending in a sob. "I'm supposed to *work* for you? Everybody knows how that comes out— Renfield eats bugs, and then Dracula kills him!"

"We put the Eye on you," Crystal said in a smug singsong. "Now you can't tell anybody about us, so we don't *have* to kill you."

"Unless," Odette added, "you say no."

Which was how Josh went into business with Odette Delauney and her "niece," Crystal Dark (a joke; Crystal, it turned out, was an avid fan of fantasy movies).

It was true: he couldn't tell anybody. When he tried to talk about the vampires, his brain fuzzed over and didn't clear again for hours. It was just as well, really. All he needed was for word to get around that Josh Burnham claimed he'd been attacked—and then *hired*—by two female vampires from out of town.

Pretending he had found a new band to hang with after work, he told his parents he'd be coming home late some nights. Luckily he was too old to be grounded. His mom put up a fight, but she left hot food in the oven for him on his late nights anyway (which was particularly important now that he was suddenly this major blood donor).

His father, absorbed in updating a textbook he was co-author of, said, "No drugs, that's all I ask."

Twice a week after hours, Josh let the vampires in through the loading doors, which were hidden from the street by the bulk of the building. In the windowless back room, they cleared space on the worktable Ivan used for fixing old furniture, and they went through whatever new stock had come in.

There was always new stuff. Business was booming. Ivan called it the "Antiques Roadshow effect"; that, and the stock market. People were desperate to put their money into solid objects, things that they thought would get more valuable no matter what.

That first week Odette bought: a tortoiseshell and ivory cigarette holder (fifteen dollars), bronze horse-head bookends (twenty-eight dollars), three colored-glass perfume atomizers (thirty dollars), a rooster-silhouette weather vane (twenty-five dollars), and a four-inch-high witch hugging a carved pumpkin, both in molded orange plastic (seven fifty).

"Your aunt," Josh said, "has weird taste."

Crystal shrugged (this was her favorite gesture). "Everything's cheap here in flyover country. In *real* cities, the Quality will pay top dollar for the same stuff, sometimes just to keep some other collector from getting it."

By "the Quality," she meant vampires.

Josh worked up the nerve to ask Odette, "Who's the pumpkin-toting witch for?"

"Some old fool I know in Seattle. We're not all rich aesthetes, Josh, whatever you may have seen in the movies."

"Aesthetes." That's how she talked. That was the kind of conversation they had, those nights that the vampires spent pawing through stacks of cartons and crates, flicking roaches aside (there were always roaches, even though Ivan had the whole place sprayed regularly) and deciding what Odette would buy the next day.

And they would each drink some of Josh's blood.

This remained skin-crawlingly horrible, but once they laid the Eye on you, you just accepted whatever they did. Instead of wigging out over it, Josh turned to working obsessively on songs about mysterious night visitors and dangerous girlfriends, with Rasputina, Theatre of Tragedy, and Voltaire playing on his iPod.

Not that Crystal herself was girlfriend material. She was

just a kid, like somebody's little sister you'd ignore completely (if not for the blood-drinking thing). Anyway, she said she was celibate right now, trying to put an edge back on her appetite for when she took up sex again. True or not (who could tell, with a vampire?), this was way more than Josh wanted to know—which was, of course, exactly why she'd told him.

Generally, though, he felt strangely upbeat. Grim lyrics poured out of him, which made a kind of sense under the circumstances. Inspiration seemed a fair exchange for a little blood. He wasn't satisfied with his work, but there were moments. Once in a while he took off on a thrill wave as his words fell together just right and he glimpsed the possibility that he could really do this—he could write songs for people to fly on.

> *"Wither my soul with your cold, dry lips*
> *So I'll have no tears to cry—"*

The only thing was, he was so *isolated.* How could his songs get better without real musicians to work with? He was writing his own lines to other people's tunes, a practice technique that could take him only so far.

He needed to get a move on, to make it to the next level. He was seventeen already! He had so much catching up to do.

Nobody breaks out as an *old* singer-songwriter.

* * *

Odette's profession was perfect: She was a masseuse. She used the Eye to draw customers to her place (a rental on Cardenas) so she never had to go out in the sunlight. Her clients came away feeling totally relaxed (as Josh knew from personal experience). Since that was the whole point of a massage, they recommended her to their friends. Odette apparently needed hardly any sleep; she kept evening hours for working people, rates on a sliding scale (why not? She could always take the difference in blood).

Crystal slept all day or else hung out at the Top of Your Game, an arcade where kids played out fantasy adventures (Odette called the Top "a casino for children"). At night, in Ivan's office, Crystal browsed antiques sites on the computer for Odette.

He asked once if she missed gossiping and giggling with other girls in school.

"Eww! Do I look crazy? Who wants to be cooped up with a bunch of smelly, spotty, horny adolescents and the teachers who hate them, in a place built like a prison?"

"Is that what you're thinking when you're drinking my blood—about how spotty and smelly I am?" (Horny just didn't come into that experience for Josh.)

"Oh," she said, "let's not go there."

He decided to celebrate his new songwriting energy by getting rid of the pathetic jumble of projects from his arts center classes (the mobile made of hangers and beer tabs, a wood-cut of crows fighting), which he had tucked out of sight in a tote bag on the floor of his closet. He might even make a few bucks by farming all this junk out for sale in the mall with whichever dealers were willing to display it. (As they said, "There's a buyer for *everything*.")

When he walked in, two cops were asking for Ivan at the register. Josh made a business of tucking the tote, with a sweatshirt stuffed in on top to keep everything from falling out, into one of the lockers by the front door, so he could listen.

They asked about a well-known local meth head who had come in the day before trying to sell some old coins.

"Stolen, right?" Ivan said.

They nodded, looking meaningfully around the nearby booths.

Ivan braced his thick hands on the glass countertop. "That's why I never buy off the street—it's always stolen goods. You won't find any valuable jewelry for sale by any of my dealers, either; too easy to steal. That kind of thing just attracts thieves.

"So," he said, relaxing now that he had declared himself totally honest, "did something happen after I kicked that kid out of here?"

"Read the papers," one of the cops said.

The *Journal* reported that the kid had been found early

that morning out by the old airport, with his throat slashed and the coins gone.

Josh, shivering, ducked into the corner reserved for books and DVDs. "Throat slashed" sounded suspiciously like "disguised vampire bite" to him. He calmed himself down with half an hour of looking at psychedelic sleeve art for old long-playing records.

Crystal showed up at midnight with a puffy, teary look and a bandage wrapped around one hand. He asked if she was okay, but she disappeared into the shadows of the nighttime mall without answering.

In the office, Odette explained in a pissed-off tone.

"A boy accosted us in your parking lot last night, trying to sell us some coins, or mug us, or both. I turned him away. Crystal was in one of her moods; she followed him. I've told her a thousand times, we do *not* drink people dry and then toss them aside like juiced oranges. It's stupid."

"She *drained* that kid?"

"She has a teenager's appetite," Odette said. "And poor impulse control."

"She told me she's seventy-five years old!"

Impatiently Odette swung the swivel chair around (with Crystal temporarily incapacitated, Odette had to find sites on the computer for herself, which made her cranky). "Years don't come into it. Crystal isn't alive the way you are, Josh. She doesn't mature with time. The parts of her brain that hadn't developed when she was turned never will. She's between thirteen and fourteen forever, in her mind as well as her body."

Imagine never being able to shed your baby fat, your zits, or your adolescent mood swings.

"Wow," he said.

"Wow indeed."

"So . . . did the guy have a knife or something? Her hand—"

Odette said, "You need to understand that I provide the only structure she has in her life, and the only security. Sometimes I must be a little harsh with her, but it's for her own sake. She doesn't survive by being a clever adult in a permanently child-like body. She's a child who survives because I protect her."

"Protect her?" Crystal, who was clearly injured—but who had also just killed someone. "From who?"

"Her own rash nature," Odette said tartly, "but also older vampires. The Quality don't like the young ones, for reasons that should be obvious. Recklessness puts us all at risk. Correction helps in the short term, but there is no curing persistently childish behavior in someone who is, essentially, a permanent child."

Crystal's prickliness began to make more sense. "Why do you keep her around, then?"

Odette jabbed irritably at the keyboard with one long, iridescent fingernail. "Youngsters are adaptable and good at modernity. She can be very helpful."

Useful, she meant.

"Well, well!" Odette's attention was caught by something on the screen. "Axel Hochauer has sold off his Grande Armée figures for a tidy sum, I see." She smiled. "Goretsky must be *livid*."

Josh knew he was dismissed.

He found Crystal crying in the bathroom. Clearing his throat nervously, he asked, "Crystal? Did she do something to you?"

"Made me hold my hand in sunlight," she blubbed, glaring up at him through her tears. "Look!"

The skin on the back of her hand was scabby and blotched with raw pink skin. She wrapped it up again quickly. "It was worse before; we heal fast. That doesn't mean it didn't hurt. I *hate* that mean old bitch!"

She had killed the meth head, but her own situation was pretty dire. He couldn't help feeling sorry for her. Not enough to hug her or anything like that, but sorry.

"Hey," he said, propping his hip against the sink. "Want to hear a new song? It's not exactly finished yet—I mean, I'm not through working on it—but I think it's a pretty good start. I'm calling it 'Love Birds.'"

He sang, mezza voce:

> "Raven hates her own harsh tone.
> She hacks and hawks to spit it out.

Swallow down her razor kiss
Salty, icy, light as bone,
To sweeten Raven's song.
She'll be your love, your turtledove,
If you sweeten Raven's song."

"'Turtledove?'" Crystal mimicked scornfully. "What century do *you* come from? Makes no sense, either. Well, that's cool. You can't eat music, and I'm starving."

She was *always* hungry, and she always had to be reminded to stop.

Next time things seemed back to normal. Crystal, Grand Theft Auto champion with a stuffed arcade bear to prove it, was on the monitor again, checking for comparables to Odette's latest find: a rare Chinese pipe, all delicately curved brass tubing and carved wood. Josh, already tapped by both vampires, dozed in a beat-up armchair on the other side of Ivan's desk.

"Oh, shit!" Crystal leaned back and yelled, "Odette! MacCardle's in Dallas!"

Odette swept into the office and tilted the monitor around to see the news photo. It featured a scrawny, self-satisfied-looking guy with suspenders holding up his pants, shaking some fancy suit's hand in an auction showroom.

Odette snarled silently, showing a gleam of fang (Josh

looked away; he hated thinking about where those teeth had been). But all she said was "Fine. He's there, we're here."

She went back to inspecting the Chinese pipe.

Crystal whispered fiercely, "Fine my foot! If MacCardle comes sniffing around here, we are *so* gone."

Josh was jolted by a stab of realization: He didn't want them gone—not without him. (God, could he really be thinking like this?)

"He looks harmless," he observed cautiously. "Not exactly a Van Helsing type."

"He's *Quality*, dummy. He comes sneaking around after Odette trying to snag the good stuff first, which makes her so *mad*! You won't like her when she's mad," she intoned, wiggling the fingers of her now-unblemished hand.

"What, she turns green and smashes the place up?"

"No joke," Crystal said.

"Okay, this is for real, right? People who live forever by drinking human blood spend their time fighting over high-priced junk?"

Crystal snorted. "Are you kidding? They *love* to feud over scraps—ugly old vases, souvenir ashtrays from Atlantic City, dried-up baby shoes. Some of them are addicted to anything from their own time. Mostly, though, it's about personal pride and protecting their investments."

"They hunt down enameled kitchenware, just like some retired bus driver desperate for something to do, and that's about pride and investment?"

"Hey, look around you," she said. "Even mass-produced trinkets get valuable if they survive long enough. A vampire can wait a century for his tin plates to become rare and then sell them for a bundle. Then there's the thrill of spotting a trend first and getting in there before anybody else. Odette's amazing at that. Timing the market is a real competition for them; they bet on each other. Gambling's always been the favorite pastime of the upper crust. Well, crust doesn't get any upper than the Quality."

An idea sparked, then glowed. "Crystal? What does Odette collect for herself?"

"What you want to know for?" She stared at him suspiciously. "Anyway, you're asking the wrong person."

"It can't all be just merchandise to her," he insisted. "What does she find in a place like this that she won't resell?"

Crystal absently twisted the ears of the trophy bear as she thought this over. "Odd stuff. One-of-a-kind things: snapshots, carvings, pictures."

"Art," he said.

"Art, and artists. If she thinks you have what she calls 'real creative talent,' you get a vampire godmother for life— whether you want it or not."

Odette hadn't asked to see his drawings again, but . . . "What about my songs?"

"The last music Odette liked was a *minuet*," Crystal said,

rolling her eyes. "And plus she has the tinnest ear ever and hates poetry."

He pressed on. "Well, what else? What does she love?" If he could find something special, something to show that he was on Odette's wavelength—that he was too *useful* to leave behind—

"Well, there's this quilt," Crystal said. "Grubby old thing; pretty hand stitching though—little strips of silk from men's ties, kimonos, and like that. She paid a lot for it. She still has it."

"But why? Why that?"

"How should I know?" Crystal scowled, then softened slightly. "I did hear once that her brother was a famous gold-smith, couple centuries back. He had a stroke, so she got to design jewelry, under her brother's name, for the rich people. It *could* be a true story, but who knows? She's not the kind who runs her mouth about her first life, like some of the Quality. Specially the really *old* ones, trying to hang on to their memories. Anyway, maybe she was talented herself, back in the day."

Josh nodded, thinking furiously. He was not going to be left behind in flyover country if he could help it.

Two more of the Quality showed up at Ivan's at the next open evening. One looked the part—tall, pale, and high shouldered like a vulture (an effect undercut by his cowboy boots, ironed jeans, and Western shirt with pearl-snap buttons). There was no mystery about what he was after: Several pounds of Indian fetish necklaces decorated his sunken chest.

The other, a chunky Asian-looking woman with a flat-top haircut, wore chains and bunches of keys jingling from her belt, her boots, her leather vest.

"What's she looking for, whips and handcuffs?" Josh whispered.

Crystal smirked at him. "Dummy. That's Alicia Chung. Odette says she has the best collection of nineteenth-century opera ephemera in America."

"She's looking for old opera posters around *here*?"

Crystal shrugged. "You never know. That's part of the challenge."

In the workroom after closing, the first thing Odette said was "If Chung is here, it won't be long before MacCardle arrives. We pack up tonight, Crystal."

Josh broke an icy sweat. He had no time for finesse.

"Odette?" His voice cracked. "Take me, too."

"No," she said. She didn't even look at him.

"Crystal travels with you!"

"Crystal is Quality, and she has no living family. Shall we kill your mother and father so they won't come searching for you?"

With Crystal's voice in his ears ("Ooh, that's *cold*, Odette!"),

Josh ran into the bathroom and threw up. He drove home without remembering to turn on his headlights and fell asleep in his clothes, dreaming about Annie Frye biting his neck. Later he sat in the dark banging out the blackest chords he could get from his keyboard.

His band was gone, nobody from school wanted to hang with him, and now even the vampires were taking off.

His mom knocked on the bedroom door at seven a.m. and asked if he wanted to "talk about" anything. "Your music sounds so sad, hon." Like he was writing his songs for her!

"It's just music." He hunched over the Casio, waiting for her to leave. How could he stand to live in this house one more day?

She stepped inside. "Josh, I'm picking up signals here. Are you thinking of leaving town with your new friends?"

He panicked, then realized she only meant his imaginary musician pals. "No."

"All the same, I think it's time I met them," she said firmly.

"Why can't you leave me alone? You're just making everything worse!"

"You're doing that brilliantly for yourself," she retorted. They yelled back and forth, each trying to inflict maximum damage without actually drawing blood, until she clattered off downstairs to finish crating pictures for a gallery show in San Jose. The hammering was fierce.

She was going out there for her show's opening, naturally.

Everybody could leave flyover country for the real, creative world of accomplishment and success, except Josh.

He slipped into her studio after she'd left. As a kid, he had spent so much time here while his mom worked. The bright array of colors, the bristly and sable-soft brushes, and the rainbow-smeared paint rags had kept him fascinated for hours. There on the windowsill, just as he'd remembered during their argument, sat something that just might convince Odette to take him with her.

Ivan had belonged to a biker gang for a few years. Later on, he'd made a memento of that time in his life and then asked Josh's mother to keep it for him (his own wife wanted no reminders of those days in *her* house).

What Ivan had done was to twist silver wire into the form of a gleaming, three-inch-high motorbike, with turquoise-disk beads for wheels. The thing was beautiful as only a lovingly made miniature can be. It looked like a jeweled dragonfly. Visitors had offered Josh's mother money for it.

Value, uniqueness, handcrafted beauty—it was perfect.

Josh quickly packed it, wrapped in tissues, into a little cardboard box that used to hold a Christmas ornament. At work, he stashed it in a drawer of the oak desk in the Victoriana booth, where he sometimes went for naps when the vampires' snacking wore him out. Odette would come tonight, after her final antiquing run through town, before she took off for good. This would be his one and only chance to persuade her.

After closing time, he dashed out for pizza. When he got back to the darkened mall, he was startled to find Crystal sitting at the oak desk with the little brass lamp turned on.

"How'd you get in?" he asked.

She gave a sullen shrug. The package sat open on the desk in front of her.

"Where's Odette?" The silent mall floor had never looked so dark.

"She's late," Crystal said. "I was tired of waiting, so I hitched a ride over from the Top. This is something of yours, right? What is it, anyway?"

"A going-away present for Odette. I got something for you, too," he added, trying frantically to think of what he could give to Crystal.

"Yeah?" Her red leather purse, heavy with quarters for the game machines, swung on its thin strap in jerky movements like the tail of an angry cat. "You were gonna give me something? You *liar*, Josh."

He wondered, with a shiver, if some of the coins making the little red purse bulge were from the meth head's haul.

Suddenly she screamed, "You think you can buy Odette with this little shiny piece of trash? You pretend to be my friend, but you just want to take my *place*!"

She lashed at him with the purse. He dodged, tripped,

and toppled helplessly. The back of his head smacked the floor with stunning force.

Crystal threw herself on top of him, guzzling at his throat as he passed out.

He woke up lying on a thirties settee outside Ivan's office, deep in the heart of the mall. In the office, the computer monitor glowed with light that seemed unnaturally bright, illuminating the little room and the hallway outside it.

His shirt stuck to his chest and his neck was stiff. He felt his throat. There was a damp, painless tear in the flesh on one side.

"Crystal is a messy eater, but don't worry, that will heal quickly." Odette, perched on a chair by the end of the settee, held the miniature bike in her hands. "I think you brought this for me? Thank you, Josh. It's very beautiful."

He sat up. His mouth tasted sharply metallic, but nothing hurt.

"Where's Crystal?"

"She ran off," Odette said. "She knows she's in serious trouble with me for killing you. Remember what I said about adolescent impulsiveness? Now you see what I meant. She won't last long on her own, not with others of the Quality starting to show up here and my protection withdrawn. It's too bad, but frankly it's for the best. I'm tired of her tantrums."

He felt a slow, chilly ripple of fear. "*Killing* me?"

"Effectively, yes, but I arrived in time to divert the process. The taste in your mouth is my blood. It's a necessary exchange that also provides a soothing first meal for you, in your revivified state. You don't want to begin your undead life crazed and stupid with hunger."

He licked his front teeth, which had a strange feel, like *too much*. His stomach churned briefly. "I thought you didn't want to . . . turn . . ."

She sniffed. "Of course not. Who needs *another* teenaged vampire? But dead young bodies raise questions, and Crystal already left one lying around out by the airport. Besides, with her gone I have a job opening. Your selection of this"—she carefully set the little bike on the table at her elbow—"shows an educable eye, at least. With coaching, I suppose you can be made into a passable member of the Quality."

Coaching? He might as well have gone back to school!

She stood, smoothing down her skirt, and picked up his canvas tote from the floor at her feet. "I found this in your locker. The sweatshirt is yours, isn't it? Take off that T-shirt and put this on. It's none too clean, but you can't walk around looking like a gory movie zombie. Then you must leave a note for your family. Say you've gone to seek your fortune."

Thoughts lit up like silent sheet lightning in his mind while he worked the blood-crusted T-shirt off over his head.

His life, his friends, his home—all that was over, and she'd just been trying to get rid of him when she'd said, before, about killing his parents. But there was no going back. The upside was, he *would* be getting out of here at last, traveling with Odette out into the real world.

Was that why he felt high, instead of all bleak and tortured about waking up undead?

Then it hit him: undead? He was finally going to get to *live*.

He punched the air and whooped. "Look out, Colin Meloy! Josh Burnham's songs are coming *down!*"

Pawing around inquisitively in the tote bag, Odette glanced up. "Forget about your songs, Josh. You *died*. The undead do not create: not babies, not art, not music, not even recipes or dress designs. I'm sorry, but that's our reality."

"You don't get it!" he crowed. "Listen, I'm still a beginner, but I'm good—I know I am. Now I have years—centuries even—to turn myself into the best damn singer-songwriter ever! So what if I never mature past where I am now, like you said about Crystal? Staying young is *success* in the music business! I can use the Eye to get top players to work with me, to teach me—"

"You can learn skills," she said with forced patience. "You can imitate. But you can't create, not even if you used to have the genius of a budding Sondheim, which you did not.

According to Crystal, your lyrical gift was . . . let's say, minor. I hope you're not going to be tiresome about this, Josh."

"Crystal's just jealous!" Buoyed by the exhilaration of getting some payback at last for his weeks of helpless servitude, he shouted, *"You're* jealous! She told me about you, how you made jewelry for rich people—"

Odette snapped, "That's someone else. I designed tapestries. As a new made, you're entitled to a little rudeness, but at least take the trouble to get the facts right."

"But the thing is, you were already *old*—your talent was all used up by the time you got turned, wasn't it? So now you can't stand to admit that anybody else still has it!"

"My talent," she said icily, "which was not just considerable but still unfolding, was extinguished completely and forever—*just like yours*—when I became what you are now." She fixed him with a dragon glare and hissed, "Stupid boy, why do you think I *collect*?"

He almost laughed: What was this, some weird horror-movie version of fighting with his mother? Fine, he was *stoked*. "It's different for me! I'm just getting started, and now I can go on getting better and better *forever*!"

With a shrug, she turned back to the contents of the tote bag. "You can try; who knows, you might even have some commercial success—"

She stopped, holding up a fantasy-style chalice he'd made in ceramics class at the arts center. It was a sagging blob that couldn't even stand solidly on its crooked foot.

"What's this?"

"You should know," he muttered, embarrassed. "You're the expert on valuable *things*. It's arts and crafts, that's all, from back when I was still trying to find my way, my *art*. I brought all that stuff in here to try to sell it, only I forgot— I've been kind of distracted, you know?"

"You made this." She ran the ball of her thumb along the thickly glazed surface, which he had decorated with sloppy swirls of lemon and indigo.

"So what?" he said. "Here, just toss that whole bag of crap." There was a trash can outside the office door. He shoved it toward her with his foot.

Odette gently put the cup aside. She reached back into the tote bag and drew from the bottom a wad of crumpled fabric.

Oh, no, not that damned needlepoint!

In his fiber arts class, he had been crazy enough to try to reproduce an Aztec cape, brilliant with the layered feathers of tropical birds, like one he'd seen in the museum. He'd just learned the basic diagonal stitch, so the rectangular canvas had warped into a diamondlike shape. Worse, frustrated that the woolen yarns weren't glossy enough, he'd added splinters of metal, glazed pottery, and glass, shiny bits and pieces knotted and sewn onto the unevenly stitched surface.

That wiseass Mickey Craig had caught him working on it once and had teased him for "sewing, like a girl." That was when Josh had quit the class and hidden the unfinished canvas in his closet where nobody would ever see it.

Yeah; his luck.

Maybe he could convince Odette that his mother had made it.

"God in heaven," Odette said flatly. "God. In. *Heaven*. If I ever catch up with that girl, I will tear off her *head*."

Her eyes glared from a face tense with fury; but he saw a shine of moisture on her cheek.

Odette was *crying*.

And there it was, the kernel of the first great song of his undead life, a soul-ripping blast about losing everything and winning everything, to mark the end of his last summer as a miserable, live human kid: "Tears of a Vampire." All he had to do was come up with a couple of starter lines, and then find a tune to work with.

All he had to do was . . . why couldn't he think?

All he had to do . . . his thoughts hung cool and still as settled fog. He found himself staring at the crude, lumpy canvas, vivid and glowing, stretched between Odette's bony fists.

He began to *see* it, this cockeyed thing that his own fumbling, amateurish hands had made. Its grimy, raveling edges framed a rich fall of parrot-bright colors, all studded with glittering fragments.

He hadn't even finished it, but it was beautiful.

Oh, he thought. Oh . . .

This was it—this was what he should have been doing all along—not drawing comics or struggling with song lyrics, but crafting this kind of mind-blowing interplay of colors, shapes, and textures. *This* was his true art, his breakout talent.

So why couldn't he picture it as a finished piece? He stretched his eyes wide open, squinted them almost shut, but he could only see it right there in front of him exactly as it was, abandoned and incomplete. His mind, flat and gray and quiet, offered nothing, except for a faint but rising tremor of dread.

Because although he couldn't describe the stark look on Odette's face in clever lyrics anymore, he understood it perfectly now—from the inside. It was the expression of someone staring into an endless future of absolute sterility, unable to produce one single creation of originality, beauty, or inspiration ever again.

If Josh wanted all that back—originality, inspiration, and beauty, only everything he had ever really wanted—he would have to get it the same way that Odette, or any of the Quality, got it.

He would have to begin collecting.

THE LIST OF DEFINITE ENDINGS
by Kaaron Warren

Sometimes partying felt like punishment. Claudia hated large groups of people, vampires included. They had secret jokes she didn't get, and the conversation always moved too fast for her.

She liked to be with one person, or two. Talking about life and the future. About the past. She met people who'd seen history being made and were alive to talk about it. This was interesting to her. Not empty nights of dancing, laughing, feasting, sex. Perhaps she was too earnest, that was the problem. The rest of them were without care or thought. She wished she could be that way, but there was too much left of her soft mortal self.

Her boyfriend, Joel, waved his hand in front of her face. "Aren't you hungry? Let's go feast." He poked her. "Stop dreaming. Let's go party. The night's coming in and you're sitting around like you don't wanna get fed."

She felt a deep gnawing in her stomach. "Yes, I'm hungry. Of course I'm hungry. But I don't feel like eating in a group."

Joel rolled his eyes. "You bore me. Do you realize that? Bored bored bored."

"Well, I'm bored with all this, too. Don't you get sick of it? The relentlessness? Don't you get tired of always being nineteen? Don't you want to know what it's like to be thirty? Forty?"

Claudia had been turned in 1942, three weeks before her final high school exams, something she'd always regretted. She'd studied hard, really hard, and she knew her stuff. She could write an essay on each of Henry VIII's wives, and on child mortality rates around the world, and on the voting systems of almost any country you could name. They didn't talk about the war in class. Their teachers said the facts changed too quickly and that they would have to wait and see. If the Germans won, then the history books would all have to be changed. Everybody knew that.

She was the first girl in her family to make it that far, one of only five girls finishing high school. Most of her friends were working in the shops, and some had even signed up as nurses, out saving the lives of brave soldiers. Finding brave, damaged husbands. Some days Claudia envied this ordinary life, others she knew she was due much more.

Her family was wealthy, always had been. It was because of shoes; people always needed shoes. Her father traveled a lot with the family shoe business, though Claudia knew there was more to it than that. He came back exhausted from his sales trips, often injured. Always his fingers covered with cuts and splinters, his eyes bruised. Scratches on his arms. While she studied, her mother fed her in a constant, perfectly timed stream of healthy and unhealthy snacks. Claudia knew the rest of the family went without so that she would have enough food to study on. A rare and beautiful apple. Thick slices of bread with butter and raspberry jam. Sometimes a piece of cake, if the neighbors pooled their resources. Claudia knew she did better than most.

Once her mother cooked a roast chicken and she put garlic all over it. Buttery garlic sauce to pour over the meat and the potatoes, fat slices of bread on the side.

This was the food she remembered now, when she thought about her past life. She hadn't tasted garlic for close to seventy years, not in vegetable form, although sometimes the blood she drank was flavored with it. She liked that.

Early on she'd tried dead blood. It made her sick and weak for days. Most vampires don't like to be around dead bodies. The smell turns them off—the waste of all that good, warm blood gone cold.

It was worth a try, though. Her vampire friends (all moved on, traveling the world) thought she was crazy, and any vampire she'd told since did as well. But every time she killed someone living, the memory of her parents lessened.

She could almost feel it; a memory breaking loose and being dissolved by the foreign blood in her veins. She didn't want to forget her parents, killed by the same vampires who'd turned her. She'd begged those monsters to turn her parents as well. Not kill them.

"We don't want any old vampires," they'd told Claudia. "No old rules, no tired old vampires. You need to be young to be one of us." Claudia thought of her dad and the thousand cuts inflicted on him by the vampires. A father's secret life as a vampire hunter come back to haunt him. He was almost dead when they dragged Claudia in and turned her in front of him. The last thing he saw was his daughter's vampire eyes.

So all she had left of her parents was the memories of them, and when she could do it with no one watching, she drank the dead blood and put up with the weakness and nausea, for the sake of keeping memory.

Joel jumped onto the couch and backflipped off it, narrowly missing the coffee table. "Can a forty-year-old do that? You can't seriously want to get old."

"I don't want to get old. But I do get tired of this stuff. This life. I've been doing it for seventy years. If they'd waited till I was twenty-one, at least. Twenty-one is a much easier age than nineteen. I could have found real jobs."

"Twenty-one is *old*," Joel said. "Who wants to be old? You

might as well be, though. You're sad and boring. Both things."
He walked away, as so many did. She'd see him around, but
they were done with a relationship.

She knew that human boys were like that as well, sudden in their decisions, uncaring about softening the blow. But
they grew up, became men. Learned how to care, be thoughtful. She'd watched it in Ken; seen him learn to love his wife,
Sonia, and his children. All of them cared about one another
and many other things.

She'd first met Ken fifty years earlier. She was out hunting with a group (she'd been a vampire twenty years, and the
group constantly changed but essentially stayed the same),
and they'd targeted a young, juicy man, sitting alone in a
bar. Stools on either side of him empty, but the rest of the
room full.

"You go," one of the gang had insisted to Claudia. "You
haven't pulled one for a while." Claudia hated this, the seduction of a victim. She hated the way they all fed off the same
veins, the same blood. But she knew she had to join in or they
might tear her apart.

She'd sat down by the lonely man. He'd looked around, as
if surprised. "Is it okay if I sit here?" she'd asked.

He'd nodded. Speechless, she thought, at the idea that
someone was talking to him. She felt terrible pity for him,
glad his life was almost over.

She ordered a Coca-Cola; she didn't want the barman asking for ID. Even in the '60s they didn't like letting minors get drunk.

"Seems quiet tonight," she said. She was really bad at this. "You meeting anyone?" She had to find out if anyone would miss him for a while.

"No. No. Just came out because the apartment gets too quiet sometimes. So what's your name? I'm Ken."

"Claudia." She didn't want to know his name. "So you live alone?"

He didn't answer.

"What do you do, then?"

"Work in the coroner's office."

"With dead bodies?"

"Yes, with dead bodies." He said it angrily, as if ready for what would come next. It must have happened many times. People walking away in disgust.

"Cool," she said. "Do you get to touch them?"

Ken took a sip of his beer. Didn't speak.

"Do you touch the dead bodies?" Claudia asked again. It seemed important.

"Yeah, I touch them. I mostly do paperwork, though. Lists and things."

"Oh."

"But I do get to touch them. Have you ever touched one?"

She could see him getting excited, thinking he might have found the right girl.

"I have." Then something he said sparked. "What sort of lists do you mean?"

"I'm not supposed to talk about it. People aren't supposed to know."

She leaned closer. Across the room, the vampires were getting impatient, bored with her. Good. Let them find their own victim. "What sort of lists?"

"We keep a list of the terminally ill. Just so we can be forewarned. So the coroner can plan ahead. But people think it sounds bad, so we don't really talk about it."

She felt something like excitement growing.

"People on the list are going to die, no doubt? They are definitely going to die?"

"There's little doubt, according to their doctors."

She liked him for not saying, "We're all going to die."

"Can we go see some dead bodies?" she said. "I'd like that."

She took his hand and led him past the vampire table on the way, and she shook her head at them, bent over to her boyfriend of the time (what was his name? She could barely remember his face), and whispered, "Leave this guy. Lives with his mother. Too much trouble."

"Where are you going then?" her boyfriend asked. She knew he didn't care.

"I'll be back. Eat without me."

The group of them physically turned their backs on her, but she didn't care. She was used to that.

That was how she got the first list of the terminally ill. It was around the time that Adolf Eichmann was hanged for war crimes, and death was a focus in the minds of many. War was coming again, and yet each death was worth grieving, each life was worth remembering.

The first person from the list she killed was a woman in her forties. Claudia had never seen anyone in so much pain, with so much suffering around her. Daily she begged to die. Daily.

As Claudia took her, she said, "Thank you."

There was no loss of memory as Claudia drank. Her parents remained clear.

Ken brought her updated versions of the list when she asked for them, never questioning what she wanted them for. Just her attention was enough. Their friendship grew even when he realized there was something up with her. He accepted it completely. They saw each other through life's events, though more so for Ken than for her. She helped him to find Sonia, and to keep her. She had never met Sonia. It was best that way. But without Claudia, Ken would never have had the confidence to make a family life. He saw her through dozens of boyfriends, mostly vampires, and disapproved of them all.

At first when she and Ken were seen together, people mistook them for brother and sister. Then father and daughter. These days it was more like grandfather and granddaughter.

He had moved beyond the morgue to other jobs, but she had learned much in her eighty years and could hack into the computers for her lists whenever she needed to.

With the thought of Joel a dull ache and Ken very much on her mind, Claudia walked down to the seawall, enjoying the wind on her face and the smell of the salt. Joel said she didn't really feel anything except for hunger, the sensation only a memory of what was. "You have a very good memory," he said as an insult.

The seawall was high and the drop on the other side long. Teenagers would tightrope the wall, and even though it was as thick as a footpath, they teetered nervously.

Claudia walked slowly in the early-evening light. She liked this time, when there was enough natural light to see by. She liked the night falling, darkness growing. Liked the way it made her focus.

She sat on the wall, her feet dangling over. Pulling out her notebook, she checked her timetable. Joel didn't know about this; none of them did. They already thought she was boring. Imagine what they'd think if they knew she had a list of future food sources, with their usual movements, phone numbers, all of it. She didn't need notes to find her meal tonight, though. She knew where he'd be. Her notes were a simple comfort, this time, giving her a sense of control.

Darkness came down, and it seemed half the streetlights didn't work. Sea spray meant the air was misty.

Up ahead, she saw someone on the wall, arms spread. There was no audience, so not a teenager showing bravado. She walked closer, saw it was Ken, his face wet.

He did not hear her approach. Tears. He was crying, passionately, as if he were emptying himself out.

"Ken?" she said. She'd been tracking him without his knowledge for six weeks now, knew his movements. After all these years of friendship, this was an odd intimacy. Watching this old man when he thought he was alone revealed nothing she didn't know, though. He was a good, kind man who picked his nose.

Every morning he would leave the house and go to sit by the seawall, tempting himself until evening drew him home.

Looking at him, she thought, He's almost the same age as I am. He remembers what I remember. The music, the movies. But he got old and I didn't. Moments like that made her glad to be a vampire. She was glad to be living young in the twenty-first century, to have enjoyed the changes in the world as a young person.

"Ken," she said again.

He turned to her voice. "Do you think I'd die if I jumped or just hurt myself?"

She climbed onto the wall, holding on tight to the edge. Looked over. "You'd hurt yourself. I guess you'd drown if you kept your face down."

He sat slumped beside her. He had an odd smell, something not quite right.

It wasn't a dead smell, not yet.

Ken, still balanced on the seawall, bent forward. "Am I on your list now?"

"Do you want me to call Sonia? The kids?" Claudia said. She knew what his answer would be.

"That wouldn't do any good. She'd only come get me."

Claudia squinted at him. "You don't want her to?"

"No. No, I don't. I don't want her to see me again. It's too hard for her."

His voice was strained, and Claudia realized he was in great pain. "Are you . . . all right?" He tilted his head and looked at her properly. "You've always been kind."

"My mum was kind. I guess it rubbed off."

"Never lose that," Ken said. "I wish I'd been kinder to everyone. Friends and strangers."

Claudia didn't say "It's never too late," because she could hear that it was.

"What's wrong with you?" she said, vampire direct. She

knew this answer as well, but he needed to say it. It was part of the process.

"Sick. Very sick. Pain ahead and long-drawn-out suffering for my kids. No kid should see a parent suffer. You shouldn't have to see it."

"What about the hospital? Can't they help?"

"With the pain. But what's the point? I want to pass quietly, peacefully, in control. Why can't I have that?"

Claudia watched him for a while, then gazed out to sea. "Have you said good-bye to everyone? Tied it all up? Dying with a loose end is no good."

He looked surprised. "Thanks. For listening, not trying to convince me." His voice was tight, so full of pain Claudia could almost feel it. "I've tied it all up. I say good-bye, I love you, every day just in case. I've left special gifts for the grandchildren and messages for the great-grandchildren. I've apologized to people. It's sorted. But I just can't . . ." He stopped, bent over, clutching his ears. "I'm too gutless to do what I need to do."

Claudia felt her teeth tingle. "I can help," she whispered. She snarled gently, then said it louder. "I can help."

He turned, saw her teeth.

"The list? This is what you use the list for?"

She nodded. "I'll be gentle," she said, and she bent forward and drank deeply from the beautiful, pulsing vein in his neck. Drank till she was done, till he was; then she sat him on the ground, propped against the wall, and called an ambulance. She didn't want him robbed, or his body stolen or damaged. His wife and kids needed to know quickly, to see him while he still looked close to life.

She watched from across the street until the ambulance arrived; then she walked home, feeling satisfied in her stomach and in the heart all the others assured her she didn't have.

BEST FRIENDS FOREVER

by Cecil Castellucci

They both smiled at each other, the way that best friends do.

Their smiles revealed different things. Gina's teeth were gray and almost translucent. They looked soft and loose. Amy's teeth gleamed bright and white even in the dimly lit room. And of course there were the canines. Long and pointy. Hollow at the tip, perfectly made for the sucking of blood.

"Would you?" Gina asked.

"Would you?" Amy asked back.

The first time Amy and Gina met was two years prior. At night school.

Amy had gone there to feed. Gina was there to get her equivalency diploma.

Amy thought she could get her feed on easily in the tunnel that linked the parking garage to the campus. Gina was the perfect prey. She was walking, oblivious to everything around her. She was listening to music much too loudly on her iPod, the sound turned up all the way spilling over and echoing thinly in the tunnel. And she was singing along. Off-key.

Even the loud clicking of Amy's go-go boots didn't make Gina notice that there was someone else in the tunnel with her.

Best kind of kill, Amy thought. Easy and there's no taste of fear in the blood. That's the sweetest.

But as Amy began to change her gait from skulking to running to go in for the kill, she gagged.

At first she chalked it up to the terrible human smells in the tunnel: the stale air, the body odor, the cigarettes, and the pee. But as she moved in, it was clear that it was the girl who stank. The rank rot smell was coming from her. Amy realized that something was wrong with the girl.

Gina turned around.

Amy doubled over and gagged again.

That was how they met.

"Hi," Gina said, pulling out one of the earbuds and letting it dangle. The music spilled out a little louder into the tunnel now. Amy recognized the song. It was old, one that Amy used to like.

"It totally smells down here, right?" Gina continued.

Amy nodded. Her teeth were extended, so she kept her

face hidden, placed her hand on the tunnel wall to steady herself as she tried to calm her frenzy and coax her teeth back down.

"I almost threw up last week," Gina overshared.

Amy nodded again. It was difficult to be understood when her mouth changed. Usually she didn't have to talk— she just ate.

"You going to be okay? I've got water in my bag if you need some."

"I just need a minute," Amy said as clearly as she could manage. "I'll be fine."

And she would. This had happened before, a stunted kill. It happened. Not all easy marks turned out to be easy. That was part of the thrill of being a hunter.

Composed, expression set back to normal, Amy stood up and turned to face Gina.

Amy noticed that Gina was very small and very thin and very pale. Even paler than her. Even paler than any vampire she'd ever known. Gina's skin was more ivory than bone. Her veins so blue that they showed uncomfortably bright through her skin. Her hair was reddish once, but it was so lifeless and dead that it lacked any prettiness to it.

Amy knew one thing for sure. This girl was a dead girl. Not actually dead. But dead soon.

"You taking a class here?" Amy asked. It was the most

normal thing she could think to ask of the girl who was supposed to be her dinner.

Gina nodded.

"I'm getting my high school diploma," Gina said.

Gina extended her slender hand. Amy took it. The hand was as cold as hers. It made her shudder. She'd never felt a human with no warmth.

"I'm Gina," the girl said. "And I love your boots. Even though I'm not so into the seventies."

Gina was wearing a royal blue velvet dress with a high neck and many tiny little buttons. It was vintage 1910. It had a lace collar. She wore white patterned thick tights and vintage boots.

"I'm Amy," Amy said.

Now that Gina had given Amy her true name, she would never feed on her. Amy had long ago decided that she couldn't feed on anyone she humanized. She could only feed on someone she thought of as an animal. They were just human meat. If they were human, like she was once before, if they had a name, she couldn't feed. Gina was no longer meat; she was now Gina, a human.

Amy was surprised to discover that they had been walking together, side by side, and that now they had arrived at the campus.

Amy knew that tonight she was not going to eat.

So she went with Gina to class.

That's how come Amy finally finished high school. It was because of her chance meeting with Gina.

Amy as a human died and was reborn as undead in 1976. She didn't want to, it just happened, in an alley in New York City. It was Independence Day and she was watching the tall boats come up the Hudson River. That night she was tripping on acid with her friends down by the Battery. She left the group alone to go find a bathroom. When she saw the vampire coming toward her, she laughed. She thought it was just a part of the trip. A great hallucination. He was cute, and she welcomed him coming close to her. He started kissing her neck. It tickled at first. Until he bit. Bit hard. Amy was still laughing when the blood was being drained out of her. Even though it hurt like hell. Even though there were explosions in the sky. Even though she was tripping like mad.

But before he killed her completely, he stopped sucking her blood. He later told her he was confused by her laughing. And also, he was hallucinating, too. He stopped and looked at her and saw every girl he'd ever loved. Every girl he'd ever killed. His mother. His aunts. His sister. His niece. His wife. And they were all doing the same thing as Amy. They were laughing. At him. And that was why he stopped. He felt remorse. He wanted to ask her why she was laughing. But he couldn't do that if she was dead. He had to turn her to get an answer.

He let her go.

Amy fell to the ground. Rolled onto her side. She could hear the fireworks.

"Is it beautiful?" she asked. She hadn't wanted to miss them, the fireworks. She had been hoping to get back to her group of friends before they started. But now she knew that something was wrong with her. She felt funny. She felt weak. She suspected it wasn't the acid anymore. She suspected that she was in danger.

"I'm going to turn you," he said. "I have to ask you if you want to be turned."

"Yes, turn me, I want a better view of the sky," Amy said. She thought if she was going to die, she wanted to do it while seeing colors light the sky.

He propped her up, bit his wrist, and dripped his blood into her mouth. She was reborn as she watched fireworks burst red, white, and blue.

Gina was a cold baby. Very cold to the touch. Her tiny hands and feet were always icy. She was always in the smallest percentile of normal. Just on the edge of being too short or too underweight.

"She just has poor circulation" was what the doctors said to reassure her worried parents. "Nothing to be done about it. Just exercise. Sunlight. Milk. She'll grow out of it. Probably have a growth spurt in late childhood. Everything will be fine."

Her parents likely realized that something was wrong early on, although they didn't want to admit it.

Gina would come inside from playing with burns that blistered and cracked her skin. At first it was just on occasion, as though it were an accumulation of too much sunshine whose toxin would finally rise and explode angrily out of her. But then, by the time she was in first grade, it was confirmed that she was full-blown allergic to the sun.

Precautions had to be taken. Thick curtains everywhere in the house. The once warm, happy family was plunged into an eternal darkness. It suffocated them. Strained their feelings to the limit. Distanced them from one another.

To help ensure that no light seeped into Gina's skin, clothing had to be UV-proof. Sunblock was worn like skin cream. Hats, dark glasses, long pants, long sleeves, long gloves became everyday parts of Gina's wardrobe.

As a child, she looked eccentric and weird from the get-go. Knowing that she'd never fit in, by the time middle school rolled around, Gina had fully embraced being a freak. She wore vintage clothing, old vintage hats, dresses, and gloves. Although she longed for them, Gina had no real friends.

When they got to class that first night, Amy discovered that the book they were reading was *The Crucible*. Amy had read it right before she'd been turned, and she was surprised to discover that she remembered the book so well. She found herself raising her hand and making comments. Perhaps it was because she hadn't been to school for thirty years and being in such a familiar environment made her kind of miss it. Back then, in 1976, she was more interested in smoking up and giving blow jobs. She was in the loser group. Part of the tough crowd. The ones that cut class, wore halter tops, feathered their hair, listened to heavy rock, and didn't give a rat's ass about school.

Perhaps it was the fact that over thirty years of feeding on humans had matured her, and so after all that time, she was finally ready for school. No matter how many years went by, she still felt sixteen inside. Which was not as fun as she thought it would be. She still had all the angst. She still had all the ups and downs. She still felt interested by things that other teenagers were interested in, even though she also now knew more about the dark side of life. More than she'd ever wanted to know.

The next class was math class, and Amy found herself slightly excited about seeing whether or not she could remember any of her trigonometry. She didn't. Not one single thing. But it was exciting to learn it all over again.

After class, she made a decision. She would officially enroll in night school. She went to the front office, used a fake name and a fake social security number. She was given a schedule and a list of textbooks she'd need.

Amy was giddy.

She didn't tell the clan about it. Every vampire in their group had their secrets. It was understood that you did what you needed to do to make the eternal life bearable.

For some it was going to prostitutes.

For some it was eating only animals.

For some it was keeping a night job.

For Amy it was finishing high school.

There was something that Gina liked immediately about Amy. It could have been her quietness. It could have been the way she wore vintage 1970s clothes. It could have been that Amy always had such an interesting perspective and point of view on things when she talked in class. Like she knew things about the world, and people. Like she'd seen things. Like she was *sophisticated*.

Amy liked Gina, too. Amy liked hanging out with Gina at the breaks between classes. Amy could tell that even though Gina was eccentric and didn't have the best social skills, she had a kindness about her. Amy was certain that if she had met Gina when she was alive, she would never have talked to her; she would only have made fun of her. But at night school, with all the others who had had something happen to them to derail them from a regular teenage life, everyone had at last found the one place where they could all be the cool girl.

Gina was a benevolent cool, welcoming everyone, including all.

It was a sharp contrast from the cool girls Amy remembered from her day. She remembered that those girls were mean. Their hair flipped perfectly, their eye shadow always the perfect shade of blue, their boyfriends always the coolest boy in school. Amy suspected that if she looked long and hard at herself, she would discover that she had been one of those mean girls. She didn't want to be that kind of girl anymore.

Here at night school, she remained quiet. Just happy to be included in the chitchat. Cheerfully chiming in when called upon. And sharing her homework with anyone who needed help.

It wasn't too long before Gina asked Amy if she wanted to hang out. They went to the movies. They had sleepovers. They went to shows. Gina and Amy were fast becoming best friends.

They told each other everything.

Well, almost everything.

Gina told her that she was allergic to the sun. But she didn't know how to explain that she was dying.

Amy told her that she was a little bit older than she looked. But didn't know how to explain that she was a vampire.

* * *

Amy had moved into the twenty-first century. Cell phone, laptop, social network profiles.

Her relationship to killing altered because now she had a friend and socialized with humans. The other vampires in her clan had told her that would happen if she mixed. It happened to all of them after a while. It was inevitable. She hadn't believed them. But in the end she had to admit that it was true.

She didn't turn to only eating animals, or working in a hospital or blood bank to get her fix, like the others. She didn't stop eating humans; they tasted too good to her. But now she ate less often, and only when people were already bleeding out, from a gunshot wound or a car accident or a stabbing or a suicide. She rationalized that those people were already dead, with no hope for life, the blood, just flowing out of them, going to waste. Feeding on them eased her conscience.

There was an older vampire in her clan who taught her how to find them, those on the brink. He taught her how to smell them from miles away. Showed her the special way to run so that it was almost flying on the wind. He had always been like that, ever since he'd turned. He called it a mercy to the dying. He said he felt like an angel.

He informed her that there was a property in vampire's mucus that acted like a sedative. Amy had never known how to use it. Her victims had always been horrified and in pain.

But he taught her how to hawk up a loogie in such a way that she could swish it around in her mouth with her saliva and spit it into the victim's mouth so that they felt a pleasant warmth as they were being drained.

This kindness that she offered made her feel better about having to kill. It made her able to look Gina and the other girls they hung out with at night school in the eyes with no guilt.

It was Gina's birthday. Gina knew that her time was coming to an end. And one thing that she had always wanted to do was go to the beach. But of course she never would be able to, because of the sun.

"Why don't you go to Abe's Tropical Paradise Tanning Spa?" one of the girls said during one of their five-minute breaks.

"You'll come, too, Amy," Gina said. "We're both so pale, we could probably use two treatments of spray-on tan."

Everyone laughed. Including Amy. But it made her miss the sun.

Abe's promised a total paradise experience in the very comfort of your own hometown. *No travel needed! Bring a beach towel! Swim in our marine-animal-free lagoon! Real imported Jamaican sand! Hawaiian-style tiki bar! Private parties available! Spray tan included!*

"It might be a fun idea," Gina said.

Everyone promised they would come. Especially Amy.

She wouldn't miss it for the world.

Gina's parents knew that there wasn't likely to be much longer, so when Gina asked for such an extravagant sixteenth birthday party, they gladly paid the $1,500 for Gina and her friends to have a private tropical experience.

All the girls packed beach bags and flip-flops and went downtown at night.

The lagoon area with tiki bar that served virgin margaritas had sand everywhere and a soundtrack of water lapping and bird calls. There were heat lamps that had no harmful UV lights in them. They just flooded the room with warmth. The only way you could tan up at Abe's was to get spray-on tan. He still had some tanning beds, but they were in a storage room and he didn't have a license for that anymore. People didn't want the skin cancer. They just wanted the tropical experience.

Amy was the first to arrive. Abe let her wander around by herself, and she opened up doors and closets as she explored.

In one room, she found the old tanning beds. They looked like futuristic coffins.

Amy could not resist. She had never slept in a coffin. She had vampire friends who swore that it was the best sleep you could ever get. You were so sealed in, with such darkness, that they were sad that it wasn't in fashion, or that having a coffin delivered to your home would call too much attention. It wasn't like the old days, when death was a part of day-to-day life and coffins were common.

Amy wanted to try it out. She opened one of the beds. Lay down. And pulled the cover over herself. It was dark. She'd checked that the machine was unplugged, to make sure that it wouldn't be accidentally turned on. Deprived of her sight, she found her hearing heightened. She could hear the heartbeat of everyone as they entered the spa. Two people. Now five. Now eleven. She could smell their sweat. She could pinpoint the person with the sweetest blood. She drooled for a second at the thought of the taste of the girl. But she would have to feed later, on a stranger. Rules were rules.

She relaxed. She breathed easy for the first time in years. She drifted off, content.

She woke when she could hear the girls moving into the room. She didn't want them to think she was weird, so she lay there, waiting for them to leave the room so that she could arrive like a normal girl, from the front door, and not emerge from the tanning bed.

"We can put all the bags and stuff in here, so they're out of the way. We don't want to see winter coats and boots in our tropical paradise," Gina said.

And that was when it happened.

The tightness in her chest. The unbearable feeling of being strapped down.

"Oh, Mom! You bought me roses!" Gina said.

"Yes, but they won't go with the tropics. Just leave them

in the bag and we'll put them in a vase at home."

The bouquet of red roses with thorns that her mother had picked up on impulse just to give to her girl on her birthday lay inside the bag. Gina innocently put the shopping bag on top of the tanning bed, trapping Amy inside.

Amy had never believed that the warning the other vampires had given her about roses was true. It seemed more like a fairy tale. Roses were too pretty a thing to net a vampire.

But here she was, stuck. Trapped in the bed.

Amy listened from her jail as Gina and the other girls pretended to swim and bask in the fake sunlight. They splashed and wiggled around in their bikinis.

The whole time that the party raged on, Amy lay ensnared in the coffinlike bed in the next room. Unable to scream. Unable to move. Unable to call for help. Hearing all the fun that she was missing.

It was death. But she was conscious.

For herself, Gina tried to have as much fun as she could. But truthfully, she was mad at Amy for not showing up to her birthday party. She swore that she would never talk to her again.

It wasn't until hours after the room had been cleaned up and the bag holding the bouquet of roses had been removed that Amy had the strength to lift off the cover and free herself from her temporary hell.

It had never really struck her that she was a vampire

before. That although she was immortal and undead, she could be vulnerable. That she really was a monstrous thing who fed on humans, who needed to be trapped. That she was an actual danger to the world. Maybe it was a kind of awakening, because that was when she knew for sure that really being dead and not just undead would be a better end than a living hell.

Amy skipped school for a week after the tanning bed incident. She was afraid that mixing with humans was dangerous to her survival. The hours in the tanning bed had traumatized her. But one night she saw Gina sitting inside a coffee shop. Gina was eating some soup.

Amy missed Gina. She hadn't called Gina to apologize, and Gina hadn't called Amy to find out where she had been. Not that she could have told her the truth. But Amy was hurt. She wasn't used to feeling hurt anymore.

Amy knocked on the window to wave Gina out to her. Instead Gina looked up and waved her in. Amy entered the coffee shop for the first time ever; after all, she'd been invited. It was a hip place, with Christmas lights strung up everywhere and overstuffed chairs and couches and impossibly hip-looking kids with colored hair, tattoos, and piercings, who sipped espressos and chai green teas with attitude.

Amy slid into a comfy chair across from Gina.

Gina didn't speak. She fiddled with her oversized soup spoon. She looked very tiny in her black dress, dwarfed by the large mustard colored cushions of the chair.

"I really wanted to be there," Amy said.

"I thought we were friends," Gina said.

Amy froze. She remembered her old life. The one with the parties and the days spent with friends at Rye Playland and the Coney Island boardwalk. She remembered the slumber parties and the doing of each other's hair and makeup. The endless flipping through fashion magazines and listening to LP records. The movie outings and the cheering on of boys at pickup basketball games in the park. She remembered her friend Stephanie, and how they couldn't wait to see each other every day, shared every intimate personal detail, wrote to each other every day over summer vacations apart, and held hands at each other's sweet sixteens.

Amy realized that she wanted to be that kind of friend with Gina. A *human* friend.

"We are friends," Amy said. *"Best friends."*

"Best friends?" Gina said. "A *best* friend would come to a friend's birthday party."

"I really tried," Amy said. How could she explain that she was there? Listening to the fun. Scared out of her mind. Trapped in a tanning bed by a bouquet of roses.

Instead she said nothing. She just stared at Gina.

"I don't have a lot of time to waste on people who are lame," Gina said.

"I know," Amy said.

That was the moment. They both looked at each other, a look that went right down to the very core. There was a moment when maybe they weren't going to share their darkest secrets. But then they both did.

"I'm dying," Gina said.

"I'm dead," Amy said.

It was a relief to them both, having the worst parts of them out in the open.

After that, they never lied to each other. They never held anything back.

"An injection every morning and an injection every evening. One helps me release the toxins, one makes my blood stronger."

"Young people taste best, children, babies. I try to stick to people who've lived a little. On occasion, though, I must admit, I have not been able to resist the tenderness of youth."

"I've kissed a boy, but I've never touched it."

"At school they used to call me the blow-job queen. I was a real slut."

"I feel worse for my parents that I'm dying than I do for me."

"My parents think that I ran away. They grew old thinking that I hated them that much."

"You know what I wish?" Gina said.

"What?"

"No, forget it. It's silly."

"I bet it's not silly. What is it?" Amy asked.

"To live."

"Isn't it funny that my deepest wish is to die?"

But they both didn't laugh.

It wasn't that funny.

Halfway through their last year at night school, it became obvious that Gina was going quickly. She became even thinner than she already was. Her skin translucent. And no amount of sweaters kept her warm anymore. She missed classes, so many the teacher informed Amy that Gina would have to take the semester over.

Amy never told Gina that. She just kept bringing Gina her assignments on the nights she missed school as though it was all going to be all right. As though Gina could catch up with a little bit of effort and extra care. Amy would patiently teach Gina everything that they had learned in class. She tutored her in all that she knew.

Gina would try to pay attention to the lessons for a while, and then fade from the effort after fifteen minutes.

Sometimes Gina would awaken and look at Amy like she wanted to ask her a question but didn't know how to properly phrase it. Gina would move her lips, practicing saying the words aloud, but whatever she was thinking, she would stop herself, crinkle her nose, then shake her head and laugh as though she thought she was about to say something stupid.

Amy could not bear to see her friend suffer.

"I could give you a new kind of life, if you wanted," Amy said slowly.

"Where I could live forever?"

"Yes," Amy said. "And you wouldn't know pain anymore. You'd be made whole, only in a different way."

"You'd give me my deepest wish?"

"Of course," Amy said. "You're my friend. But you have to ask me to turn you. I can't do it otherwise."

"Does it hurt when you turn?"

Amy tried to remember turning. She remembered a stiffening. Her muscles cracking. Her body, her organs losing control. They had all failed and then restarted. A distinct feeling that her skin had been ripped off and burned and then numbness. And after the agony, it felt like she was floating on the warmest cloud of beauty, which slowly turned to ice.

"A little bit," Amy lied. "But then you feel like you are supposed to."

"We could be vampires together," Gina said.

"Best friends forever," Amy said.

Amy placed her hands on her lap and looked down. If she had tears left in her, she might start to cry. If it was the only way that Gina could have a life free from the half life she had now, and if it was what she wanted, Amy would help her friend. Her only friend.

"Would you do it if I asked you?" Gina asked.

"In a heartbeat," Amy said. Although she didn't have one of those.

Gina smiled. Relieved that she didn't have to die if she didn't want to.

"You know, I would kill you if you asked me, too," Gina said.

"You would?"

"Yes."

"It's not easy. You'd have to cut off my head or burn me."

"I know," Gina said. "I looked it up on the internet."

They didn't mention the conversation again. Gina got sicker. Amy got busier with final exams. They saw each other less and less. Each one of them wrapped up in the difficulty of day-to-day survival.

Gina preferred to wear the long silk nightgown that had belonged to her great-grandmother, even though it was so thin that it offered no heat. That was why the hospital room was so hot. She wore a shawl, but it wasn't enough.

Amy brought Gina the fleece robe from the closet. But Gina would have none of that.

"Ugh," she said, pushing it back into Amy's hands. "I wouldn't be caught dead in that."

They watched a movie on the television. Laughed at the funny parts. Caught up on the gossip of friends. The nurse came in to turn down the blankets and adjust the IV. She took one look at Gina and told Amy that she could stay the night if she wanted.

The nurse padded out of the room.

Gina looked at Amy. Her eyes were glassy.

"Do you remember what we talked about?" Gina asked.

"Remind me," Amy said, even though she hadn't forgotten. She had to make sure that Gina was serious.

"About turning me," Gina said.

Amy nodded.

"I was thinking. You could turn me and then, once it's done, I could kill you."

Amy had never thought of that. She had assumed that if Gina turned, that would be that. She would never get her wish and she would be condemned to roam the streets of New York City for a hundred lifetimes. Only now she would have a true friend.

They looked at each other. Ready.

"Would you?"

"Would you?"

Amy let her face change. She bared her teeth.

Gina slipped her hand under her pillow and pulled out a can of hair spray and a Zippo. Amy could see the glint of a very large kitchen knife that lay there, available at a moment's notice.

They eyed each other, waiting for what seemed an eternity for the other one to say the words, to give permission, to make the move.

One of them was going to live and one of them was going to die. But not exactly in that order.

And then, as if by magic, or by complete mutual understanding and love for each other, the absolute knowledge that they would never condemn their truest friend to their lot in life, they both moved at the same time as they put their weapons away.

Amy settled back into her chair and read a magazine and lived, as undead a life as it was.

Gina settled back into her pillows, closed her eyes, and died peacefully, in her sleep.

SIT THE DEAD

by Jeffrey Ford

Luke was in his room at the computer, looking at used cars. His cell phone rang. He answered with it on speaker.

"Darene," he said.

"Gracie died," she said.

He pictured the deceased, hairdo like a helmet, overweight in flowered stretch slacks. Her earrings were disco balls; her face, a half inch of powder and pale green lipstick. He'd met her at a barbecue in Darene's backyard. "You're in for it, kid. God bless ya," she'd said to Luke, and kissed his cheek green.

"That sucks," he said.

"Is that all you have to say?" asked Darene.

"I only met her once," he said. "I'm sorry you feel bad, though."

"My father's inviting you to sit the dead."

"Sit the dead . . . ," said Luke.

"It's a family ritual."

"I don't have to touch her, do I?"

"Don't be a tool," she said. "You just have to go and sit with the body in the church for a few hours."

"Like a wake," he said.

"Yeah, but nobody else but you and one other person will be there."

"You just sit there?" he asked.

"Two members from our family have to sit with Gracie till they take her to her grave. It's a family tradition going all the way back."

"Sounds weak."

"Your shift starts at midnight."

"Me and you?"

"No, you and Uncle Sfortunado."

Luke closed his eyes and shook his head.

"This means my family is officially accepting you," said Darona. "My father says it's a test of your manhood."

Luke laughed.

"I can see you're not mature enough," she said.

Two nights earlier they were at the lake on the picnic bench. She sat on his lap facing him, her legs on either side of his. There was a cool autumn breeze, but she glowed with warmth as they kissed.

"Okay, sign me up," he said, "but my parents are gone for the weekend with the car. I'm stranded."

"I'll pick you up at eleven thirty," she said.

He turned off the computer and went to take a shower.

Luke always got stuck sitting next to Uncle Sfortunado at the Cabadula family parties. After a while the reason for it became clear to him—no one in the family wanted to. The ancient patriarch often spoke in some foreign tongue, and when he did talk English, he mumbled cryptic sayings involving animals—"The moon in the lake is for the fish" or "A spider in the mouth will empty your pockets." When Luke stared back in puzzlement, the old man would spit out the word *"gaduche,"* which Luke was sure meant "stupid" or worse. Although Darene's family went to church on the weekends, Luke could never get a straight answer as to what religion they were. Likewise, he'd asked Sfortunado what country the Cabadula were originally from. He guessed Greece, Italy, Romania, Turkey, Russia.

The old man squinted and shook his head to each.

"Are you Gypsies?" asked Luke.

"I wish," said Sfortunado.

"I give up. Where then?"

"Another country."

"Which one?"

"The old country, up in the hills," he yelled, and shook his head in annoyance.

As the shower water fell and the steam rose, Luke closed his eyes. I'm gonna have to get blazed for this, he thought.

Darene pulled up in her old Jeep Cherokee at exactly eleven thirty. Luke had never known her to be on time. He got in. She was dressed all in black—T-shirt, jacket, jeans; and he knew, even though he couldn't see her feet, that she'd be wearing black socks and sneakers. She gave him a quick kiss before he could slide across the seat and put his arms around her. Just as he reached, she turned, started the car, and pulled away from the curb.

"Put your seatbelt on," she said.

"Where are we going?" he asked, and lightly touched a ringlet of her hair.

"The church over on Gebble Street."

"That's a crappy area."

"That's our church," she said, and made a stern face.

"How about we make a detour to the lake and you can test my manhood?" he said, and laughed.

"Are you high?" she asked.

"No," he said. "I'm tired. I was asleep when you called."

She sighed, and from that point on it was silence until they pulled into the church parking lot.

"I can't go in with you," she said. She opened her door. He also got out and met her at the front of the car. She put her arms around his waist, and he leaned back against the hood.

"I know this is beat," she said, "but it means a lot to me."

She looked up and he smiled. She put the side of her face against his chest.

"You've got nothing to worry about," he said. "I'll sit the dead like my father sits the bowl."

"Seriously," she said.

"I'm all about it."

The next thing he knew, she was closing the front door of the church behind him. He stepped into a dark alcove, and a sudden smell of incense and old wood made his spine twitch. Luke looked through the open doors and down the aisle before him, past the rows of darkened pews, to the altar—white marble, crowded with statues, and holding the candlelit coffin of Gracie. He took a deep breath and moved toward the light.

Between the first pew and the altar, there was an empty folding chair set up next to Uncle Sfortunado's.

"Hello," Luke said too loud, sending echoes everywhere.

The old man turned and stared through thick glasses. He wore a gray cardigan dotted with cigarette burns. His beard was a week old and white as snow; his hair, crazy. *"Gaduche,"* he said, raised a trembling hand, and farted.

"Good to see you again," said Luke.

"This is who I get to sit the dead?" said Sfortunado, shouting into the dark. He grimaced. "The cat makes the owl bleed. . . ."

"Darene's father told me to come."

"Yeah, yeah." The old man waved a trembling hand in front of his face.

"My condolences about Gracie," said Luke.

Sfortunado laughed and pointed at the altar. "Go tell her you're sorry," he said.

Luke got up and slowly ascended the three steps to the coffin. Gracie came into view, a deflated balloon made of dough. She wore a white dress, a giant version of a little girl's party rig, pale green lipstick, and her blond hair helmet was slightly askew. A hand grabbed the side of the coffin. Luke started and then saw it belonged to Uncle Sfortunado, who stood beside him.

"Looks like shit," said the old man. "What do you think?"

Luke stalled by rubbing the back of his neck. Finally he said, "Well . . . she's dead."

Sfortunado shrugged and nodded. "This is true."

"What happened to her?"

"Something bad."

Luke went back to his chair. Sfortunado mumbled a few words to Gracie and then announced, "She smells like flowers." He threw his head back and laughed loud. The echoes rained down, and Luke considered splitting. The old man hobbled back to his chair and less than five minutes later was asleep.

Luke studied the statuary on the altar, elongated marble figures in the throes of agony gathered in a semicircle, at the center of which hung a large golden sun made of gleaming metal. He took out his cell phone and texted Darene. "Wt relign r u?" Uncle Sfortunado was swaying slightly side to side, snoring, his arms folded across his sunken chest. Darene's reply came back. "No txting. C u @ dawn."

Time stood still in the candlelight, and Luke listened to the church quietly creak. The rapid scuttling of some tiny creature echoed like a whisper from the shadows. Somewhere something was dripping. It didn't take long before the creepiness gave way to boredom. They should have a TV set up here, he thought. Eventually his mind turned to Darene.

They'd been together since the previous autumn, junior year. Whatever her culture was, it demanded an old-fashioned formality between kids their age. They went to all the parties together, movies, some concerts, but she insisted he meet her family and attend the holiday and birthday gatherings at her house.

Both his male and female friends told him he was pussy whipped, but he didn't care. Darene's hair, ringlets of black springs that seemed alive, her smooth dark complexion, her green eyes and unabashed laugh, canceled all of their scorn. She definitely knew her mind, and yet he wasn't particularly good at school or good-looking by anyone's standards. The whole thing was a mystery he enjoyed pondering.

Luke's memory returned to that night at the picnic table by the lake for quite a while, and then he checked his phone for the time, sure that at least a couple of hours had passed. He discovered that not even a half hour had gone by since Sfortunado had fallen asleep. Taking a cue from the old man, he put his phone in his pocket, folded his arms across his chest, and closed his eyes. As he began to doze, a putrid stench, the first stirrings of which he attributed to Uncle Sfortunado, slowly overcame the aroma of old incense and pervaded the place. Gracie's not embalmed was his last thought before sleep, and then he dreamed of going naked, late, to the SATs.

Gracie's not embalmed was the first thought he had upon waking suddenly at the touch of someone's hand upon his shoulder. The church was freezing, and that death stench was now thick as perfume. He looked over and caught a burst of adrenaline upon seeing a revolver in the old man's wobbling hand. Luke made a move to bolt, but Sfortunado's eyes got big behind his glasses, and he brought his finger to his lips. He waved with the gun toward the altar. "The squirrel claws my heart," he whispered.

Luke tried to get away, but the old man grabbed his wrist. "*Fashtulina*," he said, and touched the gun to his chest. He released his grip on Luke's wrist and turned to face the altar.

"Okay," said Luke, reluctantly sitting back in his chair.

"She's got it in her blood," whispered Sfortunado.

"What's in whose blood?" asked Luke.

"Gracie," said the old man. "Every fifty years or so, one of us Cabadula is born with the *gritchino* in the blood. You can't tell till they die. But this one"—he pointed at the coffin—"I always had a feeling."

"*Gritchino*," said Luke.

At the sound of the word, Sfortunado touched his yellowed left thumbnail to each lens of his glasses and then kissed his middle finger. "The breeze. Do you feel it?" said Sfortunado. Luke could feel a cold wind in his face. The candle flames danced wildly. "It's freezing," he said, teeth chattering, and he noticed his breath was now steam.

"The wind of eternity," said the old man. He pointed with the gun again, toward the altar. Luke looked up to see the lid of the coffin slowly closing. "What the hell," he said. He wanted to run but was paralyzed with fear. The wind increased, whipping around the church and screeching above in the darkened dome. Luke was shivering. Uncle Sfortunado was shivering, but when the coffin lifted slowly off its platform, the old man stood and brought the gun up in front of him.

The coffin, as if lifted with invisible strings, rose six feet off its platform. Then it began to move through the air like a slow, wooden torpedo. As it swept by above and out over the pews, Uncle Sfortunado aimed and fired at it. He pulled the trigger three times, and the echoes from the shots and splintering wood careened everywhere. As Gracie passed into the dark toward the front of the church, he said, "*Fasheel*," and tapped his forehead with the barrel of the gun.

"Let's get out of here," said Luke, trembling. He stood

and saw the coffin cruising back out of the shadows, returning toward the altar. He ducked. Sfortunado again took aim and fired two more shots in rapid succession as she passed overhead. Splinters fell into Luke's hair, and he noticed the coffin beginning to wobble in its flight. It gained speed and then took a nosedive at the altar, crashing into the metal sun and smashing the head off one of the sculptures.

As Uncle Sfortunado moved toward the altar steps, the lid of the coffin swung open on its hinges and what was left of Gracie levitated slowly into a standing position. Her blond wig was crooked, and her face drooped in lumpy folds. She was pale as milk; even her long tongue was white, and her eyes had lost their pupils. Her lopsided green smile revealed sharp canines.

"She's a fuckin' vampire," said Luke.

"Fly like the wren," said Sfortunado over his shoulder, and Luke didn't need a translation. He bolted down the aisle toward the front door of the church. He heard the gun go off again, and he stopped and turned to see the old man hobbling after him, waving him to move. On the altar, Gracie was screaming like a wounded cat.

Luke made the door, burst out into the night, and then held it for Sfortunado, who was little more than halfway, limping and scuttling with all he had. Behind him, Gracie was floating up off the altar.

"Come on!" yelled Luke, and just as the old man reached

him, he saw Gracie swoop through the air toward them. He grabbed Uncle Sfortunado by the arm, pulled him outside, and slammed the door. There was a thud against it from inside.

"She's coming."

The old man leaned back against the door and bent over to catch his breath. In between heaves, he held up a trembling index finger and said, "She's trapped in the church . . . till dawn." Then he laughed and again couldn't catch his breath. "I knew she was *gritchino*," he said. "I told them all, and they said, 'Oh, Sfortunado, he's losing his marbles.'"

"She can't get out?" said Luke.

"I already told you. Call Darene, tell her *gritchino*. Tell her to bring guns."

Luke took out his phone and did as he was told. He still wanted to run and keep on running till he was back at his house, in his room, earphones on, sitting at his computer. Darene finally answered.

"What are you doing to me here?" said Luke.

"Quit complaining," she said. "You're already more than half through the night."

"*Gritchino*," he said. "Gracie's gone wild."

Darene didn't answer, but he heard her running from her room. At a distance he heard her scream, "Dad, Gracie's *gritchino*."

Two minutes passed, and while Luke waited for Darene to pick up again, Uncle Sfortunado limped over to a stone bench to the right of the church doors and sat down with a sigh.

"Stay there," Darene finally said into the phone. "We're coming."

"Your uncle says to bring guns. Darene, what the hell?"

She hung up. Luke walked over to the bench and sat next to the old man. "This is all wrong," he said.

Sfortunado smiled. "Only wrong if we don't kill her."

"Forget we," said Luke. "I'm done."

The old man waved a hand as if to dismiss him. "Cowards get no treasure," he said.

"What treasure?"

"You kill the *gritchino,* cut off the left leg, and there's a diamond, right here," he said, leaning forward and pointing to the back of his leg. "Inside the calf muscle, a gift from the great spirit for killing the creature."

"Get out of here," said Luke.

"This big," said Sfortunado, and made a fist. "You help kill it, you get a share."

"How hard is it to kill the *gritchino?*" asked Luke.

"Ehh." The old man rocked back and forth. "Sometimes not so hard. First you shoot it, shoot it, shoot it, and then you gotta nail the head."

"What do you nail it with?"

"Brass. This long," he said, and stretched his thumb and forefinger apart six inches. "Right here." He touched his finger to the middle of his forehead. "With a hammer." He pantomimed a mighty hammer blow. "*Pfft*, finished."

"What if she gets me before I get her?"

"*Gritchino* likes the organ meat—liver, kidney, heart, you know. Likes the blood."

"What makes her do that?"

"It's in the blood. People say it's a demon, evil spirit, goblin, but this is the twenty-first century. It's a hereditary germ. It makes *gritchino* every fifty years or so."

"If it's a hereditary germ, how does the diamond get in her leg?" said Luke.

Uncle Sfortunado shrugged. "You ask too many questions. Just shut up and kill the *gritchino*."

"Was that a twenty-first-century flying coffin?" asked Luke.

"*Gaduche*," said the old man, and shook his head.

Five minutes later, Mr. Cabadula's black Mercedes pulled into the parking lot. As soon as it stopped, Darene got out of the passenger side and came running toward the bench. Luke stood up to meet her, but she passed him and went to Uncle Sfortunado. "Are you okay?" she asked, leaning down and putting her arms around him.

"Yeah, yeah, I had *gaduche* to protect me," he said, staring at Luke over her shoulder.

Mr. Cabadula walked up and began speaking in their language to Sfortunado. Darene went to Luke, took him by the arm, and moved him away from the men to the other side of the church doors.

"I'm sorry," she whispered.

"Are you kidding? She's some kind of vampire," he said.

"Once in fifty years out of all the Cabadula. Why Gracie?"

"When do we call the cops and leave?" asked Luke.

"We have to kill it," said Darene. "It's our family duty."

"That's crazy."

"You can go home if you want," said Darene. "I'll call you a cab."

"Listen, I've seen Gracie and she's nasty. Come back with me."

"I can't," she said.

"So are we ready?" asked Mr. Cabadula, now standing behind his daughter. He had a wave of graying hair and a mustache. His arms were folded across his chest.

"Luke's going home," she said to him.

"Going home," said her father in a flat voice.

"No . . . I'll help," said Luke.

"Ever shoot a gun?" said Mr. Cabadula.

"Sure," he said, though he'd never even touched one.

"Come to my car," said Darene's father.

As they followed him, she put her arm around Luke and kissed his ear.

"If I get killed, my parents are gonna be pissed," he said to her.

Sfortunado was already at the trunk of the Mercedes. Mr. Cabadula opened it and stepped aside. "Take one," he said.

Luke looked in and saw a row of six pistols lying on a beige woolen blanket. The guns didn't look like anything he'd seen in the movies. They were old, with rounded wooden stocks and silver filigree work on the barrels.

"Three shots," said Darene's father as Luke reached in and took one in his hand.

"What gun has only three shots?" asked Luke, backing out of the car and lifting the piece to inspect it.

"Three shots," Mr. Cabadula repeated. "The bullets are made with shards of witch bone."

Luke held the gun straight down at his side, afraid it might go off from either age or magic. Darene's father then handed both her and Luke flashlights.

Sfortunado had left the revolver he'd used in the church and took two pistols, as did his nephew. Darene slid hers into the waist of her jeans.

They stood by the church door, and Mr. Cabadula was giving instructions. All Luke heard was the first point, that Gracie could be lurking right inside the front door, and after that he was too scared to concentrate. Darene looked over at him and touched his shoulder. "Do you know what you're doing?" she asked. He nodded, and then Uncle Sfortunado, one gun in the pocket of his baggy pants, wrapped his fingers around the handle of the church door. Mr. Cabadula crouched slightly and took aim with his pistols. Darene drew the gun from her waist and nudged Luke back a few steps. "Now," said her father, and the door swung open.

"Flashlights," yelled Mr. Cabadula. Luke and Darene aimed their beams into the darkened foyer. "All right," he said. "Let's go in." The next thing Luke knew, he was standing in the dark with the old man, and Darene and her father were halfway down the center aisle to the altar. The place stank of death, and the temperature hadn't risen a degree.

"*Gaduche,*" said Sfortunado, "sometime before dawn."

Luke came to his senses and started toward the altar, the flashlight trained ahead. He thought of Gracie floating up by the ceiling or crouched in one of the pews, licking her green lips. He realized his index finger was near to squeezing the trigger of his pistol and tried to relax. The candles on the altar had gone out. The mysterious wind had died.

Sfortunado whispered, "Remember the diamond."

The skin on the back of Luke's neck tingled. He spun around and shone the flashlight behind them and then into the pews, up at the ceiling, at Sfortunado, who looked, himself, like he'd just crawled out of a coffin.

The old man laughed and pointed forward with his guns. On their way toward the front row of pews, Luke kept an eye on Darene's flashlight beam. She and her father had moved off to the left of the altar. Sfortunado said, "Go right," when they reached the front row of pews. Luke passed the beam of his flashlight over the altar, the fallen coffin, and the rubble around it. They moved on into a more profound darkness at the side of the church, where thick wooden beams arched toward the dome like the rib cage of a monster.

At the opposite end of the church, Mr. Cabadula yelled, "There." Luke turned to see Darene's beam aimed upward. Something flitted through it. There was a sudden flash of orange light and then a bang. Luke called, "Darene," and started back along the front row of pews.

When he reached the center aisle before the altar, he heard Sfortunado yell, "Down." Luke fell to the floor and felt the sweeping breeze of Gracie pass overhead. Two shots went off, and he winced and covered his ears. The next thing he knew, Darene was lifting him to his feet. He turned and saw Mr. Cabadula on the altar, setting the candles back up and lighting them. A glow grew around them, and even that meager light was a relief.

Out of the shadows shuffled Sfortunado, grumbling. They gathered on the altar with their backs to the wall, their pistols out. Luke said to Sfortunado, "How did you see her? I had the flashlight."

"I knew in my head that you were screwing up."

"You're psychic?"

"Did you duck?" asked the old man.

"I have to go into the back of the church and find the switch for the lights," said Mr. Cabadula. "It's stupid to challenge her in the dark. If I get the lights on, we'll finish this up in a half hour."

No one said a word. They listened to hear Gracie move, out beyond the candlelight. Luke was standing in front of the crashed coffin, trembling. Darene stood close to him.

"This place stinks," she said.

"The wind of eternity," said Sfortunado.

Mr. Cabadula put one of his pistols in his belt, removed the flashlight from Luke's hand, and descended the altar steps. "I'll be back in a minute," he said over his shoulder. When he passed into the dark, they followed him by the white beam searching above and below. Then he disappeared behind the altar.

Luke could hear Gracie purring, moving among the distant pews near the front door. Then, in the next minute, she seemed to be just out of sight beyond the glow of the candles.

"Stand back," said Sfortunado as he took a step forward. "I'll call her in."

"What do you want to do that for?" asked Luke.

"Darene, explain," said the old man in a whisper over his shoulder.

"Uncle Sfortunado is going to use the *lamentalata* to draw Gracie to us, so we can shoot her," said Darene. "Stand on that side of him, two feet behind, and have your gun ready. I'll cover this side."

Luke took his position and lifted his pistol, his hand trembling.

Sfortunado half turned to look at him. "When you pull the trigger, bullets come out," he said, and laughed. A moment later, the old man called out to Gracie in a high-pitched, wavering voice. The sound of it startled Luke, and he turned to look at Darene, who smiled.

Sfortunado paused after calling her name five times, and then he made what sounded like bird calls—whistling, gibbering, cawing, singing in a higher tone than before. Even though the threat of Gracie lunging out of the dark had him sweating, Luke couldn't keep a straight face. His nervous laughter lasted only a second before he saw a white form slowly passing into the grainy light halfway up the center aisle. The pale blob wavered with the candle flame and then became clearer—Gracie on all fours, crawling obediently toward the altar.

Spit was flying from Sfortunado's lips as he trilled and whooped. He swung his arms for more power and lifted up on his toes. His head darted back and forth, like a bird's. Luke thought the old man was going to keel over from his efforts. Gracie inched ever closer, purring in a way that made the sound echo everywhere.

When she reached the foot of the altar, she grunted and

slowly rose to her feet. Her wig had come off; she was completely bald. Her white tongue lolled down over her chin and her eyes were closed. She began snoring. Sfortunado quit his bird impersonations, stumbled backward, and fell onto the altar.

"Now," said Darene, and stepped forward with her gun out. Luke froze for a heartbeat, and in that brief space, the lights of the church went on. He blinked and brought his free hand up to block out the sudden glare. From between his fingers, he saw Gracie's eyelids slide open. Then he saw the fangs. She pounced like a flying leopard, arcing upward through the air. A shot rang out and then another, and the next thing Luke knew, Gracie had landed at Sfortunado's feet and sunk her fangs into his left calf muscle. Blood sprayed over the altar, and the old man screamed in agony.

Sfortunado's cry brought Luke to his senses. He aimed at Gracie's back and pulled the trigger. The pistol kicked in his hand and the slug went wide and dug into the altar floor. Darene took aim, fired, and hit Gracie in the side, tumbling her off Sfortunado and right at Luke's feet. He jumped back a step and the gun went off, splintering the boards. At the sound of the shot, Gracie sprang up and away from him. She bounded once, and in an instant had her hands wrapped around Darene's throat. Darene's arms were between Gracie's, and she struggled to hold back that pale, gaping mouth.

Luke sprang into action but thought, What am I doing? as

he managed to sling an arm, hand holding the stock of the pistol, around Gracie's neck. With his free hand, he grabbed the end of the barrel of the gun and pulled back, forcing it against her windpipe. Rearing away from Darene, Gracie tried to break his grip with her hands. She bucked and whipped from side to side, turned in circles. He barely held on. Her flesh was the consistency of wet clay, and she stank like rotting meat. She dug her nails into his forearms, and he head butted her as hard as he could at the base of her skull. She growled and tipped backward, losing her balance at the edge of the altar.

Luke caught a glimpse of Darene, aiming her gun at them as they fell. He didn't know whether to let go or hold on tighter. He was sure he'd lose her if she landed on him, but though he cringed in anticipation, he never slammed against the church floor. Instead, he opened his eyes as Gracie lifted off the edge of the altar and ascended. Luke looked down and screamed.

"Let go," Darene yelled.

He held tighter as they circled upward. In seconds, they'd reached the height of the dome, and Gracie leveled out, now placidly flying, like Superman, with her arms out in front of her. They orbited the inside of the dome, and amid his panic, Luke noticed the images painted on the curved ceiling—scenes of people with bird heads feasting on platters of insects, a haloed grasshopper on a throne, trees and mountains, all against a sky blue background with white clouds.

Gracie was babbling in the language of the bald dead, and Luke eased up on his grip, resting upon her back. She swept so smoothly through the air, it felt like a dream.

"Luke" came a voice from below. He roused and looked down over his shoulder from the dizzying height. Appearing like the size of grasshoppers themselves, Mr. Cabadula was standing next to Darene on the altar. Behind them, Sfortunado was writhing in pain on the floor.

"Choke her down," called Darene's father. He lifted his gun, holding it in two hands as Luke was, and pulled it in tightly toward his throat.

"Choke her down," whispered Luke. He gathered his strength and pulled back hard on the gun barrel. Gracie wheezed with the pressure and bucked her hips, trying to shake him off her back. They descended in a slow spiral.

"Keep the pressure on, no matter what," said Mr. Cabadula. Luke peered over Gracie's shoulder and saw Darene's father handing her a mallet and a long brass nail. She then turned and walked to the edge of the altar. Mr. Cabadula walked to the opposite edge and crouched down.

Gracie reached a certain altitude, and no matter how much Luke put into choking her, she'd not go an inch lower. They went into a wide orbit fifteen feet above the altar, moving in an arc out over the pews and back.

"I gotta let go," Luke yelled.

"One more minute," said Darene.

He looked down to find her on the altar as they circled toward it. He heard her father say, "Now, Darene." At this, she took off, sprinting toward him, her arms pumping, her hair flying. Luke watched her dash across the altar to her father, who had his hands cupped, fingers laced, in front of him. She placed her left foot in his hands, and at that instant, he pushed upward with his legs, lifting Darene, pitching her high into the air.

Luke saw everything, but it seemed at a distance. Once Darene was in flight, though, he noticed how closely they'd circled in toward her. He pulled back hard on Gracie, afraid that Darene would collide with them. She rose in an arc, flipping in midair so that as she passed just in front of them, she was completely upside down, her face toward them. At the perfect moment, she reached out, set the nail to Gracie's forehead, and, with one deft blow, slammed it through her skull. Luke heard the sickening crunch of bone, felt Gracie go slack, and then realized that Darene was next to him. She shoved him hard. He lost his grip and fell, screaming, into the arms of Mr. Cabadula, who set him carefully on the altar. They both immediately looked up. Darene had removed her belt and had it around Gracie's throat. She'd turned the belt tight like a tourniquet and had the ends wrapped around her wrist. She sat straight up on the back of the vanquished *gritchino*, her legs hanging down, and seemed able to direct the course of their slow descent by tugging in one direction or another.

Darene steered the remains of Gracie in a slow, meandering descent that ended in the open coffin. Luke shivered at the fantastic precision of Darene's delivery. She hopped off the *gritchino* as it fell, like an avalanche, into the box. The lid eased down of its own accord and latched with a distinct click. Then the whole casket turned to steam and evaporated.

"Forget it," said Luke, and covered his face with his left hand.

Darene and her father were on either side of Sfortunado, who was whimpering. Luke inched closer but really didn't want to see either the old man's chewed-up leg or, worse, his face. Mr. Cabadula took Darene by the arm and led her away from Sfortunado to where Luke was standing.

"Here's my keys," he said, putting the ring of them in her hand. "You go on ahead. I'll clean this up."

There were tears in Darene's eyes when she nodded.

"What's gonna happen with Sfortunado?" asked Luke. "Is he *gritchino*, like vampires make other vampires?"

"Don't worry," said Mr. Cabadula, and cocked the hammer of one of the pistols. "You watch too many movies."

"Come on," said Darene. She put her arm around Luke's back and pulled him down the altar steps and up the aisle toward the door.

Out in the parking lot, the air was so fresh. There was a ribbon of light at the horizon. A bird sang. They got into the black Mercedes. Darene started it and pulled out of the parking lot. Neither of them spoke, and Luke dozed briefly before the car eventually came to a halt. He opened his eyes and saw that she had driven them to the lake.

They sat on a bench beneath the pines, facing the water and the dawn. He had his arm around her, and she leaned against him.

"That was sick," he said. "What's with your family?"

"Do you still love me?" she said.

"I loved it when you spiked Gracie. You and your dad are like a circus act or something."

"They teach you that when you're a kid," she said.

"So what's with Sfortunado? He's not *gritchino*?" asked Luke. "I thought your father was going to ice him."

"Relax," she said, and brought her hand up to lightly trace, with the nail of her index finger, an invisible design on his forehead. Luke felt the tension leave his muscles. His eyes closed, and a moment later he was asleep. When he woke with the sunlight in his face, Darene was gone, as was the Mercedes.

Luke played sick on Monday and Tuesday and stayed home from school. He spent those days on the computer going randomly from one site to another or playing Need for Speed. The implications of the *gritchino* made him dizzy. He wanted to call Darene, at least text her, but when he reached for his phone, the memory of her flying upside down and striking that nail into Gracie's skull made her even more a mystery to him than the wind of eternity.

When he did return to school Wednesday, he found out that Darene hadn't been to class that week either. He looked for her at all the times and places they'd usually meet on a school day and asked around for her. By fifth period, he knew she wasn't there. He cut his seventh-period class and slipped out the side door of the gym. On the path through the woods, he smoked a joint. A half hour later, he stood in front of Darene's house.

The windows had been stripped of their curtains, and the whole place was sunk in that eerie stillness of the vacant. There was a FOR SALE sign in the ground next to the driveway. "She's gone," he said aloud, realizing he wasn't sure if it was for the best or worst.

Two nights later, Luke was awakened from a nightmare of the church by a light nudging at his shoulder. "Shh," whispered a voice. At first he thought it was his mother who'd heard him crying out from his dream. He turned to see her, but instead saw a ghastly visage illuminated from beneath and appearing to be floating in the dark. Luke gasped, then groaned, backing up against the headboard.

"*Fashtulina,*" said the voice. The figure moved, and the glow that had lit the face revealed itself to be a flashlight.

"Uncle Sfortunado?" said Luke.

"Who else?"

"What do you want?" asked Luke, turning on the lamp next to his bed.

The old man came into view, wearing a long black coat and a beret. "Surprised to see me, *gaduche*?" he said, turning off the flashlight and putting it into his coat pocket.

"How's your leg?" asked Luke, trying to swallow.

"The wasp makes the eye cry out," said the old man with a sigh. "That Gracie, she could bite."

"What are you doing here? Where's Darene?"

"I'm here to give you this. . . ." Sfortunado reached his gloved hand into the breast pocket of the coat and brought out a thick roll of cash circled by a red rubber band. "Three thousand," he said, and dropped the money onto the top of the nearby dresser.

"You're giving me three thousand dollars?" said Luke.

"Your cut of the diamond."

"That was real?"

"What I say?" He smiled.

"And Darene?"

"They were called back to the old country for their shame."

"Shame for what?"

"They didn't do it. I told them they should, but my nephew loves his uncle."

"You've got the *gritchino* in you now, don't you? After Gracie bit you, you got it in you," said Luke.

Sfortunado shambled over and sat on the edge of the bed.

"Are you going to eat my kidney?" asked Luke, pulling his legs away from the old man.

"Not tonight," said Sfortunado. "I came to ask you to please, now, put a brass nail into my head." He put his thumb to the spot above the bridge of his nose. "Darene and her father could not, and now they have been banished from here. I couldn't go back with them because I have the *gritchino* in me. Until I die, I'm almost the same old Sfortunado, but after that I will be as Gracie was."

Luke listened and shook his head. "Forget it," he said.

Sfortunado reached into the pockets of the long coat and brought out a mallet and a long brass nail. "You see," said the old man, "there are no Cabadula here anymore. When I come from the coffin, there will be no one to stop me. I will feast on many. This will happen."

"No way," said Luke.

"When vanquished by the nail, like *gritchino*, I will evaporate. And then I am gone, and Darene and her family can return. You miss the girl, *gaduche*, I know," he said, and reached the mallet and nail toward Luke.

"No!" yelled Luke.

Sfortunado stood up. "Do it," he growled. When his lip trembled, the sharp tips of his canines were visible. He took a step toward Luke, but from down the hallway outside the bedroom door there came the sound of footsteps on the stairs.

The old man's head turned, like a bird's, listening.

"My parents are coming," said Luke.

"Turn off the light," said Sfortunado.

The instant the dark came on, Luke knew he shouldn't have followed the order.

"Think about it, *gaduche*. When you are ready, turn on your phone and whisper my name three times. I will come with the mallet and nail."

The doorknob turned.

Sfortunado stepped back, and his silhouette melted into the dark. Then the door opened, the lights came on, and Luke's parents were there, but the old man had vanished.

"We heard voices and then you yelling, 'No,'" said his father.

"Where'd this money come from?" asked his mother.

Luke couldn't answer. He turned on his side, curled up in a ball, and pulled the blanket over his head.

SUNBLEACHED

by *Nathan Ballingrud*

"We're God's beautiful creatures," the vampire said, something like joy leaking into its voice for the first time since it had crawled under this house four days ago. "We're the pinnacle of his art. If you believe in that kind of thing, anyway. That's why the night is our time. He hangs jewels in the sky for us. People, they think we're at some kinda disadvantage because we can't go out in the sunlight. But who needs it. The day is small and cramped. You got your one lousy star."

"You believe in God?" Joshua asked. The crawl space beneath his house was close and hot; his body was coated in a dense sheen of sweat. A cockroach crawled over his fingers, and he jerked his hand away. Late summer pressed onto this small Mississippi coastal town like the heel of a boot. The heat was an act of violence.

"I was raised Baptist. My thoughts on the matter are complicated."

The crawl space was contained partially by sheets of aluminum siding and partially by decaying wooden latticework. It was by this latter that Joshua crouched, hiding in the hot spears of sunlight that intruded into the shadows and made a protective cage around him.

"That's why it's so easy for us to seduce. God loves us, so the world does too. Seduction is your weapon, kid. You're what—fifteen? You think seduction is pumping like a jackrabbit in your momma's car. You don't know anything. But you will, soon enough."

The vampire moved in the shadows, and abruptly the stink of burned flesh and spoiled meat greased the air. It had opened a wound in itself, moving. Joshua knew that it tried to stay still as much as it could, to facilitate the healing, but the slowly shifting angles of the sunbeams made that impossible. He squinted his eyes, trying to make out a shape, but it was useless. He could sense it back there, though—a dark, fluttering presence. Something made of wings.

"Invite me in," it said.

"Later," Joshua said. "Not yet. After you finish changing me."

The vampire coughed; it sounded like a snapping bone. Something wet hit the ground. "Well, come here then, boy."

It moved again, this time closer to the amber light. Its face emerged from the shadows like something rising from deep water. It hunched on its hands and knees, swinging its head like a dog trying to catch a scent. Its face had been burned off. Thin parchment strips of skin hung from blackened sinew and muscle. Its eyes were dark, hollow caves. Even in this wretched state, though, it seemed weirdly graceful. A dancer pretending to be a spider.

For the second time, Joshua laid himself on the soft earth, acrawl with ants and cockroaches, centipedes and earthworms, positioning his upper body beyond the reach of the streaming sunlight. The light's color was deepening, its angles rising until they were almost parallel to the ground. Evening was settling over the earth.

The vampire pressed the long fingers of one charred hand onto his chest, as delicately as a lover. Heat flushed Joshua's body. Every nerve ending was a trembling candle flame. The vampire touched its lips to his throat; its tongue sought the jugular, the heavy river inside. It slid its teeth into his skin.

A sharp, lovely pain.

Joshua stared at the underside of his home: the rusted pipes, the duct tape, the yellow sheets of insulation. It looked so different from beneath. So ugly. He heard footsteps overhead as somebody he loved moved around inside it, attending to mysterious offices.

* * *

Four days ago: he'd stood on the front porch of his home in the deep blue hollow of early morning, watching the waters of the Gulf roll onto the beach. It was his favorite time of day: that sweet, lonesome hinge between darkness and daylight, when he could pretend he was alone in the world and free to take it on his own terms. In a few moments he would go inside and wake his five-year-old brother, Michael, make him breakfast, and get them both ready for school, while their mother still slept in after her night shift at Red Lobster.

But this time belonged to him.

The vampire came from the direction of town, trailing black smoke and running hard across the no-man's-land between his house and the nearest standing building. There'd been a neighborhood there once, but the hurricane wiped it away a few years ago. What remained had looked like a mouthful of shattered teeth, until the state government came through and razed everything to the ground. Their own house had been badly damaged—the storm had scalped it of its top floor, depositing it somewhere out in the Gulf—but the rest had stood its ground, though it canted steeply to one side now, and on breezy days you could feel the wind coming through the walls.

It was over that empty expanse the vampire fled, first billowing smoke like a diesel engine and then erupting into flame as the sun cracked the horizon.

The vampire ran directly for his house and launched itself at the opening to the crawl space under the porch steps. Oily smoke eeled up through the wooden planks and dissipated into the lightening sky.

Joshua had remained frozen in place for the whole event, save the rising clamor in his heart.

Their mother would be late getting home from work—and even later if she went out with that jackass Tyler again—so Joshua fed his little brother and directed him to his bedroom. On their way they passed the stairwell, which was capped now by sheets of plywood hammered over the place where it used to open onto the second floor.

"You want me to read you a story?" he asked, reaching for the copy of *The Wind in the Willows* by the bedside. Michael didn't really understand the story, but he liked it when Joshua did the voices.

"No," he said, leaping into his bed and pulling the covers over himself.

"No story? Are you sure?"

"I just wanna go to sleep tonight."

"Okay," Joshua said. He felt strangely bereft. He reached down and turned on Michael's nightlight, then switched off the lamp.

"Will you cuddle with me, Josh?" he said.

"I won't 'cuddle' with you, but I'll lay down with you for a little bit."

"Okay."

"Cuddle" was a word their dad used before he moved away, and it embarrassed him that Michael held on to it. He eased back on top of the covers and let Michael rest his head in the crook of his arm.

"Are you scared of anything, Josh?"

"What, like monsters?"

"I don't know, I guess."

"No, I'm not scared of monsters. I'm not scared of anything."

Michael thought for a minute, then said, "I'm scared of storms."

"That's silly. It's just a bunch of wind and rain."

". . . I know."

Michael drifted into silence. Joshua felt vaguely guilty about shutting him down like that, but he really didn't have it in him to have the storm talk again. That was something Michael was going to have to get over on his own, since logic didn't seem to have any effect on his thinking.

As he monitored his brother's breathing, waiting for him to fall asleep, he found himself wondering about how he would feel toward his family once the transformation was complete. He was worried that he would lose all feeling for them. Or, worse, that he'd think of them as prey. He didn't think that would happen; everything he'd ever read about vampires seemed to indicate that they kept all their memories and emotions from life. But the thought troubled him nonetheless.

That was why he wouldn't let the vampire into his house until he became one, too; he wanted to be sure it went after the right person. It couldn't have his family.

The question of love was tricky, anyway. He felt protective of his brother and his mom, but he had a hard time aligning that feeling with a word like "love." Maybe it was the same thing; he honestly didn't know. He tried to imagine how he'd feel if they were gone, and he didn't come up with much.

That thought troubled him even more.

Maybe he would think of Michael and his mother as pets. The notion brightened his mood.

People loved their pets.

Michael pretended to be asleep until Joshua left the room. He loved his older brother in the strong, uncomplicated way children loved anything, but recently he'd had become an expert in negotiating the emotional weather in his home, and Joshua's moods had become more turbulent than ever. He got mad at strange things, like when Michael wanted to hold hands, or when Mom brought Tyler home. Michael thought Tyler was weird because he wouldn't talk to them, but he didn't understand why Joshua got so mad about it.

He listened as his brother's footsteps receded down the hallway. He waited a few more minutes just to be sure. Then he slid down and scooted under the bed on his stomach, pressing his ear to the floor. The house swayed and creaked around him, filling the night with bizarre noises. He hated living here since the storm happened. He felt like he was living in the stomach of a monster.

After a few minutes of careful listening, he heard the voice.

Joshua opened his window and waited. He didn't even try to sleep anymore, even though he was constantly tired. The night was clear and cool, with a soft breeze coming in from the sea. The palm trees across the street rustled quietly to themselves, shaggy-haired giants sharing secrets.

After about half an hour, the vampire crawled from an opening near the back of the house, emerging just a few feet from his window. Joshua's heart started to gallop. He felt the familiar, instinctive fear: the reaction of the herd animal to the lion.

The vampire stood upright, facing the sea. Most of its flesh had burned away; the white, round curve of its skull reflected moonlight. Its clothes were dark rags in the wind.

A car pulled into the driveway around front, its engine idling for a few moments before chuckling to a halt. Mom was home.

The vampire's body seemed to coil, every muscle drawing taut at once. It lifted its nose, making tiny jerking motions, looking for the scent.

He heard his mother's laughter, and a man's voice. Tyler was with her.

The vampire took a step toward the front of the house, its joints too loose, as if they were hinged with liquid instead of bone and ligament. Even in its broken, half-dead state, it moved quickly and fluidly. He thought again of a dancer. He imagined how it would look in full health, letting the night fill its body like a kite. Moving through the air like an eel through water.

"Take him," Joshua whispered.

The vampire turned its eyeless face toward him.

Joshua was smiling. "Take him," he said again.

"You know I can't," it said, rage riding high in its voice. "Why the hell don't you let me in!"

"That's not the deal," he said. "Afterward. Then you can come in. And you can have Tyler."

He heard the front door open, and the voices moved inside. Mom and Tyler were in the living room, giggling and whispering. Half drunk already.

"He's all I'll need," the vampire said. "Big country boy like that. Do me right up."

Someone knocked on his bedroom door. His mother's voice came through. "Josh? Are you on the phone in there? You're supposed to be asleep!"

"Sorry, Mom," he said over his shoulder.

He heard Tyler's muffled voice, and his mother started laughing. "Shh!"

It made Joshua's stomach turn. When he looked back outside, the vampire had already slid back under the house.

He sighed and leaned his head out, feeling the cool wind on his face. The night was vast above him. He imagined rising into it, through clouds piled like snowdrifts and into a wash of ice-crystal stars, waiting for its boundary but not finding one. Just rising higher and higher into the dark and the cold.

The school day passed in a long, punishing haze. His ability to concentrate was fading steadily. His body felt like it was made of lead. He'd never been so exhausted in his life, but every time he closed his eyes, he was overcome with a manic energy, making him fidget in his chair. It took the whole force of his will not to get up and start pacing the classroom.

A fever simmered in his brain. He touched the back of his hand to his forehead and was astonished by the heat. Sounds splintered in his ear, and the light coming through the windows was sharp edged. His gaze roved over the classroom, over his classmates hunched over their desks or whispering carelessly in the back rows or staring like farm animals into the empty air. He'd never been one of them, and that was okay. It was just how things were. He used to feel smaller than them, less significant, as if he'd been born without some essential gene to make him acceptable to other people.

But now he assessed them anew. They seemed different, suddenly. They looked like victims. Like little pink pigs, waiting for someone to slash their throats and fulfill their potential. He imagined the room bathed in blood, himself striding through it, a raven among the carcasses. Strutting like any carrion king.

He was halfway into the crawl space when nausea overwhelmed him and he dry heaved into the dirt, the muscles in his sides seizing in pain. He curled into a fetal position and pressed his face into the cool earth until it subsided, leaving him gasping in exhaustion. His throat was swollen and dry.

"I can't sleep," the vampire said from the shadows.

Joshua blinked and lifted his gaze, still not raising his head from the ground. He didn't think he could summon the strength for it, even if he'd wanted to.

The vampire was somewhere in the far corner beneath the house, somewhere behind the bars of sunlight slanting through the latticework. "The light moves around too much down here," it said, apparently oblivious to Joshua's pain. "I can't rest. I need to rest."

Joshua was silent. He didn't know what he was expected to say.

"Invite me in," it said. "I can make it dark inside."

"What's happening to me?" Joshua asked. He had to force the air out of his lungs to speak. He could barely hear himself.

"You're changing. You're almost there."

"I feel like I'm dying."

"Heh, that's funny."

Joshua turned his face into the soil. He felt a small tickling movement crawling up his pant leg.

"I remember when I died. I was terrified. It's okay to be scared, Joshua."

That seemed like a funny thing to say. He blinked, staring into the place where the voice was coming from.

"I was in this barn. I was a hand on this farm that grew sugarcane. Me and a few others slept out there in the loft. One day this young fella turned up missing. We didn't think too much about it. Good-natured boy, worked hard, but he was kinda touched in the head, and we figured it was always a matter of time before he went and got himself into some trouble. We thought we'd wait for the weekend and then go off and look for him.

"But he came back before the weekend. Sailed in through

the second-floor window of the barn one night. I about pissed myself. Seemed like he walked in on a cloud. Before we could think of anything to say, he laid into us. Butchered most of the boys like hogs. Three of us he left, though. Maybe 'cause we were nicer to him, I don't know. He decided to make us like him. Who knows why. But see, he was too stupid to tell us what was going on. Didn't know himself, I guess. But he just kept us up there night after night, feeding on us a little bit at a time. Our dead friends around us the whole time, growing flies."

"Why didn't you run when the sun came up?" Joshua had forgotten his pain. He sat up, edging closer to the ribbons of light, his head hunched below the underside of the house.

"Son of a bitch spiked our legs to the floor of the loft. Wrapped barbed wire around our arms. He was determined, I'll give him that. And no one came from the house. Didn't take a genius to figure out why." The vampire paused, seemingly lost in the memory. "Well, anyway, before too long we got up and started our new lives. He went off God knows where. So did the other two. Never seen them since."

Joshua took it all in, feeling the shakes come upon him again. "I'm worried about my family," he said. "I'm worried they won't understand."

"You won't feel so sentimental, afterward."

This was too much to process. He decided he needed to sleep for a while. Let the fever abate, then approach it all with a fresh mind. "I'm gonna lay down," he said, turning back toward the opening. The light there was like a boiling cauldron, but the thought of lying in his own bed was enough to push through.

"Wait!" the vampire said. "I need to feed first."

Joshua decided to ignore it. He was already crawling out, and he didn't have the energy to turn around.

"BOY!"

He froze and looked behind him. The vampire lunged forward, and its head passed into a sunbeam. The flesh hissed, emitting a thin coil of smoke. A candle flame flared around it, and the stench of ruined flesh rolled over him in a wave, as though a bag of rancid meat had been torn open.

The vampire pulled back, the blind sockets of its eyes seeming to float in the dim white bone. "Don't play with me, boy."

"I'm not," Joshua said. "I'll be back later." And he crawled out into the jagged sunlight.

He awoke to find his mother hovering over him. She was wearing her white Red Lobster shirt, with the name tag and the ridiculous tie. She had one hand on his forehead, simultaneously taking his temperature and pushing the hair out of his face.

"Hey, honey," she said.

"Mom?" He pulled his head away from her and put his

hand over his eyes. He was on the couch in the living room. Late-afternoon light streamed in through the window. No more than an hour could have elapsed. "What are you doing home?"

"Mikey called me. He said you passed out."

He noticed his brother sitting in the easy chair on the other side of the room. Michael regarded him solemnly, his little hands folded in his lap like he was in church.

"You're white as a sheet," his mother said. "How long have you been feeling bad?"

"I don't know. Just today, I guess."

"I think we should get you to a hospital."

"No!" He made an effort to sit up. "No, I'm fine. I just need to rest for a while."

She straightened, and he could see her wrestling with the idea. He knew she didn't want to go to the hospital any more than he did. They didn't have any insurance, and here she was missing a shift at work besides.

"Really, I'm okay. Besides, we'd have to wait forever, and isn't Tyler coming over tonight?"

His mother tensed. She looked at him searchingly, like she was trying to fathom his motive. She said, "Joshua, you're more important to me than Tyler is. You do understand that, don't you?"

He looked away. He felt his face flush, and he didn't want her to see it. "I know," he said.

"I know you don't like him."

"It's not that," he said, but of course it was that. Tyler had to be here so he could feed him to the vampire. He had a feeling that tonight was going to be the night. He didn't know how he could go on much more, as weak as he was.

Michael piped up, his voice cautious yet hopeful: "It doesn't matter anyway, 'cause Daddy's coming back."

His mother sighed and turned to look at him. Joshua could see all the years gathered in her face, and he felt a sudden and unexpected sympathy for her. "No, Mikey. He's not."

"Yes, he is, Mom, he told me. He asked if it was okay."

Her voice hardened, although she was obviously trying to hide it. "Has he been talking to you on the phone?" She looked to Joshua for confirmation.

"Not me," Joshua said. It occurred to him that Dad might have been calling while he was under the house, talking to the vampire. He felt at once both guilty that he'd left his brother to deal with that alone, and outraged that he'd missed out on the calls.

"You tell him next time he calls that he can talk to *me* about that," she said, not even bothering to hide her anger now. "In fact, don't even talk to him. Hang up on him if he calls again. I'm going to get his number blocked, that son of a bitch."

Tears piled in Michael's eyes, and he lowered his face. His body trembled as he tried to keep it all inside. A wild anger coursed through Joshua's body, animating him despite the fever.

"Shut up!" he shouted. "Shut up about Dad! You think Tyler is *better*? He can't even look at us! He's a fucking *retard*!"

His mother looked at him in pained astonishment for a long moment. Then she put her hand over her mouth and stifled a sob. Aghast, Michael launched himself at her, a terrified little missile. He wrapped his arms around her and buried his face in her chest. "It's okay, Mom, it's okay!"

Joshua unfolded himself from the couch and walked down the hall to his room. His face was alight with shame and rage. He didn't know what to do. He didn't know what to feel. He closed the door behind him, muffling the sounds of the others comforting each other. He threw himself onto his bed, pulling the pillow over his face. The only things he could hear now were the wooden groaning of the house as it shifted on its foundations and the diminished sound of the blood pumping in his own head.

Their father left right after the hurricane. He used to work on the oil rigs. He'd get on a helicopter and disappear for a few weeks, and money would show up in the bank account. Then he'd come home for a week, and they'd all have fun together. He'd fight with their mother sometimes, but he always went back out to sea before things had a chance to get bad.

After the hurricane, all that work dried up. The rigs were

compromised and the Gulf Coast oil industry knocked back on its heels. Dad was stranded in the house. Suddenly there was no work to stop the fighting. He moved to California shortly thereafter, saying he'd send for them when he found another job. A week later their mother told them the truth.

Joshua still remembered the night of the storm. The four of them rode it out together in the house. It sounded like hell itself had come unchained and was stalking the world right outside their window. But he felt safe inside. Even when the upper floor ripped away in a scream of metal and plaster and wood, revealing a black, twisting sky, he never felt like he was in any real danger. The unremarkable sky he'd always known had changed into something three-dimensional and alive.

It was like watching the world break open, exposing its secret heart.

His father was crouched beside him. They stared at it together in amazement, grinning like a pair of blissed-out lunatics.

Joshua heard a gentle rapping on his door.

"I'm going to the store," his mother said. "I'm gonna get something for your fever. Is there anything you want for dinner?"

"I'm not hungry."

He waited for her car to pull out of the driveway before he swung his legs out of bed and tried to stand. He could do it as long as he kept one hand on the wall. He couldn't believe how tired he was. His whole body felt cold, and he couldn't feel his fingers. It was coming tonight. The certainty of it inspired no excitement, no joy, no fear. His body was too numb to feel anything. He just wanted it to happen so he could get past this miserable stage.

He shuffled out of his room and down the hall. The vampire needed to feed on him once more, and he wanted to get down there before his mother got back.

As he passed by his brother's door, though, he stopped short. Somebody was whispering on the other side.

He opened the door to find his little brother lying prone on the floor, half under the bed. Late-afternoon shadows gathered in the corners. His face was a small moon in the dim light, one ear pressed to the hardwood. He was whispering urgently.

"Michael?"

His brother's body jerked in alarm, and he sat up quickly, staring guiltily back. Joshua flipped the light switch on.

"What are you doing?" Something cold was growing inside him.

Michael shrugged.

"Tell me!"

"Talking to Daddy."

"No."

"He's living under the house. He wants us to let him back

in. I was afraid to because Mom might get mad at me."

"Oh, Mikey." His voice quavered. "That's not Dad. That's not Dad."

He found himself moving down the hall again, quickly now, fired with renewed energy. He felt like a passenger in his body: He experienced a mild curiosity as he saw himself rummaging through the kitchen drawer until he found the claw hammer his mother kept there; a sense of fearful anticipation as he pushed the front door open and stumbled down the porch steps in the failing light, not even pausing to gather his strength before he hooked the claw into the nearest latticework and wrenched it away from the wall in a long segment.

"We had a deal!" he screamed, getting to work on another segment. "You son of a bitch! We had a deal!" He worked fast, alternately smashing wooden latticework to pieces and prying aluminum panels free from the house. "You lied to me! You lied!" Nails squealed as they were wrenched from their moorings. The sun was too low for the light to intrude beneath the house now, but tomorrow the vampire would find the crawl space uninhabitable.

He saw the vampire, once, just beneath the lip of the house. It said nothing, but its face tracked him as he worked.

The sun was sliding down the sky, leaking its light into the ground and into the sea. Darkness swarmed from the east, spreading stars in its wake.

Joshua hurried inside, dropping the hammer on the floor and collapsing onto the couch, utterly spent. A feeling of profound loss hovered somewhere on the edge of his awareness. He had turned his back on something, on some grand possibility. He knew the pain would come later.

Soon his mother returned, and he took some of the medicine she'd bought for him, though he didn't expect it to do any good. He made a cursory attempt to eat some of the pizza she'd brought, too, but his appetite was gone. She sat beside him on the couch and brushed the hair away from his forehead. They watched some TV, and Joshua slipped in and out of sleep. At one point he stared through the window over the couch. The moon traced a glittering arc through the sky. Constellations rotated above him, and the planets rolled through the heavens. He felt a yearning that nearly pulled him out of his body.

He could see for billions of miles.

At some point his mother roused him from the couch and guided him to his room. He cast a glance into Michael's room when he passed it, and saw his brother fast asleep.

"You know I love you, Josh," his mother said at his door.

He nodded. "I know, Mom. I love you, too."

His body was in agony. He was pretty sure he was going to die, but he was too tired to care.

* * *

A scream woke him. The heavy sound of running footsteps, followed by a crash.

Then silence.

Joshua tried to rouse himself. He felt like he'd lost control of his body. His eyelids fluttered open. He saw his brother standing in the doorway, tears streaming down his face.

"Oh no, Josh, oh no, oh no . . ."

He lost consciousness.

The next morning he was able to move again. The fever had broken sometime during the night; his sheets were soaked with sweat.

He found his mother on the kitchen table. She had kicked some plates and silverware onto the floor in what had apparently been a brief struggle. Her head was hanging backward off the edge of the table, and she had been sloppily drained. Blood splashed the floor beneath her. Her eyes were open and glassy.

His brother was suspended upside down in the living room, his feet tied with a belt to the ceiling fan, which had come partially free from its anchor. He'd been drained, too. He was still wearing his pajamas. On the floor a few feet away from him, where it had fluttered to rest, was a welcome-home card he had made for their father.

The plywood covering the open stairwell had been

wrenched free. The vampire stood on the top stair, looking into deep blue sky of early morning. Joshua stopped at the bottom stair, gazing up at it. Its burned skin was covered in a clear coating of pus and lymphatic fluid, as its body started to heal. White masses filled its eye sockets like spiders' eggs. Tufts of black hair stubbled its peeled head.

"I waited for you," the vampire said.

Joshua's lower lip trembled. He tried to say something, but he couldn't get his voice to work.

The vampire extended a hand. "Come up here. The sun's almost up."

Almost against his will, he ascended the stairs into the open air. The vampire wrapped its fingers around the back of his head and drew him close. Its lips grazed his neck. It touched its tongue to his skin.

"Thank you for your family," it said.

"No . . ."

It sank its teeth into Joshua's neck and drew from him one more time. A gorgeous heat seeped through his body, and he found himself being lowered gently to the top of the stair.

"It's okay to be afraid," the vampire said.

His head rolled to one side; he looked over the area where the second story used to be. There was his old room. There was Michael's. And that's where his parents slept. Now it was all just open air.

"This is my house now," the vampire said, standing over

him and surveying the land around them. "At least for a few more days." It looked down at Joshua with its pale new eyes. "I'd appreciate it if you stayed out."

The vampire descended the stairs.

A few minutes later, the sun came up, first as a pink stain, then as a gash of light on the edge of the world. Joshua felt the heat rising in him again: a fierce, purging radiance starting from his belly and working rapidly outward. He smelled himself cooking, watched the smoke begin to pour out of him, crawling skyward.

And then the day swung its heavy lid over the sky. The ground baked hard as an anvil in the heat, and the sun hammered the color out of everything.

BABY

by Kathe Koja

It's hot in here, and the air smells sweet, all sweet and burned, like incense. I love incense, but I can never have any; my allergies, right? Allergic to incense, to cigarette smoke, to weed smoke, to smoke in general, the smoke from the grill at Rob's Ribs, too, so good-bye to that, and no loss either, I hate this job. The butcher's aprons are like circus tents, like 3X, and those pointy paper hats we have to wear—SMOKIN' SPECIALIST, God. They look like big white dunce caps, even Rico looks stupid wearing one and Rico is *hot*. I've never seen anyone as hot as he is.

The only good thing about working here—besides Rico—is hanging out after shift, up on the rooftop while Rob and whoever swabs out the patio, and everyone jokes and flirts, and if Rob isn't paying too much attention, me and Rico shotgun a couple of cans of Tecate or something. Then I lean as far over the railing as I can, my hands gripping tight, the metal pressing cold through my shirt; sometimes I let my feet leave the patio, just a few inches, just balancing there on the railing, in thin air. . . . Andy always flips when I do it, he's all like, *Oh, Jani, don't do that, Jani, you could really hurt yourself! You could fall!*

Oh, Andy, I always say; Andy's like a mom or something. *Calm down, it's only gravity,* only six floors up, but still, if you fell, you'd be a plate of Rob's Tuesday-night special, all bones and red sauce; *smush,* gross, right? But I love doing it. You can feel the wind rush up between the buildings like invisible water, stealing your breath, filling you right up to the top. It's so weird, and so choice. . . . Like the feeling I always got from you, Baby.

It's kind of funny that I never called you anything else, just Baby, funny that I even found you, up there in Grammy's storage space, or crawl space, or whatever it's called when it's not really an attic but it's just big enough to stand up in. Boxes were piled everywhere, but mostly all I'd found were old china cup and saucer sets, and a bunch of games with missing pieces—Stratego, and Monopoly, and Clue; I already had Clue at home, I used to totally love Clue, even though I cheated when I played, sometimes. Well, all the time. I wanted to win. There were boxes and boxes of Grampy's old books, doctor books, one was called *Surgical Procedures and Facial Deformities* and believe me, you did *not* want to look at *that.* I flipped it open on one picture where this guy's mouth was all grown sideways, and his eyes—his eye . . . Anyway. After that I stayed away from the boxes of books.

And then I found you, Baby, stuffed down in a big box of clothes, chiffon scarves and unraveling lace, the cut-down skirts of fancy dresses, and old shirts like army uniforms, with steel buttons and appliqués. At the bottom of the box were all kinds of shoes, spike heels, and a couple of satin evening bags with broken clasps. At first I thought you were a kind of purse, too, or a bag, all small and yellow and leathery. But then I turned you over, and I saw that you had a face.

Right away I liked touching you, your slick wrinkled skin, weird old-timey doll with bulgy glass eyes—they looked like glass—and a little red mouth, and fingers that could open and close; the first time you did that, fastened on me like that, it kind of flipped me out, but then I saw I could make you do it if I wanted to. And then I wanted to.

I played with you for a long time that first day, finding out what you could do, until Mommy came and bitched me out for being "missing." How big was Grammy's house? Not very, Mommy was just mad that she had to be there at all, even once a year was too much. Mommy and Grammy never really got along. *Speak English,* Mommy used to yell at her. *This is Ohio!*

So when she yelled at me I wasn't surprised: *What are you doing up here?* with the door open and the afternoon light behind her, like a witch peering into a playhouse; I was surprised at how dark it was in there, I could see *your* face perfectly fine. I knew to hide you, Baby, even though I didn't know why, I stuck you in the folds of one of the evening skirts and *I'm just playing dress-up*, I said, but Mommy got mad at that, too: *Stay out of that stuff, all her Nazi dancehall stuff, it's all moth-eaten and disgusting. And anyway come on, we're leaving now.*

Can I take these? I said, pointing to the board games, I threw the games away when I got you home. You slept with me that first night, didn't you? You got under the blanket, and fastened on. . . . It was the first time I really had it, that feeling, like when you spin yourself around to get dizzy, or when you're just about to be drunk, but a hundred times sweeter, like riding an invisible wave. I could see into things when you did that, see into the sky, into myself, watch my own heartbeat. It was so *choice*.

It's funny, too, because I never liked baby dolls, or dolls of any kind. Grammy bought me, like, a million Barbies, but I don't think I ever played with any of them, or the Madame Maurice dolls that anyway aren't meant to be played with, Mommy ended up selling those on eBay. But you were different. It wasn't like we were playing, I wasn't the mommy and you weren't the baby, I didn't have to dress you up, or make you walk and talk. You were pretty much real on your own. . . . If I'd been a little older, I might have wondered more about that; I mean, even then I knew you weren't actually a toy. Or a "real" baby, either. You never cried, for one thing. And what you ate never made you grow.

But I knew you loved me since I got you out of that clothes box, and so you did things for me, things that I wanted you to do. Like when Alisha Parrish wrecked my Lovely Locket, and wouldn't say sorry, and you puked—or whatever that was— all over her sleeping bag! That was choice. Or when I threw Mommy's car keys down the wishing well in the park, and she told me I couldn't come home until I found them. She was surprised, wasn't she, Baby?

I let you do things, too, that you wanted, like when we found that dead raccoon out by the storage shed, remember? Or the time I was so sick with the flu that the fever made me see things, and I let you fly all around the room; you were smiling, Baby, and swimming through the air. I wondered, later, how much the fever had to do with it, and for a long time after I kept watching, to see if you would smile again, or fly. . . . It was kind of like having a pet, a pet who was also a friend.

And a secret, because I knew without even thinking about it that I could never show you to anyone, not sleepover friends or school friends or anyone, that you were only meant for me. You knew it, too. And you were happy, you didn't need anyone but me anyway.

For sure Mommy's never seen you—Mommy doesn't even go into my room—but Roger knew about you, or knew *something*; remember Roger? With the bald head and mustache? He used to look at me weird, like he was sad or something, and once or twice he asked me if I was okay: *You doing all right, Jani? You feeling all right?*

I'm fine.

Anything you want to talk about? If you're not—feeling good, or anything, you can always talk to your mom about it. Roger didn't know Mommy very well. And he didn't last very long.

Definitely Flaco knew about you, I don't know how but he did. He finally caught us in the hallway, in the Pensacola house, when Mommy was at the gym, he popped out of the bathroom like he'd been standing there waiting and *So there's your Santeria toy,* he said. *Come on, Jani, let's see it.*

He smelled like aftershave, and skunky weed; he was smiling. In the dusty hallway light, you looked yellower than normal; I could feel the heat coming off you, like it does when you're hungry. I tried to hide you under my arm.

It's just a doll, I said.

Ah, that ain't no dolly, girl, come on. That's a bat boy! A familiar. My uncle Felix had one, he called it Little Felix. We used to say it was the devil's little brother. Flaco was still smiling; the skunk-weed smell was burning my throat. *He bites when you tell him to, don't he? Does anything you tell him to.*

I didn't know what to say. I didn't know how he knew. "Familiar"? With what? *The devil's little brother.* Family. You were squirming under my arm, I couldn't tell if you were angry or afraid.

They can do some crazy shit, familiars. Come on, I won't tell your mama. Let me see— And he tried to make a grab for you, he put his hand on you and *Stop it!* I said.

Let me see, girl!

You stop it, or I'll tell Mommy you tried to touch me, I'll say you tried to touch me under my shirt.

I wouldn't never— That's a sick kind of lie, Jani! But we both knew that Mommy would believe me, Flaco was pretty much a straight-up man-whore from day one. He let us go then, didn't he, Baby? And he never said anything about you again, to me or to Mommy, even though I let you do things to him, once or twice—okay, more than that, but whatever, he was passed-out high when you did it, and anyway he deserved it, right? And even though he knew—he had to know—how it happened, those bites, he never said a word.

Flaco moved out that Christmas Eve and took all the presents with him, his and ours; *A real class act.* Mommy said, and then she threw a big Christmas party to celebrate, and get more presents. Mommy said she was tired of Flaco's drama anyway, and really tired of Pensacola, and so was I.

So I hid you in my backpack and we moved back to Ohio, Bay Ridge, Ohio, and I hated it, hated middle school, hated the girls who made fun of my jeans and called me a trash burger and a slut; I was like eleven years old, how much of a slut could I have been? Even in Bay Ridge? In Ohio you wrinkled up like a raisin, and you barely moved at all—I think it was too cold for you there, I don't think you can, like, process the cold. In Pensacola you always smelled a little bit funky, like an old sneaker left in a closet, or a dog's chew toy, but at least you could get around. Once or twice, in Bay Ridge, you were so stiff and so still in my backpack that I thought you were, you know, dead, and I cried, Baby. I really, really cried.

When we moved again, down to Clearwater, things got better; you liked it better here, too, at least at first, right? It was warm again, for one thing. And I started high school, which is a *lot* more fun than middle school, and our house is a lot nicer, too: There are two bathrooms, and the solarium with the hot tub, even if it leaks, and the home office where Mommy works, she's an online "consultant" now—

What kind of a consultant?

I'm a relationship counselor.

What kind of relationships?

—but the more I asked the madder she got, all pinched up around the mouth until she looked like Grammy; and really I don't care, right? At least we have money now, at least there are no more boyfriends wandering all over the house in their tighty whities. Not hers, anyway. . . . The first time I did it, with a boy, you knew somehow, didn't you, Baby? When I got back from the Freshman Spring Fling, you smelled all over my hands and face, and then you went all stiff at the side of the bed, and you didn't want to fasten on, you wouldn't until I made you.

And when I woke up the next morning you weren't there, even though I looked all over, and Mommy yelled at me for being late to school, *I'm not going to call in for you again, Jani, I mean it!* All day I thought, Oh, God, what if Mommy finds Baby? I couldn't imagine what she would do to you, or to me. Kick me out, or—who knows what Mommy would do.

I was pretty scared, and pretty mad, when I got home. Mommy was sleeping, so I tore the house apart again, and when finally I found you, curled up behind the washer— where Mommy could have seen you in a second, if she ever bothered to look, if she ever bothered to do a load of clothes— *Where were you?* I said. I think I shook you a little, or a lot. *Where the hell were you?*

You just rolled your glass eyes at me and didn't make a sound. All sad and cold and stiff, like—like beef jerky or something, you were *nasty*. So I stuffed you into the old backpack, I threw you into the back of the closet, and I almost didn't let you out. Almost. Except I finally did, and I let you fasten on, too. And you were happy, Baby, I could tell, that night it was like both of us were flying. After that, no matter what I did or who I hooked up with, or even if I didn't come home all night, you never ran away again. I knew you needed me, then, more than I needed you. And I realized that I didn't really need you much at all.

But that was going to happen anyway, right? Because really, the older I get, the more I can do for myself, and the less I need the things that you can do—and the things I can't get you can't get either, I mean I'm not going to send you into the liquor store, right? *Crawl up into the cold case, get me a six-pack of Tecate, Baby!* And even the fastening on—even though we still do it, and I still like it, I can get to that place without you now. Driving really fast, smoking up and then drinking—it's mostly the same feeling, not as pure or as . . . as good as with you, but I can be with other people when I get it. People like Bobby, or Justin, or Colin. Or Rico. Especially Rico.

I told Rico about you, Baby. I didn't plan to beforehand, but I did. We were in the storage room—Rob said to go unpack the napkins, there must have been like fifty boxes—but instead we were joking around, and flirting, and I was trying to think of ways to keep him talking; I wanted to stay that way, the two of us alone together, for as long as I could. I wanted to show him that I'm . . . different, from Carmen, and Kayla, and those other girls, those pervy night-shift girls, I wanted him to know something about me. To be . . . familiar with me. So I told him about you.

At first it seemed like he was impressed: *Whoa, that's some crazy shit. How'd your grandma get something like that?*

She was, like, in a war, or something. "Her Nazi dance-hall stuff"—that's creepy to think of, actually, because I'd never really thought about where you came from, or how Grampy got you. Or who might have—made you, or whatever. You weren't born like normal, that's for sure.

You saying the doll's, like, alive, Jani? For real?

Not alive-alive. But he moves around and everything. You should see him when he eats!

Rico was smiling—*That's so crazy*—but I couldn't tell if he thought it was cool crazy or weird crazy; I couldn't tell if I'd just made a big mistake. And then Rob came looking for the napkins, and bitched us both out for taking so long: *What were you guys doing in there anyway?* Everyone laughed, Rico, too. Later on, I asked Rico if he wanted to come over and use the hot tub, but he said he was busy, and maybe we could just hang out at work instead. So I guess you can't help me with Rico, Baby, after all.

And even if I wanted to ask Grammy about you, or give you back, I can't: Because she's gone, right, she finally died in that hospice in Ohio. Mommy said she found out too late to be able to go to the funeral, but she sure got there fast enough for the will, she must have taken half the furniture from that house. I wonder what happened to all of that other stuff, those old clothes, and the medical books. . . . Maybe I should have asked Flaco about you, back when I had the chance.

The thing is, Rico finally said yes, Baby, when we were up on the roof last night, I was leaning over the railing and he was standing next to me, and I told him that Friday was my last night at Rob's Ribs, that I was quitting to go back to school; it's online school, but still. Mommy said I could quit working if I take at least one class, and anyway I didn't tell him that part. *I'd like to, like, be with you,* I said to Rico. *Before I go.*

And he smiled so you could see all his dimples, God, he is so hot. And then he said, *Okay, wild child, how about I come over tomorrow? I have to drive up to Northfield, but I can be over by midnight.* Mommy might be home, but Mommy doesn't bother me, she doesn't care what I do. So I said, *Absolutely,* I said, *Come over whenever you want.*

But the thing is, you can't be there, Baby, I don't want you to be there, I don't want Rico to ask, *Hey, where's that crazy doll?* And if he does, I want to be able to say, *Oh, that? Oh, I don't have that anymore.*

But I don't want to—to bury you alive in some old clothes box, you didn't like it the first time, right, when Grammy or Grampy stuck you in there? I know you didn't. Just like you don't like living in my old backpack with the April-May-Magic stickers and the black-plaid bows, stuffed way down in the very back of my closet, behind the Princess Jasmine bed-spread. When I take you out to feed you, now, you just—look at me. I hate the way you looking at me feels. . . . I'm just too old to play with dolls.

It really does smell like incense in here, like hot, sweet

wood, burning. No one's supposed to mess with the smokers—
Rob does that himself, all the cleaning—but Andy helps the
cooks load, and he says it's not that hard; he's going to help
me, too. He doesn't know what's in the backpack, when he
asked I just said, *Memories,* and he nodded. Andy will do what
I want him to do; like you, Baby. They keep the smokers at,
like, 250 degrees, but it can go a lot higher, a lot hotter, I bet
it won't even hurt. Not like falling off the roof, right? No
Tuesday-night special, just ash, and gone. . . . I'm going to
throw in that stupid SMOKIN' SPECIALIST hat, too.

I wonder if you knew that's why I let you fasten on, last
night, for one last time? You seemed so happy to get out of the
closet, and the backpack, to be close to me again. . . . I'd take
you out again to say good-bye, right here behind the shelves,
but if I look at you, your sad glass eyes, then I won't do it,
maybe. Maybe. But I can't keep you forever anyway, and Rico
will be over tonight.

The smoke smell is everywhere in here, digging a
barbed-wire itch in my throat, in my chest, it makes me
cough. . . . Afterward, when Andy's done, I'm going to
go up onto the roof and lean over the railing, let my feet
dangle and feel like I'm flying. Flying and crying, for you
and for me: Because I *am* crying, Baby, just a little, because
I'm going to miss you a lot.

IN THE FUTURE WHEN ALL'S WELL

by Catherynne M. Valente

These days, pretty much anything will turn you into a vampire.

We have these stupid safety and hygiene seminars at school. Like, before, it was D.A.R.E. and oh my God if you even look crosswise at a bus that goes to that part of town you will be hit with a fire-hose blast full of PCP and there is nothing you can even do about it so just stay in your room and don't think about beer. Do you even know what PCP looks like? I have no idea.

I remember they used to say PCP made you think you could fly. That seems kind of funny, now.

Anyway, there's lists. Two of them, actually. On the first day of S/H class, the teacher hands them out. They're always the same, I practically have them memorized. One says: MOST COMMON CAUSES. The other says: HIGH-RISK GROUPS. So here, just in case you ditched that day so you could go down to *that part of town* and suck on the fire hose, you fucking slacker.

MOST COMMON CAUSES

Immoral Conduct

Depression

Black Cat Crossing the Path of Pregnant or Nursing Mother

Improper Burial

Animal (Most Often Black) Jumping Over Grave, Corpse

Bird (Most Often Black) Flying Over Grave, Corpse

Butterfly Alighting on Tombstone

Ingestion of Meat from Animal Killed by a Wolf

Death Before Baptism

Burying Corpse at Crossroads

Failing to Bury Corpse at Crossroads

Direct Infection

Blood Transfusions Received 2011–2013

HIGH-RISK GROUPS (HR)

Persons Born with Extra Nipple, Vestigial Tail, Excess
Hair, Teeth, Breech

Persons Whose Mothers Encountered Black Cats While
Pregnant

Persons Whose Mothers Did Not Ingest Sufficient Salt
While Pregnant

Seventh Children, Either Sex

Children Conceived on Saturday

Children Born out of Wedlock

Children Vaccinated for Polio 1999–2002

Children Diagnosed Autistic/OCD
Promiscuous Youngsters
Persons Possessing Unkempt Eyebrows
Persons Bearing Unusual Moles or Birthmarks
Redheads with Blue Eyes

I swear to God you cannot even walk down the *street* without getting turned. That list doesn't even get into your standard jump-out-of-the-shadows schtick. Like, half the graduating class have to get their diploma indoors, you know? Plus I think they just put in that shit about promiscuous youngsters because it's, like, their duty as teachers to make sure no one ever has sex. Who says "youngsters," anyway? The problem with S/H class is that, just like the big scary PCP, we all know where to get it if we want it, so the whole thing is just . . . kill me now so I can go get a freaking milkshake.

My dad says this is all because of the immigrants coming in from Romania, Ukraine, Bulgaria. I don't know. I read *Dracula* and whatever. Doesn't seem very realistic to me. Vampires are sort of something that just *happens* to you, like finals. I know people used to think they were all lords of the night and stuff, and they are, I guess. But it's, like, my friend Emmy got turned last week because a black dog walked around her house the wrong way. Sometimes things just get fucked up and it's not because there was a revolution in Bulgaria.

But I guess the point is, I'm going to graduate soon and

I'm just sort of waiting for it to happen to me. There's this whole summer before college and it's like a million years long and I have red hair and blue eyes, so, you know, eventually something big and black is just going to come sit on my chest till I die. I told Emmy, "It's not your fault. It's not because you're a bad person. It's just random. It doesn't mean anything. It's like a raffle."

So my name is Scout—yeah, my mom read *To Kill a Mockingbird*. Leave it to her to think fifth-grade required reading is totally deep. She also has a heart thing where she's had to be on a low-sodium diet since she was my age, which means while she was pregnant with me, so *thanks*, Mom. With high-risk groups, birds don't even have to fly over your own grave. It can be, like, anyone's grave, if you're nearby. It's like a shock wave. I heard about this one HR guy, like, two towns over, who was a seventh son with a unibrow *and* red hair *and* was born backward, and he just turned *by himself*. Just sitting there in English class and *bang*. That's what scares me the most. Like it's something that's inside you already, and you can't stop it or even know it's there, but there's a little clock and it's always counting down to English class.

The other night I was hanging out with Emmy, trying to be a supportive friend like you're supposed to be. In S/H class they say high-risk kids should cut off their friends if they get turned. Like it's one of those movies about how brutal high school is and we're all going to shun Emmy on Monday if she's wearing a little more black than usual. As if I would ever.

"What's it like?" I said. Because that's what they don't tell you. What it feels like. "PCP is bad, it'll make you jump off buildings." Yeah, but before that. What's it like? Before you crave blood and stalk the night. What's it like?

"It's stupid. My hair's turning black. I have to go to this doctor every two weeks for tests. And, I don't know . . . it's, like, I want to sleep in the dirt? When I get tired, my whole head fills up with this idea of how nice it would be to dig up the yard and snuggle down and sleep in there. The way I used to think about bubble baths."

"Have you . . . done it yet?"

"Oh, blood? Yeah. Ethan let me right away. He's good like that." Emmy shoved her bangs back. She had a lot of makeup on. Naturally Sunkissed was a big color that year. Keeps the pallor down but it doesn't make you all Oompa-Loompa. "What? What do you want to hear? That it's gross or that it's awesome?"

"I don't know. Whatever it is."

"It's . . . like eating dinner, Scout. When somebody goes to a little effort to make something nice for you, it's great. When they eat healthy and wash really good but don't taste like soap. When they let you. But sometimes it just gets you through the night." She lit a cigarette and looked at me like "Why shouldn't I, now?"

"Did you hear about Kimberly? She got turned the old-fashioned way, by this gnarly weird guy from Zagreb, and she can *fly*. It's so fucking unfair."

Emmy wasn't very different as a vampire. We had this same conversation after she lost her virginity—Ethan again—and she was all "it is what it is" then, too, with an extra helping of "I am part of a sacred sisterhood now." Emmy has always been kind of crap as a friend, but I've known her since Barbies and kiddie soccer, so, whatever, right?

I don't know, I suppose it was dumb, but things can get weird between girls who've known each other that long. Like this one time when we were thirteen we did that whole practice kissing on each other thing. We'd been hanging out in my room for hours and hours and rooms get all whacked out when you lock yourselves in like that. We sat cross-legged on my lame pink bedspread and kissed because we were lonely and we didn't know anything except that we wanted to be older and have boyfriends because our sisters had them and her lips were really soft. I didn't even know you were supposed to use tongue, that's how thirteen I was. Her, too. We never told anyone about it, because, well, you just don't. But I guess I'm talking about it now because I let Emmy feed off me that night, even though I'm HR, and it was kind of like the same thing.

I didn't see her much, though, after that. It was just awkward. I guess that sort of thing happens after senior year. People drift.

Back in seventh grade, right after the first ones started showing up, like every freaking book they assigned in school was a vampire book. That's when I read *Dracula*. *Carmilla* and *The Bride of Corinth*, too. *The Vampyre*, *The Land Beyond the Forest*. *Varney the Freaking Vampire*. Classics, you know—they said all the modern stuff was agitprop, whatever that means. It's weird, though, because back then there were maybe twenty or thirty vampires in the whole world, and people just wrote and wrote about them, even though there's like statistically *no way* that Stoker guy ever met one. And now there's vampires all over. Google says there's almost as many as there are people. They have a widget. But nobody's written a vampire book in years.

So I've been hanging out in cemeteries a lot lately. I know, right? I mean, before? I would *never*. Have you seen how much it costs to get up in black fingernail polish and fishnets? And now, for an HR like me, it's pretty much like slitting your wrists in the bathtub with a baby blue razor for sensitive skin. Everyone knows you're not serious, but there's a slim chance you'll fuck up and off yourself anyway. If you want to get turned, you don't have to go chasing it. Not when some bad steak will do you for about $12.50, and a guy down on Bellefleur Street will do it for less than that.

So, I'm one of those girls. Like we didn't know that already. Like you never did anything embarrassing. Anyway, it's kind of peaceful. Not peaceful, really. Just kind of flat. I don't do anything. I sit there on the hill and think about how like half my family is buried down there. Any second, a black bird could fly out over one of them. I wonder if you can see it when it happens, the affinity wave. What color it is. That's what Miss Kinnelly calls it. An affinity wave. She leads an after-school group for HRs that my dad says I have to go to now. He picked Miss Kinnelly because she's a racist bitch, or as he would put it, "has a strict policy against eastern Europeans attending." I was all "Duh, we're Jewish, and isn't Gram from like Latvia or wherever?" And he was all "Jews aren't Slavic, it's the Slavs who are the problem, why do you think they knew about all the HR vectors before we did?" And I was like "What the hell do you know about HR vectors? Your eyebrows are fucking perfect!"

Anyway, group is deeply pointless. Mostly we talk about who we know who got turned that week, and how it happened. And how scared we all are, even though if you keep talking about how scared you are, eventually you stop really being scared, which I thought was the point of having a group, but apparently not, because being scared is, like, what these people do for fun. All anyone wants to talk about is how it happened to their friend or their brother. It's like someone gets a prize for the most random way. Some girl goes: "Oh my God, my cousin totally drank three bottles of vodka and passed out at the Stop & Rob and woke up a vampire!" And even though that is *highly* retarded, and it probably doesn't work that way, at least, it doesn't work that way yet, everyone goes *oooooh* like she just recited *The Rime of the Ancient Mariner*. Oh, yeah. We had to read that one, too. It's not even about vampires, it's about zombies, which is totally not the same thing, but apparently it falls under supplementary materials or something. Anyway, Miss Kinnelly then lectures for a hundred years about how immoral conduct is the most pernicious of all the causation scenarios, because you can never know where that "moral line" lies. By the time she gets to the part about "abstinence is the only sensible choice," I want to stick her fake nails through her eyes. Once I said, "I hear you can totally get it from drinking from a glass one of them drank from." And they all gasped like I was serious. God. Before, I wouldn't have spent three seconds after school with those people. But the sports program is basically over.

This one time Aidan from my geometry class started talking about staking them, like in old movies. Everyone got real quiet. Thing is, it's not like those movies. A vampire's body doesn't go anywhere if you mess with it. It doesn't go *poof.* It just lies there, and it's a dead person, and you have to bury it, and God, burying things by yourself is practically a crime these days. There's hazmat teams at every funeral. It's the law, for like three years now. Plus, it's not that big a town. Everyone knows everyone, and you try stabbing the kid you used to play softball with in the heart. I couldn't do it. They're still the same kids. They still play softball. We're the ones who've stopped.

Sometimes, when I'm sitting up on the hill by the Greenbaum mausoleum, I think about Emmy. I wonder if she's still going to State in the fall.

Probably not, I guess.

I dated this guy for a while during junior year. His name was Noah. He was okay, I guess. He was super tall, played center for basketball, one of the few sports we still played back then. Indoors, right? I remember when the soccer teams moved indoors. It was horrible, your shoes squeak on the floor because it's shellacked within an inch of its life. The way it used to be, soccer was the only thing I really liked to do. Run around in the grass, in the sun. There's something really satisfying about kicking the ball perfectly so it just flies up, the feeling of nailing it just on the right part of your foot. I've played since I was, like, four. Every league. And then, finally, they just called it off. Too dangerous, not enough girls anymore. You can't just go running around outside like that now. You could fall down. Get cut. Scrape your knee. So now instead of running drills I have to read *The Land Beyond the Forest* for the millionth time and stay inside. God, I'm turning into one of those snotty brainy hipster chicks.

Oh, right, Noah. See, the soccer girls date basketball boys. We're the second tier. Baseballers are somewhere below us, and then there's, like, archery and modern dance circling the drain. And then all the people who cry into their lockers because they can't hit a ball. Football and cheerleaders are up at the top, still, even though it's not exactly 1957 and not exactly the Midwest, where they still play football. But some things stick. I think maybe it's because all the TV shows still have regular high school. It's a network thing. No one wants to show vampires integrating, dating chess geeks, whatever would be jam-packed with soap opera hilarity. TV is strictly *pre*. So we keep acting like what we did in sixth grade matters, even though no one actually plays football or cheers at all. It's like we all froze how we were three or four years ago and we'll never get any older.

Anyway, I remember Noah drank like two jumbo bottles of Diet Coke every day. He'd bring his bottle into class and park it next to his desk. When we kissed, he always tasted like Coke. Everyone thought we were sleeping together, but really, we weren't. It's not that I didn't think I was ready or whatever. Sex just doesn't really seem like that big a deal anymore. I guess it should. My dad says it definitely qualifies as immoral conduct. I just don't think about it, though. Like, what does it matter if Alexis let the yearbook editor go down on her in the darkroom if she found out like not even a week later that the Hep A vac she got for the senior trip to Spain was tainted and now she freaks out if the teacher drops chalk because she has to count the pieces of dust? It's just not that important. Plus, this couple Noah and I hung with sometimes, Dylan and Bethany, turned while they were doing it, just, not even any warning, straight from third base to teeth out in zero point five. We broke up a little after that. Just didn't see much point. I don't watch TV anymore, either.

But lately, I've been seeing him around. He turned during midterms. I think he even dated Emmy for a while, which, fine. I get it. They had a lot in common. I just didn't really want to know. Anyway, it wasn't any big plan. One minute I barely thought about him anymore and the next we're sitting on the swing set in Narragansett Park way past midnight, kicking the gravel and talking about how he still drinks Diet Coke, it just tastes really funny now.

"It's, like, before it was just Coke. But now all I can taste is the aspartame. And not really the aspartame but, like, the chemicals that make up aspartame. I taste what aspartame is like on the inside. I still get the shakes, though. So I'm down to a can a day."

Noah isn't exactly cute. The basketball guys usually aren't, not like the football guys. He's extra lanky and skinny, and the whole vampire thing pretty much comes free with black hair and pale skin. He used to have really nice green eyes.

"How did it happen to you?" I hated saying it like that. But it was the only thing I could think of. How it happens to you. Like a car accident. "You don't have to tell me if you don't want to. If it's, you know, private."

Noah was counting the bits of gravel. He didn't want me to know he was doing it, but he moved his lips when he counted. That's why OCD is on the high-risk list. Because vampires compulsively count everything. I think it's the other way, though. You don't turn because you're OCD. You're OCD because you turned.

"Yeah, no, it's not private. It's just not that interesting. Remember when the HR list first came out and I was so freaked because I was conceived on a Saturday and I have that mole on my hip? I was so sure I'd get it before everyone else. But it didn't happen like I thought, like when that third grader just flipped one day and the CDC guys figured out it was because her mom is a crazy cat lady and she doesn't even have a path to cross without a black cat there to cross it for her. Ana Cruz. I thought it would be like that. Like Ana.

I couldn't *stop* thinking about how it would be. Just walking down the street, and *bang*. But it wasn't. I woke up one night, and this woman was looking in my window. She was older. Pretty, though. She looked . . . kind, I guess."

"How old was she?"

"One of the oldest ones in California, it turned out, so about six? Her name was Maria. She used to be an anesthesiologist, down at the hospital."

"Were you guys . . . together? Or something?"

"No, Scout, you just kind of get to talking eventually. Afterward, there's not that much to do but wait, and she was nice. She stayed with me. Held my hand. She didn't have to. Anyway, I opened the window, but I didn't let her in. I'm not an idiot. I just sat there looking back at her. You know how they look after they're past the first couple of years. All wolfy and hard and stuff. And finally she said, 'Why wait?' And I thought, Shit, she's right. It's gonna happen, sooner or later. I might as well get on with it. If I do it now, at least I can stop *thinking* about it. So I climbed out." He laughed shortly, like a bark. "I didn't invite her in. She invited me out. I guess that's sort of funny. Anyway, you know how it works. I don't want to get all porny on you. It was really gross at first. Blood just tastes like blood, you know? Like hot syrup. But then, it sort of changes, and it was like I could hear her singing, even though she was totally silent the whole time. Anyway. It hurts when you wake up the next night. Like when your arm falls asleep but all over. My mom was really mad."

I picked at the peeling paint on the side of the swing set. "I think about it."

"Oh! Do you want me to . . . ?" God, Noah was always so fucking eager to please. He's like a puppy.

It took me a long time to answer. I totally get him. Why wait. But finally, I just sighed. "I don't think so. I have a bio test tomorrow."

"Okay." Noah lit a cigarette, just like Emmy. He looked like a total tool. Like he's the vampire Marlboro Man or whatever.

"What does blood taste like now?" I asked. I can't help it. I still want to know. I always want to know.

"Singing," he mumbled around the cigarette, and puffed out the smoke without inhaling.

The other week, my uncle Jack came to visit. He lives in Chicago and works for some big advertising company. He did that one billboard with the American Apparel kids all wrapped up in biohazard tape. My mom cooked, which means no salt, and Uncle Jack just wasn't having that. He travels with his own can of Morton's and made sure my steak tasted like beef jerky.

"Kids in your condition have to be extra careful," he said.

"Yeah, I'm not pregnant, Uncle Jack."

"You really can't afford to take the risk, Scout. You have to think about your future. There's so much bleed these days."

That should pretty much tell you everything you need to know about what a bag of smarm my uncle is. He'll use a terrible pun to talk about something that'll probably kill me. He was talking about how that list of common causes is actually kind of out of date. Like how kids used to use textbooks that said, "Maybe someday man will walk on the moon." About a year ago, some of the causes started having baby causes. Like, it doesn't have to be meat killed by a wolf anymore, it can be any predator, so hunting game is right out. Even for non-HRs. We've always kept kosher, so it's not really an issue for us, but plenty of other ones are. They've acted like sex was on the no-no list since the beginning, but I don't think it was. I think that was recent. If sex could turn you into a vampire way back in ancient Hungary, we'd all be sucking moonlight by now. Some people, who are assholes, call this "bleed." But never in front of an HR. It's just flat out rude.

My uncle Jack is an asshole. I mean, I said he was in advertising, right?

"My firm is sponsoring a clean camp up in Wisconsin. Totally safe environment, absolutely scrubbed. For HRs, it's the safest place to be. God, the only place to be, if I were HR! You should think about it."

"I don't really want to move to Wisconsin."

"We wouldn't feel right about that, Jack," said my mother quietly. "We'd rather have her close. We take precautions, we take her in for shots."

Uncle Jack made a fake-sympathetic face and started babbling the way old people do when they want to sound like they care but they don't really. "My heart just breaks for you, Scout, honey. You, especially. You must be so scared, poor thing! I feel like if we could just get a handle on the risk vectors, we could gain some ground with this thing. It's pretty obvious the European embargo isn't doing any good."

"Probably because it's not like it's the Romanian flu, Uncle Jack. You can't blockade *air*. I don't even think it really started there. Practically every culture has vampire legends."

Mom quirked her eyebrow at me.

"Come on, Mom. There's like *nothing* left to do but read. I'm not stupid."

"Well, Scout," continued Uncle Jack in a skeevy isn't-it-cute-how-you-can-talk-like-a-grown-up voice. "You don't see people here detaching their heads and flying around with their spines hanging out, or eating nail clippings with iron teeth, so I think it's safe to say the Slavic regions are the most likely source."

"And AIDS comes from Africa, right? Isn't it funny how

nothing ever comes from us? Nothing's ever our fault, we're just *victims*."

Uncle Jack put down his fork quietly and folded his hands in his lap. He looked up at me, scowling. His face was scary calm.

"I think that kind of back talk qualifies as immoral conduct, young lady."

My mother froze, with her glass halfway to her mouth. I just got up and left. Fuck that and fuck you, you know? But I could hear him as I stomped off. He wanted me to hear him. That's fine, I wanted him to hear me stomping.

"Carol, I know it's hard, but you can't get so attached. These days, kids like her are a lost cause. HRs, well, they're pretty much vampires already."

The problem is, they live forever and they can't have kids. That's it, right there. That's the problem. They don't play nice with the American dream. They won't do the monkey dance. They don't care about what kind of car they drive. They don't care about what's on TV—they know for damn sure *they're* not on TV, so why bother? Guys like Uncle Jack can't sell them anything. I mean, yeah, there's the blood thing, too, but it's not like nobody was getting killed or disappearing before they came along. Anyway, Noah says they mostly feed off each other when they're new.

Blood is blood. Cow, human, deer.

They all think I don't get it, that I'm just a dumb kid who thinks vampires are cool because they all grew up reading those stupid books where some girl goes swooning over a boy vampire because he's so *deep* and *dreamy* and he lived through centuries waiting for *her*. Gag. I guess that's why that crap is banned now. No one wants their daughters getting the idea that all this could ever be hot. But guess what? They don't have body fluids. They only have blood. You do the math. And then come back when you're done throwing up. No one dates vampires.

Anyway, I'm not dumb. It's hard to be dumb when half your friends only come out at night. I get it. Pretty soon they'll outnumber us.

And then, pretty soon after that, it'll be all of us.

Noah and I went to the park most nights. Nobody gave us any shit there—no kids play in parks anymore, anyway. It's just empty. And it was so hot that summer, I couldn't stand being inside. Even at night, I could hardly breathe.

One time Noah brought Emmy along. I wasn't freaked or anything. I knew they weren't dating anymore. Gossip knows no species, you know? I guess it must be pretty lonely to hang out with a human girl all the time and explain your business to her. They sat in the tire swing together and kind of draped their arms and legs all over each other. They didn't make out or anything, they just sat there, touching.

"Do . . . you guys need some time alone?" I asked. Okay, I was a little freaked.

"It's just something we do, Scout," Emmy said, sighing. "Share ambient heat. It's cold."

"Are you kidding? It's like ninety degrees."

"Not for us," Emmy said patiently.

"It's not just that, you know," added Noah. "Ever seen pictures of wolf pups? How they all pile together? Well, you know, some days, a bunch of us just sleep that way. It's . . . comforting."

I plunked down on one of those plastic dragons that bounce back and forth on a big spring. I bounced it a couple of times. I didn't know what to say.

"So what are you guys gonna do in the fall?"

They just looked at each other, kind of sheepish.

Noah moved his leg over Emmy's. It was just about the least sexual thing I've ever seen. "We were thinking we might go to Canada. Lots of us are going. There's jobs up there. On, like, fishing boats and stuff. In Hudson Bay. The nights . . . are really long. It's safer. There's whole towns that are just ours. Communities. And, well. You probably heard, about Aidan?"

Aidan's the kid from group who thinks he's Van Helsing. Emmy sniffed a little and sucked on her cigarette.

"Well, you know, he was kind of seeing Bethany?"

"*What?* Bethany turned like a year ago! Why would he even touch her?"

They shrugged, identically.

"So they were messing around in back of his truck and all of the sudden he just fucking killed her," Noah whispered, like he didn't really believe it. "She trusted him. I mean, God, he let her *feed* off him! That's like . . . I don't know how to explain it so you'll understand, Scout. That's serious shit with us. It's way more intimate than screwing. It's a *pact*. A promise."

Emmy and I glanced at each other, but we didn't say anything. Some things you don't want to say.

Noah's voice cracked. "And he put a piece of his dad's fence through her heart. And they're not even going to arrest him, Scout. He got a *fine*. Disposal of Hazardous Materials Without Supervision."

"It seems like a good time to clear out," said Emmy softly. Her eyes flashed a little in the dark, like a cat's.

"You could come with us," Noah said, trying to sound nonchalant. "I bet you've never even seen snow."

Well, you know what he meant by that.

"I have a scholarship. I'm gonna be a teacher. Teach little kids to do math and stuff."

Noah sighed. "Scout, why?"

"Because I have to do *something*."

* * *

Whenever people have more than five seconds to talk about this, they always come around to the same thing.

Why did it happen? Where did it start?

You know that TV show you used to like? And somewhere around the third season something so awesome and fucked up happened and you just had to know the answer to the mystery, who killed sorority girl whoever or how that guy could come back from the dead? You stayed up all night online looking for clues and spoilers, and still you had to wait all summer to find out? And you were pretty sure the solution would be disappointing, but you wanted it *so bad* anyway? And, oh, man, *everyone* had a theory.

It's like that. They all want to act like it's a matter of national security and we all *have* to know, but seriously, we're way past it mattering. It's just . . . wanting the whole story. Wanting to flip to the end and know everything.

You want to know what I think? There were always vampires. We know that, now. There's still about ten of them who've been around since before Napoleon or whatever. They're in this facility in Nebraska and sometimes somebody gets worked up about their civil rights, but not so much anymore. But something happened and all of a sudden, there were HRs and lists of common causes and clean camps and Uncle Jack's billboards everywhere and Bethany lying dead in the back of a truck and oh, God, they always told us PCP makes you think you can fly, and I'll never play soccer again and at the bottom of it all there's always Emmy's mouth on me in the dark, and the sound of her jaw moving. All of a sudden. One day to the next, and everything changes. Like puberty. One day you're playing with an Easy-Bake and the next day you have breasts and everyone's looking at you differently and you're bleeding, but it's a secret you can't tell anyone. You didn't know it was coming. You didn't know there was another world on the other side of that bloody fucking mess between your legs just waiting to happen to you.

You want to know what I think? I think I aced my bio test. I think in any sufficiently diverse population, mutation always occurs. And if the new adaptation is more viable, well, all those white butterflies swimming in the London soot, they start turning black, one by one by one.

See? I'm not dumb. Maybe I used to be. Maybe before, when it couldn't hurt you to be dumb. Because I know I used to be someone else. I remember her. I used to be someone pretty. Someone good with kids. Someone who knew how to kick a ball really well and that was just about it. But I adapted. That's what you do, when you're a monkey and the tree branches are just a little farther off this season than they were last. Anyway, it doesn't really matter. If it makes you feel better to think God hates us or that some mutation of porphyria went airborne or that in the quantum sense our own cultural memes were always just echoes of alternate matrices and sometimes, just sometimes, there's some pretty deranged crossover or that the Bulgarian revolution flooded other countries with infected refugees? Knock yourself out. But there's no reason. Why did little Ana Cruz turn as fast as you could look twice at her and I've been waiting all summer and hanging out in the dark with Emmy and Noah and I'm fine, when I have way more factors than she did? Doesn't matter. It's all random. It doesn't mean you're a bad person or a good person. It just means you're quick or you're slow.

I went down to Narragansett Park after sunset. The sky was still a little light, all messy red smeary clouds. I'd say it was the color of blood, but you know, everything makes me think of blood these days. Anyway, it was light enough that I could see them before I even turned into the parking lot. Noah and Emmy, shadows on the swing set. I walked up and Noah disentangled himself from her.

"I brought you a present," he said. He reached down into his backpack and pulled out a soccer ball.

I smiled something *huge*. He dropped it between us and kicked it over. I slapped it back, lightly, with the side of my foot, toward Emmy. She grinned and shoved her bangs out of her face. It felt really nice to kick that stupid ball. My throat got all thick, just looking at it shine under the streetlight.

Emmy knocked it hard, up over my head, out onto the wet grass, and we all took off after it, laughing. We booted it back and forth, that awesome sound, that *amazing* sound of the ball smacking against a sneaker thumping between us like a heartbeat and the grass all long and uncut under our feet and the bleeding, bleeding sky and I thought: This is it. This is my last night alive.

I kicked the ball as hard as I could. It soared up into the air and Noah caught it, in his hands, like a goalie. He looked at me, still holding up the ball like an idiot, and he was crying. They cry blood. It doesn't look nice. They look like monsters when they cry.

"So," I said. "Hudson Bay."

TRANSITION

by Melissa Marr

TOMORROW

Sebastian lowered the body to the ground in the middle of a
dirt-and-gravel road in the far back of a graveyard. "Crossroads
matter, Eliana."

He pulled a long, thin blade and slit open the stomach. He
reached his whole forearm inside the body. His other hand,
the one holding the knife, pressed down on her chest. "Until
this moment, she could recover."

Eliana said nothing, did nothing.

"But hearts matter." He pulled his arm out, a red slippery
thing in his grasp.

He tossed it to Eliana.

"That needs buried in sanctified ground, and she"—he
stood, pulled off his shirt, and wiped the blood from his arm
and hand—"needs to be left at crossroad."

Afraid that it would fall, Eliana clutched the heart in

both hands. It didn't matter, not really, but she didn't want to drop it in the dirt. *Which is where we will put it.* But burying it seemed different from letting it fall on the dirt road.

Sebastian slipped something from his pocket, pried open the corpse's mouth, and inserted it between her lips. "Wafers, holy objects of any faith, put these in the mouth. Once we used to stitch the mouth shut, too, but these days that attracts too much attention."

"And dead bodies with missing hearts don't?"

"They do." He lifted one shoulder in a small shrug.

Eliana tore her gaze from the heart in her hands and asked, "But?"

"You need to know the ways to keep the dead from waking, and I'm feeling sentimental." He walked back toward the crypt where the rest of their clothes were, leaving her the choice to follow him or leave.

TODAY

"Back later," Eliana called as she slipped out the kitchen door. The screen door slammed behind her, and the porch creaked as she walked over it. Sometimes she thought her aunt and uncle let things fall into disrepair because it made it impossible to sneak in—*or out*—of the house. Of course, that would imply that they noticed if she was there.

Why should they be any different from anyone else?

She went over to a sagging lawn chair that sat in front of

a kiddie pool in their patchy grass. Her cousin's kids had been there earlier in the week, and no one had bothered to put the pool back inside the shed yet. The air was sticky enough that filling it up with the hose and lying out under the stars didn't sound half bad.

Except for the part where I have to move.

Eliana closed her eyes and leaned her head back. One of the headaches she'd been having almost every day the past couple months played at the edge of her eye. The doctor said they were migraines or stress headaches or maybe a PMS thing. She didn't care what they were, just that they stop, but the pills he gave her didn't help that much—and were more money than her aunt felt like paying for all the good they did.

On to Plan B: self-medicate.

She tucked up her skirt so it didn't drag in the mud, propped her boots on the end of the kiddie pool, and noticed another bruise on her calf. The bruises and the headaches scared her, made her worry that there was something really wrong with her, but no one else seemed to think it was a big deal.

She closed her eyes and waited for her medicine to arrive.

"Why are you sleeping out here?" Gregory glanced back at her empty front porch. "Everything okay?"

"Yeah." She blinked a few times and looked at him. "Just another headache. What time is it?"

"I'm late, but"—he took her hands and pulled her to her feet—"I'll make it up to you. I have a surprise."

He'd slid a pill into her hand. She didn't bother asking what it was; it didn't matter. She popped it into her mouth and held out her hand. He offered her a soda bottle, and she washed the pill taste out of her mouth with whatever mix of liquor he'd had in with the cola. Unlike pills and other things, good liquor was more of a challenge to get.

They walked a few blocks in silence before he lit a joint. By the look of the darkened houses they'd passed, it was late enough that no one was going to be sitting on their stoop or out with kids. Even if they did look, they wouldn't know for sure if it was a cigarette—and since Gregory didn't often smoke, there was no telltale passing it back and forth to clue anyone in.

"Headaches that make a person miss hours can't be"—she inhaled, pulling the lovely numbing smoke into her throat and lungs—"normal. That doctor"—she exhaled—"is a joke."

Gregory slid his arm around her low back. "Hours?"

She nodded. Her doctor had given her a suspicious look and asked about drugs when she'd mentioned that she felt like she was missing time, but then she could honestly say that she hadn't taken drugs. The drugs came after the doctor couldn't figure out what was wrong. She tried the over-the-counter stuff, cutting out soda, eating different foods. The headaches and the bruises weren't changed at all. *Neither is the time thing.*

"Maybe you just need to, you know, de-stress." Gregory kissed her throat.

Eliana didn't roll her eyes. He wasn't a bad guy, but he wasn't looking for a soul mate. They didn't discuss it, but it was a pretty straightforward deal they had going. He had medicine that took away her headaches better than anything else had, and she did the girlfriend bit. She got the better part of the deal—meds and entry into every party. Headaches had taken her from stay-at-home book geek to party regular in a couple months.

"We're here," he murmured.

She took another hit at the gates of Saint Bartholomew's.

"Come on, El." Gregory let go of her long enough to push open the cemetery gate. It should've been locked, but the padlock was more decoration than anything. She was glad: Crawling over the fence, especially in a skirt, sounded more daunting than she was up for tonight.

After he pushed the gate shut and adjusted the lock so it looked like it was closed, Gregory took her hand.

She imagined herself with a long cigarette holder in a smoky club. He'd be wearing something classy, and she'd have on a funky flapper dress. Maybe he rescued her from a lame job, and she was his moll. They partied like crazy because he'd just pulled a bank job and—

"Come on." He pulled her toward the slope of the hill near the older mausoleums.

The grass was slick with dewdrops that sparkled in the moonlight, but she forced herself to focus on her feet. The world spun just this side of too much as the combined headache cures blended. At the top, she stopped and pulled a long drag into her lungs. There were times when she could swear she could feel the smoke curling over her tongue, could feel the whispery form of it caught in the force of her inhalation.

Gregory slipped a cold hand under her shirt, and she closed her eyes. The hard press of the gravestone behind her was all that held her up. *Stones to hold me down and smoke to lift me up.*

"Come on, Eliana," he mumbled against her throat. "I need you."

Eliana concentrated on the weight of the smoke in her lungs, the lingering taste of cheap liquor on her lips, the pleasant hum of everything in her skin. If Gregory stopped talking, stopped breathing, if . . . *If he was someone else*, she admitted. *Something else.*

His breath was warm on her throat.

She imagined that his breath was warm because he'd drained the life out of someone, because he'd just come from taking the final drops of life out of some horrible person. *A bad person who*—the thought of that was ruining her buzz, though, so she concentrated on the other parts of the fantasy: He only killed bad people, and he had just rescued her from something awful. Now, she was going to show him that she was grateful.

"Right here," she whispered. She lowered herself to the ground and looked up at him.

"Out in the open?"

"Yes." She leaned back against a stone, tilted her head, and pushed her hair over her shoulder so her throat was bared to him.

Permission to sink your fangs into me . . . He asked. He always asked first.

Gregory knelt in front of her and kissed her throat. He had no fangs, though. He had a thudding pulse and a warm body. He was nothing like the stories, the characters she read about before she fell asleep at night, the vague face in her fantasies. Gregory was here; that was enough.

She moved to the side a little so she could lie back in the grass.

Gregory was still kissing her throat, her shoulder, the small bit of skin bared above her bra line. It wasn't what she wanted. *He* wasn't what she wanted. He *was* what she had.

"Bite me."

He pulled back and stared at her. "Elia—"

"*Bite* me," she repeated.

He bit her, gently, and she turned her head toward the gravestone. She traced the words: THERE IS NO DEATH, WHAT SEEMETH SO IS TRANSITION.

"Transition," she whispered. That's what she wanted, a transition to something new. Instead she was stretched out in the dew-wet grass staring at the wingless angel crouched on the crypt behind Gregory. It was centered over the lintel of a mausoleum door almost as if it was watching her.

She shivered and licked her lips.

Gregory was pulling up her shirt. Eliana sighed, and he took it for encouragement. It wasn't for him, though: It was for a fantasy that she'd been having every night.

Eliana couldn't see the face of the monster. He'd found her again, though, offered her whispered promises and sharp pleasures, and she'd said yes. She couldn't remember the words to the questions, but she knew he'd asked. That detail was clear as nothing else was. Shouldn't fantasies be clear? That was the point, really: Fantasies were to be the detailed imaginings to make up for the bleak reality.

She opened her eyes, pushing the fantasies away as headache threatened again, and she saw a girl walking up the hill toward them. Tall glossy boots covered her legs almost to her short black skirt, but at the top—just below the hem of the sheer black skirt—pale white skin interrupted the darkness of the sleek vinyl and silk skirt. "Gory! You left the party before we got there. I *told* you I wanted to see you tonight."

Gregory looked over his shoulder. "Nikki. Kind of busy here."

Undeterred, Nikki hopped up on the gravestone beside Eliana's head and peered down at them. "So what's *your* name?"

"El . . . Eliana."

"Sorry, El," Gregory murmured. He moved a little to the side, propped himself up on one arm, and smiled at Nikki. "Could we catch you later?"

"But I'm here now." Nikki kicked her feet and stared at Eliana.

Eliana blinked, trying to focus her eyes. It wasn't working: The wingless angel looked like it was on a different mausoleum now. She looked away from it to stare at Gregory. "My head hurts again, Gory."

"Shh, El. It's okay." He brushed a hand over her hair and then glared at Nikki. "You need to take a walk."

"But I had a question for *Elly*." Nikki hopped down to stand beside them. "Are you and Gory in love, Elly dear? Is Gory that special someone you'd die for?"

Eliana wasn't sure who the girl was, but she was too out of it to lie. "No."

"El . . ." Gregory rolled back over so he was on top of her. His eyes were widened in what looked like genuine shock.

Nikki flung a leg over Gregory so she was straddling both Gregory and Eliana; she leaned down to look into Eliana's eyes. "Have you already met someone new then? Someone who you dream—"

"Nicole, stop it," another voice said.

For a strange moment, Eliana thought it was the wingless angel on the crypt. She wanted to look, but Nikki reached down and forced Eliana to look only at her.

"Do stone angels usually speak?" Eliana whispered.

"Poor Gory." Nikki shook her head—and then pressed herself against Gregory. "To die for a girl who doesn't even think you're special. It's sad, really."

He started to try to buck her off. "That not funn—"

Nikki pushed herself tighter to his back. "You seem like a nice guy, and I wanted your last minutes to be special, Gory. Really, I did, but"—she reached down and slashed open Gregory's throat with a short blade—"you talk too much."

Blood sprayed over Eliana, over the grass, and over Nikki.

And then Nikki leaned down and sank her teeth into the already bleeding flesh of Gregory's neck.

Gregory arched and twisted, trying to get free, trying to escape, but Nikki was on his back, swallowing his blood and pressing him against Eliana.

Eliana started to scream, but Nikki covered her mouth and nose. "Shut up, Elly."

And Eliana couldn't move, couldn't turn her head, couldn't breathe. She stared up at Nikki, who licked Gregory's blood from her lips, as the pressure in her chest increased. She tried to move her legs, still pinned under Gregory's body; she grabbed Nikki's wrists ineffectually. She scratched and batted at Nikki as everything went dark, as Nikki suffocated her.

Graveyard soil filled Eliana's mouth, and a damp sensation was all over her. She opened her eyes, blinked a few times, spit out the dirt, but that was as much as she could manage for the moment. Her body felt different: Her nerves sent messages too fast, her tongue and nose drawing more flavors in with each breath than she could identify, and breathing itself wasn't the same. She stopped breathing, waiting for tightness in her chest, gasping, *something*. It didn't come. Breathing was a function of tasting the air, not inflating her lungs. Carefully, she turned her head to the side.

She wasn't in the same spot, but the same wingless angel stood atop a gravestone watching her.

He was alive. He looked down at her with shadow-dark eyes, and she wondered how she'd mistaken him for a sculpture. *Because I couldn't see this clearly. . . or smell . . . or hear.* She swallowed audibly, as she realized what she didn't hear: The angel who had watched her die wasn't alive either.

She swiped a hand over her eyes, brushing something sticky from her eyelids. Not too many hours ago—*she thought*—she'd coated her lashes in heavy mascara and outlined her eyes in thick black liner. It wasn't eyeliner that she smeared over her temple. *No.* The memory of Gregory's blood all over her face came back in a rush.

Eliana could hear the sounds of people walking outside the graveyard, could smell the peculiar cologne the crypt angel wore, could taste the lingering mustiness of the soil that she'd had in her mouth. *And blood.* Gregory's blood was on her lips. Absently, she lifted her hand and licked the dirt-caked dried blood—and was neither disgusted nor upset by the flavor.

"Up." A boot connected with her side.

Without looking, Eliana caught the boot. She felt slick vinyl over a toned leg. Holding the boot, she looked away from the crypt angel and stared at the boot's owner.

"Nikki," Eliana said. "You're Nikki."

"Nice catch." Nikki crouched down. "Now get up."

Eliana was sober now—or perhaps completely mad. Her face was wet with blood and dirt, and she was lying in a mound of fresh soil. It wasn't a hole. She hadn't been buried *in* the ground. Instead, she was on her back on top of the ground.

Like I was when Nikki killed Gory . . . and me.

But the moonlight falling on Eliana's soil-covered body felt like raw energy, pushing away all of her confusion, re-forming her. It had saturated the soil in which she was lying, and the energy of the two pricked her skin like tiny teeth biting her all over. She wanted to stay there, soak in the moonlight and the soil, until everything made sense again.

"Get up." Nikki tangled her fingers in Eliana's hair and stood.

Eliana came to her feet, wishing she could stop or at least pause longer in the fresh-turned earth. *At least the moonlight is still falling.* It felt like a very light rain, tangible but too delicate to capture.

She stepped backward, and Nikki released her.

"You *killed* me," Eliana said. It was not a question or an accusation but something between the two. Things felt uncertain; memory and reality and logic weren't all coming together cohesively. "Suffocated me."

"I did." Nikki walked over and tugged open the door of the crypt where the angel had been perched. "Come, or you'll go hungry."

The angel from the crypt walked between Eliana and Nicole. "Kill her and be done with it, Nicole. These games grow tedious. You've made your point."

"Don't be difficult, or"—Nikki went up on tiptoes and kissed him—"you'll go hungry, too."

He didn't move, even when she leaned her whole weight against him. The angel's expression remained unchanged. "Do you think she matters? She's just some girl."

"No. Here she is"—Nikki grabbed Eliana by the arm and shook her—"*proof* that you picked her. *Again.* How many of them has it been now? Twenty? Fifty?"

"I got careless." The angel shrugged. "Tormenting her is foolish, but if it amuses you . . ."

Nikki stared at him, her hand tightening on Eliana's arm. Then, still holding on to Eliana, she walked into the crypt.

"Wash. There's water over there"—Nikki pointed to the corner where a cooler of melting ice sat—"and your outfit . . . hmm?"

As Eliana dropped to the floor in front of the melting ice, Nikki looked behind them at the angel, who'd come to stand just outside the door. She opened a wooden trunk on the floor. "What do you think?"

"Nothing you want to hear." Then the angel walked away.

Sebastian watched Eliana with growing doubt. He'd tried to pick a strong one this time. *Blood and moonlight.* That was the key. *Killed under the full moon with enough vampire blood already in them.* For two months, he'd kept her hidden, fed her, prepared her, yet here she was like a mindless sheep.

Nicole always waited to see if they woke; she knew how often he'd been unfaithful, but she always hoped. Sometimes, the newly dead girls hadn't had enough of his blood to wake back up. Nicole took those as victories, as if killing them before they'd had enough of his blood meant she was still special. She wasn't. If he could kill her himself, he would've done so decades ago, but her blood was why he was transformed, and vampires couldn't kill the one whose blood has remade them. *And mortals can't kill us.* It left him very few options.

"What are you doing?" Nicole had followed him. She shoved him face-first into the side of another mausoleum. "You don't just walk away when I have questions! How am I to get changed if I have to *guess* how I look? What if—"

"You look beautiful, Nicole." He wiped a trickle of blood from his forehead.

"Really?"

"Always." He held out the blood on his finger, and she kissed it away.

There wasn't any sense in arguing with her. It only prolonged the inevitable, and he wasn't in the mood to watch her take out her temper on the barely conscious vampire girl who watched them from the doorway of the crypt where Nicole had left her.

"She needs help." He kept his voice bland.

Nicole's gaze followed his to the shivering girl. "So dress her up. I want to go play before I kill her."

"Are you sure?"

With a vulnerability that he'd once thought endearing, Nicole asked, "Does that bother you? Does she matter then?"

"No," Sebastian murmured. "Not at all."

The angel and Nicole returned. A dim voice inside whispered that Eliana shouldn't be standing here, that being in the dirty crypt was not good, but then Nicole smiled and Eliana's mind grew hazy.

"Sebastian will tell you what to wear, Elly." Nicole held out her hand, palm up. Obediently, Eliana extended her arm, and Nicole lifted Eliana's hand to her lips.

"Don't say a word," Nicole whispered before she kissed each of Eliana's fingertips. "Okay?"

"Okay," Eliana answered.

"I"—Nikki broke a finger—"said"—and another—"not"— and another—"to speak."

Eliana stumbled backward from the pain.

Sebastian caught her. He held her against him, keeping her from falling.

"Buttons." Nicole pointed at a wooden trunk. "There's pants that button all the way up on each leg. She can wear those."

Eliana watched her leave. Once Nikki was out of sight, some semblance of clarity returned again. "I remember you." Eliana stared at Sebastian. "You were *somewhere*. . . . I know you."

He didn't reply. Instead, he held out a pair of pants with tiny buttons from ankle to hip.

"Why is this happening?" she asked. "I don't understand."

When she didn't move, he dropped to the ground, tugged off her shoes. The motions, the sense of his proximity, felt familiar. "You just woke, Eliana. The confusion will fade."

"No," Eliana corrected. She held up her hand. "Why did she kill me? Why did she hurt me?"

"Because she can." He pulled off her muddy jeans and bloody shirt, leaving her shivering in nothing but her underwear. Silently, he ripped a T-shirt that was in the trunk, dipped it in the ice water, and started washing the blood from her.

"Can you do this?" he asked. "Like I am?"

Eliana grabbed the wet shirt. The pain in her hand should be bringing tears to her eyes. *A lot of things should.* She wanted to escape, to get away from Nikki. *And him . . . I think.* Her hand throbbed, but the hunger she felt was worse. "I'm a lot more capable than you think."

Sebastian changed into a black shirt and, oddly, slipped a dark silk scarf into his pants pocket. His gaze was unwavering as he did so. "Let's not tell Nicole that."

"She killed me . . . and Gory, but"—Eliana shivered as she washed away Gregory's blood and felt guilty that the sight of it made her stomach growl "I'm not . . . she's . . . you . . ."

"Just like you. Dead. Undead. Vampire. Pick your term." Sebastian took the wet shirt back and held out a pair of pants. "Step in."

"I see why you picked her." Nikki's voice drew Eliana's attention. "It'll almost be a shame when she dies."

Eliana's gaze fastened on Nikki. *When I die?* She looked at

Sebastian. *He picked me? For what?* Neither vampire moved for a moment; neither spoke; and Eliana wasn't sure she wanted to speak her questions aloud—or if it would help.

"We're ready to go," she said.

I'm not ready for any of this. Not really. But it was here, and she felt pretty certain that getting out of the graveyard was a good first step to something. *Hopefully something that involves me not dying. Again.*

Sebastian swept Nicole into his arms. He'd watched Eliana assess both of them, seen her weigh and measure what she could glean of the situation, and he was excited. The new vampire was conscious and angry, and had no memory of him. After so many dead girls, he finally had the right one. *This must've been what Nicole felt when she found me.* It was almost enough to make him forgive her. *Almost.*

"Let's go to dinner, Nik." He couldn't keep the tremor out of his voice.

Nicole smiled and kissed him with the same passion they'd shared for decades—enough so that he debated one last tumble. But Eliana was hungry, and he was looking forward to a new future.

With Eliana trailing behind them, he carried Nicole through the graveyard and down the street. *Just as when we were first together.* On what he hoped would be the last night, he felt renewed tenderness for her. *And hope.*

No one spoke as they made their way through the streets to the party.

Sebastian lowered Nicole to the ground just outside the house, and she led them inside. She didn't doubt her superiority. *Why should she?* Eliana was no match for Nicole in a fight, and Sebastian was physically unable to strike her. Unless Eliana chose to take control of the situation, Nicole would be safe, and Eliana would die at the end of the night.

And I'll have to start over . . . again.

The humans weren't surprised to see any of them; if anything, a few of the assessing looks made Sebastian wish that he could keep both Nicole and Eliana for a while, but unless they were romantically involved, vampires of the same gender rarely had the ability to be around one another without territory issues.

The music thumped. Drunk humans danced and hooked up in shadowed corners. Finding a bite to eat was almost too easy. Sebastian missed proper hunting. Nicole insisted on staying in the graveyard, but she didn't like to hunt anymore.

The precise opposite of the way traditions should be observed.

He hated this, the tedium of plucking the humans like produce at a grocer. He hated living in the gloom and dank of graveyards. The soil was transportable. The humans were discardable, food on legs but with bank accounts. If they modernized, as he had begun to do, they could live in comfort: hunt food, gather funds, and relocate.

If she'd changed, I wouldn't have to do this. He cupped Nicole's face in his hands, kissed her, and manipulated her once more: "I can watch her while you—"

"Go find a snack"—Nicole caught Eliana's hand, though, not letting the new vampire free to find food—"since you wouldn't eat earlier. We'll *both* be here."

Eliana watched, studying him, obviously looking for the truth behind his words and actions. Lying to her would be harder. Winning her approval would be a true challenge. *Unlike Nicole.* Vampires had a peculiar protectiveness, an almost pathological adoration of the humans they turned. It was why Nicole had never killed him despite his perpetual unfaithfulness. *She's weak. I won't be.* He hadn't killed Eliana himself. It was his blood in her veins, but he hadn't murdered her.

He stared at them both. The music thrummed in the room, heartbeats beckoned, warm bodies surrounded them. Both Nicole and Eliana looked back at him, and he forced himself to look only at Nicole as he smiled. "My lady."

The hunger in Nikki's gaze as she watched Sebastian walk away was pitiful. For all of her cruelty, the vampire was desperate for Sebastian's attention.

"He's beautiful," Eliana murmured, "but he doesn't really seem that into you."

Nikki's gaze snapped to Eliana. "He's been mine for longer than you've been alive."

The possessiveness that was creeping into Eliana was less about Sebastian than about taking him from Nikki. He *was* attractive, but attractive guys weren't worth fighting over. *Especially guys who stood by while someone murdered you.*

"He seems like the sort who would sleep with whatever's handy." Eliana paused at the words. He *was* that sort; she was sure of it. All the headaches, the fantasies, they made sense. Sebastian had come to her outside the library. He'd been charming; he'd paid attention to her. He'd asked to walk with her, to kiss her, to touch her, to bite her. *He gave me his blood.* For that, he hadn't asked permission. *He made me forget.*

"The fantasies . . . they were memories. When I wanted Gory to bite me . . . that was because of Sebastian."

"Yes," Nikki hissed. Her hold on Eliana's hand tightened. "But don't think you're special. He's strayed before. He—"

"Special?" Eliana laughed. "*I* don't want to be special to him. *You* do."

He said I would be his if I was strong enough.

Sebastian stood midway up the stairs. He really was gorgeous, and if the memories that were returning to her were true, he was even more so without the clothes. She licked her lips and was amused to see an answering smile from him.

He didn't say I would be murdered.

"Nik?" He called out to Nicole, but his gaze was on Eliana,

not Nikki. "I changed my mind. Come with me?"

Eliana's stomach growled loudly, but the music was too loud for anyone but Nikki to hear it. She remembered blood, the taste of it, the number of times she'd swallowed it. He'd assured her that when she remembered, she'd be strong.

But you can't remember now, not until you wake, Elly, he'd repeated. *Then you'll be strong and clever, and you'll know what to do.*

She did know what to do. Keeping hold of Nikki's hand, Eliana shimmied through the crowd.

At the top of the stairs, a girl leaned against the wall. Eliana had partied with her a few times, but not enough that she remembered the girl's name. Sebastian was nuzzling the girl's throat. He held a hand out behind him, and Nikki took it.

He pulled her close and hooked his arm around her waist. Beside them was an open door. With one arm around the girl whose throat he'd been kissing and one arm around Nikki, he took a step toward the unoccupied bedroom.

"Hey." The girl looked at Sebastian dazedly and stepped away. "What—"

"Shh." He released Nikki and led the girl inside. "Close the door, Eliana."

He shoved the girl toward Eliana, who caught hold of her with both hands and steadied her. Eliana felt a twinge of regret, but it was quashed by hunger.

"Do you really want her to eat?" Nikki asked. Desperate

hope was plain in Nikki's expression. She reached up on her tiptoes and kissed Sebastian—who watched Eliana as he and Nikki kissed.

The drunk girl he'd found looked from Sebastian to Eliana. "I don't do the group thing. I mean . . . I'm not . . . I thought he was . . ." The girl looked over at Sebastian. "I don't know what's going on."

"Shh." Eliana stroked the girl's face comfortingly and pulled her closer. "There's no group thing. It's okay."

The girl nodded, and Eliana lowered her mouth to the girl's throat, covering the same spot where Sebastian had kissed. It was nature, not logic, that told Eliana where to bite. It was simple biology that made her canines extend and pierce skin.

Sebastian had his eyes open while he kissed Nikki, watching as Eliana bit the girl.

It wasn't disgusting. Well, it *was*, but not in a rather-die-than-eat way. It was instinct. Like any animal, Eliana hungered, and so she ate.

She didn't gorge, didn't kill the girl, but she swallowed the blood until she felt stronger. *If a bit tipsy.* The buzz that she got from drinking the girl's blood was somewhere between a good high and a delicious meal. *Familiar.* The taste wasn't new. *His blood was better.*

Eliana let the girl fall to the floor and looked at him.

Sebastian and Nikki were all over each other. Nikki had

pushed him against the wall, leaving her back to Eliana, and he was cupping the back of Nikki's head with one hand. His other hand was on the small of her back.

"Nicole," he murmured. He kissed her collarbone. Without pausing in his affections, he lifted his gaze and looked at Eliana.

The temptation to rip Nikki out of his arms was sudden and violent. It was irrational and ugly and utterly exciting. All she wanted was to tear out the other vampire's throat, not to feed, not carefully. *Like she did to Gory.* Eliana couldn't: In a fair fight, Nikki would kill Eliana.

She felt her teeth cutting into her lip and opened her mouth on a snarl.

She stepped forward. Her hands were curled in fists.

Fists aren't enough.

"I need"—she looked at Sebastian—"help."

Sebastian spun so Nikki was now the one against the wall, with his body pressed against her. With one hand he caught her wrist and held it to the wall.

Nikki looked past him to Eliana. "For centuries he's been mine. A few weeks of being with you is *nothing.*"

"Two months," he murmured as he raised Nikki's other wrist so he was holding them both in his grasp.

Then he kissed her, and she let her eyes close.

Sebastian reached back and lifted the bottom of his shirt.

In a worn leather sheath against his spine, there was a knife.

Eliana walked toward it and wrapped her hands around the hilt of the knife.

She stood there, her knuckles against his skin.

He made me this. He knew she'd murder me. Eliana remembered the blood and the kisses. He'd picked her, changed her life. *But Nikki suffocated me.*

Eliana wanted to kill them both. She couldn't, though; even if he gave her access to his throat, she couldn't raise a hand to him. She wasn't sure why, but she couldn't do it.

And with his help, I can kill Nikki.

With a growl, Eliana stabbed the knife into Nikki's throat.

Sebastian held Nikki up, his body still pressed against her, and kissed her as she struggled. He swallowed her screams, so no one heard.

Then he pulled back. He held out his arm, and Eliana moved closer. She reached up and covered Nikki's mouth with her hand, just as Nikki had done to her.

"Go ahead," he whispered.

Eliana closed her mouth over the wound in Nikki's throat and swallowed. Her blood was different from the human girl's blood; it was richer.

Like Sebastian's.

Nikki struggled, but Sebastian held her still. He held them both in his embrace while Eliana drank from her murderer's throat. For more than a minute, they stayed like that. The sounds of drinking and soft struggles were covered by the noise downstairs.

Then Nikki stopped fighting, and Eliana pulled back.

Sebastian let her go, and he sat on the bed, cradling Nikki in his arms while he drank from the now motionless vampire. If not for the fact that she was staring glassy-eyed at nothing and her arm dangled limply, it would almost have seemed tender.

Sebastian wrapped the scarf that he'd brought with him around her throat to hide her wound. Then he and Eliana washed Nicole's blood from their faces and hands. They stood side by side in the adjoining bathroom.

Back in the bedroom, he slipped a few trinkets into his pockets and grabbed a messenger bag from the closet. Eliana said nothing. She hadn't spoken since before Nicole's death.

"There are clothes in the closet that would fit you," he suggested.

She changed in silence.

He took the bloodied clothes and shoved them into the bag, lifted Nicole into his arms, positioned her head, and carried her as he had done earlier. In silence, they walked downstairs and out the door. A few people watched drunkenly, but most everyone was too busy getting lost in either a body or a drink.

Eliana was more disturbed by murdering Nikki than she had been by being murdered *by* her—mostly because she'd enjoyed killing Nikki.

She closed the door to the house behind her. For a moment, she paused. *Can I run?* She didn't know where she'd go, didn't know anything about what she was—other than dead and monstrous. *Are there limitations?* There were two ways to find out if the television and book versions of vampire weaknesses were true: test them or ask.

Instead of following Sebastian, she sped up and walked beside him. "Will you answer questions?"

"Some." He smiled. "If you stay."

She nodded. It wasn't anything other than what she expected, not after tonight. She walked through the streets in the remaining dark, headed back to the graveyard where she'd been murdered, escorting the corpse that *she'd* murdered.

Inside the graveyard, they walked to the far bottom of the hill, in the back where the oldest graves were.

Sebastian lowered Nikki to the ground in the middle of a dirt-and-gravel road in the far back of a graveyard. "Crossroads matter, Eliana."

He pulled a long, thin blade from Nikki's boot and slit open her stomach. He reached his whole forearm inside the body. His other hand, the one holding the knife, pressed down on Nikki's chest, holding her still. "Until this moment, she could recover."

Eliana said nothing, did nothing.

"But hearts matter." He pulled his arm out, a red slippery thing in his grasp.

He tossed it to Eliana.

"That needs buried in sanctified ground, and she"—he stood, pulled off his shirt, and wiped Nicole's blood from his arm and hand—"needs to be left at crossroad."

Afraid that it would fall, Eliana clutched the heart in both hands. It didn't matter, not really, but she didn't want to drop it in the dirt. *Which is where we will put it.* But burying it seemed different than letting it fall on the dirt road.

Sebastian slipped something than his pocket, pried open Nikki's mouth, and inserted it between her lips. "Wafers, holy objects of any faith, put these in the mouth. Once we used to stitch the mouth shut, too, but these days that attracts too much attention."

"And dead bodies with missing hearts don't?"

"They do." He lifted one shoulder in a small shrug.

Eliana tore her gaze from the heart in her hands and asked, "But?"

"You need to know the ways to keep the dead from waking again, and I'm feeling sentimental." He walked back toward the crypt where the rest of their clothes were, leaving her the choice to follow him or leave.

She followed him, carrying Nikki's heart carefully.

"Killing on full or new moon matters," he added when

she caught up with him.

She nodded. The things he was telling her mattered, and she wanted to be attentive to them, but she'd just killed a person.

With his help . . . because of him . . . like an animal.

And now he was standing there shirtless and bloodied.

Is it because I slept with him? She listened to the words he said now, trying to remember the words he'd said *then*. Those words mattered, too. *He planned this. He knew she'd kill me. He watched.*

"She killed me under the full moon," Eliana said.

"Yes." He wrapped Nicole's heart in his shirt. "You were born again with blood and moonlight."

"Why?"

"Some animals are territorial, Eliana." He looked at her then, and it was like stepping into her own memories. That was the same look he'd given her when she'd first gone with him, when she'd been alive and bored: It was a look that said she mattered, that she was the most important thing in his world.

And I am now.

He was looking at her the way Nikki had watched him. He brushed her hair away from her face. "We are territorial, so when we touch another, our partners respond poorly."

"Why were you with me then? You knew that . . ." She couldn't finish the sentence.

"She'd kill you?" He shrugged again, but he didn't step away to give her more room. "Yes, when she found you, when I was ready."

"You *meant* for her to kill me?" Eliana put both hands on his chest as she stared up at him.

"It was preferable that she do it," he said. "I planned very carefully. I *picked* you."

"You picked me," she echoed. "You picked me to be murdered."

"To be changed." Sebastian cupped her chin in his hand and tilted her head up to meet his gaze. "I needed you, Eliana. Mortals aren't strong enough to kill us, and we can't strike the one whose blood made us. The one whose blood runs inside us is safe from our anger. You can't strike me. I couldn't strike her."

"You wanted her to find me and kill me, so I would kill her for you?" Eliana clarified. She felt like she was going to be sick. She'd been used. She *had* killed for him, been killed for him.

"I was tired of Nicole, but it was more than that." He wrapped his arms around her waist and held tight as she tried to pull away. "We still need the same nutrients that we needed as humans, but our bodies can no longer extract them from solid food. So we take the blood from those who can extract the nutrients."

"Humans."

He nodded once. "We don't need that much, and the shock and pain makes most people forget us. It hurts, you know, ripping holes in people's skin."

She dropped a hand to her leg in suddenly remembered pain. It *did* hurt. Her entire thigh had been bruised afterward. *And her chest.* At the time, she couldn't remember what the bruises were from. *And the bend of her arm.*

He kissed her throat, softly, the way she'd fantasized about afterward when she'd believed it was just a dream, when headaches kept her from remembering more.

"Why?" she asked again. "You needed a meal and a murderer. That didn't mean you needed to screw me."

"Oh, but I *did*. I needed you." His breath wasn't warm on her throat; it was a damp breeze that shouldn't be appealing. "The living are so warm . . . and you were perfect. There were others, but I didn't keep them. I was careful with you."

She remembered him looking at her and asking permission.

"Sometimes I can't help but want to be inside humans, but I won't keep them. We're together now." He kissed her throat, not at her pulse, but where her neck met her shoulder. "I chose you."

Eliana didn't move away.

"Nikki found out, though." He sighed the words.

"So she killed me." Eliana stepped backward, out of his embrace.

Sebastian had an unreadable expression as he caught and held her gaze. "Of course. Would you do any differently?"

"I . . ."

"If I left you tonight and sank into some girl—or guy—would you forgive me?" He reached out and entwined his fingers with hers. "Would you mind if I kissed someone else the way I kiss you? If I knelt at their feet and asked permission to—"

"Yes." She squeezed his hand until she saw him wince. "*Yes.*"

He nodded. "As I said, territorial."

Eliana shook her head. "So that's it? We kill, but not under full or new moon. We drink blood, but really not so much. If we *do* kill, it's some sort of territorial bullshit."

"An area can support only so many predators. I have you, and you have me."

"So I killed Nicole, and now you're my mate?" She wasn't sure whether she was excited or disgusted.

Or both.

Sebastian whispered, "Until one of us makes someone alert enough and strong enough to kill the other, yes."

She pulled her hand out of his. "Yeah? So how do I do that?"

Sebastian had her pinned against the crypt wall before she could blink.

"I'm not telling you that, Eliana. That's part of the game." He rested his forehead against hers in a mockery of tenderness.

She looked at the floor of the crypt where Nicole's heart had fallen. The bloodied shirt lay in the thin layer of soil that covered the cracked cement floor. Moss decorated the sides where the dampness had seeped into the small building.

Transition. Eliana felt an echo of herself crying out, but the person she'd been was dead.

She looked at Sebastian and smiled. *A game?* She might not be able to kill him yet, but she'd figure it out. She'd find someone to help her—and unlike Sebastian, she wouldn't be arrogant enough to leave the vampire she made alive to plot her death.

Until then . . .

With a warm smile, she wrapped her arms around him. "I'm hungry again. Take me out to dinner? Or"—she tilted her head to look up at him—"let's find somewhere less depressing to live? Or both?"

"With pleasure." He looked at her with the same desperation Eliana had seen in Nikki's gaze when she watched Sebastian.

Which is useful . . .

Eliana pulled him down for a kiss—and almost wished she didn't need to kill him.

Almost.

HISTORY

by Ellen Kushner

"You just totally ran that red light," she says, not without admiration.

"I know." As always, he sounds smug. He downshifts and passes a van that has been in front of them for blocks. "I love driving."

He is much too old for her, but that doesn't bother her. She has never been fussy about age. She is a historian— almost. Just a couple more papers, and she'll get honors this year from their country's oldest university. What bothers her is that he won't tell her about history. "I forget," he says when pressed. "It was all a long time ago."

He knows. She knows he knows. He just won't say.

"Why do you still drive shift?" she asks crabbily.

"Everyone should drive shift. Can't you drive shift?"

"Of course I can. I just wouldn't in city traffic, if I didn't have to."

He is now weaving his way through a densely populated open square ringed by ancient buildings, where the traffic vies for road space with students late for class—brilliant adolescents who believe all cars will stop for them—and with beggars and tourists and absentminded faculty. When he first knew it, the square, it was full of students in black robes and muddy shoes, never looking straight ahead of them but always up for tavern signs, or down to avoid horse manure and rotting cabbage and the occasional peasant. These students don't look down, and they don't look up much, either.

"Out of my way, asshole!" he growls at a blond waif with a backpack who has just stepped off the curb to wait for the light.

He loves to drive, and he loves to swear. In his youth he did neither. But that was a long time ago.

He also loves rock and roll. And the blues. "American blues," he says. "There's nothing like them. Muddy Waters taught Eric Clapton all he knows."

"Have you ever been to America?" she asks.

"Once." He scowls. "I hated it."

She has learned not to make jokes about his needing his Native Soil. He really hates that. She'll do it to get a rise out of him, but that's all.

She tries to catch him when he's half awake. "Tell me about the Great War," she'll say, but he turns over, muttering,

"Which one?" or "They were all great."

"Which was your favorite, then?"

"The one with the little short guy on the horse. There he was, looking out over the plain at the smoldering campfires below at what remained of his army. They were a ragtag lot. The sun was low. He turned to the adjutant next to him and said softly, 'My friend—'"

She whacks him on the head with her bookmark. "I saw that movie, too."

They take a walk down by the river that runs through the heart of the city. People are lined up on the sidewalk along the bridge trying to sell them things: bead earrings, knockoff purses, used comics, watercolors of the cathedral. There's a caricaturist drawing portraits. Her lover *does* reflect in mirrors, but she has the sudden thought that he would not show up in caricature. What would a cartoon sketch of him look like? The things that make him most himself are not visible to the eye. She sneaks a peek off to the side, where he stands looking at the cathedral. Long, bony nose, high brow, hair swept back . . . Another thought strikes her.

"Did you ever have your portrait done?"

"I—" If he says "I forget" again, she'll smack him. But a shadowy look passes across his face.

He did. People have drawn him, sketched him, even painted him. Maybe a student in a garret did a quick charcoal sketch of him asleep. Maybe a girl sitting in a garden some-where tried to capture him in watercolors, a parasol shading her face.

He's waited too long. He knows she knows. He doesn't answer. He points at one of the knockoff purses.

"Look at that. Why would anyone in their right mind want anything in that color? It looks like how I feel with a hangover."

Does he get hangovers? He did have a cold once, for a couple of hours. He said he picked it up on the street. And that people should be forced to wear tags on their collars say-ing, DON'T BITE ME, I'M DISEASED. He was fine the next day. If she could shake off a cold that quickly, she wouldn't com-plain! He doesn't drink, or eat anything regular, really. When they go out with her friends, he takes sips at his beer, but she always finishes it for him. He likes it when she drinks; he says it helps him sleep better. He's learned to sleep at night, sort of. If she's next to him. If she's breathing slowly and deeply. Soft and warm.

His hair is long, and always smells a little of fresh snow.

She locks the door because she has a research paper due. She needs her sleep, and she needs her strength, and he's hard on both of them. He leaves little tributes outside her door, iron-rich things like spinach salad with walnuts in takeaway boxes from the fancy bistro, and half bottles of red wine. Once he even left a steak, nicely cooked, wrapped in tinfoil.

She has no idea where he sleeps when he's not with her. She really doesn't want to know. Maybe he doesn't sleep at all. Maybe sleep is another sensual luxury that he indulges in just for the pleasure with his lovers, like sex.

The truth is, she's mad at him right now. She's banging her brains against the library every night, reading through microfiche and digging around in books she needs to wear special gloves to open, trying to find out what happened to a nascent rebellion when the river froze, and wolves came down from the hills—or at least to make a reasonable argument that her theory about sumptuary laws and printing presses is correct.

But her arguments are stupid. Her theories have holes in them. Giant, fact-sized holes. The documentation's just not there.

And so she spends day after day combing through files, and night after night poring over printed texts and unedited letters of people with bad handwriting and lousy crummy ink that fades after a mere three hundred years or so, most of it insanely boring. Looking for something that might not even be there, for evidence of a fact that may never have existed in the first place.

It's not that she wants to be famous, or even to prove anything to anyone else, really. That would be nice, but that's not it. She loves knowing about things that are gone.

She wants so badly to know the truth.

And he knows. She knows he knows. He was there.

There's his hair, for one thing. It's about the right length for the period she's researching, and it stays that way, captured, like the rest of his body, at the time of his transformation. Whenever he tries to cut it shorter—and of course, he let her try it once herself—it grows right back, almost overnight.

"I'm a self-regenerating organism," he says proudly. Proud of his vocabulary, proud of his scientific factoids. *Those*, he doesn't have any trouble remembering.

Was he a scholar, before? She can bet he wasn't a peasant. Not that a peasant couldn't have been born smart, and educated himself over the years. But not him. She'd bet the farm her lover never bowed low to anyone. He was someone who was always at the center of things. His original name might not ring down through the ages, but he would have known the ones whose did.

And so she's asked him. Tell me about the wolf hunts. The Thousand Candle Ball. The plague.

"I can't remember," he says, no matter what. "It's too long ago. You can't expect me to remember that."

She is beginning to suspect that it's because it's true. He really can't remember anything. He loses his car keys, he forgets to tell her that her mother called. She's given up on her birthday. It's coming up, and she knows he hasn't a clue.

She finds herself scanning the books, not for the facts she

needs, but for old engravings that look like him. Here's a page in a book: soberly dressed men in lace collars all signing a document. The Civil Compact of 1635. Is he the one standing off to the side of the table, as if he's proofreading their signatures? She's seen that look on his face, keen and critical and mocking. Can she dig out the names of all the signers? That shouldn't be hard. There are complete lists of them; another scholar's already done that work.

She scans the list of the Compact signers. Now what? Does she try out each name on him in turn, like the poor queen with Rumpelstiltskin? Does she murmur in his ear all night, a roll call of dead politicos, until he starts up with a cry of "Present, my lord!"?

She checks the date on the picture. Damn: It's an engraving of a commemorative painting done fifty years after the actual event. The artist would have been making up what everyone looked like, or working off old portraits, or something.

She peers closer at the engraved face and realizes it's just a bunch of lines, anyway.

She misses him. First she unlocks her door, and then, as if he knows she did, he meets her outside the library and walks her home.

"Do you want dinner?" he asks. He always buys, probably from some centuries-old bank account that has multiplied like her papa always promised: "Just put a penny in, add to it every year, and when you're all grown up you'll be able to buy whatever you want!"

She doesn't want dinner. She wants him. On the stairs to her room, she's already tearing his clothes off. He has the nicest clothes. (Oh, that savings account!) He has the nicest body under them. A young man's body, skin dense and firm. An invincible body, no matter how dissolute his character or degraded his memory.

Is he going to grow old with her? Or, rather, is he going to let her grow old with him? She doubts it. A lot. ("Practice on older men," her grandmother used to say, "but marry a young one." Oh, Granny!)

He doesn't ask how her paper's coming along.

They're supposed to be going to her study partner's birthday party. It's not that far from her flat, but he's insisted on going the long way round by the river, where it curves and they'll have to cross the bridges twice. She knows he doesn't really want to go at all. He hates parties; he hates her friends. She knows he thinks they're stupid, even though they're not. Really not: They were all the smartest kids in their graduating classes. He just doesn't like listening to them talk about their lives. He doesn't say so, but it depresses him. Her friends are mostly history and literature. He can barely sit still around them. He wants to be mean to them, to skewer them with his scorn for their youth and inexperience and dreams—but if he does, she'll dump him. She's made that clear.

He has to come with her, now, because she's already been to too many parties without him, and missed too many others because of him. At first it was okay to say her busy older boyfriend was working all the time, but they've been together too long; it looks like there's something funny if he never turns up, and the last thing she wants is people worrying about her. She got him to come along tonight by telling him that Theo will be there. Theo is Anna's boyfriend, and he's in physics. He adores talking physics with Theo.

Swallows have begun darting over the river, looking for the bugs that swarm there at twilight. The air is getting blue-gray, but he's still wearing his heavy, trendy sunglasses. Light really does hurt his eyes. That much is true.

"Flower for the lady?"

It's one of those beggar kids, trying to sell long-stemmed red roses, each one wrapped in cellophane, tied with a ribbon. The kid probably thinks he's a tourist, because of the glasses.

To her surprise, he stops. He never stops for anyone. He's looking at the kid. He never does that, either.

"Hey," he says.

The kid stares back. "Flower?"

Her arm linked in his, she can feel the twitch of him

starting to reach for his wallet, then pulling back and letting go. "No, thanks."

He pulls her along with him, not looking back.

Was it someone he knew before he met her? Too young. His child by his last lover? But he can't have kids himself; he says he's sterile. (Good thing!) Suddenly she remembers when she first came here to university, feeling lonely and raw, then one morning on her way to class spotting Sophie from their soccer club back home ahead of her, on the square, waiting for the light to change. And then realizing it couldn't be, because Sophie had been hit by a car last year. It was just someone with the same shoulders, the same hair, same height. It would be like that for him all the time, the people he'd known, when he remembered. He'd see them every-where. But it would never really be them.

"No flower for me?" she says, to recapture his attention. Maybe she'll even learn something this time. He's shaken. She knows the signs.

"When I buy you flowers, they won't look like that." He loosens his grip on her arm. "Have I ever bought you flowers?"

"Sure," she says airily. "Don't you remember that huge basket of lilies and white roses?" He looks at her sideways. He doesn't quite believe her, but he's trying to remember, just in case. "And the big bunch of hydrangeas you brought when I got the honors in folklore? I had to borrow a vase from Anna downstairs to hold them all. But my favorite was the rosebuds and freesias you gave me on my birthday."

He is still walking. But slowly. She feels the tension in his arm. "Did I?"

"No." She walks past him, now, her heels clicking on the pavement. "Of course not."

He lets her get a little ahead of him, but only a little. By the time he's caught up with her, she's a little sorry. But only a little.

"Hey," he says. He takes off his sunglasses. Hair falls into his eyes. He pushes it back with one hand. "Not everyone gets honors in folklore."

"You didn't even know me then."

"I didn't know you liked getting flowers," he says innocently.

"All women like flowers. You've had how many centuries of us, and you can't even remember that one stupid thing?"

He slings a pebble from the embankment into the water. Then he steps back, to watch it fall. The river is running strong. She can't see it hit the water, but maybe he can.

"In foreign lands," he announces, "ancient heroes sleep in caves, waiting for a horn to be blown or a bell to be rung, whereupon they spring into action in their country's hour of greatest need." Moodily, he slings another pebble. "Lucky bastards. Nothing to do but dream of ancient glory till it's time for a remix. Our motherland discourages such sloth."

"Really?"

"Really. No lying around when the land is in peril. Not here. Oh, no. We've got a better system in place."

Finally! She can't believe he's telling her this. "And you're it?"

"I'm it."

She keeps her voice level, nonchalant. "I've always wondered how anyone could decide when the hour of greatest need was, anyway."

"Me, too. Every year's got plenty of hours, believe me."

"That must be a lot of work."

"All the work, and none of the glory." Another pebble. "How do you think we kept our borders intact until '41? When the Russians were boiling shoe leather?"

She shudders with delight. "You *ate* Nazis?"

"Ate?" He looks down his nose at her. "What do I look like, an ambulating garbage disposal? I just scared the crap out of them." His head, lifted against the horizon, is too perfect, like a profile on a coin, a medal of heroism. "Well, certainly I drew a little sustenance first. Waste Not in Wartime and all that." (She remembers her grandmother telling her that slogan.) "But foreign blood does not nourish like the blood of the land."

"Is that why you hate to travel?"

"One reason."

"The blood of the land?"

He draws a little closer to her. And he was close before. He puts one hand on the back of her head and bends down to smell her hair.

Her heart starts slamming like it's working for him already. She lifts her chin and reaches up to draw his head down to her. Someone passing would think they were just any couple, nuzzling on a picturesque riverbank. They might even wind up in some tactless tourist's photos. He pulls her tighter, getting her neck right up against his mouth.

"I used to be tall," he mutters. "I mean really, really tall. People would stare at me on the street. That tall. Now I'm, what, just normal?"

"You're hardly normal." She always feels a giddy, reckless joy with his mouth near her veins.

"After the war," he growls. "All that nutrition. Milk. Marshall Plan. A race of giants. And now it's vitamins. I'll end up having to date midgets my own size."

He might have said more, but she doesn't hear it because the blood is pounding in her ears. Sweet, it's so sweet letting him take her into himself. If they were home, she'd take him into her, too. She takes a deep breath of air, the best air she's ever breathed. She doesn't want him to stop, but he does.

She's lost track of time, but the birds are still swirling; it hasn't been long. She clutches at the wool of his jacket, because otherwise she knows she's going to fall. He's so tender with her, now, as he pulls away. He wipes his mouth quickly with a white cotton handkerchief. He'll never use a paper tissue, and there's never much to wipe, but he always does it anyway.

He puts an arm around her, letting her lean against him as they walk along the river. He's buzzing with life energy, as the sun is going down. "Come home," he says. "Come home with me. Come home."

He's always up for it when he's had a drink. He can't even function when he hasn't.

She's fuzzy, and she lets a possible clue go by, still thinking of what he said before. "You're a hero," she says dreamily. "You patrol the borders in time of need."

"That's right. And now I know you want to express your gratitude."

"The Siege of '83? Was that you?"

"Now, which '83 was that?" he teases.

She nuzzles his shoulder. "You know. The one with the Turks. The coffee siege."

"Oh, look!" He stops suddenly, in the middle of the street. "I used to have a house here!"

She looks. They've stopped in front of a kebab joint on the

border of the tourist and the red light districts. The houses are old, but so is most of the city.

"Or maybe it was a little farther down. Hey, this place used to be a bakery. It smelled like heaven in the morning. . . ."

Diversionary tactics. She lets it pass, because even more than truth and history right now, she wants to get him home and get him into bed.

They can be late to the party. It's not like it hasn't happened before.

He brings her flowers that week. And the week after that. On her actual birthday.

"You're getting sentimental," she says, and he answers, "You're addictive." She tries to lie awake figuring what that means, but she always falls asleep with him beside her, warm with the gift of her blood. Little, tiny gifts, like sips of fine old cognac. He enjoys her thoroughly and deeply, in ways no man ever has before, or will. He'll do a lot for her. She's figuring that out. He's beautiful, but he's not young. He does what he can.

But she still can't leave it alone. "Tell me," she says, sometimes with his mouth still at her throat. "Tell me about the last king's court. Tell me about the Spanish Embassy and the Treaty of Ockrent. Tell me whether the duchess Octavia really had an affair with her governess and her maid."

"It was a long time ago. What's at the movies? Let's go out."

"Tell me the first time you saw electric lighting. Tell me how long it took to walk across the city in 1708."

"You can't expect me to remember that."

"Tell me what your mother liked to eat. How did you learn to drive? Did you ever fight a duel? Tell."

"I can't remember," he says.

He knows. She knows he knows.

"Will you remember *me*?"

"Of course," he says. And maybe he even means it.

THE PERFECT DINNER PARTY
by Cassandra Clare & Holly Black

1. RELAX! GUESTS WON'T HAVE FUN UNLESS THEIR HOSTESS IS HAVING FUN, TOO.

You walk into the dining room, alone. You're wearing a green shift, pale as grass, and have pulled your hair back into a glittering barrette. You're biting your lip.

"Lovely," Charles says, and you look pleased. You dressed up for him, after all.

You explain that you're sorry that your friend Bethenny couldn't come. She had a dance recital and besides, she was too chicken to sneak out of the house. Not like you.

I bet you met Charles the way he always meets girls. He hangs around the mall just like he used to when he was alive. Back then, he wore skinny ties and listened to new wave. He's excited that skinny ties are back. See? He's wearing one tonight.

You look over at me nervously. You probably think I'm too young to drink the bottle of wine you stole from your parents. You think I'm not going to be any fun.

Or maybe you're just wondering what happened to the rest of the guests.

When I smile at you, you look away uneasily. That just makes me smile wider.

When I was a littler girl than I am now, there was this boy who would always hang around. One day he was over at the house annoying me (he would do this thing where he put his finger on my chin and asked me, "What's this?" and when I looked down, he would bop me in the nose and laugh), and I realized the cupboard had a package of almond-flavored tea in it.

Since this was back in the eighties, cyanide was in the news a lot. We all knew it tasted like almonds. It was a pretty simple thing to make us mugs of tea—mine, plain, his, the almond-flavored kind.

Then I started telling him how sorry I was that I'd poisoned him. I kept it up until he started crying. Then I kept it up some more.

Our dinner parties always remind me of how much fun that was.

2. A FEW SIMPLE CHANGES TO YOUR USUAL DÉCOR WILL GIVE YOUR HOUSE THAT PARTY FEELING.

Charles pulls out your chair and that seems to reassure you that things are going just the way you thought they would.

You see a pair of teenagers, dressed up in their church clothes, using their parents' good china to have a dinner party in the middle of the night.

A grown-up party, with candles burning brightly in silver candlesticks and glass stemware and napkins folded into the shape of swans. Charles pours from the bottle of wine he's already decanted an hour ago.

You take a big sip. That's the first strike against you. Clearly you have no idea what to do with good wine—how to catch its scent, how to swirl it around the glass to see the color. You glug it like you're washing down a handful of pills.

You put the glass down with a bang on the table. I jump. "That was great!" you say. There's lipstick smeared on your teeth.

Charles looks over at me. I frown at him. Disapproving. He could have done better, my look says.

Charles gets up. "I'll get the first course."

Silence falls between us as soon as he's out of the room. I don't mind. I can be silent for hours. But you're not used to it. I see you squirm in your chair. Put your hands up to fiddle with your barrettes, unclasp them, close them again. Fiddling. You say, "So you're Charles's little sister, huh? How old are you, anyway?"

"Fourteen," I lie. I try to keep the bitterness out of my

voice, because there is nothing worse than a disagreeable hostess, but it's hard. Charles is nearly grown, old enough to pass for an adult, while I am struggling to pass for fourteen.

With your flat chest and wide eyes, you look fairly young yourself. Another strike against you.

Charles comes back a moment later with bowls of soup. He places yours down first. That's proper. He's turning into a real gentleman, Mr. DuChamp would say.

"Are your parents on a trip?" you say. "They must really trust you to leave you here alone."

"They trust Charles," I say with a sly smile.

That makes you smile at Charles, too, entrusted to take care of his little sister. And it makes me think of my parents, down in the dirt basement, buried six feet under with pennies in the sockets of their eyes.

Mr. DuChamp said that that was so they could pay the ferryman to take them to the shores of the dead. Mr. DuChamp thought of everything.

3. CHOOSE GUESTS WHO ARE INTERESTING AND FUN, AND WHO WILL INVIGORATE THE CONVERSATION.

You pick up your spoon and dig it into the soup like you're scooping out a melon. I am fairly sure that when you do start eating, you will make slurping sounds.

You do. Strike three. I look over at Charles with my

eyebrows up, but he is ignoring me.

"So," you say, around your soup, "did Charles tell you where we met?"

I shake my head, although I know. Of course I know. It's always the same. I can't imagine why you think I'd be interested. Mr. DuChamp always used to say that guests should never talk about themselves. They should make polite conversation on topics of interest to everyone.

"It was at a concert." You say the name of a band. A band I've never heard of.

"They were okay," said Charles, "but *you* were amazing."

Only the fact that it would be a massive breach of etiquette prevents me from making a gagging sound.

You both get into a long, dull conversation weighing the merits of Ladyhawke, Franz Ferdinand, Le Tigre, the Faint, and the Killers. Charles forgets himself so far as to exclaim how happy he is that Devo are making another album. Your blank stare is warning enough for him to clear his throat and suggest that you would like more wine.

You would. In fact, you drink it so fast that he pours yet another glassful. A fine bright color has come into your cheeks. Your eyes shine. I doubt you have ever looked lovelier.

Mr. DuChamp always used to say that appearances weren't everything. He said that the way a woman carried herself, the way she spoke, and the perfection of her manners were more important than how red her lips and cheeks were, or how shining her eyes. "Looks fade," he said, "except, of course, in our case." He would raise a glass to me. "'Age cannot wither her,'" he would say, "'nor custom stale her infinite variety.'"

Whatever that meant.

I lift the soup spoon to my mouth, smile, and lower it again. It was Mr. DuChamp who taught me how to pretend that I was eating, how gestures and laughter distracted your guests so that they'd never notice you didn't take a bite of food.

Mr. DuChamp taught us lots of things. He taught Charles to stand up when a lady entered the room, and how to take a lady's coat. He told me never to refer to an adult by his or her first name and to sit with my legs uncrossed, always. He didn't like pants and didn't approve of girls wearing them. He taught us to be punctual for all social engagements, even though once he moved in with us, the only social engagements we ever had were with him.

When he first came, it was horrible. I woke in the middle of the night because I heard something downstairs. I thought it was my parents fighting—they fought a lot: about the house, which always needed repairs, about her habit of hiding booze and pills, about girls in the office who called him on the weekends. I padded down to the kitchen in my nightgown to see the new Corian countertops splashed with blood.

Mom was on the floor with a strange man hunched over her. All I could see of Dad was his foot sticking out from behind the island.

I must have gasped. Mr. DuChamp looked up. The lower half of his face was red.

"Oh," he said. "Hello."

I made it all the way to the stairs before he caught me.

4. DON'T SCRIMP ON FOOD AND DRINK. ARRANGE IT ATTRACTIVELY AND LET GUESTS HELP THEMSELVES!

Charles clears our soup bowls and returns carrying the main course. It's lasagna, which is the only thing I know how to cook. I know Mr. DuChamp would say I ought to learn more elegant cooking: how to make pâté, clear soups, coq au vin, lamb stuffed with raisins and figs, maybe in a sweet plum sauce. But it's hard to learn when you don't have much money for ingredients and can't taste what you've made.

The lasagna is a little burned around the edges, but I don't think you'll care. You're too tipsy, and anyway, hardly anyone makes it through the main course.

As you dig into your food, I wonder if you notice that there are heavy curtains across all the windows here and that they are thick with dust. I wonder if you notice the strange scratch marks on the floor. I wonder if you notice that nothing in the house has been updated since 1984.

I wait for Charles to move, but he doesn't. He just grins at you like an idiot.

"Can I see you in the kitchen?" I ask Charles in a way where it's not really a question.

He looks over at me like he's only just remembered I'm here at the table, too.

"Sure," he mumbles. "Okay."

We push back our chairs. Mom used to complain about our kitchen because it wasn't the cool, open-plan kind. She wanted to knock down one of the walls, but Dad said that was too expensive, and anyway, who wanted an old Victorian house with a modern kitchen.

I'm glad it's the old kind, so I can close the door and you can't hear.

"We don't have any dessert," I tell Charles.

"That's okay," he says. "I'll go down to the corner store for ice cream."

"No," I say. "I don't like her. She doesn't pass the test."

He slams his hand down on the counter. "No one passes your stupid test."

I look at Charles in his skinny tie and shiny, worn shirt. I am so tired of him. He is so tired of me. It's been so long.

"It's a big deal," I say. "Turning someone into one of us. They'll be with us forever."

"*I* want her with me forever," Charles says, and I wonder if you know that, that he feels that way about you. And I wonder if Charles knows that he said "me" instead of "us."

"She's smart," he says. "She's funny. She likes the same music as me."

"She's boring. She has bad manners, too."

"Manners," Charles says, like it's a swear word. "You and your obsession with manners."

"Mr. DuChamp says—," I start, but he cuts me off.

"Mr. DuChamp killed our parents!" he yells, loud enough that maybe you might hear. "And anyway, we haven't seen him in months. He's off being vizier or chamberlain or whatever it is he does."

Charles knows perfectly well what Mr. DuChamp does. He looks after the household of the greatest vampire in our state. He has his ear. It is a very lofty position. He used to tell us over and over the story of how he rose from a lowly nestling to planning the state dinners where he entertained members of the elite from New Orleans to Washington. Charles found the stories boring, but I was always fascinated.

Even though I didn't like Mr. DuChamp, I liked hearing about how he succeeded in drawing the threads of power around himself. He seized opportunities other people wouldn't even have recognized as opportunities. I liked to think that in his position, I would have seized my chance, too. I guess that's what everyone likes to think.

"Mr. DuChamp taught us how to behave," I say. "Our parents weren't going to do that. If you don't know how to behave, then you're no better than anyone else."

Charles looks stubborn. "Fine, if you want to do everything that guy said, remember that he said we should make more like ourselves."

"Only if they're worthy! He said some people don't care about bettering themselves."

So many lessons. At first, how to hold a wine glass, a fork, not to ever eat with your knife, no chewing gum, speaking when you're spoken to, sitting with your hands in your lap, to say please and excuse me. Later: to kill quickly, to be subtle in finding your prey, not to make others clean up your mess, and the three Bs: to bite cleanly, then to burn and then bury the remains, unless you wanted more like yourself.

"It's not for everyone," I say. "He warned us."

"This isn't about him," Charles says. "You're the one who doesn't want anyone else around. You're the one who doesn't want more of us. How come I always have to be the one who hunts? How come we always have to eat the girls I bring home? What about your friends? Oh, right, you don't have any."

I make an involuntary sound, like the hiss of air going out of a balloon. "I can't—," I start, then take a deep breath and start again. "When I walk around the mall alone, all the other girls are with their mothers. I used to go into this one arcade, but the boys there wouldn't even talk to me. They're not interested in girls, at least not girls my age. *You* can go out in the world alone. *You* can pretend to have a young-looking face, but I'm a *child* to everyone I meet."

"Look," Charles says. "You know I feel bad for you. I try to be a good brother. I bring girls to your stupid dinner parties and let them sit around like stuffed bears while you pour out pretend tea. All I want is for tonight to be different, Jenny. Just one night. For me."

"Fine." I whirl around and stalk back into the dining room. I stop short, so short that Charles, just behind me, almost walks right into my back. If he didn't have such good reflexes, he would have.

You are still sitting where you were, at the table, and I think of what Charles said about tea parties. You look stiff as a doll with little red spots on your cheeks like paint. Mr. DuChamp is standing beside you, one hand on the back of your chair. He smiles when he sees us.

"Hello, children," he says.

5. EVERY PARTY NEEDS AN ELEMENT OF THE UNEXPECTED TO MAKE IT UNFORGETTABLE. THINK FONDUE!

"There's a place set for you," I say, even though, really, the place was for your friend.

He laughs, probably unconvinced, and runs his finger through the dust on the sill. "Regrettably, I have already eaten."

"Oh," I say; then, remembering my manners, "How do you do?"

He smiles indulgently. "Very well, thank you, excepting one thing." Then his demeanor changes, his face darkens, and he stands, still clutching your hand. You stare at him in horror. "Excepting that you were supposed to bring my master tribute *not six months past.*

"I have tried to contact you and *nothing.* You, my charges, embarrass me. Did I not instruct you better than this? If I, who manage all my master's affairs, cannot manage you, what must I look like?"

I look over at Charles. His expression is determined but not surprised.

"Charles?" I say. "What tribute?"

He shakes his head. "Six living girls."

I turn back to Mr. DuChamp. He is frowning, like he's trying to puzzle out something. "You did not receive my message?"

"I received it," Charles says. "I tore it up."

"That is unacceptable," says Mr. DuChamp.

"I don't understand." It's you, speaking in your tinny little human voice, like the voice of a fly. "What's going on?"

Mr. DuChamp turns to me. "Ladies," he says. "Perhaps if you were to retire to the parlor, I might speak to Master Charles in private."

I already know you're not going to go along with it. You don't understand that requests for privacy must always be honored. You are already sputtering as I take hold of your arm. I squeeze, just a little, and you turn white.

"Ouch," you say. "Ouch, what are you doing to my *arm?*"

"Nothing," I say. "I'm not doing anything." My mother used to do that when I misbehaved in the supermarket. She would pinch the skin in the crook of my arm and smile a syrupy smile like the one I'm smiling now. Although she couldn't pinch as hard as I can, now. "Ladies retire to the parlor after dinner."

You're looking at Charles. "I'm not going anywhere with your creepy little sister."

"I'll be there in a minute," Charles tells you. "Stay with Jenny."

You go, but not quietly. Whining the whole way.

All the furniture in the parlor is covered in big white sheets. It's more convenient that way. When they get blood on them, we can take them away and launder them and put them back clean. The sofa looks like a fat white iceberg, surrounded by smaller icebergs, floating in the darkness. You cough and sneeze a little, choking on all the dust. There's a fireplace full of dead ashes and windows that have had plywood hammered over them. I wonder if you're starting to realize this isn't a normal sort of house.

I push you down on the couch and go back over to the door. If I stand just behind it, I can hear Charles and Mr. DuChamp, but they can't see me.

"It's not right," Charles is saying. "It's one thing to kill people because we have to, because we've got to live, but those girls were so scared. And I didn't know anything. I hurt that one girl real bad because I didn't know how tight to knot the rope. And another girl just sobbed for the whole five-hour drive. I hate it. I'm not doing it again."

"That is the very point of etiquette, Charles. It instructs us as to how to do things we don't want to do."

"I *won't* do it," Charles says.

"That is very rude. And you know I do not tolerate rudeness."

"What's going on?" you say, tremulously, from behind me.

"He's going to kill Charles," I say. My voice doesn't sound all that different from yours.

"What are you?" you ask. You must be sobering up. "What's *he*?" You point at Mr. DuChamp.

I bare my teeth at you. It's the easiest way, really, to show you what I am. I've never done it before in front of someone I wasn't intending to kill right away.

Your eyes go wide when you see the fangs, but you don't step back. "And *he's* one, too? And he's going to hurt Charles?"

You're so stupid. I already told you. "He's going to kill him."

"But . . . why?"

"For not following the rules," I tell you. "That's why rules are so important."

"But you're just kids," you say. You're used to second chances and next-time-there'll-be-consequences-young-lady. You've never had your mother killed in front of you. You've never drunk your brother's blood.

"I'm old," I say. "Older than you. Older than your mother."

I know why Charles didn't tell me about the tribute, though. It's because some part of him still thinks of me as little too. He's been protecting me from that, just like he's been protecting me by staying in the old house, even though he no longer wants to. It's not fair. He was right before when he said he was a good brother. He shouldn't get killed for that.

"Well, do you have a stake?" you ask.

I don't point out that this is like asking a French aristocrat if they have a guillotine around. Instead I point toward the fireplace.

You are surprisingly quick on the uptake. Not sophisticated, of course, but with a sort of rough intelligence. Street smarts, Mr. DuChamp would say. You grab the fireplace poker and without a second glance head out the door into the dining room.

I lean around the door. Mr. DuChamp has Charles up against the wall. His big hand is around Charles's neck, and he is squeezing. He can squeeze hard enough to crush Charles's neck if he wants to, but that wouldn't be fatal. Right now he's just having fun.

When we were just starting to learn how to feed, the hardest part for me was moving out of the stalk and into the strike. There's an awkward moment when you get close to your victim but haven't actually lunged. It can seem an impossible gulf between planning and actually doing, but if you hesitate, you'll get noticed.

You obviously don't have that problem. You swing the poker against the side of Mr. DuChamp's head hard enough to make him stagger back. Blood runs down his cheek, and he opens his mouth in a fanged hiss.

Before he can get his bearings, I clamp my mouth on his throat like a lamprey. I've never drunk the blood of one of my kind before. It's like drinking lightning. It goes zinging down my throat, and all the time Mr. DuChamp's fists are beating on my shoulders, but I don't let go. He's roaring like a tiger in a trap, but I don't let go. Even when he crashes to the ground, I don't let go, until Charles leans over and detaches me, pulling me off the corpse like an engorged tick so full and fat it doesn't even care.

"Enough, Jenny," he says. "He's dead."

6. NEVER START CLEANING WHILE YOUR GUESTS ARE STILL PRESENT.

A lot of people think that when vampires die, they explode or catch on fire. That's not true. As death sets in, our kind subside slowly into ash, like a bowl of fruit ripening into mold and rot on speeded-up film. We all stand in a sort of triangle, watching as Mr. DuChamp starts turning slowly black, the tips of his fingers beginning to crumble.

You start crying, which seems ridiculous, but Charles takes you into the other room and talks to you softly like he used to talk to me when I was little.

So then it's just me, witness to Mr. DuChamp's final end. I take the little broom from the fireplace and sweep what's left of him among the scorched wood and bones.

When you and Charles come back out, I'm standing there with the broom like Cinderella. Charles has his arm around you. You look blotchy and red nosed and very human.

"We're going to have to run away, Jenny," he says. "Mr. DuChamp's master knew where he was. He'll come looking for him soon enough. I don't know what he'll do when he finds out what happened."

"Run away?" I echo. "Run away to where?" I've never been

anywhere but here, never lived anywhere but in this house.

You explain that you have an uncle who has a farmhouse upstate. You and Charles plan to hide out there. I am welcome to come along, of course. Charles's creepy little sister.

This is what Charles always wanted—a real girlfriend, someone who will love him and listen to music with him and pretend that he's a regular boy. I hope that you do. I hope that you will. You might be stuck with each other for a long time.

"No," I say. "I'm okay. I've got somewhere else to go."

Charles furrows his brow. "No, you don't."

"I *do*," I say and give him the evilest look I can manage.

I guess he doesn't really want me to come to the farm-house, because he actually drops it. He goes upstairs to pack up his stuff, and you go with him.

The remains of dinner are still on the table. The glasses full of wine. The four plates, only one of them with food on it. The remains of our last dinner party.

When I'm done cleaning up and I've said good-bye to you and Charles, when you've given me the address in case I change my mind, when you've hugged me, even, my neck so close to yours that I can smell your blood through the pores of your skin, then I'm going to get ready, too.

Six girls is nothing to me. I can ask them to help me find my mother in parking lots, to look for lost kittens, to pick me up after I fall from my bike and skin my knee. I don't care if they scream or cry. It might be a little annoying, but that's it.

The hardest part is going to be driving while sitting on a phone book. But I'll figure out a way. If I want the job, I'm going to have to show the master I'm just as good as DuChamp. I know every detail of the story of his rise to power. I've heard it a hundred times. Everything he did, I can do.

As I leave town, I'll drop this letter in the mail, just so you know what my plans are.

Thank you very much for coming to my party. I had a lovely time.

SLICE OF LIFE

by Lucius Shepard

I've never done it with another girl, but Sandrine gets me thinking how it would be. She's got the kind of body I wish I had, long legged and lean, yet with enough up top to keep boys happy. Her nose is too big and beaklike for her narrow face, but after you study on her awhile, it seems to settle in above her generous mouth, becoming part of her beauty. The light that shines her into being, reflecting off God knows how many shards of mirror, makes it difficult to judge—most times she's scarcely more than a sketch with a few hazy details—but I figure if all her color was restored, her hair would be jet-black and her eyes dark blue like the ocean out past the sandbar on a sunny day.

She says I'll never leave her, that we're two of a kind, and who knows, maybe she's right.

If you're born in these parts, in one of the sad, savage, broken towns along the St. John's River, now reduced to cracker slums . . . shells of old mansions with fallen-in roofs and busted-out screens on the front porch and people inside gray as the weathered boards, moldering amid live oaks and scrub pines. Surrounded by a prefab debris of bait shops and trailer parks and concrete block roadhouses where redneck coke dealers shoot nine ball for crisp new hundreds and bored fifty-dollar hookers sit at the bar wishing for a Cadillac to bear them away on one last windy joyride. Towns like this, towns like DuBarry, Sandrine says, they stain you with their colors and make you vulnerable to their deceits. You can go to Dallas or New Orleans or somewhere they speak a foreign language, you can live there the rest of your days, but that won't change a thing. No matter how far you travel or how long you stay, you never feel real anywhere else and you're always living a measly cheat of a life that makes you think you've got to get over on folks even when you're doing just fine playing it straight.

I've never been south of Daytona or west of Ocala or north of Jacksonville, so I'm no expert, but maybe Sandrine's got a point. People who return to DuBarry after years of being away, you can see the relief in their faces, as if the pressure is off and they can't wait to start dissolving in the heat and damp of the town, like the pigs' feet atop the counter down at Toby's, mutating in their jar of greenish brine.

Take Chandler Mason.

After graduating from FSU she headed for New York,

where she hired on at ESPN. She started out reading the news on one of their sports talk shows and before long she landed a job as a sideline reporter for NBA games; then, a few years later, suddenly, with no reason given, she was back in DuBarry, strutting her stuff in designer clothes. Whenever she strolled by, the men sitting in rusted lawn chairs out front of Toby's would develop a case of whiplash. Following a whirlwind courtship, she married Les Staggers, an ex-marine who teaches phys ed and algebra at County Day, and popped out three kids, put on fifty, sixty pounds, and now when she passes, the men in the lawn chairs say something like "Must be time to water the elephants," and share a big laugh. She goes on a liquor run a couple of times a week, weaving an unsteady path to the ABC store, wrapped in a cloud of diaper stink, and on Sundays she accompanies Les to Jacksonville Beach, where he's a deacon in some screech-and-holler church. Otherwise she stays home with the blinds drawn and her brats yowling, drinking gin and Fresca, the TV on loud enough to drown out the twenty-first century.

Sandrine says that's the best I can hope for, unless I help her, unless she helps me, and I can probably expect a whole lot worse, considering my reputation.

—Go fuck yourself, I tell her.

—That's all I ever do, says Sandrine.

* * *

This matter of my reputation has come under fire from predictable quarters. Boys who I won't let touch me write my name on bathroom walls and talk about the things I've done with them, things they've only heard about. They go to singing "Louie, Louie" whenever they see me coming. Louie's short for Louise—it got tacked on me in grade school for being a tomboy, and ever since they started with that dumb song, I've been trying to convince my friends to shorten it further and call me Elle. Not that the singing bothers me so much . . . but it's annoying and I think Elle's a name I'll grow into someday. Old habits die hard, though. I expect I'll be stuck with Louie for as long as I hang around DuBarry.

Momma told me once that the tales people carry about me make her cry herself to sleep.

—Excuse me, I said. I sleep right across the hall and what I hear coming from your room don't sound a thing like crying. What it sounds like is you and Bobby Denbo bumping uglies. Or else it's Craig Settlemyre. I can't keep those two straight.

—I'm a grown woman! I've got the right to a life!

—Some life, I said.

My faculty advisor at County Day, Judy Jenrette, has expressed sincere concern that my promiscuity is an outgrowth of low self-esteem. I tried to nip this concern in the bud by assuring her that my self-esteem was just dandy, but judging by the way she pressed her lips together, her chin wobbling, I suspected that she thought to see her younger self in me and was repressing an Awful Secret that tormented her to this day. Before I could prevent it, she unburdened herself of a dismal story about teen pregnancy and its consequences that I must have watched half a dozen times on Lifetime Television for Women, only this came without the hot guys.

—I appreciate you letting me hear that, I said. I honestly do.

Judy snuffled, dabbed her eye with a tissue, and forced a shaky smile.

—That story don't apply to me, though, I said. We're different breeds of cat. You were in love. Me, I fuck because I'm bored. And living here, if I'm awake I'm bored.

—Language, Louie!

—I'm taking birth control and no one gets near me without a condom. If I got pregnant, you better believe Momma would drag me to the clinic and sign those abortion papers. Having me around is bad enough for her love life. A baby would just about finish her off.

Judy said that pregnancy wasn't her only worry, that sexing it up so young would cause me to have emotional issues. She handed me a pamphlet on Teen Celibacy with a photo on the front of cheerleader types who appeared to be overjoyed by not getting any. I read enough of the pamphlet to get the basics—if you saved yourself for marriage Jesus would love you, Coke would taste better, etc.—and then Googled the company that produced it. They turned out to be the subsidiary of a corporation that made its mark selling baked goods. This led me to speculate that doing without caused you to eat more cupcakes and that a generation of diabetic Teen Celibates were victims of a duplicitous marketing campaign. Who knew there was profit to be had from negative pimping?

Where Sandrine lives is off a blue highway a couple of miles south of DuBarry, a tore-down, two-room fishing shack tucked into a hollow on the riverbank, camouflaged by ferns and fallen beards of Spanish moss, hidden by chokecherry bushes and a toppled oak out front. You'd never spot it unless you were looking for it, and you wouldn't go near it unless you'd lost your mind. What's left of the place is roofless, crazy with spiderwebs and rotting boards so crumbly you can rip off pieces with your hands. If you go inside, you'll find that every inch of the walls and part of the floor is covered with glued-on shards of mirror, and if you trespass on a night during a period between three days either side of the full moon, chances are you won't be coming out again. Sandrine can't compel you like once she could, but she's got enough left to slow you down. You'll see her stepping to you and you'll stumble back in fright, even though you're not sure she's real, and then you see the hungry glamour in her eyes, and that holds you for a second.

A second's all it takes.

She won't talk much about the past—she prefers to hear

about my life, a life I'd gladly leave behind. Some nights, though, I get her going and she tells me things like she was born in 1887 in Salt Harvest, Louisiana, a little Acadian town, and was turned when she was twenty-three by a fang who left her to figure out on her own what she'd become. She's been living in the shack since 1971, sustaining herself on whatever animals happen along. Frogs, mainly. She hardly ever supplies much detail, but we were sitting on the toppled oak one night, right at the boundary beyond which she cannot pass, watching the water hyacinths that carpet the majority of the river undulate with the current, their stiff, glossy green leaves slopping against the bank, and I asked how she'd come to be stranded there. She had just fed and was more substantial than usual, yet I could see low stars through her flesh and, when she shifted position, the neon lights of a roadhouse on the opposite bank. Sweet rot merged with the dank river smell, creating an odor that reminded me of the rained-on mattress in Freddy Swift's backyard.

—Diadadjii, Sandrine said, I've heard them called other names, but that's what Roy called them. He's this fang I traveled with in '71 . . . and for a while before that.

—What's jajagee?

—Not jajagee. Djadadjii.

Mosquitoes plagued us, but Sandrine didn't seem bothered. She looked off south toward the roadhouse.

—They look like humans, but they're not—they mimic

humans. Roy heard that this old Jewish magician bred them in the seventeenth century to hunt fangs. They're stronger than fangs and they can do one piece of magic. That's what binds me here. Why I'm like this. The Djadadj that ate Roy, he couldn't eat anymore, so he salted me away for later.

—And left you here forty years?

—Maybe he got hit by a bus. Or maybe he forgot. They're not very smart. But sooner or later, he'll remember where he stored me, or else another one will sniff me out.

She nailed me with a stare I felt at the back of my skull. That's the best can happen unless you help me, she said.

—Do we have to talk about this every time I come out? I'm thinking about it, okay?

She kept staring for several seconds and then sighed in dismay.

—It's not the easiest thing to wrap your head around, I said. Becoming a serial killer.

—I do the killing.

—Yeah, but I have to lure them here. That's even more disgusting.

—Listen, Louie. I . . .

—Elle!

—I'm sorry. Elle.

A distant plop came from the center of the river, where there was open water.

—I only need five, she said.

—I know what you need. It's not like you never tell me.

—One a night for five nights. Then I'll be strong enough to break free. There must be five people you hate in town. Five like that first one.

—You have to give me more time.

We sat quietly, caught in our bad mood like two flies in a puddle of grease. I thought to say I had to go, but I didn't want to go. Sandrine wrestled with a hyacinth stem and snapped off a lavender bloom and offered it to me. When I accepted it, her fingers brushed mine and I felt a blush of heat, like I'd rubbed my fingertips fast over a rough surface.

—Does Djadadjii magic work on regular people? I asked.

—No. They don't care about you, anyway. They're only interested in fangs.

—Suppose you get clear of this. What'll you do?

—Maybe South Carolina. There's a group of fangs there who're well protected. They're not fond of outsiders, but I'm tired of being on my own. It might be worth the risk.

—What if you weren't on your own?

—If you were with me, you mean?

I shrugged. Yeah.

—I'd probably stay here.

That alarmed me. In DuBarry?

—No, no. Florida. Most of the fangs in this hemisphere

are in Latin America and . . .

—How come?

—It's easier to get away with killing there. Of course it's a trade-off. Since most fangs are there, most of the Djadadjii are, too. The one that caught me, he's only the fourth I've seen up here . . . and the first three were over a century ago.

A bug crawled from beneath a petal of the bloom Sandrine had plucked, and I laid it on the oak trunk.

—You all right, *cher*?

—Tell me some more about the Djadadjii.

—I don't know much more. They all have wide mouths. . . . Their mouths expand. They could swallow a football if they wanted. They could bite it in half. And they have a refined sense of smell. If a fang's been near you, they'll pick up the scent. Roy told me they're all beautiful and the ones I've known were beautiful . . . and dumb. Dumb as chickens.

A fisher bird swooped low above the hyacinth, and the faint chugging of a generator came from somewhere upriver.

—Take off your top for me, said Sandrine.

—I . . . I don't . . .

—I won't touch you. I know you're shy and you're not ready, but I want to look at you this once. She pretended to pout. It's not fair you can see me and I never see you.

Hesitantly, I reached back and undid the strings of my halter. I fitted my eyes to the red winking light atop a water tower across the river and held the halter in place for a second; then I let it fall.

—God, she said. I'd forgotten.

—What is it? I asked. Is . . .

Shh! She reached down to the river and cupped her hand and scooped up some water and let it trickle between her fingers onto my breasts. Cool and lovely, little rivers spilling over my contours. I felt beautiful and grand, a hill divided by tributaries. My skin pebbled where the water touched me. One nipple poked up hard.

The halter slid off my lap. Sandrine handed it to me and told me I could put it back on.

—No, it's okay. My hair curtained my face, hiding my excitement. It's nice . . . sitting here like this.

One afternoon when I was fifteen and feeling downhearted, I hitched out to the old boneyard set in a fringe of Florida jungle south of town and sat beside the big gray angel, drinking from a pint of lime-flavored vodka I'd lifted from Momma's stash. Forty years ago a bunch of DuBarry kids went skinny-dipping at night in the ocean near St. Augustine. Their bodies were never found (it's assumed they were caught in a rip-tide) and the town put up the angel beneath a twisted water oak for a memorial. They must have skimped on the sculptor, or else they were going for something different . . . or maybe getting vandalized four or five times a year has taken a toll, because except for more-or-less regulation wings, it resembles the husk of a half-human female insect nine feet high. The grave tenders have gotten slack about scraping paint off it, and the statue has acquired a crusty glaze over the head and torso that makes it look even weirder. Used to be there were some goth kids who lit candles and sang to the angel, but that provided an evangelical preacher with an excuse to rev up his campaign against devil worship and their parents smacked the goth out of them. Now kids come there to bust bottles on the headstone and howl and dry heave and screw, and I guess some believe they gain power over death by pissing on the angel or smearing it with paint, behavior the town apparently deems more in keeping with the moral standard.

I got pretty smashed and lay on my back, thoughts drifting from one depressing topic to the next, watching the dusk and then darkness settle in the oak boughs. A car purred along the dirt drive, its engine so quiet I heard the tires crunching gravel. Headlights swept over me. I figured it for kids and didn't pay any attention. Someone came to stand above me—the salesman who had given me a ride out, a chunky middle-aged bald guy in a madras jacket.

—You still here? he asked.

—Naw, I said, wondering foggily what he was doing there—he'd told me he had stops to make in Hastings and Palatka.

He toed the empty vodka bottle and then stuck out a

hand. Come on. I'll ride you into town. This ain't no fit place for a young lady.

Calling me a young lady must have pushed my daddy button, because I let him haul me to my feet. He had doused himself with cologne, but I could smell his sweat. He pulled me close and ran a hand along my butt and said thickly, Man, you are one sweet-looking piece of chicken.

I started to freeze up but recalled Momma's advice.

—There's a motel down near Orange Park that don't ask no questions, I said.

I didn't think he bought my act. He held me tightly and seemed confused; then a smile split his doughy face.

—Damn! he said. I was halfway to Hastings before I realized you were putting out signals.

All I'd done in his car was not look at him and grunt answers to his questions. He gave my breast a squeeze and I rubbed against him and said in a breathy voice, Ooh, yeah!

—You like that, huh? he said.

With my free hand I hiked up my T-shirt, exposing the other breast. He played with it until the nipple stiffened, then grinned like he was the only one who could work that trick.

—I been watching you for must be an hour and a half, he said. Here we could have been having some fun.

He placed his hand on the small of my back, the way you'd squire a prom date, and steered me toward his car—a crouching animal with low-beam eyes. I broke free and kneed him in the crotch. He puked up a groan, grabbed his jewels, and bent double. A string of drool silvered by the headlights unreeled from his lips. He went down on all fours, breathing heavy, and I kicked him in the side. That's where I departed from Momma's plan of action. Instead of running like hell, I grabbed the vodka bottle and busted out the bottom on a headstone and told him if he didn't get the fuck gone I'd slice him. He came at me in a clumsy run, a hairless bear in a loud sport jacket, cursing and reaching for me with clawed hands. I slashed his palm open and lit out for the trees, leaving him screaming in the dirt.

For a time I heard him shouting and battering through the underbrush. I moved away from the noise and tried to circle behind him but lost my bearings. After hiding for half an hour or so, I thought he must have given up. A big lopsided moon was on the rise and I could smell the river but had no other clue as to where I stood in relation to the graveyard. I located the river and trudged along the bank, detouring around thickets, figuring I'd head north until I recognized a landmark. Crickets sizzled, frogs belched out loopy noises, and beams of moonlight chuted down through the canopy, transforming the bank into a chaos of vegetable shapes spread out across the irregular black-and-white sections of a schizophrenic's checkerboard.

If I hadn't cut him, I told myself, he would have probably slunk away. It don't do to piss off that kind more than you have to, Momma said. Otherwise they're liable to get obsessed.

I pushed back a palmetto frond, ducked under it, and stopped dead. The salesman stood about forty feet away in a slash of moonlight, thigh deep in weeds and gazing out across the river with a pensive air, as if he were rethinking his goals in life. He'd shed his jacket and was shirtless—the shirt was wrapped around his left hand, the hand I'd sliced. A thin shelf of flab overhung his belt.

I retreated a step, letting the frond ease back into place, and he looked straight at me. I could have sworn he didn't see me, that he had simply caught movement at the corner of his eye and been put on the alert. Then he sprinted toward me. I ran a few steps and pitched forward down a defile, gonging my head pretty good. Dazed, I realized I'd fetched up among ferns sprouting beside an abandoned shack. The door hanging one-hinged. Roofless. The moon shone down into it, but the light inside was too intense for ordinary moonlight—it cast shadows that looked deep as graves and flowed like quicksilver along spiderwebs spanning broken windows and gapped boards. Shards of mirror covered the interior walls, reminding me of those jigsaw puzzles that are one color and every piece almost the same shape. I picked myself up and was transfixed by the image of a bloody terrified girl reflected in the mirror fragments.

—Bitch!

The salesman spun me around, gut-punched me, and slung me through the door. Next I knew he had me straddled, pinning my arms with his knees and fumbling one-handed with his zipper, telling me what he had planned for the rest of our evening. When I made to buck him off, he slammed my head against the floor. He gaped at something behind me and I rolled my eyes back, wanting to know what had distracted him.

A ghost.

That was my first thought, but she had more the look of animation, a figure with just enough lines to suggest a naked woman, her colors not filled in.

The salesman scrambled to his feet, and she seemed to flow around him like a boa constrictor, locking him into an embrace and drawing him toward the back room, where they vanished, slipping through a seam that opened in midair and then closed behind them, leaving no trace. I don't believe he made a single sound.

I had a strong desire to leave and got to my knees, but the effort cost me and I blacked out. When I came to, I heard her humming an aimless tune. I slitted my eyes and had a peek. She sat cross-legged by my side. She was more defined and her colors were brighter, though they were still ashen . . .

except for a single drop of blood below her collarbone. She smiled, exposing the points of her fangs. I scooted away from her, but she had me and I knew it.

—Don't fret, *cher*, she said. I won't hurt you.

She noticed the blood drop, touched her finger to it, and licked the tip clean. I was too scared to speak.

—That man, she said. You're safe from him now.

My head had started to clear and I felt the creep of hysteria. Is he dead?

—Not dead. He's . . . waiting for me.

—Where is he? What's going on?

—He's where I sleep. Go slow, now. Calm yourself and I'll tell you all about it.

Just her saying that had an effect on me—it was like she'd turned down my temperature.

—I'm Sandrine, she said. And you are . . . ?

—Louie.

She repeated the name, pronouncing it like she was giving it a long, slow lick.

—If you want to go, I won't stop you, but it's been such a long time since I had someone to talk to. Sit with me? For a little while?

I didn't have any run left and I felt drowsy, scattered. My eyes skated across the mirror pieces. In each of them was Sandrine's face—pensive, fearful, frowning, in repose, moving as if alive. Hundreds of Sandrines, almost all of her, were trapped in those fragmented silver surfaces.

I must have spoken, because Sandrine laughed and said, I've been talking to them forty years and they haven't answered yet. For a pretty girl like you, though, they might just whisper a little something.

Cracker Paradise lies about four miles east of DuBarry on State Road 17 and consists of a spacious one-story structure of navy blue concrete block set on a weedy patch of white sand that's round as a bald spot and surrounded by slash pine. It doesn't sport a huge neon sign like some roadhouses, just a little plastic MILLER HIGH LIFE sign above the door, and it has a slit window that's been painted over so you can't see in. When I was younger, Momma would leave me locked in the car while she partied, assuming glass would protect me from the men who peered in. I used to create fantasies about the place based on glimpses I had of the interior when the door swung open. Even today, now I've been inside a few times, it remains a kind of fantasy. I'll hang out in the parking lot, sipping on a wine cooler slipped me by one of Momma's friends, and picture slinky waitress queens dancing barefoot on sizzling short-order grills and serving slices of fried poison to travelers in bathroom fixtures, while out on the purple-lit bash and rumble of the dance floor, checkout girls from the Piggly Wiggly, acne-blemished counter girls from Buy-Rite, pretty-for-a-season Walmart girls with clownish face paint and last decade's hairdo, they shake themselves into a low-grade fever, they make suggestions with their hips that turn the loose change in men's pockets green, they slice hearts and pentagrams on the beer-slickered floor with their spike heels, looking to give it up for love-only-love and a cute duplex in Jax Beach.

A few nights ago, a hot July night with the moon causing the sand to give off sparkles and silvering the hoods of the cars encircling the club, and a couple of hundred rednecks jammed inside, I stood in the parking lot smoking with two girls from New Jersey, Ann Jeanette and Carmen, who intended to compete in the wet T-shirt contest later that night. They were good-looking, gum-snapping, tough-talking girls in their early twenties, with frosted hair and big boobs, and they wore bikini thongs and Cracker Paradise T-shirts. They told me they were on the run from Ann Jeanette's boyfriend, who was connected and owned a recycling company in East Orange. Both girls were secretaries with the company, and they had stumbled across some paperwork they weren't supposed to see. The boyfriend ratted them out to a Mafia guy, and they had to leave town in a hurry. Since then they'd worked their way down the East Coast, heading for Miami, where Carmen had friends, entering wet T-shirt contests to pay for a few months out of the country. They claimed to win most of the contests they entered and considered themselves pros on the circuit.

Carmen nudged my breasts and said, You should enter, hon. They're paying out to fifth place.

I told her I was sixteen.

—Sixteen! My gawd! Ann Jeanette flicked ash from her Kool—her fake nails were gold with tiny black diamonds. You're very mature for sixteen. Don'tcha think she's mature, Carmen?

—Extremely, Carmen said. You gotta watch it with a figure like yours. Ann Jeanette's little sister was wearing a C cup in junior high and by the time she's your age, she needed a reduction.

—I'll be seventeen soon, I said. I don't think they're going to get much bigger.

—Oh my gawd! Ann Jeanette rolled her eyes.

—All the women in her family are big, said Carmen. You should see her mutha. The poor creetcha! Believe me, hon. They can get a lot bigger.

Two high school boys leaned against the bed of a pickup farther along the row, watching us. When they started singing "Louie Louie," Ann Jeanette took note of my embarrassment. She strolled over to the pickup and talked to them for half a minute. By the time she came back, they had hopped into their truck and were trying to start the engine.

—What'd you say? I asked delightedly.

—Fucking winkie dicks, she said.

Carmen gave her a hug and kissed her cheek and said, Ann Jeanette's badass!

—I hate fucking winkie dicks. Ann Jeanette inspected her nails and appeared satisfied. Men suck! It's true, they can be stimulating, but most of 'em are winkie dicks.

—We should go in, Carmen said. That guy runs the contest is a real pisser. We could lose our spot.

—The scrawny bitches they got in there, they can't afford to lose us. Now if Louie here were competing, we'd be in trouble. Ann Jeanette planted a sloppy kiss on my mouth, startling me, and said, Maybe we'll see ya after, doll.

They fluttered their hands in a wave and walked away arm in arm, wobbly in their high heels on the uneven ground.

I hopped up on the fender of a car and shut my eyes and thought about Sandrine. She'd be angry at me for not visiting her, but I was sick of being pressured and thought that when I visited her tomorrow night, the pressure would be off—no way I could bring her five live bodies in the next couple of days, so she wouldn't pester me about it and we could relax. I heard a blast of music and crowd noise as the door opened and looked in time to see it swing shut. This blond guy had stalled in midstride outside the door and was staring at me. After a second he came over. He was too old for me, twentysomething, but he was way beyond cute. He had blue eyes with long pale lashes, and his mouth was so wide and beautifully shaped I wanted to touch it, to make certain it was real. He was almost pretty, like a gay guy, but he didn't have that vibe. I thought I might expand my age limit for him. When he leaned against the fender, I felt the temperature go up a notch.

—I like the way you smell, he said.

—That's because I shower regularly.

He nodded soberly, as if a daily course of hygiene was an intriguing concept, something he might one day consider. His conversational skills seemed limited, but I figured he was nervous, so I said, What do you mean, I smell nice? Do I smell springtime clean or minty fresh or what?

He appeared to struggle with the question.

—Where you from? I asked.

—Up north, he said. I have a job.

I scrunched around, brushing his arm with my hip. His skin was hot, but he wasn't sweating.

—Is your job with the CIA? I asked. That's why you're being circumspect? Because you're a spy and you've been trained to guard against the likes of me?

His mouth hung open—I thought his circuits might be fried. To test my theory, I asked his name.

—Johnny, he said. Johnny Jacks.

The notion of doing a moron with a retarded name like Johnny Jacks . . . it didn't sit well. The last guy I'd gone with on the basis of his looks alone lay there afterward, thumping the side of my breast again and again, laughing to see it jiggle.

—Well, Johnny. I slid off the fender. I'll catch you later.

He started to follow me toward the door, and I turned on him and yelled, Stay! Sit! Don't follow me, okay?

I opened the door a crack and asked Wayne the bouncer if he cared to join me for a smoke and help fend off someone annoying. Wayne said, It's too damn hot. You can sit inside.

The AC made me happy—my sweat beads popped like champagne bubbles. Ted Horton, the radio deejay who oversees the wet T-shirt contests, did his spiel, the microphone blatting and squealing. The crowd whistled and yelled. Wayne wouldn't let me peek around the corner at the stage, and all I got to see were the geezers shooting pool at the rear. I played with Wayne's ink stamp, pressing it to my wrists, imprinting several dozen blurry Cracker Paradise logos. He scowled and snatched it away. Ted announced the winners—I couldn't make out the names—and the crowd turned ugly. They cursed Ted and he cursed them. "Fuck you" were the first words of his I heard clearly. Wayne shoved me back out into the heat.

The parking lot was empty, and I was both relieved and disappointed. I'd been modifying my position on Johnny Jacks, but it seemed he had lost interest. People boiled out of the club, several of them bleeding, escorted by Wayne and his colleagues. I spotted Ann Jeanette and Carmen beside a white SUV. Their soaked-through T-shirts drew lots of male attention, but the men who approached them hurried away as if scorched. I asked how they'd done.

—That muthafucka! Ann Jeanette had to take a breath, she was so angry. He give first prize to his Goddamn girlfriend!

—Ted Horton? I asked.

Carmen said, The bitch don't have enough to fill a training bra and stands here shivering when they pour the water . . . and she won? Puh-leese!

I assumed they were talking about Sarafina, Ted Horton's fiancée, a dark-skinned Cuban girl who was flat as an ironing board.

—I swear to God, I'll kill her, Ann Jeanette said. I'll kick the shit out of her.

I asked again how they had done.

—We come second and third. Carmen lit a cigarette. I thought there was gonna be a riot, people were so pissed.

She seemed ready to let go of her anger, and I explained that Sarafina had recently lost her job and like as not Ted was trying to help her out.

—Fuck her unemployed ass! Ann Jeanette scanned the lot. That don't mean she can take money out of my pocket.

—We get this sometimes, Carmen confided. There's a lot of jealousy, you know. We realize we're not gonna win all of 'em, but this was fucking ridiculous.

—There they go! Ann Jeanette shouted.

Ted, a runty guy with a Mohawk, was hustling toward

the rear of the lot, accompanied by a dark-skinned girl shrouded in a beach towel. They had their heads down and kept close to the wall. Ann Jeanette made a beeline for them, with Carmen at her heels. Ted turned at the last second, too late to prevent Ann Jeanette from spinning Sarafina around and decking her. Carmen leapt onto Ted from behind, riding him piggyback style to the ground, and Ann Jeanette began kicking him.

It was the first serious fight initiated by women that I'd seen, and I was impressed. A crowd closed in around them, cheering the girls on and blocking my view. Between bodies I caught sight of Ann Jeanette rifling Sarafina's purse. The cops would be coming soon, and reluctantly I headed for the highway, hoping to catch a ride with someone pulling out of the lot. Somebody wrapped me up from behind. I squirmed about and saw Johnny Jacks.

—Let me go, I said.

Something surfaced in his vacant, beautiful face, a flicker of emotion gone too quickly to identify.

—Let me go, fucker!

I managed to wriggle free of the bear hug, but he kept hold of my wrist. His grip was tight and hot like an Indian burn. I tried to pull away and said, I'll scream if you don't let go.

—I like you, he said.

The idea that he liked me was suddenly scary.

—Let her go, dude, said a rumbly voice at my shoulder.

It was Everett, my favorite of Momma's exes, a lanky muscular guy with a gloomy, bony face, gray hair tied in a ponytail, a motorcycle helmet in his right hand, a trucker wallet chained to his jeans. He planted his left hand, big as a frying pan, on Johnny Jacks's chest and gave him a hard shove—Johnny released my wrist, but the shove didn't move him as far as I might have expected.

—Yeah? Everett inquired of him. There something you want?

—I like you, Johnny Jacks said to me.

He walked off, his eyes on me, and merged with the crowd.

—What was that? Everett asked.

—Another Friday night at Cracker Paradise. Can I catch a ride?

—C'mon.

I locked my hands around Everett's waist, tucked my head onto his shoulder, and listened to his flathead growl, to police devils whining like sirens, the wind ripping my hair, wishing the ride would wind up somewhere anywhere different from a crummy Florida bungalow with a weedy patch of grass enclosed by a chain-link fence. The windows were dark when we arrived, and Momma's car wasn't in front. A yellow streetlight buzzed overhead and the moths were out in force.

—Thanks, I said, climbing off the bike.

—Somebody ain't always going to be around to protect you, said Everett. You aware of that?

—Yeah, I guess.

He stared at me gravely—he was the only one of Momma's boyfriends who looked me in the eye and not about a foot, foot and a half lower.

—You know I bought into that custom parts shop over in Jacksonville?

—Momma told me.

—Whyn't you come on up? I'll give you a job in sales. You can stay with me 'til you get a place.

—Everett! I batted my lashes. I didn't know you cared.

—Least there'd be somebody looking after you. You ain't doing nothing here you can't do there.

—You serious? I don't know anything about bikes.

—Ain't that much to know. It might give you a chance to get your bearings.

—I'll think about it, I swear I will.

—Don't think too long. We need people now. He gunned the engine. You're a smart girl, Louie. How come you treat yourself like you do?

I started to tell him my name was Elle, but it didn't seem important right then.

—I got self-esteem issues, I said.

* * *

Momma slept in the next morning. There wasn't anything to eat in the house, so I walked down to the convenience store and bought orange juice and pancake mix and made myself breakfast. After that I cleaned the living room, straightened the furniture, removed fast-food cartons and ladies' magazines and empty diet pill bottles, and vacuumed the rug. It was still a slum furnished with sprung sofas and patched easy chairs, but I felt accomplished. I watched TV for a while, surfing through a mix of get-right preachers and cartoons. Long about one o'clock I heard the toilet flush.

—Don't look at me, said Momma, coming into the room, carrying a glass of juice and wearing a robe with a design of winning poker hands. She closed the blinds all around until the room was half dark and plunked herself down in the recliner.

—I must look terrible, she said.

I wanted to tell her she was a female version of Dorian Gray's portrait, because whenever I saw her, I saw myself in about twenty years, but she would have asked was this Dorian some boy I was fooling with. Actually, she was a pretty woman yet, despite the pills and booze.

—You could at least lie to me, she said.

—You look fine, Momma.

A sigh. What'd you do last night?

—Nothing. I ran into Everett.

—Did you tell him I wanted him to call?

—Forgot.

—Jesus, Louie!

—Elle, I said.

—What*ever*. Don't you listen to a word I say?

I turned up the volume on the TV.

—Here! Let me have that. She pointed at the remote. There's a real good movie on. We can watch together.

The movie had started. It concerned two girls in a nuthouse—they didn't appear to like each other and took lots of meds. I tried not to relate it to my home life.

—That Angelina Jolie's so pretty, Momma said. I wish I could get my hair like hers.

The telephone rang.

—Can you grab that?

I answered and a mellow voice said, How you doing, sugar britches?

—It's for you. I passed Momma the phone.

—Hello. She sang the word.

After a few seconds of giggling and going, Uh-huh, uh-huh, Momma got up and said to me, I'm gonna take this in the bedroom. Fix me a piece of toast, sweetie. Okay?

I showered, put on cutoffs and a T-shirt, and went out, walking down the middle of the street barefoot, seeing how long I could take the hot asphalt before I had to hop onto a patch of grass. The parked cars were thousand-dollar shit boxes with smeared windshields that made the reflected sunlight look dirty. Every house was the same sort of rat hole; some had Tonka toys and Big Wheels half buried in the yellowish grass. A kid in a diaper stared at me from a doorway, holding an empty Coke bottle in his grubby fist, the TV jabbering in the gloom behind him. It was the fucking Third World.

The guys at Toby's would sneak me out a beer in a paper sack, but I didn't feel social and went to the park instead— a scrap of shade with some big azalea bushes and diseased palms and a fountain that gurgled like someone dying. I sat on the retaining wall, digging at a sand spur I'd picked up in the pad of my foot. Ants were scavenging a squashed beetle on the sidewalk. A gleaming black car with smoked windows breezed past. Two women talked in front of the grocery store, both shielding their eyes from the sun, as if saluting each other. A tabby cat emerged from under an azalea bush and stared at me with moderate interest.

—What's up? I asked.

Nothing, bitch, he said in cat language, and walked off, his tail straight up, showing me his ass.

The black car again—it slowed and stopped beside me. The window rolled down and Johnny Jacks peered out. I wondered how a loser like him had copped such a sharp ride.

—What's your name? he asked.

—Now that would have been a terrific follow-up question last night. Did it just occur to you?

No response.

—Are you on a holy quest? That would explain your minimalist style. You must be focused on prayer all the time, right?

Nothing.

—Do I still smell nice? I asked.

He tipped his head back—his nostrils flared. Dial soap, he said.

My detectors started beeping. Momma's favorite movie was *Silence of the Lambs*. I'd caught Hannibal Lecter's act.

—Okay, I said. Good-bye.

—Let's go for a drive, he said, climbing out of the car.

—Are you crazy? Fuck off!

I moved away along the wall.

He came after me, and I said, I'll scream.

—Why? I mean you no harm

The words "I mean you no harm" weirded me out even more—he seemed to have learned his English from a phrase book.

He stepped close, and I felt heat streaming off him. Please, he said.

—Leave me the fuck alone!

I crossed the street, glancing behind me to make certain he wasn't following, and nearly got splattered by a panel van.

—Hey! What's your problem? The driver stuck his head out. Your life not worth living?

I drank a couple of beers out front at Toby's, letting the geezers eye-fuck me, and that's when I began putting together Johnny Jacks and the Djadadjii. Once I started thinking about it, I couldn't get it out of my head, and by the time I arrived at Sandrine's, I was busting to tell her. She was nowhere to be seen, and I knew she was hiding because I hadn't visited the night before.

—Sandrine, I called.

The river made chuckling noises, rubbing against the bank. Clouds hedged the moon, but it sailed clear. The shack held only moonlight and mirrors. I studied the foliage, trying to find her outline among the tangles of leaves.

—Don't be pissy, I said.

—I know everything you're thinking.

I still couldn't find her.

—You think because you don't visit me one night, two nights, I won't mention what I need. What you promised me.

I whirled about, thinking she was behind me, and said, I didn't promise anything. I said I'd try.

—How can I expect such a stupid girl to understand what I've endured? You tell me how alone you are, how much you hunger for life, yet every day you talk to people, you fill your belly, you taste life.

—Everything's relative.

—You could have more life with me than you can possibly imagine.

—Don't go there! You tricked me. You made me feel things.

—Oh! Now you're going to pretend you feel nothing for me? That I put those feelings into your head? All I did was unlock a door you never realized existed. I've seen how you look at me.

She melted up from the chokecherry, a paring of a woman seeming no thicker than onionskin, drifting toward me on the breeze—she touched her gauzy breasts, caressed almost imperceptible hips and thighs. A firefly danced behind her forehead, hovered for an instant in one eye.

—I see you looking now, she said.

Frightened, I backed away from her until my shoulders touched the wall of the shack.

I've been patient with you, she said. I could be patient forever and it wouldn't do any good.

—The Djadadjii, I said. Do they feel hotter than normal people?

Her face emptied.

—I met this guy, I said. He's new in town. Super good-looking, but a retard. He can barely talk and his skin feels like an oven door. Sound familiar?

I'd meant to warn her about Johnny Jacks, but she had frightened me, and now I wanted to tell her in a way that made her heart race.

—First thing out of his mouth was he liked the way I smelled, I said. Think he smelled you on me?

—Lou . . . Elle. You have to help me!

—What can I do? Bring you five people? I doubt there's time.

Fear sharpened her indistinct features. She looked this way and that, agitated, searching for an out.

—Maybe I could do with four, she said. Four might be sufficient.

I realized then what a danger she was to me, and I bolted for the fallen oak, vaulted over it, landing among the hyacinths at the edge of the water.

—Louie!

—Four? You been drilling it into me ever since we met how you needed five.

—You don't understand!

—Of course I don't. I'm such a stupid girl. I must be really fucking stupid to trust you. Maybe it's only three people you need. Two plus me.

We were slightly more than an arm's length apart, but it might have been in different countries.

—Don't leave, Sandrine said. Without you I'll die.

I slogged a few paces through the water, the leathery

hyacinth roots snagging my ankles.

—I can explain!

I kept going.

—I'll show you things, she said. Incredible things. I'll tell you my secrets. I should have been open from the start, but I thought I'd lose you. I'll never keep anything from you again.

I clambered onto shore.

—You're taking my heart!

I slipped on something slick and sat down hard.

—Whore! she screamed. You filthy, disgusting whore! Go ahead! All you are is flabby tits and stinking blood! Touching you makes me sick! You hear? I feel like puking when I'm near you! Do you know what you smell like?

She told me. In detail. I could hear her screaming corrosive insults long after I entered the brush, and perhaps I heard them even after I had gone beyond the range of her voice.

I tracked down Johnny Jacks in the parking lot at Cracker Paradise. He took me into the shadows alongside his car, and there he choked me a little and slapped me. I told him he didn't have to use force, he could have everything he wanted. We drove to a spot not far from Sandrine's, and we walked down to the river. Big chunks of anger, boulder sized, were in my head, damming up everything except a leakage of bitterness. I ignored thoughts of what he might do to me—I wanted something to happen, and I didn't care what so long as it was violent. He hardly spoke, and I couldn't tell what was on his mind. He might have been no different from the rest of us, mostly urge and raw need, and simply was less capable of expressing it.

We reached Sandrine's, and he climbed eagerly over the toppled oak. I waited in the river, mud oozing between my toes. The moon was so bright the blue sky was almost a day color. I felt it shining inside me, generating hatred, a cooler emotion directed at her, at all things. Hyacinths with foot-high purplish blooms bobbled against my knees. Johnny Jacks glanced at me, his face expressionless as ever. I thought he would say something, but Sandrine melted up from the rotting boards of the shack, a female pattern emerging from the wood grain, and appeared to coil around him. She didn't draw him inside the shack, into the place where she slept; she bore him to the ground and sank her fangs into his neck and drank. He moaned once, a frail sound. Every now and then his hand twitched or an arm jerked. As he grew paler, she grew more real. It wasn't what I had expected, or maybe it was. Part of me was disappointed he wasn't what I'd hoped. Another part would have preferred to be horrified. Mainly I had a sense of . . . I don't know. Closure, maybe. Not the feeling you get when you're over a crush or have gone past some pain, but like the feeling you have the morning after your first time with a boy. Anxious and a little shaky, worried that you've screwed up, but with a bigger anxiety removed, and you're ready to become this new person you see in the mirror.

Johnny Jacks was still alive when Sandrine lifted her head. Blood flowed from the puncture wounds on his neck, anyway. She flipped hair back from her eyes—blood filmed over her chin and lips, dark and thick as gravy.

—The Djadadjii are cool to the touch, she said. But you knew he wasn't Djadadj, didn't you? At the least you suspected.

I had nothing to say.

—Not this month, she said. But next month, the month after . . . soon we'll be together.

She lowered her head and drank again, just a sip, and then said, I'm not angry with you. You needed a push, so I pushed you. If he had turned out be Djadadj, well . . . life is risk. It was only a tiny risk, though.

She closed her eyes and arched her neck, sated and languorous. On her hip a speckle of mud like a beauty mark. She stroked Johnny Jacks's blond hair.

—He's beautiful, though. Beautiful enough to be Djadadj.

She rested her cheek against his, her lips parted, baring the tips of her crimson fangs—a scene from one of my mind movies brought to life.

—Go home now, she said. Come again tomorrow night . . . or wait a month. It's no matter. Go home and think about what you must do.

When I turned from the tableau of the shack and the two figures lying in the grass and mud, it was as if I'd never seen

the river and the sky before—they were so vast and unfamil-
iar, they almost flattened me.

—Good night, Elle, said Sandrine.

My father's a battered gray suitcase. He left me with no photographs, no scars, no good-byes, no promises, no postcards,
no phone calls on my birthday, no memories whatsoever; but
he did leave me that suitcase. To my mind he might as well
be a battered old thing whose last name is Samsonite. I lay
the suitcase open on the bed and begin stuffing everything I
own into it. As I cross back and forth between the closet and
the bed, I catch glimpses of myself in the mirror. I see Louie,
small-time and ordinary, a bright, slutty girl, still hopeful,
soul somewhat in hock to a regulation Sunday school dream,
with a nice enough face and body to make it happen. And
I see Elle, spooky and hot to trot, with her hungry mouth
and Xed-out eyes and reckless ways. She strikes me as a fraud,
though I can't say why. I avoid staring at the reflection, not
wanting to see which one will become dominant, disliking
both equally.

I latch the suitcase and picture myself working with
Everett in the parts store—it seems I already know how that
story ends, and it's the same with every other story I imagine.
I realize there are better stories out there, ones with happier
endings, but I have no idea how to go about achieving those
fantasies of wealth and fame. Chandler Mason could tell me,

probably, but look where she wound up.

Momma's entertaining tonight. The bed frame creaks, the springs shriek, the headboard hammers out a factory rhythm, a relentless machine fury, *blam-blam-blam*ming against the wall. Her flutelike outcries provide a breathy counterpoint.

When I was little, I'd scrunch down outside her door and try to interpret the noises, worried about what was happening. After I discovered sex, I envisioned demons atop her. Monsters. Wild animals. Men with beards and hairy thighs and cloven hooves. Now I close my ears to it. For a murderous instant I see myself appearing naked in her doorway, displaying my fangs.

Lugging the suitcase down the hall is a chore and toting it along the riverbank would be a real pain. Maybe, I think, its weight will determine my destination. I crank open the blinds and the vivid indigo of predawn invades the room. The thrift store furniture looks opulent in the half-light. I perch on the recliner, thinking that if I were Sandrine, I'd have handled my seduction more efficiently and the matter would not be in doubt. Sandrine's stronger than me, she knows more, she's more experienced, but how smart can she be? She got herself caught by someone as dumb as a chicken . . . and she intends to let Elle into her life. Elle's quick on her feet and rat crafty. A fast learner. She's capable of using a user like Sandrine.

Who am I kidding?

I'll fuck up wherever I'm going.

At first light I'll step outside and hitch a ride to Jacksonville. I can always change my mind. It comes as a revelation, the recognition that Elle is driving this indecisive decision and that it's Louie who is reluctant to go. I thought it would be the other way around. They're all scrambled in my head, these roles I understudy, these half-formed characters I inhabit, but I understand now that Elle is frightened of life's sudden dips and swerves. She endangers herself only when she thinks— sometimes mistakenly—that she's in control. Louie's the scary one, the one who Sandrine wants, the one who wants Sandrine. She's the dreamer, the believer. She'd tattoo a heart on her heart and be true for no reason. She could live on a dime's worth of hope and make love with a shadow. She's the kind of girl who'd sacrifice for love.

She'd kill to sustain it.

MY GENERATION

by Emma Bull

Curfew is at sunrise.
Mornings were get going, get up, get dressed, get to
   school
Get get get
Wait 'til you get home—
No soft kindly dawn to miss.
Sunset brings forgiveness
Smoothing out the flaws;
Even rusted cars shine after dark

The date moves forward on the fake ID.
Leather, Lycra, latex, linen
Unmarked in them all
Dance every song
Dance full out
And never shake or ache or gasp for breath.

Bass and kick drum put a heartbeat
Inside every dancer's ribs.

Best friends dropped the needle down
On that track each time:
Hope I die—he sang.
But they got old.
The track wore down, the tape stretched
While new songs throbbed unnoticed.
Ruts grow deep and deeper
Until they reach six feet
Then shovel dirt in.

Life is change.
New songs, new bands,
New stories, new dreams.
Death is one old song on repeat play.
The living, lazy, choose to die
Before the beat stops in their chests.

Greedy for life after life,
Gulping fresh tunes whole,
Grabbing more,
Glorying in each new night, new dance:
I will never die.

WHY LIGHT?

by Tanith Lee

PART ONE

My first memory is the fear of light.

The passage was dank and dark and water dripped, and my mother carried me, although by then I could walk. I was three, or a little younger. My mother was terrified. She was consumed by terror, and she shook, and her skin gave off a faint metallic smell I had never caught from her before. Her hands were cold as ice. I could feel that, even through the thick shawl in which she'd wrapped me. She said, over and over, "It's all right, baby. It's all right. It will be okay. You'll see. Just a minute, only one. It'll be all right."

By then of course I too was frightened. I was crying, and I think I wet myself, though I hadn't done anything like that since babyhood.

Then the passage turned, and there was a tall iron gate—I

know it's iron, now. At the time it only looked like a burned-out coal.

"Oh, God," said my mother.

But she thrust out one hand and pushed at the gate, and it grudged open with a rusty scraping, just wide enough to let us through.

I would have seen the vast garden outside the house, played there. But this wasn't the garden. It was a high place, held in only by a low stone wall and a curving break of poplar trees. They looked very black, not green the way the house lamps made trees in the garden. Something was happening to the sky; that was what made the poplars so black. I thought it was moonrise, but I knew the moon was quite new, and only a full moon could dilute the darkness so much. The stars were watery and blue, weak, like dying gas flames.

My mother stood there, just outside the iron gate, holding me, shaking. "It's all right . . . just a minute . . . only one . . ."

Suddenly something happened.

It was like a storm—a lightning flash maybe, but in slow motion, that swelled up out of the dark. It was pale, then silver, and then like gold. It was like a high trumpet note, or the opening chords of some great concerto.

I sat bolt upright in my mother's arms, even as she shook ever more violently. I think her teeth were chattering.

But I could only open my eyes wide. Even my mouth

opened, as if to drink the sudden light.

It was the color of a golden flower and it seemed to boil, and enormous clouds poured slowly upward out of it, brass and wine and rose. And a huge noise came from everywhere, rustling and rushing—and weird flutings and squeakings and trills—birdsong—only I didn't recognize it.

My mother now hoarsely wept. I don't know how she never dropped me.

Next they came out and drew us in again, and Tyfa scooped me quickly away as my mother collapsed on the ground. So I was frightened again, and screamed.

They closed the gate and shut us back in darkness. The one minute was over. But I had seen a dawn.

PART TWO

Fourteen and a half years later, and I stood on the drive, looking at the big black limousine. Marten was loading my bags into the boot. Musette and Kousu were crying quietly. One or two others lingered about; nobody seemed to grasp what exactly was the correct way to behave. My mother hadn't yet come out of the house.

By that evening my father was dead over a decade—he had died when I was six, my mother a hundred and seventy. They had lived together a century anyway, were already tired of each other, and had taken other lovers from our community. But that made his death worse, apparently. Ever since, every seventh evening, she would go into the little shrine she had made to him, cut one of her fingers, and let go a drop of blood in the vase below his photograph. Her name is Juno, my mother, after a Roman goddess, and I'd called her by her name since I was an adult.

"She should be here," snapped Tyfa, irritated. He too was Juno's occasional lover, but generally he seemed exasperated by her. "Locked in that damn room," he added sourly. He meant the shrine.

I said nothing, and Tyfa stalked off along the terrace and started pacing about, a tall, strong man of around two hundred or so, no one was sure—dark haired as most of us were at Severin. His skin had a light brownness from a long summer of sun exposure. He had always been able to take the sun, often for several hours in one day. I too have black hair, and my skin, even in winter, is pale brown. I can endure daylight all day long, day after day. I can *live* by day.

Marten had closed the boot. Casperon had gotten into the driver's seat, leaving the car door open, and was trying the engine. Its loud purring would no doubt penetrate the house's upper story, and the end rooms that comprised Juno's apartment.

Abruptly she came sweeping out from the house.

Juno has dark red hair. Her skin is white. Her slanting eyes are the dark bleak blue of a northern sea, seen in a foreign movie with subtitles. When I was a child I adored her. She *was* my goddess. I'd have died for her, but that stopped. It stopped forever.

She walked straight past the others, as if no one else were there. She stood in front of me. She was still an inch or so taller than I, though I'm tall.

"Well," she said. She stared into my face, hers cold as marble, and all of her stone still—this, the woman who trembled and clutched me to her, whispering that all would be well, when I was three years old.

"Yes, Juno," I said.

"Do you have everything you need?" she asked me indifferently, forced to be polite to some visitor now finally about to leave.

"Yes, thank you. Kousu helped me pack."

"You know you have only to call the house, and anything else can be sent on to you? Of course," she added offhandedly, "you'll want for nothing, *there*."

I did not reply. What was there to say? I've "wanted" for so much *here* and never gotten it—at least, my mother, from *you*.

"I wish you very well," she coldly said, "in your new home. I hope everything will be pleasant. The marriage is important, as you're aware, and they'll treat you fairly."

"Yes."

"We'll say good-bye then. At least for a while."

"Yes."

"Good-bye, Daisha." She drew out the *ay* sound; and

foolishly through my mind skipped words that rhymed—fray, say . . . prey.

I said, "So long, Juno. Good luck making it up with Tyfa. Have a nice life."

Then I turned my back, crossed the terrace and the drive, and got into the car. I'd signed off with all the others before. They had loaded me with good wishes and sobbed, or tried to cheer me by mentioning images we had seen of my intended husband, and saying how handsome and talented he was, and I must write to them soon, email or call—not lose touch—come back next year—sooner— Probably they'd forget me in a couple of days or nights.

To me, they already seemed miles off.

The cream limousine of the full moon had parked over the estate as we drove away. In its blank blanched rays I could watch, during the hour it took to cross the whole place and reach the outer gates, all the nocturnal industry, in fields and orchards, in vegetable gardens, pens, and horse yards, garages and workshops—a black horse cantering, lamps, and red sparks flying—and people coming out to see us go by, humans saluting the family car, appraising in curiosity, envy, pity, or scorn, the girl driven off to become a Wife of Alliance.

In the distance the low mountains shone blue from the moon. The lake across the busy grasslands was like a gigantic vinyl disk dropped from the sky, an old record the moon had played, and played tonight on the spinning turntable of the Earth. This was the last I saw of my home.

The journey took just on four days.

Sometimes we passed through whitewashed towns, or cities whose tall concrete-and-glass fingers reached to scratch the clouds. Sometimes we were on motorways, wide and streaming with traffic in spate. Or there was open countryside, mountains coming or going, glowing under hard icing-sugar tops. In the afternoons we'd stop, for Casperon to rest, at hotels. About six or seven in the evening we drove on. I slept in the car by night. Or sat staring from the windows.

I was, inevitably, uneasy. I was resentful and bitter and full of a dull and hopeless rage.

I shall get free of it all—I had told myself this endlessly since midsummer, when first I had been informed that, to cement ties of friendship with the Duvalles, I was to marry their new heir. Naturally it was not only friendship that this match entailed. I had sun-born genes. And the Duvalle heir, it seemed, hadn't. My superior light endurance would be necessary to breed a stronger line. A bad joke, to our kind—they needed my *blood*. I was *blood*stock. I was Daisha Severin, a young female life only seventeen years, and able to live daylong in sunlight. I was incredibly valuable. I would be, everyone had said, so *welcome*. And I was *lovely*, they said, with my brunette hair and dark eyes, my cinnamon skin. The

heir—Zeev Duvalle—was very taken with the photos he had
seen of me. And didn't I think *he* was fine—*cool*, Musette had
said, "He's so *cool*—I wish it could have been me. You're so
lucky, Daisha."

Zeev was blond, almost snow-blizzard white, though his
eyebrows and lashes were dark. His eyes were like some pale,
shining metal. His skin was pale, too, if not so colorless as
with some of us, or so I'd thought when I watched him in
the house movie I'd been sent. My pale-skinned mother had
some light tolerance, though far less than my dead father. I
had inherited all *his* strength that way, and more. But Zeev
Duvalle had none, or so it seemed. To me he looked like what
he was, a man who lived only by night. In appearance he
seemed nineteen or twenty, but he wasn't so much older in
actual years. Like me, a new *young* life. So much in common.
So very little.

And by now "I shall get free of it all," which I'd repeated
so often, had become my mantra, and also meaningless.
How could I *ever* get free? Among my own kind I would be
an outcast and criminal if I ran away from this marriage,
now or ever, without a "valid" reason. While able to pass as
human, I could hardly live safely among them. I can eat and
drink a little in their way, but I need blood. Without blood I
would die.

So, escape the families and their alliance, I would

become not only traitor and thief—but a *murderer*. A human-slaughtering monster humanity doesn't believe in, or *does* believe in—something, either way, that, if discovered among them, they will kill.

That other house, my former home on the Severin estate, was long and quite low, two storied, but with high ceilings mostly on the ground floor. Its first architecture, gardens, and farm had been made in the early nineteenth century.

Their mansion—castle—whatever one has to call it—was colossal. Duvalle had built high.

It rose, this *pile*, like a cliff, with outcrops of slate-capped towers. Courtyards and enclosed gardens encircled it. Beyond and around lay deep pine woods with infiltrations of other trees, some maples, already flaming in the last of summer and the sunset. I spotted none of the usual workplaces, houses, or barns.

We had taken almost three hours to wend through their land, along the tree-rooted and stone-littered upward-tending track. Once Casperon had to pull up, get out, and examine a tire. But it was all right. On we went.

At one point, just before we reached the house, I saw a waterfall cascading from a tall, rocky hill, plunging into a ravine below. In the ghostly dusk it looked beautiful and melodramatic. Setting the tone?

When the car at last drew up, a few windows were burning amber in the house cliff. Over the wide door itself glowed a single electric light inside a round pane like a worn-out planet.

No one had come to greet us.

We got out and stood at a loss. The car's headlamps fired the brickwork, but still nobody emerged. At the lit windows, no silhouette appeared gazing down.

Casperon marched to the door and rang some sort of bell that hung there.

All across the grounds crickets chirruped, hesitated, and went on.

The night was warm, and so empty; nothing seemed to be really alive anywhere, despite the crickets, the windows. Nothing, I mean, of *my* kind, our people. For a strange moment I wondered if something ominous had happened here, if everyone had died, and if so, would that release me? But then one leaf of the door was opened. A man looked out. Casperon spoke to him, and the man nodded. A few minutes later I had to go up the steps and into the house.

There was a sort of vestibule, vaguely lighted by old ornate lanterns. Beyond that was a big paved court, with pruned trees and raised flower beds, and then more steps. Casperon had gone for my luggage. I followed the wretched sallow man who had let me in.

"What's your name?" I asked him as we reached the next

portion of the house, a blank wall lined only with blank black windows.

"Anton."

"Where is the family?" I asked him.

"Above" was all he said.

I said, halting, "Why was there no one to welcome me?"

He didn't reply. Feeling a fool, angry now, I stalked after him.

There was another vast hall or vestibule. No lights, until he touched the switch and grayish, weary side lamps came on, giving little color to the stony, towering space.

"Where," I said, in Juno's voice, "*is* he? He at least should be here. Zeev Duvalle, my husband-to-be." I spoke formally. "I am insulted. Go at once and tell him—"

"He does not rise yet," said Anton, as if to somebody invisible but tiresome. "He doesn't rise until eight o'clock."

Day in night. Night was Zeev's day. Yet the sun had been gone over an hour now. Damn him, I thought. *Damn* him.

It was useless to protest further. And when Casperon returned with the bags, I could say nothing to him, because this wasn't his fault. And besides, he would soon be gone. I was alone. As per usual.

I met Zeev Duvalle at dinner. It was definitely a dinner, not a breakfast, despite their day-for-night policy. It was served in an upstairs conservatory, the glass panes open to the air.

A long table draped in white, tall old greenish glasses, plates of some red china, probably Victorian. Only five or six other people came to the meal, and they introduced themselves in a formal, chilly way. Only one woman, who looked about fifty and so probably was into her several hundreds, said she regretted not being there at my arrival. No excuse was offered, however. They made me feel like what I was to them, a new house computer that could talk. A doll that would be able to have babies . . . yes. Horrible.

By the time we sat down, in high-backed chairs, with huge orange trees standing around behind them like guards—a scene on a film set—I was boiling with cold anger. Part of me was afraid, too. I can't really explain the fear, or of what. It was like being washed up out of the night ocean on an unknown shore, and all you can see are stones and emptiness, and no light to show the way.

At Severin there were always types of ordinary food to be had—steaks, apples—we drank a little wine, took coffee or tea. But a lot of us were sun born. Even Juno was. She hated daylight but still tucked into the occasional croissant. Of course there was Proper Sustenance, too. The blood of those animals we kept for that purpose, always collected with economy, care, and gentleness from living beasts, which continued to live, well fed and tended and never overused, until their natural deaths. For special days there was special blood. This being drawn, also with respectful care, from among the human families who lived on the estate. They had no fear of giving blood, any more than the animals did. In return, their rewards were many and lavish. The same arrangement, so far as I knew, was similar among all the scattered families of our kind.

Here at Duvalle, we were served a black pitcher of blood, a white pitcher of white wine. Fresh bread, still warm, lay on the red dishes.

That was all.

I had taken Proper Sustenance at the last hotel, drinking from my flask. I'd drunk a Coke on the road, too.

Now I took a piece of bread and filled my glass with an inch of wine.

They all looked at me. Then away. Every other glass by then gleamed scarlet. One of the men said, "But, young lady, this is the best, this is *human*. We always take it at dinner. Come now."

"No," I said, "thank you."

"Oh, but clearly you don't know your own mind—"

And then *he* spoke. From the doorway. He had only just come in, after his long rest or whatever else he had been doing for the past two and a half hours, as I was in my allotted apartment, showering, getting changed for this appalling night.

What I saw first about him, Zeev Duvalle, was inevitable. The blondness, the *whiteness* of him, almost incandescent against the candlelit room and the dark beyond the glass.

His hair was like molten platinum, just sombering down a bit to a kind of white gold in the shadow. His eyes weren't gray, but green—gray-green like the crystal goblets. His skin, after all, wasn't that pale. It had a sort of tawny look to it—not in any way like a tan. More as if it fed on darkness and had drawn some into itself. He was handsome, but I knew that. He looked now about nineteen. He had a perfect body, slim and strong; most vampires do. We eat the perfect food and very few extra calories—nothing too much or too little. But he was tall. Taller than anyone I'd ever met. About six and a half feet, I thought.

Unlike the others, even me, he hadn't smartened up for dinner. He wore un-new black jeans and a scruffy T-shirt with long, torn sleeves. I could smell the outdoors on him, pine needles, smoke, and night. He had been out in the grounds. There was . . . there was a little brown-red stain on one sleeve. Was it *blood*? From *what*?

It came to me with a lurch what he really most resembled. A white wolf. And had this *bloody* wolf been out hunting in his vast forested park? What had he killed so mercilessly—some squirrel or hare—or a deer—that would be bad enough—or was it worse?

I knew *nothing* about these people I'd been given to. I'd been too offended and allergic to the whole idea to do any research, ask any real questions. I had frowned at the brief movie they sent of him, thought: So, he's cute and almost albino. I hadn't even gotten that right. He was a *wolf.* He was a feral animal that preyed in the old way, by night, on things defenseless and afraid.

This was when he said again, "Let her alone, Constantine." Then, "Let her eat what she wants. She knows what she likes." *Then*: "Hi, Daisha. I'm Zeev. If only you'd gotten here a little later, I'd have been here to welcome you."

I met his eyes, which was difficult. That glacial green, I slipped from its surface. I said quietly, "Don't worry. Who cares."

He sat down at the table's head. Though the youngest among them, he was the heir and therefore, supposedly, their leader now. His father had died two years before, when his car left an upland road miles away. Luckily his companion, a woman from the Clays family, had called the house. The wreck of the car and his body had been retrieved by Duvalle before the sun could make a mess of both the living and the dead. All of us know we survive largely through the wealth longevity enables us to gather, and the privacy it buys.

The others started to drink their dinner again, passing the black jug. Only one of them took any bread, and that was to sop up the last red elements from inside his glass. He wiped the bread around like a cloth, then stuffed it into his mouth.

I sipped my wine. Zeev, seen from the side of my left eye, seemed to touch nothing. He merely sat there. He didn't seem to look at me. I was glad of that.

Then the man called Constantine said loudly, "Better get on with your supper, Wolf, or she'll think you already found it in the woods. And among *her* clan that just *isn't* done."

And some of them sniggered a little, softly. I wanted to hurl my glass at the wall—or at all their individual heads.

But Zeev said, "What, you mean this on my T-shirt?" He too sounded amused.

I put down my unfinished bread and got up. I glanced around at them, at him last of all.

"I hope you'll excuse me. I've been traveling and I'm tired." Then I looked straight at him. Somehow it was shocking to do so. "And good night, *Zeev*. Now we've finally met."

He said nothing. None of them did.

I walked out of the conservatory, crossed the large room beyond, and headed for the staircase.

Wolf. They even *called* him that.

Wolf.

"Wait," he said, just behind me.

I can move almost noiselessly and very fast, but not as noiseless and sudden as he apparently could. Before I could prevent it, I spun around wide-eyed. There he stood, less than three feet from me. He was expressionless, but when he spoke now his voice, actor trained, I thought, was very musical. "Daisha Severin, I'm sorry. I've made a bad start with you."

"You noticed."

"Will you come with me—just upstairs—to the library? We can talk there without the rest of them making up an audience."

"Why do we want to? Talk, I mean."

"We should, I think. And maybe you'll be gracious enough to humor me."

"Maybe I'll just tell you to go to hell."

"Oh, *there*," he said. He smiled. "No. I'd never go there. Too bright, too hot."

"Fuck off," I said.

I was seven steps up the stairs when I found him beside me. I stopped again.

"Give me," he said, "one minute."

"I've been told I have to give you my entire *life*," I said. "And then I have to give you children, too, I nearly forgot. Kids who can survive in full daylight, just like me. I think that's enough, isn't it, Zeev Duvalle? You don't need a silly little *minute* from me when I have to give you all the rest."

He let me go then.

I ran up the stairs.

When I reached the upper landing, I looked back down,

between a kind of elation and a sort of horror. But he had vanished. The part-lit spaces of the house again seemed void of anything alive, except for me.

Juno. I dreamed about her that night. I dreamed she was in a jet-black cave where water dripped, and she held a dead child in her arms and wept.

The child was me, I suppose. What she had feared the most when they, my house of Severin, made her carry me out into the oncoming dawn, to see how much, if anything, I could stand. *Just one minute.* What he had asked for, too, Zeev. I hadn't granted it to him. But she—and I—had had no choice.

When I survived sunrise, she was at first very glad. But then, when I began to keep asking, "When can I see the light again?" Then, oh then. Then she began to lose me, and I her, my tall, red-haired, blue-eyed mother.

She never told me, but it's simple to work out. The more I took to daylight, the more I proved I was a true sun-born, the *more* she lost me, and I lost her. She herself could stand two or three hours, every week or so. But she *hated* the light, the sun. They *terrified* her, and when I turned out so able to withstand them, even to like and . . . *want* them, then the doors of her heart shut fast against me.

Juno hated me just as she hated the light of the sun. She hated me, *loathed* me, *loathes* me, my mother.

PART THREE

About three weeks went by. The pines darkened and the other trees turned to copper and bronze and shed like tall cats their fur of leaves. I went on walks about the estate. No one either encouraged or dissuaded me. They had then nothing they wanted to hide from me? But I don't drive, and so there was a limit to how far I could go and get back again in the increasingly chilly evenings. By day, anyway, there seemed little activity, in the house or outside it. I started sleeping later in the mornings so I could stay up at night fully alert, sometimes until four or five. It was less that I was checking on what went on in the house castle of Duvalle than that I was uncomfortable so many of them were around, and *active*, when I lay asleep. There was a lock on my door. I always used it. I put a chair against it, too, with the back under the door handle. It wasn't Zeev I was worried about. No one, in particular. Just the complete feel and atmosphere of that place. At Severin there had been several who were mostly or totally nocturnal— my mother, for one. But also quite a few like me who, even if they couldn't take much direct sunlight, as I could, still preferred to be about by day.

A couple of times during my outdoor excursions in daylight, I did find clearings in the woods, with small houses, vines, orchards, fields with a harvest already collected.

I even once saw some men with a flock of sheep. Neither sheep nor men took any notice of me. No doubt they had been warned a new Wife of Alliance was here, and shown what she looked like.

The marriage had been set for the first night of the following month. The ceremony would be brief, unadorned, simply a legalization. Marriages in most of the houses were like this. Nothing especially celebratory, let alone religious, came into them.

I thought I'd resigned myself. But of course, I hadn't. As for him, Zeev Duvalle, I'd been "meeting" him generally only at dinner—those barren awful dinners where good manners seemed to demand I attend. Sometimes I was served meat— I alone. A crystal bowl of fruit had appeared—for me. I ate with difficulty amid their "fastidious" contempt. I began a habit of removing pieces of fruit to eat later in my rooms. He was only ever polite. He would unsmilingly and bleakly offer me bread and wine, water. . . . Sometimes I did drink the blood. I needed to. To me it had a strange taste, which maybe I imagined.

During the night, now and then, I might see him about the house, playing chess with one of the others, listening to music or reading in the library, talking softly on a telephone. Three or four times I saw him from an upper window, outside and running in long wolflike bounds between the trees, the paleness of his hair like a beam blown off the face of the moon.

Hunting?

I intended to get married in black. Like the girl in the Chekhov play, I too was in mourning for my life. That night I hung the dress outside the closet and put the black pumps below, ready for tomorrow. No jewelry.

Also I made a resolve not to go down to their dire dinner. To the older woman who read novels at the table and laughed smugly, secretively at things in them; the vile man with his bread cloth in the glass. The handful of others, some of whom never turned up regularly anyhow, their low voices murmuring to one another about past times and people known only to them. And him. Zeev. Him. He drank from his glass very couthly, unlike certain others. Sometimes a glass of water, or some wine—for him usually red, as if it must pretend to be blood. He had dressed more elegantly since the first night, but always his clothes were quiet. There was one dark white shirt, made of some sort of velvety material, with bone-color buttons. . . . He looked beautiful. I could have killed him. We're easy to kill—car crashes, bullets—though we can live, Tyfa had once said, even a thousand years. But that's probably one more lie.

However, tonight I wouldn't go down there. I'd eat up

here, the last apple and the dried cherries.

About ten thirty, a knock on my door.

I jumped, more because I expected it than because I was startled. I put down the book I'd been reading, the Chekhov plays, and said, "Who is it?" Knowing who it was.

"May I come in?" he asked, formal and musical, alien.

"I'd rather you left me alone," I said.

He said, without emphasis, "All right, Daisha. I'll go down to the library. No one else will be there. There'll be fresh coffee. I'll wait for you until midnight. Then I have things I have to do."

I'd gotten up and crossed to the door. I said through it, with a crackling venom that surprised me, I'd thought I had it leashed, *"Things to do?* Oh, when you go out hunting animals and rip them apart in the woods for proper fresh blood, that kind of *thing,* do you mean?"

There was silence. Then, "I'll wait till midnight," he flatly said.

Then he was gone, I knew, though I never heard him leave.

When I walked into the library it was after eleven, and I was wearing my wedding dress and shoes. I told him what they were.

"It's supposed to be unlucky, isn't it," I said, "for the groom to see the bride in her dress before the wedding. But there's no luck to spoil, is there?"

He was sitting in one of the chairs by the fire, his long legs stretched out. He'd put on jeans and a sweater and boots for the excursion later. A leather jacket hung from the chair.

The coffee was still waiting, but it would be cold by now. Even so, he got up, poured me a cup, brought it to me. He managed—he always managed this—to hand it to me without touching me.

Then he moved away and stood by the hearth, gazing across at the high walls of books.

"Daisha," he said, "I think I understand how uncomfortable and angry you are—"

"*Do you?*"

"—but can I ask that you listen. Without interrupting or storming out of the room—"

"Oh, for God's—"

"*Daisha.*" He turned his eyes on me. From glass green, they too had become almost white. He was flaming mad, anyone could see, but unlike me, he'd controlled it. He *used* it, like a cracking whip spattering electricity across the room. And at the same time—the *pain* in his face. The closed-in pain and . . . was it only frustration, or despair? That was what held me, or I'd have walked out, as he said. I stood there stunned, and thought, He hurts as I do. Why? Who did this to him? God, he hates the idea of marrying me as much as *I* hate it. Or—he hates the way he—*we*—are being used.

"Okay," I said. I sat down on a chair. I put the cold

coffee on the floor. "Talk. I'll listen."

"Thank you," he said.

A huge old clock ticked on the mantelpiece above the fire. *Tock-tock-tock*. Each note a second. Sixty now. That minute he'd asked from me before. Or the minute when Juno held me in the sunrise, shaking.

"Daisha. I'm well aware you don't want to be here, let alone with me. I hoped you wouldn't feel that way, but I'm not amazed you do. You had to leave your own house, where you had familiar people, love, stability"—I had said I'd keep quiet; I didn't argue—"and move into this fucking monument to a castle, and be ready to become the partner of some guy you never saw except in a scrap of a movie. I'll be honest. The moment I saw the photos of you, I was drawn to you. I stupidly thought, This is a beautiful, strong woman who I'd like to know. Maybe we can make something of this pre-arranged mess. I meant make something for ourselves, you and me. Kids were—are—the last thing on my mind. We'd have a long time, after all, to reach a decision on *that*. But you. I was . . . looking forward to meeting you. And I *would* have been there, to meet you. Only something happened. No. Not some compulsion I have to go out and tear animals apart and *drink* them in the forest. Daisha," he said, "have you been to look at the waterfall?"

I stared. "Only from the car . . ."

"There's one of our human families there. I had to go

and—" He broke off. He said, "The people in this house have switched right off, like computers without any electric current. I grew up here. It was hell. Yeah, that place you wanted me to go to. Only not bright or fiery, just—*dead*. They're dead here. Living dead. *Undead*, just what they say in the legends, in that bloody book *Dracula*. But *I* am not dead. And nor are you. Did it ever occur to you," he said, "your name, *Daisha*—the way it sounds. *Day*—sha. Beautiful. Just as you are."

He had already invited me to speak, so perhaps I could offer another comment. I said, "But you can't stand the light."

"No, I can't. Which doesn't mean I don't *crave* the light. When I was two years old, they took me out—my dad led me by the hand. *He* was fine with an hour or so of sunlight. I was so excited—looking forward to it. I remember the first colors—" He shut his eyes, opened them. "Then the sun came up. I never saw it after all. The first true light—I went blind. My skin . . . I don't remember properly. Just darkness and agony and terror. Just one minute. My body couldn't take even that. I was ill for ten months. Then I started to see again. After ten months. But I've seen daylight since, of course I have, on film, in photographs. I've read about it. And music—Ravel's 'Sunrise,' from that ballet. Can you guess what it's like to long for daylight, to be . . . *in love* with daylight . . . and you can never see it for real, never feel the warmth, smell the scents of it, or properly hear the sounds, except on a screen, off a CD—*never*? When I saw you, you're like that, like real daylight. Do you know what I said to my father when I started to recover, after those ten months, those thirty seconds of dawn? *Why*, I said to him, why is light my enemy, why does it want to kill me? *Why light?*"

Zeev turned away. He said to the sunny bright hearth, "And you're the daylight, too, Daisha. And you've become my enemy. Daisha," he said, "I release you. We won't marry. I'll make it clear to all of them, Severin first, that any fault is all with me. There'll be no bad thing they can level at you. So, you're free. I regret so much the torment I've unwillingly, selfishly put you through. I'm sorry, Daisha. And now, God knows, it's late and I have to go out. It's not rudeness, I hope you'll accept that now. Please trust me. Go upstairs and sleep well. Tomorrow you can go home."

I sat like a block of concrete. Inside I felt shattered by what he had said. He pulled on his jacket and started toward the door, and only then I stood up. *"Wait."*

"I can't." He didn't look at me. "I'm sorry. Someone . . . needs me. Please believe me. It's true."

And I heard myself say, "Some human girl?"

That checked him. He looked at me, face a blank. *"What?"*

"The human family you seem to have to be with—by the fall? Is that it? You want a human woman, not me."

Then he laughed. It was raw, and real, that laughter. He came back and caught my hands. "Daisha—my *Day*—you're insane. All right. Come with me and see. We'll have to race."

But my hands tingled; my heart was in a race already.

I looked up into his face, he down into mine. The night hesitated, shifted. He let go my hands, and I flew out and up the stairs. Dragging off that dress, I tore the sleeve at the shoulder, but I left it lying with the shoes. Inside fifteen more minutes we were sprinting, side by side, along the track. There was no excuse for this, no *rational* reason. But I had seen him, *seen*, as if sunlight had streamed through the black lid of the night and shown him to me for the first time, light that was his enemy, and my mother's, *never* mine.

The moon was low by then, and stroked the edges of the waterfall. It was like liquid aluminum, and its roar packed the air full as a sort of deafness. The human house was about a mile off, tucked in among the dense black columns of the pines.

A youngish, fair-haired woman opened the door. Her face lit up the instant she saw him, no one could miss that. "Oh, Zeev," she said, "he's so much better. Our doctor says he's mending fantastically well. But come in."

It was a pleasing room, low ceilinged, with a dancing fire. A smart black cat with a white vest and mittens sat upright in an armchair, giving the visitors a thoughtful frowning scrutiny.

"Will you go up?" the woman asked.

"Yes," Zeev said. He smiled at her, and added, "This is Daisha Severin."

"Oh, are you Daisha? It's good of you to come out too," she told me. Zeev had already gone upstairs. The human woman returned to folding towels at a long table.

"Isn't it very late for you?" I questioned.

"We keep late hours. We like the nighttime."

I had been aware that this was often the case at Severin. But I'd hardly ever spoken much to humans—I wasn't sure now what I should say. But she continued to talk to me, and overhead I heard a floorboard creak; Zeev would not have caused that. The man was there, evidently, the one who was "mending."

"It happened just after sunset," the woman said, folding a blue towel over a green one. "Crazy accident—the chain broke. Oh, God, when they brought him home, my poor Emil—" Her voice faltered and grew hushed. Above also a hushed voice was speaking, barely audible even to me. But she raised her face and it had stayed still rosy and glad, and her voice was fine again. "We telephoned up to the house, and Zeev came out at once. He did the wonderful thing It worked. It always works when he does it."

I stared at her. I was breathing quickly, frightened. "What," I said, *"what* did he do?"

"Oh, but he'll have told you," she strangely reminded me. "The same as he did for Joel—and poor Arresh when he was sick with meningitis—"

"You tell me," I said. She blinked. "Please."

"The blood," she said, gazing at me a little apologetically, regretful to have confused me in some way she couldn't fathom. "He gave them his blood to drink. It's the blood that heals, of course. I remember when Zeev said to Joel, it's all right, forget the stories—this won't change you, only make you well. Zeev was only sixteen then himself. He's saved five lives here. But no doubt he was too modest to tell you that. And with Emil, the same. It was shocking"—now she didn't falter—"Zeev had to be here so quick—and he cut straight through his own sleeve to the vein, so it would be fast enough." Blood on his sleeve, I thought. Vampires heal so rapidly . . . all done, only that little rusty mark . . . "And my Emil, my lovely man, he's safe and alive, Daisha. Thanks to your husband."

His voice called to me out of the dim roar of the water-falling firelight, "Daisha, come up a minute."

The woman folded an orange towel over a white one, and I numbly, speechlessly, climbed the stair, and Zeev said, "I have asked Emil, and he says, very kindly, he doesn't object if you see how this is done." So I stood in the doorway and watched as Zeev, with the help of a thin, clean knife, decanted and poured out a measure of his life blood into a mug, which had a picture on it of a cat, just like the smart black cat in the room below. And the smiling man, sitting on the bed in his dressing gown, raised the mug, and toasted Zeev, and drank the wild medicine down.

★ ★ ★

"We're young," he said to me, "we are both of us *genuinely* young. You're seventeen, aren't you? I'm twenty-seven. We are the only actual young *here*. And the rest of them, as I said, switched off. But we can do something, not only for ourselves, Day, but for our people. Or my people, if you prefer. Or *any* people. Humans. Don't you think that's fair, given what they do, knowingly or not, for us?"

We had walked back, slowly, along the upper terraces by the black abyss of the ravine, sure-footed, omnipotent. Then we sat together on the forest's edge and watched the silver tumble of the fall. It had no choice. It *had* to fall, and go on falling forever, in love with the unknown darkness below, unable and not wanting to stop.

I kept thinking of the little blood mark on his sleeve that night, what I'd guessed, and what instead was true. And I thought of Juno, with her obsessive wasted tiny blood-drop offerings in the "shrine," to a man she had no longer loved. As she no longer loved me.

She hates me because I have successful sun-born genes and can live in daylight. But Zeev, who can't take even thirty seconds of the sun, doesn't hate me for that. He . . . he doesn't *hate* me at all.

"So will you go back to Severin tomorrow?" he said to me as we sat at the brink of the night.

"No."

"Daisha, even when they've married us, please believe this: If you still want to go away, I won't put obstacles in your path. I will back you up."

"You care so little."

"So much."

His eyes glowed in the dark. They put the waterfall to shame.

When he touched me, touches me, I *know* him. From long ago, I remember this incredible joy, this heat and burning, this refinding *rightness*—and I fall down into the abyss forever, willing as the shining water. I never loved before. Except Juno, but she cured me of that.

He is a healer. His blood can heal, its vampiric vitality transmissible—but noninvasive. From his gift come no substandard replicants of our kind. They only—*live.*

Much, much later, when we parted just before the dawn inside the house—parted till the next night, our wedding day—it came to me that if *he* can heal by letting humans drink his blood, perhaps I might offer him some of my own. Because *my* blood might help him to survive the daylight, even if only for one unscathed and precious minute.

I'll wear green to be married. And a necklace of sea green glass.

As the endless day trails by, unable to sleep, I've written this.

When he touched me, when he kissed me, Zeev, whose name actually *means* "wolf," became known to me. I don't believe he'll have to live all his long, long life without ever seeing the sun. For that was what he reminded me of. His warmth, his kiss, his arms about me—my first memory of that golden light that blew upward through the dark. No longer any fear, which anyway was never mine, only that glorious *familiar* excitement and happiness, that *welcomed* danger. Perhaps I am wrong in this. Perhaps I shall pay heavily and cruelly for having been deceived. And for deceiving myself, too, because I realized what he was to me the moment I saw him—why else put up such barricades? Zeev is my sunrise out of the dark of the night of my so-far useless life. Yes, then. I love him.

ABOUT THE AUTHORS

NATHAN BALLINGRUD lives with his daughter just outside Asheville, North Carolina. His stories have appeared in *Inferno: New Tales of Terror and the Supernatural*; *The Del Rey Book of Science Fiction and Fantasy*; *Lovecraft Unbound*; *SCIFICTION*; and *The Best Horror of the Year, Volume Two*, and will be forthcoming in *Naked City: New Tales of Urban Fantasy*. He recently won the Shirley Jackson Award for his short story "The Monsters of Heaven."

CHRISTOPHER BARZAK's first novel, *One for Sorrow*, won the Crawford Award for Best First Fantasy. His second book, a novel-in-stories called *The Love We Share Without Knowing*, was placed on the James Tiptree Jr. Award's Honor List. His stories have appeared in the young adult anthologies *The Coyote Road*, *The Beastly Bride*, and *Firebirds Soaring*. He is at work on his third novel and teaches fiction writing at Youngstown

State University in Youngstown, Ohio, where vampires have begun to fight for equal rights. You can find out more about him at www.christopherbarzak.wordpress.com.

STEVE BERMAN began writing and selling weird stories when he was seventeen. His novel *Vintage: A Ghost Story* was a finalist for the Andre Norton Award for Young Adult Science Fiction and Fantasy and made the Rainbow List for recommended gay-themed books for young readers by the American Library Association's GLBT Roundtable. His favorite vampire movie is *Near Dark*. And if you email him at sberman8@yahoo.com and ask for more vamp-slaying adventures for Saul, he just may write them.

HOLLY BLACK writes bestselling contemporary fantasy for readers of all ages. She is the author of the Modern Faerie Tale series, The Spiderwick Chronicles, and the graphic novel series The Good Neighbors. Currently she is hard at work on *The Black Heart*, the third book in the noirish caper series The Curse Workers.

EMMA BULL grew up in California, Texas, Wisconsin, New Jersey, and Illinois. As soon as she finished school and headed out on her own, she started collecting more states and a Canadian province. She's been writing since elementary school, when she discovered that turning in a short story when the teacher asked for an essay got her an automatic A.

She's been in five bands, plays lame guitar, and likes to sing. She lives (for now, at least) in Arizona with her husband, Will Shetterly, and cats Toby (best cat) and Barnabas (worst cat).

CECIL CASTELLUCCI has published four novels for young adults: *Rose Sees Red*, *Beige*, *The Queen of Cool*, and *Boy Proof*, and a picture book, *Grandma's Gloves*. She also wrote the graphic novels *The PLAIN Janes* and *Janes in Love*, illustrated by Jim Rugg, which were the launch titles for the DC Comics Minx line. She has had numerous short stories published in various places, including *Strange Horizons*, *The Eternal Kiss*, *Geektastic* (which she coedited), and *Interfictions 2*. Her books have been on the American Library Assocation's Best Books for Young Adults, Quick Picks for Reluctant Readers, and Great Graphic Novels for Teens lists, as well as the New York Public Library's Books for the Teen Age and Amelia Bloomer lists. Upcoming books include a graphic novel for young readers, *Odd Duck*, illustrated by Sara Varon, and two new novels, *First Day on Earth* and *The Year of the Beasts*. In addition to writing books, she writes plays and opera libretti, makes movies, does performance pieces, and occasionally rocks out. For more information, go to www.misscecil.com.

SUZY McKEE CHARNAS grew up on the West Side of Manhattan when pizza was fifteen cents a slice. She escaped into the wider world by joining the Peace Corps fresh out of college, and was sent to Nigeria to teach. Home again, she taught junior high until she was lured away to write curriculum for a drug abuse treatment program founded on two ideas: that teachers should stop telling lies about drugs to students, since the students knew more about drugs than they did, so lying just made the teachers look ridiculous; and that teachers and students have a common interest in making school less boring, since they are the ones stuck in classrooms together for years on end.

She married in 1969, and she and her husband went to live in New Mexico (for the big blue sky and high desert horizons), where she began writing science fiction and fantasy full-time. Her books and stories have won her various awards over the years, and a play made from her best-known novel (about a vampire who teaches college) has been staged on both coasts. She lectures and teaches about fantasy, SF, and fiction writing whenever she gets a chance to, and blogs about everything on Live Journal. Her website is www.suzymckeecharnas.com.

CASSANDRA CLARE is the internationally bestselling author of the Mortal Instruments and the Infernal Devices series of young adult urban fantasy novels. She lives with her husband and two cats in western Massachusetts, where she is currently writing *Clockwork Prince*, the last in the Infernal Devices trilogy. She has always liked vampires.

ELLEN DATLOW has been editing short stories in the science fiction, fantasy, and horror fields for thirty years. She was fiction editor of *OMNI* Magazine and editor of *SCIFICTION*, as well as editing anthologies throughout those years and continuing to do so today. Her most recent anthologies include *Poe: 19 New Tales Inspired by Edgar Allan Poe*; *Lovecraft Unbound*; *Darkness: Two Decades of Modern Horror*; *Tails of Wonder and Imagination: Cat Stories*; *Haunted Legends* (coedited with Nick Mamatas); *The Beastly Bride*; and *Troll's-Eye View* (these last two with Terri Windling). Forthcoming in 2011 is *Naked City: New Tales of Urban Fantasy*. She coedited *The Year's Best Fantasy and Horror* for twenty-one years and has been editing *The Best Horror of the Year* for three years. Datlow has won multiple World Fantasy Awards, Bram Stoker Awards, Hugo Awards, Locus Awards, International Horror Guild Awards, and the Shirley Jackson Award for her editing. She was named recipient of the 2007 Karl Edward Wagner Award for "outstanding contribution to the genre."

Ellen Datlow and Matthew Kressel curate the long-running New York monthly reading series Fantastic Fiction at KGB. She lives in New York City with two opinionated cats.

Her website is at www.datlow.com, and she blogs at http://ellen-datlow.livejournal.com.

JEFFREY FORD is the author of the novels *The Physiognomy, Memoranda, The Beyond, The Portrait of Mrs. Charbuque, The Girl* *in the Glass*, and *The Shadow Year*. His short fiction has been published in three collections: *The Fantasy Writer's Assistant*, *The Empire of Ice Cream*, and *The Drowned Life*. His fiction has won the World Fantasy Award, the Nebula Award, the Edgar Allan Poe Award, and the Grand Prix de l'Imaginaire. He lives in New Jersey with his wife and two sons and teaches literature and writing at Brookdale Community College.

NEIL GAIMAN is the Newbery Medal–winning author of *The Graveyard Book* and a *New York Times* bestseller, whose books have been made into major motion pictures, including the recent *Coraline*. He is also famous for the Sandman graphic novel series and for numerous other books and comics for adult, young adult, and younger readers. He has won the Hugo, Nebula, Mythopoeic, World Fantasy, and other awards.

KATHE KOJA's books for young adults include *Buddha Boy*, *Talk*, *Kissing the Bee*, and *Headlong*; her work has been honored by the International Reading Association, the American Library Association, and the Humane Society of the United States. She lives in the Detroit area with her husband, Rick Lieder, and three rescued cats. Visit kathekoja.com.

ELLEN KUSHNER grew up in Cleveland, Ohio, attended Bryn Mawr College, and graduated from Barnard College. She worked in publishing in New York City, then quit to write her first novel, *Swordspoint: A Melodrama of Manners*, which took a lot longer than she thought it would. When it was finished, she moved to Boston to be a music host for WGBH Radio and eventually got her own national public radio series, *Sound & Spirit*, which has been running ever since.

Her second novel, *Thomas the Rhymer*, won the Mythopoeic Award and the World Fantasy Award. She has returned to the world of *Swordspoint* in two more novels, *The Fall of the Kings* (written with Delia Sherman) and *The Privilege of the Sword*, plus a growing assortment of short stories. Her children's book *The Golden Dreydl* was adapted by Vital Theatre as *The Klezmer Nutcracker* and has become a holiday favorite. Most recently, she and Holly Black coedited a new anthology of stories set in the world of Terri Windling's Bordertown.

She lives in Manhattan, travels a lot, and can never remember where she put anything. www.ellenkushner.com.

TANITH LEE has written nearly one hundred books and more than 270 short stories, besides radio plays and TV scripts. Her genre crossing includes fantasy, SF, horror, young adult, historical, detective, and contemporary fiction. Plus combinations of them all. Her latest publications include the Lionwolf Trilogy: *Cast a Bright Shadow*, *Here in Cold Hell*, and *No Flame but Mine*; and the three Piratica novels for young adults. She has also recently had several short stories and novellas in publications such as *Asimov's SF Magazine*, *Weird Tales*, *Realms of Fantasy*, *The*

Ghost Quartet, and *Wizards*. Norilana Books is reprinting all the Flat Earth series, with two new volumes to follow.

She lives on the Sussex Weald with her husband, writer/ artist John Kaiine, and two omnipresent cats. More information can be found at www.tanithlee.com.

MELISSA MARR is the author of the *New York Times* bestselling Wicked Lovely series (a film of which is in development by Universal Pictures). She has also written a three-volume manga series (Wicked Lovely: Desert Tales) and her first adult novel, *Graveminder*. All her texts are rooted in her lifelong obsession with folklore and fantastic creatures. Currently she lives in the Washington, D.C., area with one spouse, two children, two Rott-Labs, and one Rottweiler. You can find her online at www.melissa-marr.com.

GARTH NIX was born in 1963 in Melbourne, Australia. A full-time writer since 2001, he has previously worked as a literary agent, marketing consultant, book editor, book publicist, book sales representative, bookseller, and part-time soldier in the Australian Army Reserve. Garth's novels include the award-winning fantasies *Sabriel*, *Lirael*, and *Abhorsen* and the YA SF novel *Shade's Children*. His fantasy books for children include *The Ragwitch*; the six books of the Seventh Tower sequence; and the seven books of the Keys to the Kingdom series. His books have appeared on the bestseller lists of the

New York Times, *Publishers Weekly*, *The Guardian*, the *Sunday Times* of London, and *The Australian*, and his work has been translated into thirty-eight languages. He lives in a Sydney beach suburb with his wife and two children.

LUCIUS SHEPARD's short fiction has won the Nebula Award, the Hugo Award, the International Horror Guild Award, the National Magazine Award, Locus Awards, the Theodore Sturgeon Award, and the World Fantasy Award.

His most recent books are a short fiction collection, *Viator Plus*, and a short novel, *The Taborin Scale*. Forthcoming are another short fiction collection, *Five Autobiographies*, and two novels, tentatively titled *The Piercefields* and *The End of Life as We Know It* (the latter young adult), and a short novel, *The House of Everything and Nothing*.

DELIA SHERMAN's most recent short stories have appeared in the Viking young adult anthologies *Firebirds*, *The Faery Reel*, and *Coyote Road*, and in the adult anthologies *Poe: 19 New Tales Inspired by Edgar Allan Poe* and *Naked City: New Tales of Urban Fantasy*. Her adult novels are *Through a Brazen Mirror* and *The Porcelain Dove* (winner of the Mythopoeic Award), and, with fellow fantasist and partner Ellen Kushner, *The Fall of the Kings*.

She has coedited anthologies with Ellen Kushner and Terri Windling, as well as *Interfictions: An Anthology of Interstitial*

Writing, edited with Theodora Goss, and *Interfictions 2*, edited with Christopher Barzak.

Changeling, her first novel for younger readers, was published in 2007, followed by *The Magic Mirror of the Mermaid Queen* in 2009. She is a past member of the James Tiptree Jr. Awards motherboard, an active member of the Endicott Studio of Mythic Arts, and a founding member of the Interstitial Arts Foundation board.

Delia has taught writing at Clarion, the Odyssey Workshop in New Hampshire, the Cape Cod Writers' Workshop, and the American Book Center in Amsterdam. She lives in New York City, loves to travel, and writes wherever she happens to find herself.

Born in the Pacific Northwest in 1979, **CATHERYNNE M. VALENTE** is the author of more than a dozen works of fiction and poetry, including *Palimpsest*, the Orphan's Tales series, *Deathless*, and crowd-funded phenomenon *The Girl Who Circumnavigated Fairyland in a Ship of Her Own Making*. She is a winner of the Tiptree Award, the Mythopoeic Award, the Rhysling Award, the Andre Norton Award, and the Million Writers Award. She has been nominated for the Pushcart Prize and the Spectrum Awards, and was a finalist for the World Fantasy Award in 2007 and 2009 and for the Hugo Award. She lives on an island off the coast of Maine with her partner and two dogs.

GENEVIEVE VALENTINE'S fiction has appeared or is forthcoming in *Clarkesworld Magazine*, *Strange Horizons*, *Fantasy Magazine*, and anthologies *Federations*, *The Living Dead II*, and *Running with the Pack*. Her first novel, *Mechanique: A Tale of the Circus Tresaulti*, about a mechanical circus troupe, is coming in 2011 from Prime. She has an insatiable appetite for bad movies, a tragedy she tracks on her blog, www.genevievevalentine.com.

KAARON WARREN'S third novel, *Mistification*, was published by Angry Robot Books in 2010, following the award-nominated *Slights* and *Walking the Tree*. Her short fiction has appeared in a number of publications edited by Ellen Datlow, including *Haunted Legends*; *Poe: 19 New Tales Inspired by Edgar Allan Poe*; *The Year's Best Fantasy and Horror*; *The Best Horror of the Year, Volume Two*; and *Tails of Wonder and Imagination: Cat Stories*. She lives in Canberra, Australia, with her family.

TERRI WINDLING is an editor, artist, folklorist, and essayist, and the author of books for both children and adults. She has won nine World Fantasy awards, the Mythopoeic Award, the Bram Stoker Award, and the SFWA Solstice Award for outstanding contributions to the speculative fiction field, and her book *The Armless Maiden* was placed on the short list for the Tiptree Award. She has edited more than thirty anthologies of magical fiction (many of them in collaboration with Ellen Datlow); she created the Borderland series (a pioneering work of urban fantasy); and she's been a consulting editor for the Tor Books fantasy line since 1986. As a painter, she has had her art exhibited in museums and galleries in England, France, and the United States; she is also codirector of the Endicott Studio, a transatlantic organization dedicated to mythic arts. A former New Yorker, Terri now lives in a small country village in the west of England with her husband, stepdaughter, and a lively black dog. For more information, please visit her website, www.terriwindling.com; her blog, http://windling.typepad.com/blog; and the Endicott Studio's website, www.endicott-studio.com.